THE EGYPTIAN PRINCESS

A STORY OF HAGAR

THE WOMEN OF VALOR

BOOK ONE: THE EGYPTIAN PRINCESS

THE EGYPTIAN PRINCESS

A STORY OF HAGAR
THE WOMEN OF VALOR SERIES

BY
KD HOLMBERG

The Egyptian Princess
Published by Mountain Brook Ink
White Salmon, WA U.S.A.

The website addresses shown in this book are not intended in any way to be or imply an endorsement on the part of Mountain Brook Ink, nor do we vouch for their content.

This story is a work of fiction. All characters and events are the product of the author's imagination. Any resemblance to any person, living or dead, is coincidental.

The Team: Miralee Ferrell, Alyssa Roat, Hope Bolinger, Nikki Wright, Cindy Jackson
Cover Design: Indie Cover Design, Lynnette Bonner Designer

Mountain Brook Ink is an inspirational publisher offering fiction you can believe in.
Printed in the United States of America.

Dedication

For KEH with love from KDH
and
In memory of Sylvia LeMerle Robershaw

Acknowledgments

I am incredibly humbled by the confirmation from Miralee Ferrell and the team at Mountain Brook Ink that helped bring my vision of Hagar to life. From editing to proofreading and cover design, I found extraordinary encouragement in our collaboration. Thank you all from the deepest places in my heart for making this possible.

My agent, Linda Glaz, was the first in the professional world of writing to believe in me and open doors that I couldn't independently. Thank you, Linda. I'm eternally grateful to you for seeing whatever you saw and launching me as an author.

My family and friends never wavered in their breathtaking support. My husband, Keith Holmberg, is my greatest patron and the best editor a girl could ask for. Thank you for your generosity of spirit and for always being in my corner. I could not have done this without you. I love you, KEH.

Brittney Hallenbeck is the dream promotion and social media guru. Thank you for your fun, unending ideas for my launch team and for giving me the gift of time to spend on my craft. Every author needs a brilliant Brittney!

I never grow weary hearing my children, Zak, Ryne, Tyler, Breanna, and Brittney, say, "I'm proud of you, Momma." My precious family, thank you. I love you all so much.

To Mosab Hassan Yousef, who inspired my first steps on the trail of discovering who Hagar may have been. Thank you, and Gonen Ben-Itzhak, for finding the familial bond that should unite all children of Abraham and showing it's possible for Palestinians and Israelis to love one another.

I want to thank friends and family who have not only encouraged but prayed for me over the years, remaining steadfast as I discovered more about Hagar. Sharon Robershaw, LeVerle O'Neal, Orit Holmberg McConnell, Pat Lunsford, Ruth Lefebvre, Cheri Fine, and Sharon Horn. They all joined my launch team, Hagar's Habibis, along with Meagan Held, Jill Kelly, Heidi Nunes, Kathy Gomez, Janice Harris, Deni Corbett, Al Fadi, Colleen Krashesky, Jane Sangalis, Valerie Bantz, Keli Wherritt, Lauren Valdez, Emily Fontenot, and Paula Schubert Russell. Your friendship and support mean everything to me.

My critique group always offered invaluable insights; Sandra Merville Hart, Deborah Sprinkle, Bonnie Sue Beardsley, Starr Ayers, and Linda Dindzans. Thank you all for your wisdom and input throughout this often arduous journey.

DiAnn Mills and Eva Marie Everson, my two mentors, were never afraid to tell me the truth. Thank you for your honesty, red ink, and reassurance over the years. You both have blessed me and so many others more than you will ever know. Big, big crowns in heaven.

A special thank you goes to Jeanie Hoover. She read my early drafts (only writers know how incredible a friend has to be to do that!), brought unending encouragement, prayed over me in the dark moments, and even came up with the title. Thank you, Jeanie. You are the flame that never flickered.

I also have to acknowledge Ellie, Micah, Maddy, Callie, Katie, Tessa, Blair, and Raya, because they are the light in my life. The older grands encouraged me to, "Keep up the good work, Grandma!" So, so sweet. They are my biggest blessing.

And to Hagar, who I can't wait to meet in heaven one day. My prayer is that this is the first step in reclaiming who you were; a woman of intelligence, faith, and valor. I feel incredibly blessed to tell your story.

Thank you, reader, for taking an interest in my work. You are what it is all about. I would love to hug every one of you and tell you how much you are appreciated.

The Egyptian Princess marks an incredible milestone in my life. As the debut novel of a "woman of a certain age," I can only encourage you never to think you are too old or too young for God to show you purpose and hope for your life. The Lord is good, and to Him only goes the glory.

Historical Note from the Author

Approximately four thousand years ago, a young Egyptian woman named Hagar found herself embroiled in a fateful, contentious love triangle that changed the course of history. The story of Abraham, Sarah, and Hagar produced two sons—Ishmael and Isaac. Two nations—the Hebrews and the Arabs. And three major religions—Judaism, Christianity, and Islam. Even the roots of the modern Arab-Israeli conflict are bound up in this event.

The Bible introduces Hagar in Genesis 16 as the Egyptian handmaid Sarah used as a surrogate to produce an heir for Abraham. Hebrew and Islamic tradition take her story deeper and claim she was the daughter of the king of Egypt, making her a princess before she became a servant.

Abraham moved his tribe from Canaan to Egypt to escape a great drought. Sarah, being the most beautiful woman since Eve, was a perfect prize for Pharaoh. She soon ended up in his harem, which resulted in a web of intrigue and conspiracies. This is where she probably met Hagar and when the twist-and-turn-filled story of their relationship may have begun.

Life for a princess in ancient Egypt saw little change through the dynasties. Royal children—boys and girls—received equal educations that included mathematics, reading, writing, the arts, and even politics. As the daughter of a king, the handmaid in Genesis 16 would have grown up in an opulent court, full of privilege and power, becoming an accomplished, refined, and cultured woman.

As a closing note, Abraham and Sarah were initially named Abram and Sarai until God changed their names in Genesis 17:5. Since my timeline is before this, I refer to them as Sarai and Abram.

Chapter One

Henen-nesut, Egypt
10th Dynasty
2085 BC

THE SUN SEARED MY FACE, BUT I couldn't steer my eyes away. I gripped the silver amulet bound to my wrist and tried to count the boats as they raced toward the royal quay. *Four score, perhaps five.* Faster vessels overtook slower ones—some still far off and blurred from my vantage point on the palace balcony. My chest tightened. Not one appeared to yield. Only the expert maneuvers of those piloting the boats averted collisions.

I quickly lost count and began again.

A familiar hymn rang out from the array of river-going vessels that trailed my father's splendid royal barge, glorious in a deep glow of gold and sunlight. Citizens from all over Egypt filled flat-bottomed ferries, cargo ships, and fishing boats from bow to stern, singing a song of praise to our god, Heryshaf. All sails were set and the strong breeze abated the need for the powerful arms of any oarsmen. It pushed the vessels and voices easily against the current of the Nile.

A whiff of longing rose in me. I crossed my arms and pressed my lips together. Why were the gods so cruel? My hot-blooded twin brother, Merikare, commanded the royal boat with its white sails unfurled. He had sailed north and explored where the Nile branched out like fingers into the streams of the delta.

It should have been me. I emerged first from the womb and still had the scarlet thread the midwife tied around my wrist to prove it. But I was cursed from my first mouthful of air for being female.

The gods had favored Merikare.

The gods and Pharaoh.

One word of blessing from the king was all I needed to receive the respect and authority my brother obtained by virtue of his manhood. But Father refused. Even though I worked tirelessly for his approval and yearned for nothing more than to be valued by him.

"Give me your verdict, Princess Hagar. Do you believe the rumors to be true?" My father's high vizier, Rensi, leaned close, his warm breath pungent with beer.

For a moment, I had forgotten him.

"You think the Sumerian woman Merikare found for Pharaoh's harem could be the goddess Isis incarnated?" I bristled. "Isis is Egyptian. She would never come to us in foreign skin."

"Your people believe it." He wiped the sweat from his bald head. "They follow the royal boat hoping to get a glimpse of her."

"And how unwise of Merikare to allow them to do so." My voice was as sour as my stomach. "His parade could have been mistaken for an invasion. Imagine the alarm caused if you had not come ahead of them. He will be king one day and should not act like a fool."

Rensi kept his scrutiny on the Nile. "Careful, Princess. The wind does not keep secrets. Our tombs are full of those who have criticized kings."

"But you know he will not be a good king. He is too controlling and never allows anything to get in the way of his own pleasure. You know it. I know it. I have known it all my life." I turned to him. "Mother said you argued for Merikare and me to ascend the throne together."

He raised his hand. "Your brother is strong and determined. If he can learn to control himself, there is no reason he will not become a great pharaoh. He pushes the boundaries, but I have seen him stand up quite forcefully for the things and people he cares about." Rensi paused and faced me. "And say no more about sharing the throne. It will not be done. The law is clear and gives royal sons precedence over their sisters. The throne will be your brother's someday, and he is holding on to it with both hands." He sipped his beer. "If only you'd been born a boy."

"Then I would be the next pharaoh."

"And if you were, would you allow Merikare to rule with you?"

His question stole my breath. "I would *never* share the throne."

"Then there is no purpose stirring it up."

A shudder went through me. Rensi was right. I would never sit on the throne, even though I had dreamt of it my entire life. There was no point in desiring it any longer. "I am sorry, Rensi. My mouth should not be set against my brother." The sun glittered on the royal barge and caught my attention again. "You have seen the woman. What is your verdict, High Vizier?"

He laughed briefly. "You want me to determine if she is a goddess? That is work for the high priest, not for the simple overseer of your father's business. But I admit, I have beheld her and have never seen the female form more wonderfully fashioned. There is nothing but light and beauty in Sarai."

I frowned and turned so he couldn't see my face. It didn't bother me that he thought she was beautiful. It bothered me that I had not been able to rest since I received his missive about the new woman the crown prince found for Pharaoh's harem. *Sarai.* My heart pounded. That name had converted my deep and dreamless sleep into restlessness and distinct visions.

A sigh escaped me. "I have never had trouble sleeping, Rensi, not even as a child. And now I become anxious when dusk falls." My chin dipped. "I know that makes me sound like a child afraid of the dark. But I have become quite undone by black dreams and abrupt awakenings."

"That is why I'm here." He wiped his bald head again. "How does the high priest explain your visions? There is no one in the world more skilled in hidden things than him."

"Meti said the gods have chosen to linger with me, although he is unable to unravel the meaning. He bound this amulet to my wrist to pass the power of the vision to me, and for my protection." I touched the inlaid red jasper stones, symbols of Isis's shielding blood on the silver cuff fettered to my wrist. My hand appeared slightly swollen and blue from the weighty shackle's tightness, but I would endure the temporary discomfort. "The apparition that visits me is getting stronger, Rensi, the closer Sarai gets." I glared at the royal boat. "And we are no closer to the message it is trying to convey. They seem somehow ..."

"Connected?"

"Yes. Connected." I felt the cuff again. I didn't know why, but for a moment, the potent magical object not only irritated my skin but chafed my soul as well. Rubbed it raw. I slid the cuff up and down my arm for a looser fit and thought perhaps I would prefer to be free of it after all.

"Dreams are where the gods speak to us. Where they show us what they are about to do. Think of it as a gift, Hagar."

A gift?

"Even when I bolt upright with eyes wide open and scream things that no one understands? Or walk to my garden in my sleep, and my servant girls have to lead me back to bed? Let me tell you if it is the gods, their meddling is pure misery." My voice sounded petulant and I didn't like being petulant. I took a deep breath.

Rensi regarded me with that ruminating concentration of his. "It would be foolish to ignore—"

Zadah, one of my servant girls, cried out in high glee. "Isn't it a sight to behold?" She approached with a gold pitcher filled with beer and nodded toward the Nile, her lips plumped, her nose pert.

The high vizier's eyes flashed fury and his lips twisted with displeasure.

Zadah looked up at him, and her face curdled like spoiled milk. She fell on the floor at my feet, the pitcher spilling its contents on my sandals. "Forgive your irksome slave for speaking before she had permission."

I fixed my gaze on Rensi's shiny bald head, amazed as it grew as red as his face.

He opened his mouth to chastise Zadah, but I intervened. "It is futile to punish this one, Rensi. She abandons proper speech when her heart is churned. She cannot be silent." I let out a sigh. "Rise, Zadah, and mind your tongue. I'd rather the high vizier not have it removed." I slipped out of my wet sandals and stepped to the side of the puddle. "I'll need dry shoes, but bring Rensi refreshment first."

Zadah kissed my feet several times and backed away stiffly, repeatedly bowing, emphasizing the nakedness of her small frame. Like all of our servants, she only wore a beaded collar and a short black wig. Her bright brown eyes belied the deep melancholy brewing beneath them.

Rensi took me by the hand. My fingers tensed and then relaxed in his grip. "I should hear this vision for myself and draw my own conclusions," he said. "But out of the sun. This cloudless sky and prickly heat are too much for me."

I hesitated an instant and stared off at the shimmering Nile. My eyes swept back and forth over the royal barge and rested on the outline of my brother on the bow. My heart stopped in my chest. "The gods so like to vex me," I muttered and turned to follow Rensi.

He led me to a gilded couch in the adjoining room, the stone floor cool under my bare feet. We sat silent for a moment. From outside came the sounds of a busy palace preparing for the great banquet that evening. Voices murmured in excitement, footsteps hurried, and someone strummed a lute. Moisture trickled between my shoulder blades even though fan-bearers flanked us, waving huge ostrich feathers. The air they roused offered little deliverance.

Zadah approached carefully and presented fresh cups of beer. Rensi took one, but I waved her away. He sipped without a sound.

I wiped wet palms on my linen dress and thought about why I had requested this audience. True and deep, from the bottom of my heart, I wanted the high vizier to make the gods leave me alone. He would know what actions to take to put everything right again. I shook my head slowly. Not even the high priest had been able to do that. The gods would do with me as they pleased.

The pause helped me gather my wits.

Rensi furrowed his brow. "I never expected to pass this life in peace, Hagar. Do not seek to spare me now."

I pushed aside beaded plaits from my wig and met his gaze. "The truth is, I believe I am going mad. Nothing like this has ever happened to me before."

He nodded in that get-on-with-it sort of way and settled into his seat.

I stiffened slightly. Did I have another choice? No. He would have confidence in me, or he would confirm that sickness had taken hold of my mind. "I am certain a god speaks to me, spins the fate of Egypt, and then departs to his own place. He leaves me awake and wallowing in confusion. I fret for hours, convince myself it meant nothing, and then see it all again the moment I close my eyes to rest."

"I know you've taken this black dream before our gods. What did they say?"

I pondered a moment how truthful I should be with Pharaoh's most trusted advisor as he peered into my face for a hint of something I held back. Oho! He knew me so well and would seize even subtle traces of anything I left out. But it was the fondness tucked inside my heart for Rensi that gave me a moment of clarity. I would never lie to him about anything. His brilliant mind and honest spirit kept this short man, with a moon-shaped face and belly to match, at the right hand of a king. And I trusted him too. If a perfect answer existed, Rensi would know it.

"The gods are silent. As usual." *There. I said it.*

He toyed with the thick gold collar that lay on his bare,

clean-shaven chest. "The gods are always silent to me. Not once have they given me a tale to tell before it happens."

My mouth fell open.

Zadah returned with dry sandals and a platter filled with dates, cheese, and flatbread. Rensi took a handful of dates and a piece of bread. I waved her away again.

"Well, actually, there was one the gods gave me," Rensi said. "When your royal father lifted me to the position of high vizier, for near a season, I dreamt I was falling. I thought it certain that soon I would be cast down."

He popped a date in his mouth, spit the stone into his hand, and gave me a faint smile. "One day, I tripped on a floor-length linen robe my wife insisted I wear. 'You need to dress to our new station,' Tameri claimed. I tumbled down the stairs of the temple and landed at the feet of the king of Egypt." His eyes twinkled. "The king said to me, 'You are already the highest official in the palace, Rensi. I cannot advance your rank further. No matter how well you express your devotion to me.'" Rensi slapped his belly and laughed out loud.

I loved the sound of it and laughed along with him.

"That dream never came upon me again," he said.

Rensi ate another date, spit out the stone, then focused his attention on me. "Shift the load onto my back, Hagar. I will have no peace until you have peace. Sages have foretold the future from dreams since the beginning of time. Often, what came from their mouths occurred. Tell me about your vision from the beginning, and I will determine what to do."

Chapter Two

"THE DREAM ALWAYS BEGINS THE SAME." I clutched the silver amulet around my wrist. "I am standing in the middle of the Nile."

"On the water?"

I shook my head. "The river is completely dry. Not a drop of water in it. All the ships that float on her are grounded." My voice turned thick. "It is noontide, and the sun blazes fiercely. Bloated and bloodless carcasses of fish and animals of the river are everywhere. The air is unbearable, rank with the smell of death."

"You could smell the air?"

"O, Rensi. Vividly. The first time I woke from it, I looked around to see from where the stench came. Then I realized it arose from the dream."

He nodded for me to continue.

I shut my eyes. "Suddenly, the desert sand rises up and roars. It rolls toward me like an angry wave from the sea. I try to scream but can't cry out. I try to run, but my feet won't move. The wind howls so loudly I cover my ears, close my eyes, and crouch into a ball. The sand whips my body, about to crash down and swallow me whole. And then silence. Not a sound. I steal a look. The wave is frozen and stays in place as though sculpted, and all of its power is taken away. I stand slowly. The grains of sand—I can see each one—fall to the ground and slither back into the desert like a belly crawler.

"I remain still, and relief floods my body for a moment … until I realize the silence has become so dominant, it is as though the entire earth has gone quiet. It presses into me like a great weight, and my heart thrashes in my chest. I look from the eastern shore to the western shore and watch the tall papyrus grass that grows along the Nile *bow* as though in reverence." I lowered my voice. "Then a great shadow falls upon me, and I look up to see what was blocking the light. Hanging between heaven and earth is a mighty wooden ankh, Rensi. It is our symbol of eternal life, but I don't know what it means in my dream."

I opened my eyes and waited for his reply, but when he gave none, I continued. "Below the ankh appears a giant statue of Amun-Ra hewn of stone, great and exulted, resting on the dry riverbed." I took a breath. "Now, in the coolness of the shadow, my eyes grow heavy, and I want to sleep. But then a blinding light falls upon me and the great statue crumbles to the ground and blows away as though it were nothing but dust. In its place stands what I believe is a god in the form of a man, not made of stone, for the breath of life was in him. I try to look at his face and shade my eyes, for it was like trying to stare at the sun.

"Then the silence is broken by a voice as soft as a feather falling, yet it seems to fill the whole earth. He says, 'Hagar.'

"'Yes, it is me,' I answer.

"'Remove the shoes from your feet, for in my presence, you stand on sacred ground.'

"I want to flee but am rooted to that very spot," I barely whispered. "Then suddenly my feet are bare. I fall to my knees, hide my face, and shake with fear. But he speaks to me tenderly and calls me by name. He says, 'Consider me, Hagar, Princess of Egypt. Fear not, for my face is toward you, and my heart is inclined to you. My word will live in you forever. The Lord has heard the outcry of the afflicted in your land. O, house of Egypt, come and walk in my light.'"

Rensi waited for me to continue, but this time when I stayed silent, he asked, "Then what happens, Hagar?"

My eyes locked with his. "I awake screaming for someone. Anyone."

Rensi gaped at me blankly. His round face collapsed in on itself as his flawless composure appeared to forsake him. "Truly, Hagar, I grant you that is not what I expected."

"It was unlike anything I've ever heard before. His words

were clear and distinct and seemed to come alive in me, Rensi. How is that possible? How can words *live*?" My voice sounded hushed and odd, even to me.

He craned his head and appeared to study the ceiling as he considered the question. "A word from your father and a man may live or die."

"But then the man lives or dies. Not the word."

Rensi shrugged. "I guess even being the highest official in the land does not give me the wisdom to answer that riddle."

I tried to mask the disappointment on my face.

He took a deep breath. "The animals. Is there a crocodile?"

I nodded.

Rensi shuddered. "Crocodiles always mean high officials. Bloated and bloodless?"

I nodded again. "There is a hippopotamus." My throat clenched.

"The royal family. What if you have foreseen the fall of your father's dynasty? Or even of Egypt?"

"Don't utter such things, High Vizier." My voice rose. "Surely there is another purpose besides the destruction of all I know and love."

"O, Hagar," he said, urgently. "Are you sure you don't know which god spoke to you?"

Salty tears seasoned my lips. "I did not recognize him, but I could not look upon his face. No more than I could stare at the sun." The room seemed to spin slowly around me, as though clogged with thick honey, and I suddenly wanted to be alone. I believed it would feel good to talk to Rensi about the vision. But it didn't. Whatever relief I thought I would find vanished with one look at his ashen face. He stared right at me but didn't seem to see me.

I sat stunned and couldn't hear another sound except the pounding of my heart. But it was too late to take it back. Too late to escape.

"The Nile is the mother that feeds all of Egypt. If she ceases to water and fertilize the fields, it would be the end of us. May the gods have mercy." Rensi paused as Zadah approached to refill his cup. Her hand trembled, and her lips and chin quivered. I realized it was the first time she had heard the disturbing dream. Until now, I had shared it only with the high priest and the gods. She managed not to spill a drop and hurried away. Rensi took a long, deep drink and wiped his mouth. "Did this god you saw demand or request an act of devotion?"

"He asked for nothing except that I should *consider* him."

He exhaled deeply. "We will give all the gods an abundant offering. It must be one of them, so we will appease all of them." His face told me he was sure of himself. "It seems you have found favor with this god, so you must be the one to take it. No one else. It must be you."

I stood and took a few steps away to consider how I would say what needed to be said. "Meti and I have offered prayers and offerings to each of the gods already. We did not overlook even the least among them. But they were as silent as they have ever been." I turned to face him. "I told you, this one was not silent. He *spoke* to me and called me by name. Even before I went to the temple, I knew I would not find his image. And I was right."

He patted the empty seat next to him. "If you could not look upon his face, how can you be so sure?"

I dropped beside him, helpless as a baby bird falling from its nest. "I have spent my life gazing on the gods of Egypt." The truth tumbled from my lips and numbed my insides. "This is the first time a god gazed *upon me*."

His face pinched. "Then I am perplexed on how we might win the favor of this god who has seen you. Unless we petition our gods to act for us and put ourselves in their hands."

"They can do nothing unless this god allows it," I said with absolute certainty. "It seemed to me that he was not one god among many, High Vizier." I held my breath. Should I say the heretical thought aloud? "More that he *alone* is God."

Rensi released the remaining dates in his hand, and they

hit the floor with soft, repeated thumps. He reclined on the couch and tipped his neck, staring upward. No words came from his mouth for a long time.

I squirmed in my seat and wished I had never uttered my vision.

Not to him.

Not to anyone.

"I have long come to suspect a single, divine power is behind all things and is present in all other deities. That each of them are followers of one great God." His words were nearly inaudible. "As a young boy, I had a recurring dream that one unconquerable spirit commanded all gods. But I have never spoken that out loud."

"Why?" I whispered.

"Because I was a child. I had no real interest in trying to envision the realm of the gods then. And I wasn't sure I believed it," he conceded. "Until now."

"Rensi, you must do one thing for me."

He gazed at me vacantly.

"We can't have the people bow to the Sumerian woman or offer her worship. No one can see Sarai on her progress to the palace."

"How?"

"Have her conveyed in a litter with the curtains pulled. And please, keep silent about my dream. If it is a foretelling, and this woman is entangled, I'll know soon enough."

"Now that I have heard your black dream, Hagar, I would be surprised if they are connected. I doubt you'll find any evil hidden in her."

I took a deep breath. "I have not slept since I first heard the news of her, Rensi. The timing makes me curious. I can't ignore it."

"I won't tell the crown prince a falsehood," he replied firmly. "What should I say is the reason for the litter? Your brother is very proud of his discovery, and you know he thrives on attention. I doubt he will readily agree to hide her from the world."

"Tell him you have been commanded that no one should see her before Pharaoh does." I faced him fully. "That is what I am doing now. Commanding you. He will think the order came from the king himself."

Rensi laughed. "I will do as you say because I agree the king should be the first to lay eyes on her. I think Merikare will too."

Drums pounded out a beat amid cheering that called our attention outside. We stood and hurried back to the balcony. I narrowed my eyes in the bright sun as its heat quickly settled on my skin. Stern-mounted oars slapped the river as vessels slowed to run up on shore. The luxurious royal barge swept forward with my brother standing on the bow, arms crossed, chin high. But the pilot pulled into the quay too hard and raked the side of the boat. Merikare lost his feet and stumbled to one knee.

I laughed out loud.

Rensi covered his mouth.

I took a deep breath and shook my head, gazing at all the boats in this, my brother's latest spectacle. They pulled in or anchored up and down the shoreline. Droves of people poured onto the long, thin strip of black, fertile land that outlined the Nile banks. And they all headed for the gates of Henen-nesut.

"What was Merikare thinking?" My voice was barely a whisper. "Where will they sleep, and what will we feed them? Those are thoughts I'm sure never crossed my brother's mind." I bit my lip to say no more.

Rensi only shrugged.

The city already burst with townsfolk and farmers from the small villages that surrounded Henen-nesut. It was the first day of the new year, Wepet Renpet, and no one would miss the Festival of Heaven and Earth. Heryshaf had blessed us with a generous yield of corn, barley, and wheat. Even spelt and emmer grew in abundance. We were beyond grateful. At midday, a statue of Heryshaf adorned with magnificent jewelry would be carried in procession on a large stretcher that rested on the shoulders of a score of priests. From the temple, through the city's streets, the gold and silver and precious stones would flame in the sun and make the god look otherworldly and majestic. The sight had stirred me as a small child and even made me believe I could feel some hidden soul in the silent, lifeless figure.

After the parade, everyone would follow the priests to the temple gardens, Wepet Renpet being the only time the common people were admitted. There they would present their gifts and sacrifices to the gods. It was a somber and sacred time, until evening when the communal affair of drunken revelry began.

I grabbed the balcony and squeezed my eyes shut as an ominous foreboding swept over me. I understood something in my bones. We would not rest in all of this plenty. Before long, it would be forgotten in the land of Egypt. The gods would forsake us and leave us helpless. We stood stuck in a trap and about to stumble into a bottomless pit.

Rensi reached out with sturdy fingers to hold me steady. "What is wrong?"

"I don't know."

"Perhaps we should get you out of the sun."

I unclenched my jaw and let out a slow breath.

"Take a sip," he said, handing me a cup.

I drained the liquid.

He moved closer to me. "It would be a mistake for me to be blind to the vision you have seen, or deaf to all I have just heard. I promise to deal seriously with your foretelling. As a thirsty man is to finding water, I will give this my full attention." Then he made a broad sweep with his arm. "But look around. All of these people have come to celebrate and give thanks to the gods. Trouble is always nigh, Hagar, so let's not bring it into a day when it is not already present." He seemed to draw strength from some inner pool of royal duty. "The front of the house puts fear in the back. And we are the front of your father's house."

I gave him a thin smile. "No one is better at pretending a situation is more agreeable than it really is than me, High Vizier. I have practiced it my entire life."

Chapter Three

I SLIPPED BENEATH THE LIMESTONE ARCH at the Great Audience Hall entrance to wait for my brother to arrive. The warm, rich scent of fragrant wood curled into the air from lit incense in large bronze braziers that lined the entry. I leaned against the wall and crossed my arms.

The voice of a female singer drifted from the front of the massive room and lured my eyes forward. Enormous stone columns stood two-by-two in rows like giant sentries, and ceremonial raised reliefs decorated the walls' entire length. Each scene depicted our king hunting wild animals or slaying enemies in battle. A border of incised hieroglyphs listed all of Pharaoh's titles: Lord of the Two Lands, High Priest of Every Temple, Son, and Beloved of Amun-Ra.

My lord father.

Ruler of Egypt. Half man. Half god.

And it was easy to believe he was a god.

Pharaoh sat supreme on a throne covered in sheets of gold and crusted with precious stones. His arms rested on replicas of fierce lion heads with open jaws displaying piercing teeth, the legs cast in the exact shape of huge paws with sharp claws. Horus, the patron god of Egyptian pharaohs, sat perched on top of the backrest in the form of a golden falcon, the ruling king's guardian.

The king wore an intricately pleated, fine linen shendyt kilt and a false beard plaited into one thick braid. A royal-blue striped nemes headdress covered the crown and backside of his head. Two parts of the cloth lay behind his ears and extended to his shoulders. On top of the nemes coiled a gold, upright cobra, warning his enemies, he could strike with deadly venom at any time.

I had witnessed many such moments.

My mother, the Great Royal Wife, glided in from a side

door and took her seat to my father's left. I stood straight. Mother's long, regal neck held her head high as she turned her striking face toward me. Her beautiful large eyes of golden amber, meticulously outlined and ornamented, flickered with recognition as they landed on me. Her full mouth turned up in affection, and she raised her hand in quiet greeting.

The Great Royal Wife dressed in a sheer pleated gown that draped her slender frame. She wore wide, matching gold and lapis lazuli armbands above her wrists and sandals made of feathers on her feet. An elaborate black wig of long, overlapping curls sat on her head, along with a gold crown with a rearing cobra—hers represented the goddess Wadjet, the royal protector.

Mother was *my* Wadjet.

Meti, the high priest, followed Mother in and stood to the right of my father. He cut a noble figure, long-legged and tall with a broad chest and shoulders. His skin matched the color of the ebony tree, his eyes black and intuitive. He wore a knee-length linen shendyt and a leopard robe. His long-tailed Vervet monkey, Sobek, sat quietly on his shoulder with an open-mouthed stare on his black face surrounded by grizzled gray fur. Fan-bearers waved feathered standards in perfect unison over their heads.

A small army of minor wives and consorts of my father bustled through the entry with their offspring. Some fanned themselves. Some murmured greetings. All moved quickly.

Ana, my four-year-old half-sister, broke from the crowd and rushed into my arms. When she was barely two, she had slipped her tiny hand in mine and commanded, "Walk." My heart went out to her that day, and I have obeyed her ever since. Her mother, a minor wife, had an unusual face with high cheekbones and gray eyes under heavy lids that always made her look sleepy. She bowed to me and urged Ana along.

Rensi entered in his station's formal clothes, a short shendyt secured by a knotted gold belt, thick bracelets wrapped around his wrists, and a broad gold collar around his neck. His noble wife, Tameri, walked beside him, her hand placed firmly on his arm, tugging him forward. "Come, don't stop," she said. A head taller than the high vizier, she carried a pouty, entitled look frozen on her face.

I felt a pang of discomfort, seeing the high vizier given our honest and transparent conversation earlier. But Rensi smiled warmly at me and even took a moment to bow in respect.

Tameri frowned slightly, nodded, and tugged his arm again to compel him onward.

Scores of nobles and their wives clamored through behind them, smiling and chatting amiably. Many nodded as they passed me, but no one stopped to visit, hoping to get a good position as they made their way to the front.

The excitement in Henen-nesut was so ripe I could taste it. The news that Merikare found a living goddess spread like robust climbing ivy. Its tendrils gripped everything in its path. Even the priests and priestesses who followed behind the nobles shuffled swiftly for a suitable place to see the attraction my brother brought from afar.

Every person who entered the Great Audience Hall knelt before Pharaoh and kissed the ground at his feet. "Life, health, and strength be to you," they said according to custom.

All of the royal children took turns and approached the king on the platform, some slow and apprehensive, others lightly bounced up the steps. I watched my father affectionately hug and kiss each one before their nurses guided them to their mothers.

On most occasions, I enjoyed being a princess.

But not today.

As I watched my father embrace my younger siblings, I noticed the extra moments he spent with the boys and how he regarded them with pride and interest. The girls were briefly pressed to his bosom, patted on the head, and quickly pushed away.

Ana resisted, clinging tightly to my father.

Pharaoh pushed a little firmer. Her nurse grabbed her by

the arm. My stubborn little sister stared at our father, her head tilted, a finger in her mouth. As her tiny shoulders sagged, she reminded me of a wilted flower bud.

My heart ached.

It had always been like that.

I remembered the gentle push, the tug from my nurse, and the curious sensation of emptiness left in its wake. Then I watched Merikare be lifted onto Father's lap, where he was allowed to sit as long as he wanted. He would pretend to rule until he was bored with the game and trotted off to do whatsoever he pleased. But it was the sparkle in Pharaoh's eyes when he gazed at my brother that baffled me. I wondered what he saw in the boy. What hidden depths to my brother had I missed? Until the realization hit that it was merely because he was a boy. Anything he did, no matter how small, would always overshadow me. His value simply surpassed mine.

The knot in my stomach tightened.

A male servant, tall for Egyptian standards, effete and pretty, passed by carrying a tray of blue faience cups filled with wine. He handed me one, his good-humored face flushed as though he had over-sipped his offerings before serving them. I settled back against the wall, took a drink, and frowned when the young wine touched my lips. Always used when there was a multitude to serve, it was second-rate.

Like me.

I motioned to Zadah, who always shadowed me. "Take this and throw it away. Bring me a cup of our finest royal wine."

She nodded and hurried away as the sounds of raucous laughter and someone whistling a tune approached the hall. I stood straight again.

Merikare had arrived.

Chapter Four

ZADAH TAPPED MY ARM AND STARTLED ME.

She giggled.

"You had this ready?"

She nodded eagerly and handed me fine wine served in a solid gold cup.

"Well, good for you. And thank you," I whispered as complete silence rang loud in the vast hall and seemed to echo off the limestone walls. News that the crown prince was about to appear rolled like a wave from the cavernous room's back to the front. Now, I could hear not even a murmur.

A sullen mood gripped me, and I shook my shoulders to relax.

Merikare entered the pillared hall with swagger and a brazen smile full of bright white teeth. He paused long enough for all eyes to fall on him. Handsome, tall, and thickly built with rich nut-brown skin, his square jaw was interrupted only by a dimple in his chin—a copy of our father's. A single plait of hair remained on one side of his shaved head, and black kohl outlined his eyes and darkened his lashes and brows.

Two mountainous men flanked the crown prince. I'd never seen either before, but they appeared to be soldiers of rank. They loomed large, towering over my tall brother, and made him look small in comparison, with their leather helmets, massive shields, and long spears. Both dark brown, square-built, and rock-hard, one as ugly as the other was pleasant to look upon. Merikare would have personally chosen and established these men as royal companions to walk beside him.

"Merikare," I shouted and strode forth boldly, the gold cup dangled from my fingers.

An enormous hand grabbed me, and my wine splashed the floor. I jerked my face upward as the ugly guard stood close enough I could smell his rank breath. My eyes burned into his.

"You cannot touch me."

He didn't move.

A ripple of gasps and uneasy stirring passed through the hall.

I addressed my brother. "Have your royal companion remove his hand from me before I have his hand removed from him."

Merikare stopped, hesitated, then nodded. "Lose your grip or lose your hand. You've seized a princess and my betrothed."

"At once, my lord."

Merikare and I had been betrothed since birth. As the king's eldest royal daughter, it was my duty to marry the heir to the throne. The gods married their sisters, and so did the pharaohs. It set them apart from the average man and increased the royal blood in the next line.

I gritted my teeth against the deep red marks left on my skin, rubbed my arm, and cast a malevolent glare at the huge man. He would not meet my eyes and bore a barely perceptible smug smile.

I took a deep breath, smoothed imaginary wrinkles from the front of my dress, and sidled next to my brother. He walked with long strides, and I struggled to keep up while the royals and nobles carefully cleared a wide path.

"Speak, brother," I said. "Ease my curiosity. Did you really bring us the blessed goddess Isis in the flesh?"

Merikare clenched his jaw. "Peace be upon you, Hagar. It is good to see your beautiful face, sister." His manner did not match the sentiment of his words.

He smelled of fresh water and sunshine. I imagined him standing on the open deck of the royal barge, smiling at all the possibilities life held for him. And then envisioned shoving him overboard.

"Peace be upon you, dear brother," I said. "Forgive my manners. But we weren't expecting you for two weeks, nearer the inundation. And then you provided us hours of entertainment with your floating parade." My voice mocked.

"Tell me, good prince, since you allowed all of Egypt to sail home with you, did you consider for a moment where those people will sleep? Or what we will feed them? Did you even *think* about those things?"

Merikare stopped short and grunted. I had successfully nudged his famous sharp temper. "The pilgrims came in search of answers to their prayers and to celebrate the Festival of Heaven and Earth in the city where their pharaoh resides. There is nothing wrong with that." He glanced across the room, then back to me. "See our old wet nurse over there?"

I kept my gaze on his. "What of her?"

"Perhaps she could instruct you on what kings' daughters do to pass the time. Like spinning, weaving, and suckling babies. I don't answer to you, Hagar." He picked up his gait as a cackle of laughter rose from the royal companions. "You will never wield power and influence in Egypt. So stay away from the affairs of men."

My stomach flipped inside out as the bravado I began with wavered. But, because of my dark vision, I needed answers.

I sweetened my tone. "Beloved prince. I did not mean to trouble you."

"Really?"

"Perhaps I'll even consider your advice if our father does not bend to the guidance of his advisors. Regarding the best way to rule Egypt after he is gone, of course." *I already know Father's answer. Why am I not backing down? I should be backing down.*

Merikare snorted.

I stepped in front of him and stopped. "But I have questions now that I need you to unravel for me."

He looked down on me, and I cringed under his full frame. "I know you'd go to great lengths to strengthen your false claim to the throne, sister." He drew me close. "You've been caught again," he whispered and scowled. "First our mother, and now the high vizier, trying to make a case for you to share the throne with me." He released me. "You were so determined to be born first you tore your way out of the womb before me. But not even that profited you. There are many critics of female rulers, and Father is one of them."

The barb, and its gut-wrenching truth, hit its mark. But I determined to let his arrows pass by without effect, one after another.

"Whatever the gods and our father decree, I will accept. But this is important, brother. The woman you brought, did you take her by force? Is her family still among the living?"

I glimpsed motion from the corner of my eye and knew many in the Great Audience Hall closely watched the confrontation between their princess and crown prince. Merikare realized it as well. We forced strained smiles and kept our voices low.

"Your web of emissaries is impressive, Hagar. Is there anyone in the kingdom who does not seek your favor?"

I started to place my hand on his arm and then drew back. "Please tell me you did not break our laws of hospitality to obtain her."

"Step aside."

I didn't move.

His face seemed carved from stone. "Her family lives," he yielded.

My heart thumped beneath my breast. "I am relieved to hear it."

"Some traveled with us, including her brother, to give his consent."

"I did not know that." I gave way, and he started walking again, faster than before, staying a pace or two ahead of me. "But I heard you took her without ceremony. That her brother was reluctant to give her away and wished to prolong the negotiation for her hand."

Merikare released a guffaw that carried the hall's whole length, which caused our parents to look up at us. My brother nodded at them and smiled. They nodded in return. "Oho,

Hagar," he whispered. "You have been talking to *someone*, sister. Her kin wasn't anxious to consent to this marriage. But we offered him riches and a treaty befitting a future brother-in-law of the pharaoh."

"Was he free to resist or offer any outrage?"

Merikare stopped again, and I nearly stumbled into him.

I gestured toward his formidable guards. "With your mighty band of followers, he was at your mercy, brother. We would not ... we *cannot* ... do anything to violate the ways of the gods."

My brother's eyes narrowed, and his hands curled into fists. "Don't scold me, sister. And stop screeching in my ear. They came to Egypt starving, from the severe famine in Canaan. His tribe will return home with more than the bread and water they came looking for." He released his fists and gave me a contented smile. "Trust me. It was all well done. He's a wealthy man now." He leaned down. "Do not be cross with me. We are to be wed soon," and kissed my forehead.

I pushed him away and shuddered as the kiss burned my brow.

A young nobleman, slim, dark, and richly dressed, stepped forward to give Merikare a cup of wine. The royal companions acted quickly to restrain him. But Merikare raised a hand, and they stopped. He nodded at the nobleman, took the cup and a good gulp of it, and gave the cup back. Another nod toward the man, and Merikare began to walk again.

I hurried alongside, trying to keep up.

"That nobleman bid fiercely for the living treasure I brought for the king," he explained calmly. "If I had not acted quickly, she would have ended up in his household. My actions were not without reason. So, don't try to seize this moment from me."

"Merikare, stop a moment. Please." I needed to step with care and take another path.

He raised a hand, and his companions halted briefly.

"Brother, forgive me. That is not what I intended. You are

the most honorable of men," I gushed. "I know you would not take advantage of the misfortune of others."

Merikare looked at me dubiously. "Although sending Rensi with the curtained litter was shrewd. I let your order stand because it was right that Pharaoh be the first to cast eyes upon her."

I gasped, thinking the high vizier had not kept my confidence. I knew it was best to own the ruse at once. "The people want to believe she is Isis. Aside from Pharaoh, it is not wise for men to worship mortals as gods." My voice sounded like a child's. "It was a cautionary act to not anger the gods. Nothing more." I raised my brow. "I hope it did not trouble you."

Merikare smiled peevishly. "So, it was you."

I drew a deep hot breath, as though I inhaled fire, sucking in burning air. He had never outdone me before.

"My duty is always to our king, Hagar. And to the throne he sits on which will one day be mine alone. You act like it was me who neglected to give you what you desperately desire."

"And what would that be, brother?"

"The parts of a boy instead of a girl. It was the gods who refused you manhood and made me heir." His scowl gave me pause. "Don't undermine me again, sister."

"Old habits, I guess."

He began to walk. "But nothing can trouble me today, Hagar. Wait until you see the unearthly beauty of the Sumerian woman. I almost claimed her for myself and spent many nights thinking about the pleasures of bedding her."

I flushed.

He winked wickedly at me. "But how could I deny our king that right?"

I chose my words with care. "You never have been one for feeble pieties. I'm happy you showed such wise restraint, dear brother. We wouldn't want Father to be cross with you." An awful smell suddenly filled the heated air. "What other exotic things did you bring?"

He shrugged. "Wild beasts, mushrooms, pomegranates, and the largest mandrakes I've ever seen. Their fleshy root looks just like the human form." His eyes flashed an iciness I had never seen before. "I swear, when you pull them from the ground, they shriek like the girls we chased throughout our journey." He glanced at his royal companions and laughed.

The royal companions laughed rowdily too. Although they spoke not a word, what I saw when they locked eyes, made my skin crawl. I had the unsettling thought of them gnawing flesh off bones like pariah dogs that dragged the dead from shallow graves.

"I am pleased you enjoyed your journey, Merikare." I wanted to back away from him but stood fast.

I scrutinized my twin and noticed something I had not seen before. Something dark and dangerous, a truth that hid behind his good looks and midnight-black eyes. Besides being prickly and pompous, he was vindictive and vulgar. Dread stirred in me just thinking about becoming his wife.

I had always believed my half-sisters from lesser wives had a worse fate. They would become nothing more than a medium of exchange for goods or services to Pharaoh. Their husbands would be Egyptian nobles of great wealth and probably ugly older men who shook with palsy and dribbled at the mouth. I shuddered. Then shuddered again when I looked at Merikare's hostile dark eyes and knew that someday soon I would be in his bed.

It was a profoundly distasteful thought.

Chapter Five

I REMEMBER THINKING I SHOULD STEP away and leave him to bask in his glory alone. Seeing him in this new light chilled me, but I couldn't surrender now. "Merikare, answer me this …"

He paused, and our eyes met.

"How does a word live?"

His expression momentarily indicated that the riddle caused him to think, but then his temper flashed. "Sister, you lack the one quality men admire most in a woman."

"And what would that be, dear brother?"

"The ability to know when to stop talking. Hear me now. After we wed, you will be a passive and *silent* complement to me."

My body recoiled. "You have never threatened me like that before." I lifted my head. "You will rule Egypt, and me, soon enough. That has been determined. But now, open your mouth and answer my question."

"I will be the next king of Egypt, Hagar, and its sole ruler," he stated. "I know you have always believed you are wiser than me. My first memories are filled with your jealous, sullen looks because Father preferred me to you. How hard you tried to get his attention, even cutting your hair and dressing in my clothes." He thrust out his chest. "All I had to do was walk into the room where he resided."

"I was not jealous, Merikare. Only confused. Until I realized that all it took was a male frame to garner his attention." I swallowed hard and lowered my face, remembering the account told of the birth of the crown prince. My father despaired when I was born because his first child was a girl. But moments later, a son slid from our mother's womb, and his sorrow turned to joy. It was this story that prompted my frequent masquerades as a boy. I only wanted my father's attention and was always frustrated that things did not go my way. I shook my head. *Who am I fooling? Despite everything, I still hunger for Father's attention. And the frustration remains alive within me.*

Merikare snapped me out of my brief reverie. "You probably think a pointless riddle will baffle me. But it won't. Words only live if they are spoken out loud or in silence. It does not matter. Once uttered, they cannot die." He bent toward me. "Heed that wisdom, Princess."

A day in school would profit you, brother. Words disappear as soon as they are released, and only the gods do not die, I thought as we knelt before Pharaoh and kissed the ground. The cool floor pressed against my forehead.

"Life, health, and strength be to you," we spoke in unison.

Pharaoh leaned forward. "Rise, my sacred twins."

Quiet fell on the Great Audience Hall except for the high-pitched wail of a young child. Pharaoh looked up. Racing feet on the stone ground told me a panicked nurse hurried her charge out of the hall.

"My beloved daughter." Our father turned his attention to me. "Meti tells me you are dreaming of darkness."

"Yes, Father." His interest surprised me, and warmth tingled through my limbs. "It is a recurrent dream, and we don't yet know what it means. I pray it only concerns me, but we are trying to determine—"

The king lifted a hand to silence me. "I, Pharaoh, have come here to dance and sing and to see all that is brought by your brother who is foremost among you."

My ears and cheeks burned red as though he had set flame to them. I lowered my face. Images of bound captives decorated the floor, designed so those who approached the throne symbolically trampled the king's enemies. I gazed at the painted faces rendered in sheer despair and disappeared into the mural, another of Pharaoh's vanquished foes.

"But I want to see you well and happy and troubled no more," Father said, his voice tender.

I lifted my head and held my breath. His words held such promise.

"Do not fight the dark, little one," he continued. "Light a candle, and it will flee because darkness cannot conquer even the tiniest light. Let it go. Enjoy the goodness of this day." He gestured toward a pillow by my mother's feet. "Please, join the Great Royal Wife. It is time for me to receive gifts from my son."

My arms fell to my sides, lifeless. Nothing ever prepared me for the aching familiarity of being dismissed by my father. Mother bowed her head. Father's words seemed soft, even loving, but spoken to diminish me beside my brother. *Light a candle, silly girl, and all your problems will flee.* Maybe Merikare was right. Because if I gave those words life, they *would* live in me forever. But could I do that? Give them life?

Merikare glanced at his royal companions, who gawked at me, and thrust his dimpled chin into the air, and released a booming laugh.

My face went red. I crept up the steps of the royal platform and sat on the pillow as instructed while tears bit at my eyes.

Mother placed a gentle hand on my shoulder and squeezed. I stared hard at her with wide-opened eyes to keep the tears from spilling over. The last thing I needed was a river of black kohl dripping down my face. She gave me an understanding nod. I forced a smile. She patted my shoulder and relaxed in her seat.

Zadah stood not far away in the crowd holding a small pitcher, which I assumed held more of the excellent wine I spilled on the floor while being crudely gripped. I motioned to her, and she grinned, silently slipped up the steps, and refilled my cup. "Stay, Zadah," I whispered, and she sat at my feet.

"My son," our father began. "O, excellent one. I am pleased you are in good spirits." I couldn't see them but knew Pharaoh's midnight-black eyes gleamed.

My brother had our father's eyes. I had our mother's. It was as if the gods were so happy with the creation of our parents, they used the same molds to create them again. The two of us, Merikare and me, made new in their image.

"Good prince, your travels have profited you. My heart is straight when I say I have never been prouder." The king stretched out his bronzed, muscular legs and smiled. "It is a day to celebrate."

Bile filled my throat. I didn't resist, ready to retch the warm sourness all over my brother's perfect day. Instead, it slipped down my throat and burned as it went.

"My loyal representatives that traveled with you report that you led your expedition with the promise of becoming a great king," Pharaoh continued. "It is said that all went very well, and you deserve a fine reward. Now, show me what, and *who,* you have found for me in my kingdom."

I wondered who the flatterers were who were false with the king. My informants whispered that my brother had traveled the country behaving like a bully and a thief.

Merikare stood a moment and basked in the glow of our father's pride. I'd never seen him look happier.

O, hiss and spit.

I gripped my cup of wine so tightly it would have burst in my hands had it not been made of gold.

My brother chased adventure. I chased wisdom. He sought pleasure for his own heart. I desired to understand history, medicine, and the gods. He drank too much. I never lost myself in strong drink. He consorted with scoundrels like the two dogs who guarded him. My companions were priests and scribes. And it had always been so.

Yet, our father gazed at Merikare with delight and awe. Today the king even had oxen and fattened fowl slaughtered for him like a gift to a deity. The crown prince had returned home safe and victorious and was treated like a god.

What a fool I am.

At that moment, our little sister, Ana, slipped from her nurse's embrace. She ran to Merikare and grabbed his hand.

The nurse reached for her. "Come back, little one," she said too late.

"Leave her," the crown prince snapped and lifted Ana into his arms. "Wait until you see what I brought you, little princess."

Ana squealed and hugged his neck. In the blink of an eye, several other small siblings vaulted toward him. Merikare laughed as they clung to him like the high priest's monkey. I squinted coolly at the crown prince for a moment, then glanced away. He never disappointed our younger brothers and sisters and always brought something special for them from his adventures. It was as though he had created a circle that they were all in but me. And only there did he show any tenderness.

I took a long sip of wine and hid my face in the cup.

My father insisted I misunderstood my brother. And times like this did not help my argument against him. Pharaoh called him a risk-taker. One who focused on practical matters like making sure the royal family had enough goods and power to oversee Egypt's wellbeing. It was why Pharaoh had shrugged his massive shoulders and blessed this expedition to the delta. "Why not?" he had said.

"Isn't our safety more important?" I asked the king before Merikare departed on his latest journey. "Shouldn't we know if our southern border is secure?" There had been rumors that Waset was threatening the villages there again. But Pharaoh patted my hand, and as he had done when I was a child, gently pushed me away.

Now, Merikare raised Ana in the air. All whispered conversation ceased. "Clap three times," he told her. She released a delighted squeal, her eyes wide, and then lifted her delicate hands to do as instructed. His royal companions followed her claps by pounding their long spears on the ground. Once. Twice. Three times. The sound echoed through the air and made me twitch.

I rolled my eyes. Merikare employed too much bluster and bravado for me, but our father seemed to enjoy this behavior as did Ana and the rest of our siblings.

An angry roar thundered. The crowd in front of us parted. Wives hid behind their husbands, and children behind their mothers or nursemaids. Ana seized Merikare's neck.

My brother smiled as the first cages entered the vast hall. They held two great lions, one male and one female, and both extremely agitated. Their long, sharp claws were useless as they desperately tried to swipe through the tight bars. Animal offerings always pleased the gods, and lions held magical powers. They would be taken to the temple, killed, and mummified in the name of paying believers.

The big, wild cats came as no surprise. My brother made many conquests, and often they were ferocious beasts, nubile young women, or a combination of both.

I took another sip of wine.

Behind them came a pair of panther cubs, black as night and pleasing to look upon. The Great Royal Wife requested to hold one. Merikare nodded at one of his companions, who grabbed a cub by the scruff of the neck and handed it to my brother. Merikare let Ana hug it and then laid it on Mother's lap. She lifted the adorable little cat, rubbed noses with it, and laughed when a long tongue slipped out and licked her face. She pushed it toward me. I blinked and reached for the cub, hesitated, and drew back my hands. I very much wanted to hold the cub, yet I refused to take any pleasure in Merikare's ridiculous performance.

Mother handed it to Merikare, then reached down and squeezed my shoulder again. This time with a not so gentle pinch. When I looked up, she cocked her head and narrowed her eyes. I gave her an apologetic smile and found the grace to lower my eyes. Then I heard the crowd murmuring as though mystified by my behavior. I knew I behaved foolishly, petty and bitter. *Is this the person I am becoming?* I should have pretended delight with the cub and given everyone less to wonder about.

What is happening to me?

Sleep.

That's what I needed. My muddled mind might clear if I could rest, but the thought of my bed nearly knocked the breath from me. A being haunted my sleep, and I found no comfort there, only a nightly struggle.

I shivered.

I took a final swig of wine and handed the empty cup to Zadah. My thin linen dress stuck to my skin. The rising temperature and sharp smell of fresh excrement from the untamed exhibition soiled the air. I thought of the cool water in my plunge pool and the sweetly scented flowers of my private garden. Perhaps I could escape there forever and be free as a trailing rosebush.

I shook my head.

Even roses were forced to go the way their keepers choose.

The panther cubs' mother had already been skinned and was now ceremoniously laid in front of Pharaoh. This was symbolic and would please Mafdet, the goddess who protected the king. She ripped out the hearts of his enemies and delivered them to his feet.

It also pleased the king. He smiled a flash of white teeth.

Two mother cheetahs followed with their cubs. The adults growled low while their young meowed loudly like palace cats.

"The adults we have brought for your menagerie, my father," Merikare gushed. "My men tamed them to hunt for you. But the cubs will make fine pets. With your permission, may I gift them to my brothers and sisters in your royal harem?"

"You may," Pharaoh said.

Squeals of delight came from all the children.

Ana slid from Merikare's embrace and followed the cats out, her nurse on her heels.

The animal waste was swept away, along with the black flies that had quickly swarmed the mounds of dung. Large rush baskets of blood-red pomegranates were placed before us, followed by globe grapes, dates, all types of nuts, and olives.

Clay pots filled with wine came after that, the name of the vineyard pressed clearly into each one. And then beer. Jugs and jugs of beer.

The maidens came next wearing thin nets made of gold as their only garment. Merikare always returned with peasant girls looking for new jobs and opportunities in the royal household. Selected for their abilities and attractiveness, some would become cooks or servers, some musicians or dancing girls, others weavers or washerwomen. They were tall and short, dark and light, young and younger, each fair and pleasing to look upon.

One charming maid with long, flowing hair followed behind. She wore a simple ankle-length sheath dress of sheer linen with two thick shoulder straps just wide enough to cover her breasts. A copper collar made of rows of beads shaped like flowers hung around her neck. It complemented two thick copper armbands and a pair of copper flower earrings.

She stole a sideways glance at my twin.

He met her eyes for the briefest moment and then looked away slowly. *She pleased him.* It was likely she would come into the Royal House of Women, the harem, as a concubine to the crown prince.

Trailing behind them came twelve huge men with dark skin like freshly turned soil. They wore leather loincloths, nothing more, gripping the plated gold handles as they carried the curtained litter fashioned from ivory and ebony I had sent to fetch a goddess. The silken pavilion on top was closed tight. They placed the carry chair on the ground in front of my father, kissed the floor at his feet, and vanished into the crowd.

I glanced up at Mother. She sat still as though fashioned from stone. I knew she would prefer to be anywhere but here, welcoming a new woman into her husband's bed. She once confessed to me that no matter how many times she had done so, it never became easy. She wanted him all to herself, like when they were children. She was his half-sister, born to a minor wife not long after my father's birth. They had been raised together, and unlike Merikare and me, had always been close. She had been possessive of him then, always wanting to be his only companion, pouting if other siblings played with him. But now that made her feel selfish. He was the king. His seed needed to be spread to ensure royal heirs, strengthen relationships, and even avoid wars.

I always believed my parents loved each other. Even though countless women joined the harem, my father's consideration toward Mother never wavered. He deprived her of nothing, and her offspring were always foremost in his life. For that, she had told me, she hid the ugly flicker of jealousy that forever sparked at times like these.

At my feet, Zadah shifted and nudged my ankle.

Merikare stepped to the litter. I held my breath along with everyone in the hall as he pulled back the curtain.

Zadah scurried to her knees and bowed her head to the floor.

"Sit up, you little fool," I whispered harshly. As the girl slowly sat up, I glanced at the litter.

The most magnificent pair of eyes met mine.

Chapter Six

HER LOVELINESS HAD NOT BEEN EXAGGERATED. She was beautiful. Her sky-blue eyes stared at me and almost appeared violet, catching the color from a large amethyst suspended from her delicate neck. Lips, red as garnet, graced a heart-shaped face with a complexion the color of goat's milk and honey. Plaited sable hair wrapped around her head like a soft crown, topped with a shimmering gold lotus flower. She dressed modestly in an ankle-length, deep purple gown with a fringed amber robe showing only her right arm and shoulder. A failed attempt to discourage lust from male appetites, I imagined.

The king caught his breath. He appeared so taken aback, if a fan-bearer touched him with an ostrich feather, he'd knock him off his throne. Merikare, with a satisfied smile, offered his hand, and she stepped off the litter as a majestic ornament on his arm.

It was impossible not to stare.

But it wasn't only her beauty that made it hard to glance away. Her stunning face and quick eyes glowed with radiance. Rensi had been right. Light dwelled in this woman. The room strangely brightened with each step she took.

Then I sensed something I could not hold on to, like trying to remember a dream that had already fled. My skin rose in gooseflesh as a chilling sense veiled my body. She had not come to us alone. There seemed to be a *presence* with her. *A specter.*

The woman walked with the gods, or the dead, I was sure of it.

My mind seemed stuck inside a swirling fog. Maybe she did have something to do with my nightmares. Weariness made my bones heavy as bronze and difficult to discern. But the hollow sensation in my stomach convinced me that something was wrong.

Sweat beaded on my forehead.

I frantically watched my parents.

Merikare.

The high priest.

And then out at the large number of people gathered. No one's countenance had changed. No one seemed alarmed. I tried to meet Rensi's eyes, but even his expression remained the same. Perhaps the wine had gone too quickly to my head.

The divine woman lay face down before Pharaoh and lingered there.

Merikare beamed. "Father, I present Sarai, sister of Abram of Ur of the Chaldeans." He took her hand and helped her to stand. "I pray that you rejoice in seeing the fair goddess who joins our family this day."

Sarai's movements were languid and graceful. Although, under all of our scrutiny, she appeared anxious. She blew out a few quick breaths as her cheeks blushed like the blooming of a thousand roses. Her gaze darted between Pharaoh and the Great Royal Wife as she clutched the amethyst necklace.

"There are many occasions for a king to display his joy of life. Today there is double joy in my heart," Pharaoh said, clearly besotted. He motioned for Sarai to step closer. "My perfect one," he began, "you have overpowered my heart. Behold, you are fairer than all the women in my kingdom. You are a lily among thorns. My heart dances upon the Nile with one look at you."

Merikare could not contain his grin, and his chest swelled. I didn't dare look at Mother but noticed the narrowed eyes and taut lips from the minor wives and concubines. The backlash against Sarai in the harem would be fierce. It would tear through the Royal House of Women like fire.

Although, I didn't feel the least bit offended. Father's words were valid.

"Those who brought you to me will be rewarded with many good things," Pharaoh continued. "Let us spend the day rejoicing and feasting with the entire palace." The King of Egypt reached out to take Sarai's hand, but his own hand froze in midair as he did. His fingers curled and turned ashen, wilted before my eyes like a thirsty plant in the hot sun.

I sprang to my feet. "What manner of black magic is this?" I shouted. "Are you employing the powers of a god upon the king?"

Sarai's eyes grew huge as a flicker of knowing crossed her beautiful face. She understood everything. Wordless, she stared at me, rubbed her arms, and trembled as though it had suddenly grown cold.

The veins exploded in Merikare's thick neck. "*Black magic?* Princess Hagar! What do you accuse me of?" His guttural roar sounded like the lions he had brought for the temple.

I searched the Great Audience Hall. No one stirred. Only the magnified buzzing of a fly, so loud as to consume all the space in the room, could be heard. In my bewilderment, my hands rushed to cover my mouth. My eyes finally met Rensi's. He pressed a finger to his lips and barely shook his head. But I understood too late. No one else, except perhaps Sarai, had seen what I believed I saw.

And it was too late to change my unfavorable outburst.

I descended the steps and fell at the feet of my brother. My behavior was inexcusable, poorly done, especially for a princess. "Forgive me, my lord," I sobbed. "I did not mean to be so discourteous. I've had no sleep, and the heat is too much for me today. I've eaten nothing and only sipped wine. It must have gone too swiftly to my head." I blurted every excuse I could think of. "Please, please forgive me."

He appeared so taken aback, and probably thought I planned it. Maybe deep inside, I had. I couldn't be sure of anything anymore.

I laid flat, face on the ground before the king. "O, Pharaoh.

Life, health, and strength be to you. My father, I *beg* forgiveness. Please allow me to go to the Royal House of Women and rest and eat. The nights have been pitiless and I have found no kindness or sleep in them."

"My king. My royal husband," the Great Royal Wife said in a firm voice, "as you know, our beloved daughter has been plagued these many weeks with a vision in the night that will not cease. The lack of sleep must be causing her to see things that are not there."

I glanced up at them.

"You know our royal child would never intentionally insult or upset this court," Mother continued. "Consent to let her go back to her rooms. I'm sure she will be refreshed and more like herself by this evening."

A mother's love and protection—older and greater than all magic and gods bound together. My heart was grateful for it.

The king only nodded, his face a mix of confusion and anger. I kissed the floor in front of his feet and stood. My brother scowled, with his chin high, legs planted wide, and fists on his hips.

What have I done?

"I'm sorry," I mouthed.

His face flushed furiously, and he turned as though dismissing me.

No one moved. No one breathed.

Signaling to Zadah to follow, I hurried off, stumbled, and found my feet before further humiliating myself. I passed Rensi, who extended his hand to me, but his noble wife Tameri took it in her own and restrained him.

I rushed down the center aisle, past the six and thirty stone columns, toward the arched entryway. Everyone gaped at me with open mouths as fingers touched their parted lips and stares seared my core. This would tear through the harem like fire too. Everyone would take sides. Those who believed I planned it, and those who would not think so. It all depended on how they felt about me.

I kept moving forward as quickly as I could and glanced at the long sculpture on the wall of a flock of geese in flight. *Wings. Why can't I have wings instead of feet so I can fly through the air and escape?* I stopped just outside the Great Audience Hall to take a breath. My hands trembled as I wiped tears away. I had wanted it to end, to be away from my brother's cocky superiority and our father's gushing pride.

But not like that. I behaved like a fool. My face burned, knowing Merikare would find satisfaction in that.

Several armchairs lined the walls. Movement from the farthest end caused me to flinch. A man, unknown to me, sat on one of the chairs. He'd been hidden in sunlight when I'd first entered, but now his form seemed drawn into the setting— as though an artist painted him there. His elbows rested on his knees, and his head lay on clasped hands. He tipped his neck, and upon seeing me, abruptly sat up.

I waited a moment and then started to move past him, but I paused when he took a knee before me and bowed his head. He wore a deep red, knee-length tunic and a ropelike leather belt wrapped around his waist. A golden-brown vesture covered his tunic. Fine leather sandals shod his feet.

"Forgive me," he said and looked up. "I did not mean to offend the hospitality of this house." He spoke my native language, flawlessly. Vulnerable brokenness scored his pleasing face and disappeared into a long gray beard. As handsome and fair as Sarai was beautiful, I could see they were kin.

Her brother.

He took my breath away.

His bearing loomed larger than life, even kneeling before me. I took one look in his bottomless deep brown eyes and wanted to remain there forever. I nearly said to the man, "Take my heart, my lord."

Thankfully, my lips did not utter those words.

"Please … stand," I said, reeling. First, with the fresh

image of my father's withered hand, and now with this handsome stranger. Maybe it hadn't happened after all, and I imagined it. Conceivably it was a mix-up with the wine and my lack of food and sleep. My mind flickered like the dim waver of a candle flame. I fought to regain composure and worried the black kohl that outlined my eyes now smeared across my face.

I steadied myself. "Forgiveness is not required here. You must be Sarai's brother."

He rose before me and stood tall and lean and comely. "I am Abram of Ur. Sarai is my blood. You must be Princess Hagar. I recognize you from the high vizier's description. He often spoke of your fine mind and beauty."

A flush crept across my cheeks. "Thank you, my lord," I gushed, my voice high-pitched. "I must remember to thank the high vizier for his kind words regarding me."

Why am I so charmed by him?

Abram was much older than my father but still fine-looking and powerfully built. Unlike the men of Egypt, long hair covered his face and head. Yet, the closeness of this foreigner gave me a strange pleasure. *What is happening to me?* My hands trembled, and my stomach fluttered.

Then my head jerked slightly. The *presence* I sensed near his sister surrounded me here. It lingered near her brother too.

Gooseflesh covered my skin.

He gave me a kind smile that did not reach his eyes, and my thoughts slipped back to him. I'd seen profound sadness in family members before. "Silent grief," we called it. It occurred the moment loved ones grasped that once their daughter or sister entered my father's harem, their goodbye was forever. Although, more oft, families delighted in having a relative connected to the royal household. The tremendous benefits and prestige eased the loss.

Zadah walked up and stood beside me. She giggled, knowing Abram averted his eyes because of her nudity. I gave her a stern look, and she knelt before him. "May this bothersome slave offer you wine or any other refreshment?"

He shook his head.

She stood and slipped behind me.

I paused a moment to observe his face further. "You must think we are strange people, my lord. With our naked servants and clean-shaven bodies."

"Again, offense is not intended, Princess. In our tradition, women do not mix with men when they have laid aside their garments. And to mutilate a beard by shaving is considered a great disgrace in our culture."

My posture stiffened, being unsure if he slighted me. "Have you not lived among my people long enough for our practices to no longer bother your traditional sensibilities? Our climate is so warm, how can you find disgrace in shaving for relief from the heat? And do your women and men not dispense with clothing at least for some purposes?"

Zadah giggled behind me.

"Even though we live in your land, we keep to our own tribe. We do not judge your practices. We only seek to be faithful to our own. We believe that the outer appearance reflects the inner spirituality. With no disrespect, Princess."

"None taken, my lord."

Abram courteously tried to keep his eyes on me, but his worried gaze often flicked toward the Great Audience Hall.

"Do not fret on account of your sister," I said in a soothing tone. "I promise you, Sarai will come to no harm here. She is truly extraordinary and will be prized among the dark daughters of Egypt."

Unless I find she employed magic powers upon the king.

"I appreciate your consideration, Princess." Abram took a deep, pained breath, closed his eyes, and stood unnaturally still. "Unfortunately, it doesn't make this easier."

"Pharaoh was pleased with her and will reward you with riches beyond your dreams." I smiled. "She is very welcome here, and we are happy to have her with us. I pray you will find some solace in that."

His chin dipped to his chest, and his posture slumped. I went over everything I knew about his situation. I had a feeling I missed something. He appeared to be grieving, but there was something else.

He looked *guilty.*

He would leave Egypt a prosperous man when the famine in Canaan was over. But Sarai would remain here until her dying day. Why would he care so much about a woman who was not his wife? I twisted the amulet on my wrist.

Perhaps I read too much into it.

Chapter Seven

WE STOOD THERE IN SILENCE, IN a kind of stupor, until the sound of soft footsteps came from behind. Flowery perfume saturated the air. I knew it belonged to Rensi's chinwag wife, Tameri, before I turned. Like her, it was sharp and unpleasant. She had a small head, a broad nose, and a big mouth.

Rensi walked beside her, and I watched them make their way to us.

"O, Princess Hagar. What did you imagine you had seen? That beautiful woman casting spells?" She planted one hand over her heart, her eyes glowing, and trilled, "Most people think you intended to make trouble for your brother on his triumphant day. But not me. I know you would never intentionally spout evil charges toward the crown prince. In public view, anyway."

Rensi cringed. "Wife, you forget yourself. Hold your tongue."

Tameri, an idle busybody, often visited the harem and wandered from room to room to absorb gossip and spread it as farmers do manure. I usually ignored her, but Abram looked alarmed. My face burned again, and I bit my bottom lip to keep silent. Only my affection for Rensi kept my wrath from her.

"Has it anything to do with Sarai?" Abram focused on me.

I started to answer, but Tameri rushed in, her dark, weasel-like eyes darting from Abram to me. "O, yes. When Pharaoh reached out to touch Sarai, Princess Hagar stood and accused her and the crown prince of black magic. A scandalous scene." She snorted.

"Tameri, you will not speak of the royal family like this. Be silent," Rensi said evenly and watched me with concern.

She ignored her husband and wormed her way between us. "You are Sarai's brother." She gave Abram a long look. "I see the resemblance. Is it true you hid your sister in a trunk so no one would see her?" Tameri did not wait for a reply. "And begged my husband not to look? He cracked it open, and a bright light emanated from it. Out came a woman that makes all other women look like monkeys." She shrugged. "I don't mind saying so, for it is the truth." Rensi moaned, and Tameri glared at him. "I had to gather these tidings from my own agents. My noble husband did not choose to share this information with me."

Rensi's face pinched. "That story is greatly exaggerated. It grows larger with each telling. Especially when *you* tell it."

I wondered. When Sarai stepped off the litter, the room appeared brighter to me. And the *presence* I sensed. It must be magic, maybe *black* magic. A conjuring revealed only to me and hidden from everyone else.

Why?

I examined Abram's pleasing face for evidence that he could harness the powers of the supernatural. It disclosed nothing. Instead, his warm, beautiful eyes focused on mine and stayed there. They appeared to search me, all the way to my soul. We stood silent again, the two of us, a thick stillness between us as something took up residence in my heart. For the first time in my life, I longed for something that would never exist for me—the love of a good man.

"Princess Hagar." Tameri's shrill voice pierced the quiet. "I feel obligated, since we are the highest nobles in the land, that I should offer my help. This new favorite of the king needs to be at her best when she goes in to pleasure him. I will make sure of that."

All color in Abram's face fled, and his eyes moved to the Great Audience Hall. He clearly did not want this union to take place. My heart fluttered in my chest. I didn't know a man could care more for a woman than Pharaoh's gold. *O, how easily you could possess me.*

"Tameri, please." Rensi shrugged helplessly. "It is not your place."

Tameri waved a hand at him but said nothing more.

"Noblewoman Tameri. How kind of you to offer," I said. "You are welcome to attend Sarai. Perhaps you would consent to accompany her to the harem? Make sure she has all she needs to be comfortable in her new home."

Rensi nodded gratefully and addressed Abram. "Pharaoh has asked for you. He is ready to pay the bride-price."

Abram took a step backward, away from the doorway.

"My lord Abram. There is no danger here. You will find only friends among us." I looked at the high vizier. "Make certain of that, Rensi?" I knew too well how the promises made by my brother could change. Thoughts of honor seldom troubled Merikare.

He bowed to me. "It shall be done."

"You are thoughtful, Princess Hagar," Abram said, also bowing. "I am not afraid of your people. I only fear my loss. And spending each day of my life without Sarai in it."

Heart be still!

Everything in me softened. "Tameri. Bring Abram's sister to my private quarters. She will stay with me until the overseer can provide her own accommodations." I locked eyes with Abram. "I will watch over Sarai myself and treat her as my own dear sister."

My words vexed Tameri. "O, Princess. Do you mean to take the task of caring for the king's new favorite from my hands?"

Royal manners made my words to Tameri kinder than I'd have liked. "Please, dear noble wife of the high vizier, act according to my wishes. I will still appreciate your presence and council concerning Sarai in my chambers."

"I will do all you ask and whatever you command," Tameri said, bowing low before me.

"And in silence," added Rensi.

"You have been a good friend on this day of distress," Abram said to me and managed a small smile. "I will not forget your compassion and remember you often to my God."

Warmth tingled in my limbs as I watched Abram walk

toward the Great Audience Hall with the high vizier. This great man promised to remember *me* often. But had he misspoken when he said "my God"? Surely, he meant "the gods."

My mind recalled the god in my dream. What had I said to Rensi about him? *It seemed to me he was not one god among many, more like he alone was God.*

Excited humming, like a happy hive of honeybees, buzzed from the crowded hall as Abram, Rensi, and Tameri reached the entrance. They paused under the limestone arch for a moment, and the noisy room settled instantly. Sorely tempted, I considered returning to watch what would take place.

Zadah pleaded to do just that. "Can we only peek our heads in? Court has never been so exciting."

I shook my head. I could not return. Mother had pleaded for me and allowed me to escape in haste. In no way would Merikare, or our father, wish to see my face so soon. I turned and strode toward the private apartments of the royal family.

Zadah lingered a moment, then reluctantly followed me.

I needed my garden and the tranquil water of my pool to gather my thoughts and compose myself. I would think about what I had seen and what I believed Sarai had seen as well.

Oho, she can't deny it. She better not deny it.

The thought twisted in my belly like a blade as my heart beat frantically. *O, what have I set in motion?* I humiliated my brother, angered my father, and saw worry and pity in the eyes of my mother and Rensi. I desperately needed to fix this. If an average citizen, or even a powerful noble, spoke out like that, they would have been dragged out and burned alive that very instant. Merikare could still insist that I be hauled into the streets and beaten. He had every right to dishonor me publicly.

Tears stung my eyes, knowing the gods were not in my favor today.

Perhaps Merikare was right—once uttered, words could not be taken back. Speaking did seem to give them life. It wasn't lost on me that I would likely live with them longer than I wanted to. But I would find a way to repair the rift between my brother and me. Whatever it took.

My heartbeat quickened as I recalled Abram and his boundless brown eyes. I smiled. I realized I wanted more than anything, no, needed more than anything, to think about Sarai's brother. I felt myself blush. How could a man older than my father and with facial hair fascinate me so? The *presence* that emanated from Abram and his sister must have cast a spell on my affections. It had to be magic. No man had ever caused passion to rise in my emotions. I wanted to believe that there had been something between us in that brief encounter. Something more than we shared with everyone else.

The thought startled me.

And Father's withered hand flashed in my mind.

I promised Abram I would take care of his sister. But I had been false with him. If I discovered any hidden thing, a hostile shade invoked, or an incantation used against my father, I would not hesitate to see her punished. I would feed his sister to wild beasts or drown her in a swift current myself. I would wash my hands in her blood and rejoice in doing so.

Chapter Eight

ZADAH LOOKED UP AND SMILED AT two dark, brawny palace guards as if she'd asked them to play. Her gaiety would have been infectious if she hadn't swung so widely between laughter and grumbling about the excitement we missed in court.

The guards stood stone-faced and still in front of twin freestanding pillars that led into the harem quarters. Their eyes, rimmed in black, at no time flickered toward us. Both wore a linen shendyt just above the knees, a headcloth pulled tight across the forehead and tied in the back, thick copper cuffs high on muscular arms that crisscrossed bare chests, and a flat leather club held in one hand.

A vivid image of Pharaoh with all of his wives and royal children adorned the wall in sunken relief through the length of the long-pillared hall. I stopped a moment at the remarkable likeness of my father.

Zadah crept behind a column.

I kissed the tips of my fingers and touched his face. A fresh flood of tears streamed down my cheeks. *I disappointed him.*

Zadah touched my arm with a small cloth, and I wiped my runny makeup and nose. I let myself linger a moment more, because his portrait could not push me away, and then continued to the vast and rambling Royal House of Women.

Divided into a southern and northern wing, both with adjacent cultivated gardens, ponds, and pools, the north wing's shade and a fit breeze made it more desirable. It housed the most prominent women. Being the Great Royal Wife, my mother presided over the entire household from there with Bunefer, the Overseer of the Royal House of Women. Mother had moved me near her years ago, giving me one of the best apartments when I was a small child. We shared the northern wing with a handful of father's minor wives who delighted him the most with their attentions, until they lost his esteem, or he favored another more.

The king's mother lived here in opulence, similar to the Great Royal Wife until she passed to the afterlife years ago. A spiteful old woman, many believed a look from her could make wine sour and a womb unfruitful. Tittle-tattle lingered that she had cast a spell on her quarters to curse anyone who entered after she died. So, her luxurious rooms had sat empty for far too long. It would not surprise me if they prepared her lavish lodgings for Sarai. Any woman would be delighted to live in such extravagance. Abram did not need to concern himself with her wellbeing any longer.

Unless, of course, she caused the king's hand to shrivel.

I wished I didn't have to think about it. I wanted to keep my promise to Abram and hoped Sarai would live with the lesser wives and concubines away from me. But I doubted that would happen.

The southern wing, as vast and luxurious as the northern wing, was less desirable because it stayed warm in the summer months. It lacked shade and a breeze, and the noise level could be deafening. All the royal children lived there. It accommodated the Royal Nursery and the Kap, the school for princes and princesses, and the offspring of favored high officials.

Except for Merikare and me, as Meti, the high priest, personally conducted our education.

The southern wing did not seem the right place for Sarai, the king's new favorite. She may not be a goddess, but she would be treated like one.

I entered my private living quarters and nearly tripped on Bastet, my spotted silver cat who lay stretched out on the cool limestone floor. I leaned down, scratched behind her ears, and watched the tip of her tail rise and fall. She purred and straightened, pushed her claws out, but did not open her eyes or attempt to stand.

I left her to her leisure and walked into my private garden

with Zadah on my heels, who still murmured complaints about missing court. I inhaled the fragrant cloud of sweet and spicy flowers—my wild roses—and stood a moment under the shade of a willow tree to take it in. Then I heard voices. My fingers trembled and my lips clenched. I marched past grapevines that clambered up mud bricks that enclosed the garden and plots of blooming flowers that shone in the intense sunlight. I halted near a long ornamental pond with white and blue lotus flowers drifting along its surface with a graceful pair of pintail ducks.

I crossed my arms and stared.

My personal attendants splashed carefree in my small swimming pool. Their noisy jests and laughter spilled out, flowed over, and drenched the peace and quiet of the garden.

Zadah clapped her hands. "Out, out. Now. You are not allowed in there. Princess, tell me what you would like me to do to them." She was little but fierce.

The girls scrambled from the pool and stood before me. I dispensed the same glare my mother used, the one that had made me wobbly when I was naughty.

Kiya, tall, willowy, and shy, appeared as though she might be ill. Dendera, pretty and plump, kept her head lowered. Water dripped from their naked bodies and created puddles on the ground.

They both shivered in the burning sun.

"Is this a thing you do in secret? Use my garden as your refuge?" It was hard to fault them. The cool shade, the heavy fragrance from the flowers, and the refreshing water were alluring. But they should have obtained permission first. "What punishment shall fall upon you?"

Kiya bowed before me and pressed her forehead to the ground. Dendera did the same. "Forgive our transgression, beloved Princess," Kiya said. "We only wanted a moment of escape from the heat and dust." She began to sob.

Zadah broke off a twig from a young sycamore tree and smacked it across Kiya's bare bottom. Kiya muffled a scream as a long, fiery-red welt rose on her skin. "Shall I slay them for you, Princess? Shall I turn the water red with their blood?"

I hid my surprise from the tiny warrior. "I have no desire to bathe in blood."

Two bodies shook before me, and neither girl dared look up.

I could lash out because right now, my spirit was vexed. But at myself. Not them. "Now that you are refreshed, rise and go quickly. Bring me something to eat. Whatever the cooks have prepared. And be swift about it before I change my mind and loose Zadah upon you."

They moved with the fleetness of the wind.

Zadah frowned as she removed the thick silver amulet from my wrist. She shook her head as she slid off my wig made from a mass of naturally curly human hair. The silver and lapis lazuli beads woven through it jingled lightly as Zadah sighed and placed it on a red granite bench.

"You need to be firm with the servants lest they no longer fear you. If you let me spill a little of their blood, they would not take advantage of your kind nature like this."

I couldn't help but smile. Zadah had been with me since we were children, so I elevated her rank above my other servants, a status she took seriously.

"I was not trying to amuse you, Princess," she huffed as she slid my linen sheath from my shoulders.

"I know, Zadah. Your words have not fallen on deaf ears." I stepped into the pool and floated on my back with my eyes closed. The water lapped over me and cooled my body. I tried not to move and let it calm my spirit. "Quiet now. Let me rest here in peace. The nights have not been kind."

"There is no rest for us today, Princess Hagar." The voice was shrill and unmistakable.

I frowned. "Tameri," I said, keeping my eyes closed. I did not stir.

"You cannot enter Princess Hagar's garden without invitation," Zadah said.

I righted myself in time to see Tameri's hand descend

effectively across my tiny servant's cheek.

"I come on the king's business, and that does not require an invitation," Tameri blazed. Egypt had many perils, but none as dangerous as Tameri when she believed someone usurped her rank.

As I had done the day before she wed Rensi.

I was a young child in need of attention, and she was about to marry the man who gave it to me in abundance. I worshipped Rensi even then. When I overheard gossip that she was from a lower social class than Rensi, I openly objected to the union on those grounds. After all these years, she had yet to forgive me. And my guilt still allowed her to get away with things that no one else could.

Zadah rubbed her cheek. Tears welled in her eyes, and she turned away as if to run.

"Don't go far, Zadah," I said gently. "I will need to dress soon."

Tameri sat on the granite bench next to the pool and pushed my wig aside with an expression of repugnance, as if it were unpleasant to her touch. The beads jingled softly. "Hagar, you should see the jewels the king has bestowed upon Sarai. Not even the Great Royal Wife has adorned herself with such as these." She gave a half-smirk. "Yes, Sarai will put them on, and your father will take them off."

I decided to ignore that and glanced up at the sun, which looked down on us from the middle of the sky like a giant, solitary eye filled with fire. Still barely past noontide.

"Tameri," I said absently. "How does a word live?"

She leaned forward and crossed her arms. "We have no time for riddles or games. I've ordered your servant girls to draw a bath for Sarai in your room. They were reluctant to obey me as they seemed to be running some errands for you. I had to clout the chubby one when she refused. I assured them they did not want to cause a delay in the king's desires."

That's what happened to my wine and repast.

"Your servants need a strong hand, Hagar."

So I've heard.

"My servants never balk when I give them an order. They certainly would never speak to a noble or royal like that little one just did."

I do not doubt that.

She stood and tapped her foot on the edge of the pool. "Please get out. There is much to be done. We have to transform a Sumerian princess into an Egyptian royal bride in time for the new year's great festival. Tonight, we feast and dance until the Nile dries up."

I bristled. *Does she jape about my dream? Would Rensi have shared my secret with her?* I examined her predatory eyes. No. It must have been a chance use of words. "Tameri, I promise my feet will hurry behind you as you go."

She offered a mocking half-bow—given only when my parents weren't around—and stalked away.

Chapter Nine

SARAI STEEPED IN A WARM, SCENTED bath, her head tilted back, eyes closed. I nearly opened my mouth to say what I thought, that she had the loveliest face I had ever seen. Perhaps she was a goddess after all. Thankfully, I remembered myself as many women of the harem now filled my room.

Dendera scrubbed Sarai's skin with coarse grains of sea salt mixed with beeswax. Kiya poured water over her to rinse the salt away, and a sweet, clean aroma flowed with it. Sorrow seemed to seep from Sarai as she soaked in the tub, and she stiffened when the cool water touched her skin. She kept her eyes closed, and I noticed her lips moved a bit, almost indiscernible as though she prayed.

Are you reciting an incantation? Or casting another spell upon my people, Sarai?

I glanced around the room as noblewomen, minor wives, and concubines—drawn here like scarabs to a flame—reclined against large, luxurious cushions scattered on the floor. They chatted amiably, and everything seemed normal. I tried hard to discern any unnatural presence. But there was nothing, not one withered hand or disfigured feature in the group.

Normal.

My gaze returned to Sarai.

As though she sensed my stare, Sarai opened her astonishing eyes and looked straight into mine. I tensed and held my breath, caught in a deep inspection of her. She smiled with tender melancholy but no bitterness or ill will. Her attempt to hide her apparent misery moved me, and my heart sympathized with her.

Tameri sat beside the tub and instructed the servants who bathed me several times a day. She always seemed compelled to teach others the best way to do things, even simple, mundane tasks. "Pour like dew descending from the sky. Not like you are drowning the meadows when the riverbanks are flooded," she snapped. She carried a small hand-fan, which she used as a spear to stab Kiya on her backside. The girl flinched and slowed the flow of water to a trickle.

My face burned, but I held my tongue. After the wedding misfortune, I swore to Rensi that I would respect his wife's position for the rest of my life. *O, but how she has tested me all of these years.*

Tameri closely viewed every inch of Sarai. "How shapely are her breasts and how lovely all of her whiteness. Her arms are goodly to look at, and her hands, how perfect. Her legs, how beautiful and without blemish."

"And what do you think of my tail?" Sarai jested, a small, choked sound in her voice. She spoke our language without a flaw, but I noticed her words came through a rigid smile.

"You have a tail?" Tameri inquired, falling into the trap.

"Just like the monkey your high priest carries on his shoulder," Sarai said, her voice terse.

I laughed along with all the other women.

Tameri stood abruptly right as Bastet tried to jump onto her lap. Her fan waved wildly in one hand, and she nervously fingered a turquoise pendant around her neck with the other. "You tease the noble wife of Rensi, the high vizier?" Her mouth gave an unpleasant twist as she pushed Bastet away with her toe.

Sarai opened her mouth as though to say something but appeared to think better of it. She released a deep sigh. "Maybe a little." Her tone gentled. "Please, Tameri, my sister, sit beside me. There is a score of women standing among us—all with shapely bodies, breasts, and braids. Even you, who has given birth many times, are beautiful of face and form. Sit and tell me about your husband and your children. My heart will be refreshed by it."

Tameri, her chin high, retook a seat. She clapped her hands several times and commanded to no one in particular, "Go and find the delicacies that the king offers. Fetch Tigernut Sweets and dates and honey cakes. Bring some of the figs, pomegranates, and grapes Merikare brought from the delta. And procure the best wine in the palace." She looked at me. "We may be here a while, and I will stay with Sarai until his majesty summons her."

When you will expect gifts from Pharaoh for tending to his favorite, I thought, but only nodded at Kiya to do as she said.

Then I noticed Sarai's troubled expression, like one waiting for a death seen coming. Tameri noticed it too.

"O, fairest among women," Tameri said, "do not fear your wedding night. The king's fruit will be sweet to you. You have been like a garden enclosed. A hidden fountain. But tonight, your garden will open, and your spices will flow out."

All the women giggled. Tameri, clearly enjoying the audience, continued. "The king is a lusty bull. He has been the lover of many women, why most of those here have aroused Pharaoh's passions and desires." The women giggled again. "But with one look at you, Pharaoh was hopelessly in love. It could just be lust—oft it is hard to tell—but I don't think so." More giggles. "I saw the same look on Princess Hagar's face when she laid eyes on your attractive brother, Abram. That was love at first sight. I'm sure of it."

Sarai, along with everyone else in the room, looked at me. My neck flamed unbearably hot, rising to my cheeks. I'd had enough humiliation for one day. "Tameri, what is this mood?" I said, giving her an unruffled smile. "Is this a thing you should do? Start rumors regarding the royal family? Perhaps you are not as keen-sighted as you believe."

"I am only an attendant and a true friend—a mere servant in the Royal Harem. You are the most highly praised among all the daughters of Egypt. And the most *watched*." The residence was hushed. "I will not deny what I saw when you looked upon Abram."

Tameri's tongue had no equal. *I wonder if Rensi would mind if I cut it out and feed it to the cheetahs Merikare gifted the harem with.* I pressed my lips together to keep my mouth silent.

Sarai's magnificent blue eyes remained on me. Bastet paced the room, purring and rubbing against the women seated on the floor.

"But that is a marriage not even the gods could arrange," Tameri said and turned toward Sarai. "Pharaoh often marries foreign princesses to strengthen political bonds. But since earliest times, no daughter of the king of Egypt has ever been given in marriage to a foreigner. It is forbidden."

Bobbing heads from the host of wives and concubines in the room confirmed what we all knew. "It is forbidden," many of them whispered.

Sarai had nothing on her beautiful face to read.

"It's never made sense to me though," Tameri said, animated. "You'd think Pharaoh would make better use of his daughters. One naked woman has far more influence over any man than ten kings put together."

The swarm of women laughed. I suppressed a smile.

"You are fortunate that Princess Hagar is so kindly, Noblewoman Tameri," Zadah said sweetly. "A short-tempered woman might have attacked you for your remarks."

"I am as accurate as the scales, straight and true. I know what I saw." Tameri raised her eyebrows and gave Zadah a stern look. "Princess, why is your ignorant servant opening her mouth to me?"

I hope I am near you on the day of pain, Zadah, for there will be pain. Tameri will not forget this. I rubbed my right temple where a headache began to grow. "Zadah, you know better than to address the royals and nobles in my chambers."

She bowed in compliance.

"Tameri, do you claim to know the secrets of the pharaoh and his daughter?" My voice was sharp. "That which we hold in our hearts? Enough of this. Do not involve me in your tittle-tattle." I could not have a tale that I had fallen for a foreigner spread. But with a glance at the riveted women around the room, I knew it would nonetheless.

Dendera helped Sarai from the tub and quickly dried her off. Zadah rubbed the finest unguent made from the sweet-scented Moringa flower into her skin. She stood before us bare, her wet hair cascading to a tiny waist.

Sarai stepped into a linen sheath Dendera placed before her. Zadah lifted it to her shoulders and secured it with two jeweled brooches. She held her place as they outlined her eyes in black kohl and rubbed red ochre on her lips.

How vain we are to believe we could improve her in the slightest.

Sarai passively let the girls do as they pleased. Her eyes met mine and seemed to have questions. I could not release myself from her gaze.

Would she want to ask a virgin princess how to please a man? Not when Tameri sat so near ready to share all that pleasured her husband. Did she wonder if Abram had indeed roused my heart? I enjoyed even thinking about his name. *Does my face reveal that to you, Sarai?*

One of Tameri's servants, a swarthy, large-boned woman, entered the room but remained by the door. She gave her mistress a crisp nod. Tameri went to her unhurried, fanning herself along the way, her free hand casually anchored on her hip. The woman whispered in her ear and handed her a small scroll. Tameri raised an eyebrow as she unrolled it. She surveyed the contents and let out a deep, haughty sigh.

"It is done," she declared from the doorway. "You belong to Egypt now, Sarai." Tameri slinked to the center of the room, waving the papyrus scroll. "Surely there has never been such a bride-price given. Your brother will be among the richest men in Canaan."

"O, Tameri, don't let your mouth shun our ears. Out with it," insisted Aria, my father's long-legged and elegant second wife. Bastet stretched out beside her, and Aria rubbed her stomach as she spoke.

Tameri tossed her head and fanned herself leisurely. She stared at the scroll between her fingers and looked down her nose at Aria. "Lo. I am so sorry. It is not something I can tell. I'm privileged to know only because my husband is the high vizier."

Bastet purred, but the rest of the room was silent.

Chapter Ten

"OHO, TAMERI. I DON'T KNOW WHY you opened a scroll delivered to my room," I said. "But I will overlook your breach if you will just read the contents of the papyrus." *And if you don't, I'll see you plucked and gutted like a quail.* My head throbbed.

Tameri gazed at me through narrowed eyes. "It is written to me by my husband, the noble Rensi." Her foot tapped the limestone floor, and her smile thinned, but she did not surrender the scroll.

Aria unfolded her long legs and began to stand. "Hand it to me, and I will share it." Bastet, whose stomach Aria had been rubbing, looked up and mewed.

Tameri recoiled, focused her cold eyes on Aria, cleared her throat, and read, "The King of Egypt has set his affections on Sarai of Ur. Desiring to marry her, he has this day paid the bride-price of fifty valiant men, all experts in war, five score male servants, five score female servants, sheep, oxen, donkeys, and camels, a number so large they will look like a mighty cloud moving across the land." She paused, letting the enormity of the bride-price be absorbed.

The women leaned in with eyebrows raised and lips parted.

"There are also trunks of gold, silver, and precious stones. Most important of all, Abram's tribe will live in peace in the land of Egypt." Tameri paused. "This is curious ..." She paused again. "He also says that Abram has been given leave to enter into conversation with the most learned among the Egyptians." She stared at the papyrus as though she didn't understand. "His virtue and reputation have become conspicuous. He is one of great wisdom, being able to discourse on any subject he undertakes." She shrugged and rolled up the scroll. "Surely, he is not as wise as Rensi."

The room erupted in squeals, laughter, and chatter.

Sarai lowered her head as if the news carried unbearable weight. I wanted to help her but had no idea what to say or do. The truth was, for women, master and servant fared alike. All of us were bartered and enslaved in one way or another. Our hearts could do nothing but submit.

My head throbbed again.

I needed a few moments to close my eyes. "Royal and noblewomen," I said, "it would please me if you would go and leave us to prepare for the Feast of Heaven and Earth." They protested. "It is futile to complain. Nothing more will happen here today."

They mumbled unhappily but rose and stretched and began to saunter out except for Tameri, who took a seat at my table even though I dismissed everyone.

I watched Bastet follow Aria toward the door.

"You wicked cat," I mused. "Is there a worse traitor in the palace than you?"

Aria heard me and considered her new companion. "I don't care a wit for them, but they are all fond of me." She picked up Bastet and brought her to my arms. "Tameri is a quick-witted wag, always eager to tell all she knows about anybody," she whispered. "But none of us take her seriously." She smiled and turned to go.

Bastet teetered, then jumped down, her dappled silver fur shimmering, and followed Aria.

I put my hands on my hips, shook my head, and laughed.

But the light moment did not last. The longhaired beauty who had made eye contact with Merikare in the Great Audience Hall left the room behind Aria and Bastet. She bent her head and grinned wide-eyed at me on the way out.

Why hadn't I noticed her earlier?

"Zadah, that girl, the one my brother brought from Zoan, who is she? What is her purpose here? Moreover, why would she be in my chambers?"

"You put forth a lot of questions to this ignorant slave,"

she simpered, stealing a glimpse in Tameri's direction. "Which would you like me to answer first?"

Tameri ignored her.

I rubbed my temples. "Answer what you can."

Zadah glanced around the room at Kiya and Dendera, who looked at the floor. "Prince Merikare has provided a private suite for her in the palace. In the southern wing of the Royal Harem. I don't think he has given her attendants yet, but he is looking."

An icy coldness swept through my body. I opened my mouth, but no words came from it.

"Is he not a man? Is he not alive?" Tameri said. "You will gain nothing by complaining about men and their conquests. It is a burden all women must bear, but me. My Rensi has never needed another woman in his bed. He only plows in this plot."

"Tameri, you know this is about much more than a conquest or seducing a man," I said. "I was to be his first wife and become the Great Royal Wife, like my mother. The succession to the throne is to come through me. Merikare should never have done anything to give another cause to dispute that."

"O, Princess." Tameri's lively voice made it appear she enjoyed this. "Of all people, I know how captivating the right man can change a woman's passage in life. It leaves one to wonder if that lowborn girl also knows."

"She was presented in court as a commoner." I sat on a low armchair, no longer trusting my legs. "That lowly status limits her to becoming a concubine. So how was she able to marry a future pharaoh? What was Merikare thinking?" I shook my head. *What was Father thinking? Merikare could never have done this without his approval.*

The room fell quiet. My servants didn't move and looked as if they were afraid to breathe. Sarai sat on the end of a gilded couch and remained still. Only the shrill cry of an infant somewhere in the distance penetrated the thick air.

Is this to be my punishment? To be honest, I had found a

strange, if not twisted pleasure in having cast a pall on Merikare's great day. Yet now it appeared he had bested me again.

"Why do you believe she is a wife and not a concubine?" Sarai said softly. "What distress could this possibly bring a princess of Egypt?"

"Concubines do not receive private rooms and servants in the harem," Tameri said as she picked up a Tigernut Sweet from the table. "While they live in the same area as the wives, they share rooms and attendants."

"That is true," I said. "To be given a private room is all our custom requires to receive rank as a legal wife. Merikare is making it clear that she is important to him."

"*That* gives her power." Tameri nibbled lightly at the ground almonds that covered mashed dates rolled in honey.

"But surely this common girl could not gather enough power to become the future queen of Egypt," Sarai said.

"It is all about influence," Tameri mumbled through a mouthful of dates and nuts. "The two most influential women in Egypt are the Great Royal Wife, *usually* the first wife, and the King's Mother, the woman who bears the crown prince. Hagar's mother is both. And she has more living sons, so no one can usurp her rank."

In unison, my servant girls recited an old chant to Isis, the goddess of motherhood. "The world lies at the feet of the mother who gives birth to heaven and earth." Their heads bobbed as they scuttled about and straightened up the room. They returned the pillows used by the royal women to their places and cleared picked-over plates of food. Wisely, they avoided anything left in front of the high vizier's wife.

Tameri fanned herself with one hand and picked up another Tigernut with the other. "This little girl can claim she is the Great Royal Wife when Merikare succeeds to the throne since he is giving her status as *first wife*. Things get murky if she gives birth to a son before Hagar. She could petition to make him the recognized legitimate heir. Hagar should have had the opportunity to provide an heir before Merikare took another wife."

Why does Tameri prattle on so?

"Enough of such talk." I aimed a look toward her. "You know royal blood is required to birth an heir. That is how it has always been done in Egypt. That will not change for Merikare and his new favorite." I reached inside for a breath. "Besides, Father had to allow this." I rubbed my temples again as I stood. "He would not have done anything that would jeopardize my position in the royal family. My son is to become the crown prince no matter how many sons Merikare has with other wives and concubines. That is Pharaoh's will."

"Assuming you have a son and Merikare keeps the desires of your father after he becomes king." She seemed pleased to disagree.

"O, Tameri, your speech bristles." *I could curse your tongue—it is everywhere.*

Tameri turned her attention to Sarai. "The harem can be a dangerous place. Many women have hatched conspiracies here, Sarai. In the sixth dynasty, one mother plotted the murder of the king by convincing his own bodyguards to kill him. In doing so, she seized the throne for her son."

"He never became a legitimate king," I muttered. "And incurred the wrath of his successor. I doubt they found it worth it in the end."

"There have been many other harem intrigues over the years," Tameri continued. "Such as consorts who simply disappear." Her eyes danced. "Here this day and gone the next. Some wives have strangled other wives in their sleep or used poison to get rid of their rivals." She stared warily at the Tigernut Sweet in her fingers, shrugged, and took a bite.

"Tameri, there is nothing poison in this room except your tongue," I said. "Those are all stories from the past." I turned to Sarai. "Tameri is overdoing the truth. There are squabbles and quarrels here, as you would expect, but nothing more disturbing than that."

Sarai gave the slimmest smile. She seemed to have discerned that Tameri's idle talk needn't be taken seriously.

"Hagar, how can you talk to me thus when I've done so much for you and Pharaoh?" Tameri retorted. "You know there are a lot of malicious and jealous women here." She inched closer to our guest. "Sarai, you will learn all about that after your first bedding with the king. That is when the claws come out. It is important to learn the rhythm of the harem like Egypt has learned the rhythm of the Nile if you want to survive."

Sarai clutched her neck as though seeking to finger the amethyst that no longer hung from it. Not finding it, she didn't seem to know what to do with her hands. She turned her gaze to the floor as though her face might betray what was within.

Chapter Eleven

ZADAH BOWED TO THE GROUND BEFORE me. "There is more you need to know, Princess, about the new wife of the crown prince."

"Then rise and tell me," I urged.

She stood, hesitated a moment, and delivered the news. "She claims royal blood. She says her mother is the great-niece of Neferkare, who ruled before your father's father."

"What are you babbling about?" Tameri spat. "Where did you hear such nonsense? Did she arrive with attendants? Or receive a bride-price to marry a future king?" She flicked her fan toward Zadah as if the action would remove her words from the air. "Surely, there is no truth in it."

"She whispered it in the ear of Pharaoh's concubine, Herneith." Zadah sent a silent glance toward Tameri, but her gaze didn't linger. "I overheard them myself. Since no one sees me, I can get close enough to most gossip in the harem." Zadah watched me for my reaction. I nodded, and she continued. "She and Herneith are from the same province in the Nile delta and know some of the same people."

"Which one is Herneith?" Sarai turned toward Tameri.

"Herneith is not one of the concubines you need to concern yourself with, Sarai," Tameri said. "She has never become a favorite of the king. She's just one of many concubines we would not miss if they disappeared."

Tameri's cold words rang true. I stared at her and realized I was more connected to her than to the women who shared rooms and air with me. I knew very little about Herneith. She was pleasant enough when our paths crossed, but her social rank was so low that no reason had presented itself for me to acknowledge her. The concubines seemed light, frivolous, and changeable to me.

Sarai's full lips parted a crack, as though she was about to say something, but Tameri raised her voice. "She will need to *prove* she is more than common-born to be placed in the most important role available to women in Egypt."

"Prove to whom, Tameri?" I crossed my arms. "You've gone to great lengths to provoke me. But now your fate may be ensnared with mine and you are alarmed?"

"You know I only jest with you, Hagar," Tameri said. "Do not use my words against me. I am always your true friend. But, if claims of royal blood are verified ..." She fitfully fanned herself. "The entire hierarchy we have grown comfortable with could be upturned. Rensi may have remained high vizier with you and Merikare on the throne. But who knows what sway this girl will have on a young king?"

At that, I moved closer to her. "We both may need true friends in this uncertain time, Tameri." I touched her shoulder and hoped it would be enough to close the gap between us.

"Does your father know about this claim of royal blood?" Tameri didn't wait for a response but answered her own question. "Of course, he must. Merikare could not have withheld that. That's how he received permission to give her private quarters. So, there must be truth to it." She looked at me. "What of your mother? Why would she not say a word to you?" Her face tightened. "My Rensi must have known."

Tameri's mouth made my heart race. I tried to perceive all possible conditions my brother could have presented to gain permission to take a wife before me. And she was right. My mother and Rensi would have known. Yet neither spoke to me regarding it. I had always believed myself safe within these walls, and trusted in my position within the royal family. Now my foundation seemed as secure as a house built on the banks of the Nile before the inundation.

"How shall you live your life with this threat lodged so close to you?" Tameri said. "How shall I? Have you ever dreamed you might have to defend yourself in your own home?"

"Of course not, Tameri." Could she ever be silent? "It

seems even I may need to learn a new rhythm in the harem to survive."

"It is intolerable that my husband, the high vizier, has kept such a thing from me. I swear I will bring the wrath of all our gods upon him for this." She started to stand.

"Please, Tameri, stay here with Sarai and assist her as needed," I said. "Your noble husband has requested that I spend time offering sacrifices and prayer in the temple today. I should not delay in doing so any further." Plus, I needed to visit my brother.

"If that is your wish, then my place is with Sarai." She sat and looked at Zadah with cold eyes. "I am yours to command as always, daughter of my king."

"Do *not* lay another hand on my attendants," I said.

Zadah flaunted an appreciative smile.

"I will do as you command. Although your brazen slave deserves a beating." She gave Zadah a long, hard look. "But I am only an attendant and true friend. A mere servant in the Royal Harem."

I stopped near the door and spoke absently over my shoulder, "Sarai?"

"Yes." Her voice ran the slight distance between us.

"How does a word live?"

Silence followed. I stood still and could feel her eyes on my back, those eyes that shone like gemstones. Sweat gathered on my brow, but I didn't move to wipe it away.

"Princess, surely you must give me time to consider such a question." She paused as I turned.

"Take all the time you need."

She searched my face as though trying to reason how serious I was. "Well, to live, a word would need to become flesh. Perhaps it would be something we could behold, maybe touch, or hear." Her voice trembled with emotion. "Your people believed me to be Isis incarnated. Think if the breath of life really filled a god. I believe the words it spoke would live as we inclined our hearts to it."

I froze. I could scarcely believe my ears. Or my heart. Her words rang true in both. I knew there was no trickery here. "When you hear a dream, can you interpret it?"

"Interpret, Princess?"

"Can you tell if it is a prophetic warning or only a nightmare?"

"If my Lord allows it. Dreams and visions take on many forms, but the nature of prophecy can be complicated."

Fury and fear warred within me, but I still moved close to her. I needed more. There must be more. "I have had a vision of great turmoil in the land and need to know why. The *presence* that stays close to you and your brother, is that a dark spirit? What kind of deity entered Egypt with you?" I stood still as stone. "Have you cast a spell on the king?"

Tameri and my girls turned their attention to us.

Sarai looked at me intently. "I'm telling you with the tongue of my flesh and the breath of my mouth, I bear no bitterness toward Egypt. I certainly do not have the ability to cast spells, nor would I want to. The spirit of the one true God entered Egypt with me, to bring divine truth." Her eyes stayed fixed on me as she added quietly, "But I do not know how El will judge what has transpired here."

El? She speaks as though this El is the only god, like the one that haunted my dreams. A stirring intruded on the room. Or was that in my heart? My skin prickled. Had Tameri felt it too? I looked at her. She had returned to picking through the Tigernuts. "Answer truly, Sarai. Are you saying a troubled spirit has followed you to Egypt? Does he intend to do us harm? Are you a priestess of the god to who the spirit belongs? His magician? His goddess? Do not be false with me."

Tameri pointed a finger at her. "Oho, you belong to the temple. It weighed on me so much, why you are no longer a young maid and still a virgin."

Sarai's face reddened. "I am not a priestess or a magician. I'm certainly not a goddess. I don't always understand the ways of the God of Abram, but I know the Lord has a purpose for my life. And my hope and faith remain in promises He made to me."

The God of Abram? A surge fired through my entire body, hearing her brother's name. My thoughts flashed to when he had knelt in front of me, just a touch away. Then I wondered why he and this god had the same name, but I waited silently for her to continue.

"I was overwhelmed with fear when I realized I would be leaving my tribe. Then the Lord comforted my heart and told me not to be afraid. I confess it is difficult for me. But I know He is with me and will protect and defend me."

I twisted the silver amulet on my wrist. *Is that what I saw when Pharaoh reached for her? A god defending her?* "This god of yours, why does he share a name with your brother?"

"They do not share a name. They share a promise. God has a plan for the ages and set that plan in motion by calling Abram out of Ur. The Lord promised to bless Abram with land and descendants." She hesitated a moment and swallowed hard. "And that through his seed, the entire world will be blessed."

I stiffened. "I desire to behold this god of yours. Where is he? What does he look like?"

"He cannot be seen," she said softly. "No more than you can stand at noontide and turn your face to the sun and gaze upon it."

I gave a mordant snigger. "He's imaginary then. At least that makes him well suited to travel with nomads." Tameri laughed out loud, and my servant girls giggled.

"I did not say He was imaginary," she replied. "More like … He is hidden."

"But, if he is hidden, how do you know of his existence?"

She stared at me as though we were the only two in the room. "You have seen His power, Hagar, and felt His spirit in this place. Have you not?"

I caught the wary expressions of my girls. "You are speaking nonsense."

"You cannot understand the mysteries of the one true God

without the ears to hear or the eyes to see."

"What do you mean I cannot understand the mysteries? There is very little I do not grasp."

There was no humor on her face. "You must be ready to allow the Lord into your life to be able to recognize Him when He is in front of you."

I turned away from her.

Tameri sighed. "You both speak gibberish to me."

"Who repairs your gods when they break?" Sarai said.

"Meti, the high priest, hires the most skilled craftsmen in the land," offered Tameri. "Sometimes he repairs them himself."

I could feel Sarai's penetrating eyes still upon me.

"Why is it hard to believe in a hidden God, whose power you have felt, when you believe in gods who cannot mend the statues they inhabit? Could they truly have created the earth and the heavens and the stars that shine in them? Could they have hung the sun and the moon in the sky?"

The room grew quiet.

I glanced around and realized everyone waited for my answer. I gave my servants a stern look, and they quickly moved to resume their duties. Zadah lit heavy, woody incense as though the swirling smoke would remove the unseen spirit. Tameri picked up yet another Tigernut, her face blank, her eyes only on the sweet confection. I knew she was unaware of the distress I believed was coming to our people. Unaware how my black dream—if it came to fruition—would afflict us all.

I stepped closer to Sarai and whispered, "I know you saw my father's hand wither when he tried to touch you."

She didn't flinch. "God promised me protection in this new land."

She *was* the reason for the ominous foreboding in my dreams and my bones. "I do not care about this god you worship." My voice held a threatening edge. "You do not belong to him anymore. You belong to the king. Your prayers will be only to the gods of my father. To the gods of Egypt."

Or I'll see you butchered and burned. I took a breath. "It is blasphemy to speak otherwise. And in Egypt, blasphemy means death."

She remained motionless. "I will kneel before the king. But can you compel me to eat or to sleep? How will you force my heart to change what I hope in? What I praise? What I know is the truth? Princess Hagar, if my death will satisfy you, so be it. But I will not allow my soul to be cast down. It will remain unbroken." Her stunning eyes flashed purple fire and did not waver from mine.

I was the first to look away.

Chapter Twelve

A BLAST OF HEAT FROM THE sun kindled my body and escorted me along the processional path that led to the temple proper. I knew I looked flushed and wilted, but I didn't care. I departed the harem in haste and desperately in need of the comfort and familiarity of my own gods. I would lay my hands on each of them, feel their solid figures of stone, and say their names aloud.

"Amun-Ra. Isis. Horus. Osiris. Set." I repeated over and over.

I would talk to the high priest, Meti. I would tell him everything Sarai said and everything I saw. Even about the *presence* that disturbed the room when she was in it. I would not hold back one detail. I shook away the thought of what might happen to Sarai and Abram. Maybe to their entire tribe. It would be swift and final, something terrible but necessary to protect the king.

To protect Egypt.

The massive pylon gateway that marked the boundaries of the temple now loomed above me. It was one of only two entries through a large enclosure wall, built with mud bricks twenty cubits thick and painted white. Twin, mottled-rose obelisks stood in front and flanked two massive gray statues of Pharaoh and his Great Royal Wife standing on pedestals. I looked at the likeness of my father. It was extraordinary. Someday my brother's face would replace his. I examined the one of my mother, a remarkable resemblance too. *But whose face will replace hers?* My stomach stirred, thinking about it. Never before had I considered any image but my own sculpted there.

A dark, weathered peasant wearing only a kilt of rough linen jostled my body, and my thoughts returned to the present. He apologized profusely and stepped around me. He quickly moved toward the assembly of people who besieged the sacred water basins near the entrance.

Above the gateway, huge glyphs decreed, "May He Who Enters the Temple Be Pure." Long rows of enormous round washbasins cut from alabaster blocks were provided for this purpose. No one could enter until they removed all impurities by cleansing their hands, arms, and thoughts.

I stood alone and watched a moment. Being a festival day, commoners were permitted to enter the temple courtyard and stroll the renowned gardens, although they could not cross the sanctuary threshold. And because of all the people Merikare let follow him home, the basins teemed with merchants, craftsmen, fellahin, and other people of low birth who bathed their limbs in the hallowed waters beside royals and nobles. Dress, hairstyle, and jewelry distinguished them.

I approached one of the water basins, and no matter what class they belonged to, the people stepped aside for me. Most moved on to other basins, but a few stood near and watched as though I came to perform for them. Perhaps they heard of my behavior in court that morning, or maybe they had never been so close to high-ranking royalty before.

I lifted my chin and looked for Zadah. For the first time, I realized she was not with me. I had never left the palace without a servant in tow. I stared at the ground, and my mind halted. Moisture gathered on my forehead. My exhaustion of the past week made me too susceptible to tears, but I determined not to let any more fall.

But this is too great for me today. My wits have deserted me.

"Princess, may I attend you in this?" The voice was soft but firm.

My jaw clenched. Merikare's longhaired beauty stood before me. Her large, sensual eyes appropriately avoided mine, and her delicately-shaped mouth smiled sweetly.

"Did you follow me? Answer me truly, or may Amun-Ra blast you where you stand."

"No, Princess. And may Amun-Ra hear my speech and defend me today," she said, still avoiding my eyes.

Her skin glowed in the sunlight. Long, dark brunette hair flowed over the simple full-length linen dress she still wore. But now, thick gold earrings hung from her delicate ears instead of the copper ones she had worn earlier. A lavish string of lapis lazuli and gold beads adorned her graceful neck—gifts from my brother, no doubt.

"I have come to visit the temple gardens today, mistress, as a good servant does who is useful to her lord," she said. "They are celebrated among my people in the north, and I was fortunate to see them as a small child. Since my path in life has led me here, I could not wait to see them again." She may have married a future king, but her thick, coarse accent implied a low birth all the same.

I narrowed my eyes and crossed my arms. "Who are your people in the north? And how did you end up with the crown prince? He did not present you at court as one of royal birth."

She lowered her eyes, her lashes like feathers against the bronze of her cheeks. "I was not born a royal. My father is an old field hand with knotted and gnarly fingers. But he was kind to me." Anger crept into her voice. "My mother is not one I would weep for. She sold me to your brother for a loom. I've spent most of my life with a spindle, spinning flax fibers into thread for her from my body's sweat. My sisters and I wove the finest cloth in Zoan." She bit her lower lip as her chin trembled. "I grieve for my mother's children. We all have scars from her, some you can see, some you can't. She is the most wretched woman on all the earth."

I thought about pressing her regarding the overheard conversation with Herneith and her claim of royal blood. She would soon learn that the harem walls had ears of their own. I started to ask if my brother had indeed given her private quarters but decided against it. I would have that conversation with Merikare.

Her face was square, almost perfect, with delicate features

and a straight nose. Perhaps her forehead was a little too high, but I looked hard to find an imperfection. Her manner was not brazen or impudent, nor was she servile. She lacked certain comportments of the higher ranks, but she still possessed a natural, effortless grace. It was easy to see how she beguiled my brother.

"I noticed your servants are not with you, and you seem a little out of sorts," she said, seeming eager to please. "I would be grateful if you would allow me to assist you. Unless I am mistaken."

There wasn't any malice in her words. *Be kind. She is humbled before you. Perhaps she doesn't understand how she threatens my position.* I opened my mouth as though to explain but found no words. I did not owe an explanation to anyone, especially her. If ever I needed to reassert myself as a royal, it was now. I held out my arms and nodded.

She gently removed the wide, tight amulet representing Isis's protective blood from my wrist. Then she slid several rings, made of emeralds and pearls, from my fingers. Lastly, she took off two upper arm cuffs made from burnished gold and inlaid carnelian.

"What is your name?"

She raised her brows, and I wondered if I had seen a spark of triumph in her eyes.

"Imi," she answered.

I turned away from her and heard the scuffle of her feet as she moved to an appropriate distance to allow me privacy. I took my time washing in the consecrated water, letting its coolness slow my heart and lower the anxiety coming from the innermost part of me.

But I found it hard to shut the hearsay of Imi and Merikare from my mind, especially with her standing so close behind me. A test from the gods? I centered my mind on Amun-Ra, took several deep breaths, and fought to push all other thoughts from my head.

I slid my fingers across the smooth inner surface of the

basin, cupped one hand, and gathered the sacred water. I spread it across the opposite arm and watched it trickle into the sink. I repeated the process with the other hand while chanting, "Hail to thee, Amun-Ra, lord of the thrones of the earth, the oldest existence, the ancient of heaven. Cleanse me, maker of all, that I may give my adoration to thee and all other gods that have come after you. Welcome me, father of the gods, Lord Amun-Ra."

I raised my arms and turned to Imi, who stood with a linen cloth ready. She dried my arms entirely and returned my rings, cuff-bracelets, and amulet to where she had removed them.

I didn't utter a word. I kept my mind on Amun-Ra and the other gods I had come to touch. And fervently prayed they would touch me too. I only nodded my gratitude to Imi and left her behind.

Sand and stone crunched under my feet as I crossed the threshold of the temple gates. Worshippers abounded everywhere, many of them grinding the ingredients of incense and tossing it into the burning coals of elevated braziers. The smoke plumes filled the air with the aroma of frankincense and myrrh and carried spewed prayers to the gods. Other citizens lingered in the cool shade of the sycamore trees, walked amid roses and jasmine, and sat beside a long pond stocked with fish and floating water plants. Many nodded courteous bows as I passed, but I didn't linger anywhere, steadfast in my determination to get to Meti.

And speak to him about Sarai.

I made my way up the steps of the temple and carefully avoided the reed offering mats bearing gifts to the gods. At the top stood the altar of sacrifice where a priest slashed the throat of a small, bleating goat. I was close enough to hear its final breath escape through the cut and catch the mordant scent of death. I watched the priest sever the head from its body and curse the evil that resided within. There would be a lot of decapitated heads today. Tonight, they would be cast into the Nile for crocodiles and other predators to devour and consume the ill omens into their own bodies.

All sorts of beasts—geese, antelopes, cattle, and more goats—festively adorned with flowers, lined the steps and waited to be sacrificed by their owners. Several priests walked among them and inspected the offerings closely for purity. A red-hot branding iron, shaped like a temple signet ring, was pressed into their rump or belly if they passed the priest's scrutiny. The penalty for sacrificing an animal not sealed meant death to the offender.

The smell of blood and raw animal flesh overwhelmed me as I passed a calf being disemboweled. A priest patiently waited to stuff it with consecrated loaves of bread, raisins, and figs. He would cover it in oil and impale it on a rod to hold it over a sacrificial fire. It would smolder there and then feed the poor this evening as we celebrated the opening of the new year at the Festival of Heaven and Earth. This would please the gods and ensure their goodwill.

The hordes of people began to unnerve me. I took a deep breath and stepped inside the temple to an open hypostyle court, with columns shaped as papyrus plants. I exhaled as the world around me became still and quiet. I made my way to the sanctuary and saw Rensi sitting on a marble bench outside the small chapel we called the inner temple. The king and high priest were the only ones allowed to enter this sacred shrine to the most-high god, Amun-Ra.

As a small child, I slipped into the chapel before I understood the sacredness of the place. I clearly remembered every royal cubit of it, along with every single terrifying moment expecting to be caught by Meti or dashed on the wall by Amun-Ra himself. Sweat poured from my young forehead into my eyes and caused them to sting. I had to squint at the decorated walls and saw a series of reliefs recounting my father's divine birth, along with hymns that focused on the life cycle of man and nature.

In the center of the inner temple sat a large gold throne with the seated image of Amun-Ra, father of Osiris, Isis, Set, and the pharaoh of Egypt. I recalled Amun-Ra's bone-chilling silence that filled my childish heart with fear. His mysterious form sat before me and seemed otherworldly.

But only for a few moments.

When he did not stir and hurl me across the room, I became bold and openly stared at him. I even ran my fingers across his smooth figure. He never seemed to see me or even acknowledge my presence. And I didn't sense any actual power or real potency. Nor had he ever told my father or Meti that I breached the sanctity of his home.

Even still, no one knew.

Chapter Thirteen

I RAISED A HAND TO ACKNOWLEDGE Rensi. My smile wavered as the sight of him made me wonder why he'd never whispered a word to me about Imi. *He had to know. Why keep it from me? What else has he withheld from me?*

He nodded and smiled, then inclined his head as though he sought to discern my subdued reaction. "Princess, I was beginning to lose hope of seeing you."

"I was delayed getting Sarai settled, I'm afraid." I tried to return his wide smile but failed by half, finding myself doubting his loyalty to me. Something else I had never questioned.

I walked past him with quiet footsteps and approached enormous images, carved from Nubian sandstone, of Egypt's most important gods and goddesses. I stopped before the one nearest to me and prostrated myself, reverently pressing my forehead against the floor. "O, Anubis," I said to the Protector of the Dead. "Mighty Anubis." I stood before the black form with the head of a jackal and the body of a man. But he stared straight ahead, and like Amun-Ra years earlier, he did not appear to see me.

Next, I bowed before Isis. "Mighty Mother. Daughter of the Nile," I whispered. Isis appeared like a beautiful human queen and wore a headdress shaped like a throne. She held an ankh in her hand, the key of life, the symbol of eternal life. I pondered it for a moment.

I remembered the mighty wooden ankh hanging from the heavens in my dream and the blazing figure of a man that stood beside me. I could not look upon his face, yet there was no doubt his eyes had fallen upon me. He called me by name and asked me to consider him and that his word would live in me.

"A word would have to become flesh to live," Sarai had said. I believed she wasn't literal, of course, more figurative.

As though her god brought some special revelation, and his words held wisdom more remarkable than all other gods. Words that could live as though they were in a person and alive.

I laid a hand gently on Isis. Hard, grainy, and cold, she would never become flesh. She would never live or utter a word. I shuddered, sure of it, and turned the silver amulet on my wrist.

I moved in front of a green-skinned man with a beard like a pharaoh wearing a distinctive crown with two large ostrich feathers. "Osiris," I whispered to the god of the afterlife. I reached up and touched the crook and flail he held. But no life stirred in him—he spoke no words to my heart—and I wasn't even moved to remove my shoes in reverence. "Put off your shoes from your feet, for in my presence you stand on holy ground," the being in my dream had commanded. And I knew it was so. I stood on holy ground before him. *But who was he?*

I moved down the line bowing before the great gods and goddesses, touching them, speaking their names. "Set. Nut. Geb." I asked each one if they had visited me in the night.

Earthy incense clouded the warm air as I faced Horus, the falcon-headed deity that had the power to give or take away Egypt's crown. My stomach twisted, realizing he would be the god who preferred Merikare to me. "O, Sky Lord," I said and laid on the ground before him. "Great falcon that flies the horizon. Did you come in the night to judge me in light of the kingship? I pray you find me worthy. But if not, if I do not wear the crown of a god's son, I will find peace where you assign me."

I stood and brushed sand from my linen kalasiris and cast another look at Horus. He stood stone-faced and silent. *No. It was not you who gazed upon me.*

Lastly, I kneeled before Heryshaf, the god of the riverbanks and patron of Henen-nesut. He stood before me with the form of a king and the head of a long-horned ram.

"O, Heryshaf, Ruler of the Shores, whose rising

illuminates the earth. My heart is on your water and belongs only to you. Protect me. Protect Egypt. Repulse our enemies so no one may rise against us."

I waited.

Nothing.

"Was it you I saw in my sleep? Come out of your high seat and let me feel your divine presence. Please, do not remain silent now."

I remained on my knees, praying he would not stay quiet. Time passed slowly. And still nothing.

I gathered all my strength not to weep as I made my way to the bench where Rensi sat and slumped next to him. "Why are they so silent?" I whispered.

Rensi nodded. "And why do they always have to be placated? They seem to be either spiteful and angry as a ferocious lion or generous and gentle as a palace cat. Does what we give them influence their mood so much?"

I ducked my chin. "Rensi, you surprise me. Are you not afraid to talk thus? It's like you have a desire to be struck with disaster. What if the gods heard you? Or worse yet—" I jerked my head toward Meti, who chuckled as he walked out of the inner temple.

"I learned long ago to ignore the high vizier in matters of the gods, Princess," he said before he bowed respectfully before me.

"Meti," I said, rising. "Teacher, there is no need for that."

"Sit, dear girl. Sit. Sit. You are my sovereign, and I will always be dutiful to you in that. But as your teacher, I must warn you of listening to the irreverent ways of our friend here."

"You are fortunate to instruct the children of Pharaoh, Meti," Rensi said, his voice light. "And wise to warn them of my sacrilegious behavior. Although you and the gods know I jest."

"Oho, we know, High Vizier," Meti chuckled again. "And I only instruct his clever children. Most of his offspring will forever flounder in darkness."

"Meti." I feigned outrage.

He smiled at me. "But not you. Your cleverness snared me from the beginning. When you were two, you were already three. When you were three, you were already four. I knew from the start that the nobles of the land would know your name."

"Thank you, High Priest," I said.

Rensi nodded. "Yes, truly blessed is he to whom she was born."

I felt his gaze on me but could not return it. I didn't want him to see my heart brimming with judgment against him.

Meti slid his long leopard robe off his shoulders and laid it across the end of the bench. "It is to Pharaoh's credit that he turned your education over to me. You used to follow me around and pretend to be a great priestess. You even swore to be one when you grew up." Meti's grin wrinkled his cheeks.

I would still prefer the temple to Merikare's bed. I wished I could say it out loud.

"But you were nursed to be a conqueror. You are a king by nature," Rensi said.

"A king destined never to have a kingdom," I said with certain testiness. "You were both in court this morning. Yes, the nobles will know my name for being a fool. I can't seem to get out of my own way anymore. I don't know what to do, and the gods are silent and good for nothing."

"Hagar, mind your thoughts. Perhaps you've sat too long next to Rensi," warned Meti.

"I am sorry, High Priest. I am a wretch." I ran my hand across the soft spots on the leopard robe. "Sometimes, I struggle with … my purpose." *Purpose and promises. Things Sarai said her god gave her.* I stroked the furry skin and found comfort from the motion. "Something is missing in my life. I feel lost. I don't know where I belong, even in my own home."

"Are you speaking of the lowborn girl Merikare has raised up?" Rensi said. "I knew it would not take long in the harem for her position to become known. You may not share the throne with your brother, Hagar, but you will be the Great Royal Wife. That is your purpose, and no one will seize it from you. Your father and I made sure there would be no risk of the line of succession being altered before he gave the crown prince permission to make her a wife."

There it is. It is all true. How long have you known, High Vizier? And why keep such a secret from me? My temper darkened.

"I think her concern is of the spirit, not of the succession, Rensi. She rightly came to me after the first night she had the vision. And a god speaking directly to us can be alarming," Meti said as Sobek, his monkey, scampered over on his two legs and used his long arms to climb Meti like a tree. "But we will figure it all out in time."

Something about the calm certainty in his voice bothered me. As though he may be withholding things from me as Rensi had. I looked in his black, intuitive eyes but could not see secrets hidden in them. "My place with the royal family weighs on me, that is true. Pharaoh has made it clear that I mean less to him than Merikare because I was born female." I took a deep breath. "But I desperately need a deeper connection with our gods. I'm just not sure how to get it."

"You have always revealed your true self with honesty and humility, Hagar," Meti said gently. "Take comfort from my words, little one. The gods are not through with you. They have big plans for you … of that, I am quite certain."

He turned and walked toward the inner temple and reverently set pellets of incense alight in the two small braziers that flanked the door. I watched the fragrant streams of smoke as they danced their way to the heavens.

Rensi and I remained silent. I didn't want to think about the secret he had kept from me, but I couldn't help it. For the first time in my life, I found myself unsure of him. And something else bothered me too. I intended the first words from my mouth upon seeing Meti to be about Sarai and the *presence* with her.

Yet, I remained silent.

Meti pointed to the inner temple's steps, and Sobek obediently scurried down and took a seat. He looked at Rensi and me, pulled his lip aggressively, and jerked his head and shoulders forward. A warning, I supposed, not to try and breach the sacred temple.

I turned my eyes toward Meti and watched him move before each of the carved statues as I had done. He bowed reverently before each one, and his lips moved with whispered supplications.

And the gods of stone remained quiet and unresponsive.

When he finished his priestly duties, Meti picked up his robe, slid it over his shoulders, and came to sit beside me. "I understand the immense inner turmoil you are going through, Princess. I want you to know that. It can be disturbing when the gods speak to us in our dreams. But trust me when I say that you are blessed to be chosen." He patted my hand before he continued. "I appreciate that you always speak truth from your heart."

And then he spoke to me as if I were a child.

"I remember when you were just a wisp of a girl, one of the idols broke. You sat and intently watched me fix it. Then you asked if I was the creator of the gods. You told me the idols should bow to me and not the other way around. 'How could they exist if you had not formed them into being, dear Meti?' you said." He laughed quietly.

A sudden coldness hit my core. I had forgotten that day. The afternoon I watched him fix one of the same pieces of stone he had taught me to bow to. I thought of Sarai's words. *"Why is it hard to believe in a hidden God, whose power you have felt, when you believe in gods who cannot mend the statues they inhabit? Could they truly have created the earth and the heavens and the stars that shine in them? Could they have hung the sun and the moon in the sky?"*

I looked at the large figures that surrounded us and couldn't imagine that they had ever created anything. I realized that even as a child, I seemed to know the truth. They were just silent stones.

"Meti, how does a word live?" I implored him.

He thought a moment. "Words are like dry quicksand, which yields easily to weight and pressure. Deeds and wisdom are like the rope thrown to us when the quicksand threatens to swallow us. They save us from drowning. They save us from danger. They are all that remains of a man after death, and are set beside him like a treasure." He nodded as though the answer was undeniable. "Yes, deeds and wisdom can live, but a word cannot."

His words only added to my bewilderment. Meti and Rensi were the wisest men I knew. Neither provided an answer that laid on my heart as Sarai's did. I decided to stop talking about my dream, a word that could live, and the *presence* that surrounded Sarai. No one could understand it.

I trembled.

"What is wrong, little one?" Meti said. He looked deep into my eyes. "What are you running from, Princess?"

I silently cursed that he could see into me so easily. *Truth, Meti,* I wanted to shout. *A truth I feel in my heart. In my spirit.* Instead, I said, "Why do you think I'm running from something?" I wanted to turn from the scrutiny in his eyes but held steadfastly.

"Hagar, I know you as well as I know myself," he said. "The black dreams weigh on you. But, child, I sense there is more."

There is much more. "It is difficult to speak about, dear priest," I said carefully. "I wonder why the gods won't reveal themselves to me. I have come here today looking for answers. But they gave me nothing. Except for you, no one extols them as I do. I always enter the temple and work tirelessly to be found worthy. Yet, not one of them has sought to touch me the way I touch them."

My beloved teacher's mouth was agape, as though he could not discover the right words to come out of it. Had our gods ever awakened in him what Sarai's god aroused in me? Her god may be hidden, but he was present. He went where she went and didn't need a temple in which to hide. I glared at the silent stone statues around me.

Enough was enough.

"Hagar, you have always been the most spiritually sensitive person I know," he said. "But, beware of loosening the cords in your soul."

I desperately wanted to tell him about the magic that entered Egypt with Sarai—that otherworld *presence*—and her haunting words. To open my mouth and unburden my sober spirit and explain my outburst that morning. I saw my father's hand wither when he tried to touch Sarai, and now she claimed a great god was protecting her.

But instead, I remained silent and looked away.

"Princess, the offerings have been made," Rensi said. "You have said your prayers. Come with me now. A little rest will do you good." A worry line appeared between his dark brown eyes.

Meti rose from the bench and kneeled before me. "Yes. You are too much underfoot today," he said lightly and patted my hand again. "Do as Rensi says. Go now, set aside your concerns for the kingdom, rest, and find a way to enjoy yourself."

He struggled to rise, so I took both of his hands in mine and stood with him. It was the first time I noticed that he was no longer firm on his legs.

Meti looked deep into my eyes again. "Don't let the words of the wise flee without delay. Beware, my dear girl. Beware."

I smiled kindly. "I hear your words and will let them rest in my heart."

Chapter Fourteen

RENSI AND I WALKED OUT OF the temple in silence, his hand snug on my elbow. I wondered why I had said nothing to Meti about Sarai after all. I remained as silent as the gods of Egypt. I also wondered why Rensi had kept silent regarding Imi. He held that secret for days at least, and it hurt to think on it.

We stopped at the top of the steps and marveled at all our people ambling through the temple gardens. I drew in a breath, thankful for the distraction below us. "They look like a colony of ants."

Rensi nodded. "Each carrying a crumb of food to offer the gods."

"A little wind carries the ship. A little bee brings the honey. A little ant carries the crumb," I said, reciting an old childhood rhyme.

Rensi added the last line. "A little locust destroys the vine."

"Little forces often have a significant effect." I smiled. "Our wet nurse oft complained of Merikare being like a little locust." My gaze drifted toward Rensi's face, but I remembered the secret he had kept from me and turned my face from him. *What else have you held out from telling me? Why now? Am I worthless to you since I have no chance of sharing the throne with my brother? Have I been dismissed from your confidence?* Heat surged in me as I watched the crowd.

Just like ants, they continued along manicured paths in an orderly fashion to the temple steps. They laid their crumbs on reed offering mats, which we sidestepped as we descended. Rensi kept his hand securely on my elbow. I wanted to shake it off, but I didn't.

"I'm surprised to find you have come here alone, Hagar."

"I left in haste and was not thinking." My answer was curt

as I recalled my encounter with Imi. I wanted to shout at him for not telling me about her. But I stayed silent. He had been my friend and confidant my entire life. *Can I trust he had his reasons?*

Rensi scowled, a deep furrow formed between his brows, as we pushed against the tide of people like fish swimming against the current. The crush of citizens that followed Merikare home were from towns between here and the delta, and none of them appeared to recognize the high vizier or me. Not one gave way to us or bowed.

As we jostled for space, the heat, the crowd, and the smoke from incense and sacrifices began to overwhelm me. Gritty sand in my sandals chafed my feet, my mouth was bone dry, my tongue a parched lump, and my linen sheath clung tightly to my skin. *A cool rinse, a light meal, and rest. That will be the order of things as soon as I get home.* I didn't want to think about anything else.

Sarai.

She would be there, in my home, with her otherworldly *presence.* A ghost who accompanied her to Egypt and—I was beginning to believe—found his way into my dreams. I bit my lip as the hair lifted on the nape of my neck.

Rensi absently released his grip on me. I looked at him, but he appeared lost in his own thoughts. We walked on in silence as I twisted the amulet on my wrist that seemed to feed the struggle within me. Meti had bound it to me for protection, and yet, I sensed trouble and withheld what I knew. I didn't say a word to the high priest. *Why? Am I trying to protect Sarai? Or Abram?* The name slipped into my thoughts even though I wanted to keep it tucked deep within. *I promised him I would take care of her. Am I trapped in that promise?* No. Not at the expense of Egypt. I couldn't explain it, except that I needed more answers from her before tossing their fate to the wind.

And then there was Imi. My fists clenched, and a pinch of something ugly reared in me, a feeling of rivalry in the harem. I had never been affected by it, always able to rise above it because of my rank. But now she would make her nest among my people, and who knew what this strange bird would breed?

Merikare. I still needed to discuss Imi with him. And perhaps even my father. A moment to rest did not seem possible now.

We made it out through the massive gateway, passed the sacred washbasins, and strode toward the palace entrance. I stopped and turned toward the high vizier. "Rensi, how long have you known that Merikare planned on taking a wife before me?" I tried, but I couldn't keep silent about it.

"Princess," Rensi said stiffly, "I have known since Zoan. Once Merikare laid eyes on her, she consumed his thoughts. As though a noose had been cast with her hair and captured him with her eyes and smile. Imi was all we heard about. At first, he said she would be a concubine. As you know, I left the delta ahead of him to alert Pharaoh to what was to come. Before I departed, Merikare approached me with the desire to make her a wife."

"But you breathed not a word to me, Rensi. All this time, since you returned home. I had to hear it first from my servant girl, Zadah."

"O, yes, the one with the busy tongue. That is unfortunate. It should not have unfolded like that." He paused and tilted his head, his warm eyes focused on mine. "I am your true friend, Hagar. I advise you when I can. And oft I don't hesitate to keep you informed on matters of the kingdom." His expression remained firm. "But I am your father's man first. The king had wished to speak to you himself regarding Imi. I was not at liberty to discuss it."

I crossed my arms. "Father has had many opportunities, Rensi. Yet, he failed to mention it. He had to know the news would reach me as soon as she entered the women's quarters."

Rensi wiped his bald head and shifted his feet. "I am truly sorry that was the way of it. The truth is, the king cannot deny your brother anything. I drafted an agreement that Merikare had to sign to secure your position as his Great Royal Wife.

But I won't be false with you." He stopped and looked around. "When your father goes to the afterlife, your rank will be subject to your brother's whims, regardless of the order in which he takes wives. That is why your mother and many of us argued to make you co-regent. Thus far, your father has been unwilling to bend to our pleas."

A red-footed falcon glided low over the land above us and released a high-pitched shriek as it searched for prey. I looked at the bird, known for being watchful and alert, and realized I had been the opposite—blind and unaware of what happened right before me.

The high vizier watched the bird too. He touched the gold collar around his neck, his short, thick fingers stroked the yellow metal. His face looked strained, and my heart softened. He loved me and fought for me. I would never doubt his loyalty and friendship again.

My hand closed gently on his arm. "You are faithful and true, dear Rensi. But it may go better for you if you did not worry on my behalf any longer." I fought a painful tightness in my throat and tried to keep my voice steady. "My father's regard for me seems to be waning, even though I have achieved all and more than he has ever requested of me."

"His affection for you has not waned as much as you may think. You are as skillful with your mind as Merikare is with a spear. Your father knows that, Hagar."

"Yet, it never appears to be enough."

"It all matters little compared to what I have to say to you next. I am trusting my life to you." He looked around again. "I saw what happened to the king when he tried to touch Sarai."

I gasped as my head jolted back.

Rensi stood stoic. His eyes searched my face. "But it is fundamental to our existence that we remain blind to it. Promise me, Hagar, to keep silent and discuss it no longer until we discern what it is we have seen."

I grabbed his arm. "We?"

He nodded. "There are others."

"But only I shouted out in the Great Audience Hall."

"Which may have saved us. No one, not even me, would have survived accusing the crown prince of black magic. Your shout allowed me time to gather my wits as it did with those who have confided in me that they saw it too. Your mother's quick thinking saved you." His voice softened. "And Pharaoh. He loves you, Hagar. It would have grieved him deeply to have punished you."

"Yes, my lord, but who are the others?"

"The answer to that will go to the tomb with me," he said steadfastly. "But complete silence going forth, Princess. Promise me."

Chapter Fifteen

RENSI AND I ENTERED THE NORTHERN wing of the harem and found it eerily quiet. We stepped lightly into the hall, knowing the other occupants must be resting. That was not unusual. The high heat of the day always stifled any desire for activity. The guards standing erect with glazed stares and sweat glistening on their exposed chests were the only sign of life.

A sudden giddiness settled on me knowing I was not going mad after all. *Others* saw my father's hand wither and discerned the *presence* that arrived with Sarai. I would never again ask for names from the high vizier. But the burden of unraveling Sarai's mysteries and secrets had lessened for me by half. I no longer carried it alone, which filled me with gratitude. I uttered silent thanks to the gods and determined to relax in my tub and let it all sink in.

We approached my chambers and heard Tameri's laugh, which sounded like the clipped howl of the spotted hyena. I caught the soft giggles of my servants too.

The high vizier winked at me and whispered, "Let me find favor in your sight and relieve you of your *help.*" He stepped through the door. I followed. He cleared his throat. "Tameri, my dear wife, come along. It is time to go."

Zadah, Kiya, and Dendera sat on the floor beside my couch, where Sarai rested. All three looked up and visibly brightened at his words.

"Rensi, my husband. A shameful deed is occurring, and you are the offender," Tameri protested. "I am needed here. With Sarai. Do not interrupt this service I do for our king."

Deeds. According to Meti, they last longer than words. They can live.

Tameri rose from her seat at a low table filled with assorted delicacies as Rensi stepped close and took her hand in his. "I would like a few moments alone with my noble wife on this festive day." He looked enchanted with her. "Come with me. I've had a visit from the royal jeweler."

She bit her lip and appeared to melt, soft as warm candle wax for a brief moment.

"Noblewoman Tameri, thank you for your help," I said amiably. "I appreciate all you have done for the king and Sarai. The entire harem is resting now before the feast begins at twilight. Go with your honorable husband and enjoy some time with your family on this great day of celebration."

Tameri took a step back from Rensi. "But I am the one in charge of Sarai. She is my responsibility for the king."

Rensi stood firm. "Tameri, act according to my wishes. The king knows of your faithful sense of duty to him. He will be grateful for all you have already done." They looked into each other's eyes. "We don't oft have time to ourselves."

"What my husband desires must be done." She slipped her arm through his and nodded at me.

I watched them as they walked away and marveled at the power Tameri seemed to have over Rensi. And then I felt a hint of something—*jealousy again?* Yes. I was jealous of what they had together. It seemed to work. They made it work. She was a difficult woman. No one, not even Tameri, denied it. Yet, she had the undying love of a good man. Rensi adored his wife. He made jests of her faults, and I believed Tameri frustrated Rensi at times, but he often talked about her wicked sense of humor, and valued her advice. He said she could take details and figure out solutions to problems that no one else could perceive. I had yet to see those traits in her but enjoyed seeing their devotion to one another.

"When the wife appears, the husband must not forget to rejoice," I heard him say many times. "True wisdom that has lived through the ages." Then he would laugh.

Was it as simple as that? Perhaps even Merikare and I could find a way to be happy together.

Merikare.

I had forgotten him again.

Then I recalled Abram. The way his eyes absorbed mine when he listened to what I said as I studied his handsome face. How he captured my heart over his tender concern for his sister. If he only knew how much I had wanted to embrace and comfort him.

Imi had been charming and humble toward me at the temple. It was hard to believe she could become a real threat. *Merikare can wait another day,* I decided. The heat had sapped the fight out of me, for now. And I wanted to relax a while with thoughts of Abram in my head.

A cool rinse, a light meal, and rest. That was the order of things.

I stood by the door and realized my servants did not bother to stir when I entered. They remained on the floor next to my luxurious couch, where Sarai reclined. She looked like a burnished, rare jewel, the couch her setting, gleaming in the muted light.

The talk had been light and lively when Rensi and I walked in. They had all been laughing. But now, even the cheerful countenance at the prospect of Tameri leaving disappeared. They regarded me carefully, and no one smiled. *My* presence seemed to cast a dark aura in my own home.

It appears there is already a new rhythm in the harem.

I rubbed my temples and pressed my lips together, that niggling headache threatening to return.

"Dendera … my bath. Fill it now," I commanded.

She started to rise, but Zadah stood first and walked toward me. "My mistress. Sarai has been telling us stories of her travels from Ur and Canaan. Her tales are fascinating and amusing. Perhaps you would join us, and your bath could wait a few moments?"

I slapped Zadah with all of my might.

She clasped her hand to her cheek and whimpered like a wounded kitten.

"How dare you disrespect me."

Zadah immediately crumbled to my feet.

Sarai sat up and looked as if she wanted to say something.

My mouth tightened. "Do you not discipline the slaves in your tribe, Sarai?"

Sarai remained on the couch and looked as though she carefully considered her words. "My answer may offend, Princess Hagar," she finally said.

"No more than Zadah has already done. They are my servants and should not be distracted in their duty to me. Besides, it is not wise to be lenient with servants. It fosters laziness and disrespect. If you are not firm with them, they no longer fear you. Isn't that right, Zadah?"

The tiny girl quivered as tears streamed down her face. In truth, I had never struck her before. She said nothing, and a knot tightened in my stomach.

"I heard Tameri say the same thing. But I find it hard to believe you side with the wife of the high vizier on much, Princess," Sarai said. "Kindness will not leave you vulnerable."

"Did you learn that from your hidden god?" I mocked.

"Not exactly, but I don't think striking slaves is necessary. Especially this little one, who praises you without your knowing," she said softly.

"I would never flout you, Princess," Zadah cried as she pressed her forehead to the ground at my feet.

"Get up, Zadah," I said. What was wrong with me? Why had I become so wroth and my heart so vexed? And why did I take it out on Zadah?

I rubbed my temples. "Leave me for a while, Zadah. Take my silver bucket and fill it with water from the Nile. I want to add it to my bath after the celebration tonight to honor Heryshaf."

Zadah's face turned ashen. Her plump lips and chin trembled. "Princess, there are many dangers in the river. My dreams are full of crocodiles … please don't make me go near there."

I slapped her again. "Take my silver bucket and fill it with water from the Nile," I spoke through clenched teeth, "and do not spill a drop until you return to me. Kiya, go with her."

Zadah grabbed the silver bucket, looked at me with tear-filled eyes, and backed out of the room trembling. Kiya and Dendera exchanged a glance, but neither said a word. Kiya followed Zadah out, and Dendera moved quickly and silently to fill my tub. Her hands shook as she removed my sheath and wig, the amulet, and other jewelry, and helped me slide into the bath.

The cool water and light scent of white Moringa flowers floating on the surface eased my bad temper. I closed my eyes and inhaled deeply.

"If my presence troubles you, Princess Hagar," Sarai said, reminding me again that she was in my home, "I will go anywhere you wish to be out of your sight."

Her voice held such gentleness, my cheeks burned thinking about my behavior.

"Your rooms will be ready soon enough, Sarai," I said without opening my eyes. "You are welcome here until then. Besides, I promised your brother, Abram, that I would take care of you." His name sounded pleasant when it fell from my lips. If I wasn't betrothed to a young fool like Merikare, perhaps I could have loved the older man.

"I feel as though my presence inflames your mood. I don't wish to do that to you any further."

"Forgive me, Sarai. I promise you only peace from now on." I opened my eyes and looked at her. "But answer one question. How did you come to believe so deeply in your hidden god? Like Egypt, Ur has many gods they bow to. How did you toss them aside for a god you cannot touch?"

Sarai stood and smiled as she walked toward me. "The city of Ur was the chief center of worship for the moon god, Nanna. As a small child, I would lie on my back outside on clear, warm summer nights and be filled with awe at the moon god."

She took the seat next to the tub, the one Tameri had occupied earlier, and continued her story.

"Nanna could shed so much light and illuminate the

darkness much more than all of the other stars in the sky. 'This is god,' I whispered to myself, and then worshiped the moon all through the night. But in the morning, with the dawn, the sun god, Utu, came out of his underground sleeping chamber and blotted out the moon. Nanna seemed to lose his power. Then all day, I would worship the sun god and believed that everything only existed because of the light and warmth of Utu." She paused. "Do you want me to go on?"

"Yes, please do," I said and thought about Zadah for a moment. Sarai's storytelling was spellbinding. No wonder my tiny servant didn't want to be disturbed. I took a deep, pained breath. *I will make it up to her.*

"Then in the evening," Sarai continued, "Nanna would reappear with all the stars in tow. My heart became confused. Abram had also been watching the sun, moon, and stars coming and going. Each in its own time."

At the mention of Abram, I sat up in the tub and leaned toward her. The water stirred around me. My heart beat a little faster as I fought to suppress a smile.

"He also noticed that Utu gave way to Nanna, and then Nanna gave way to Utu. Abram reasoned that there must be a power above and beyond the gods we worshipped, one who controlled all of the others. On my own, I too had reasoned that both the sun and moon must have a master. That perhaps they weren't gods at all, but do the bidding of another, true God."

I gasped.

It was precisely what Rensi had said.

If Sarai heard me, she didn't let on. She kept on with her story and looked enchanting doing so. Her face was lit as if from candlelight, and her hair tumbled across her bare shoulders. Now, like Zadah, I did not want anything to disrupt this moment. Thinking of her made my cheeks burn again.

"One day, Abram took an axe and destroyed all of our father's idols but the largest one. Father had many because he was an idol merchant. When he saw all of his idols shattered, he accused Abram. Abram denied it. He said the largest idol had killed the others over an offering given to them." Sarai paused again and laughed tenderly. "Our father said such a thing was impossible since the gods lived in houses of stone and wood. Therefore, they could not fight." She smiled, her lovely eyes warm and inviting. "It was at that moment that all in our household sought to follow the one, living God." Sarai let that rest in the air a moment. "The odd thing was, with that single act of humbling ourselves before God, we felt as if we all remembered something that was planted within us. Something written on our hearts from the beginning of time. We just needed to be reminded that He, that *El*, was there."

My breath caught in my throat. I found myself so mesmerized by her grace and warmth and knew I had to protect her. Rensi's warning flashed in my head.

"O, Sarai," I said gravely. I raised my arms, resting them on the edge of the tub. Water trickled and pooled. "You were right. I cannot compel you to worship our gods in your heart. And I will not concern myself with what god you worship in private. But heed my warning. In public, your prayers must be to the gods of the King of Egypt. They are the gods who make a man a king and who make a king a god." I shifted in the tub, the water dancing around my naked body. "If you utter such things to others, your life, and the lives of everyone in your entire tribe, will be in great distress."

Chapter Sixteen

THE DRY DESERT AIR COOLED RAPIDLY as what remained of the day disappeared. I stood on the balcony outside the Great Festival Hall and stared at the black sky that possessed only a splinter of a silver moon. The bright stars burned blue and white and took my breath away. They lingered so near, I imagined collecting them like shells on the shore of the Nile.

I caught sight of Abram inside and heat rose in my cheeks. I lowered my head to hide the emotions he stirred in me. A rumor had surfaced that the king invited him to stay for the Feast of Heaven and Earth. Until now, I did not know if he had accepted or declined.

I only hoped in my heart.

I composed myself and raised my face to take him in. He stood, full-bearded and splendid, exuding the vigor of youth even at his advanced age. Several other women gazed at him with adoring looks too, and my cheeks burned even hotter.

He talked with my pompous, clean-shaven brother as though they were the only two in the room. The difference was staggering. Abram's eyes never left my brother's, while Merikare's attention wandered from Abram and back again. The crown prince appeared blind to the great man's value and behaved dismissive, making it clear he viewed Abram as inferior.

I remained in solitary silence under the pristine sky and tried to sense the spirit that traveled here with Sarai. Nothing stirred. I let the growing noise from the banquet fall away and allowed the silence to deepen within me—still nothing. My limbs began to tremble, and I was surprised by the fear and disappointment that filled me.

And how lost I felt.

I looked up and met Abram's gaze and shivered all over.

A servant, squat with dark eyes and skin, approached and

offered me a cup of wine as percussion instruments called us to feast. I took the cup and let the servant lead the way to my seat. My every movement slowed when I realized I'd sit at the same table as Abram. I faced him with wide eyes and only produced a nod.

He smiled, and it was as though the sun rose in his face alone.

My body became rigid. My thoughts held captive, and I could no longer breathe. *Silly, silly girl.*

He wore the same type of sweltering clothing he had earlier, but now a brightly colored scarf was wrapped around his head. He waited until I was seated on one of the luxurious pillows that surrounded the low table and then sat to the left of me.

I still had not taken a breath.

Bare-chested Merikare sat on my right, sloppily gulping a cup of wine. A gold amulet, full of topaz and garnets, hung around his neck to protect him from evil spirits. His head bore a short-cropped human hair wig with a gold, rearing cobra perched on top. Which meant he had shaved the single plait of hair on his head, that last symbol of youth removed because he was married now. He roughly grabbed a passing servant, yanked a pitcher of wine from his hands, and shoved him away so hard the poor fellow fell to the ground.

Merikare laughed.

My chin dipped.

Another servant rushed to help the young man to his feet.

I sat stunned, staring at my hands. Abram cleared his throat, diverting my distress, and everyone's attention from Merikare's appalling behavior. He introduced his nephew, Lot. Lot sat across from Merikare and next to Tameri, with Rensi on her opposite side. He was as handsome as Abram, but a smaller man, with dark olive skin, light brown eyes, and a cheery grin on his face.

We muttered greetings as musicians strolled by with handheld drums, keeping rhythm with lithe male and female dancers. The performers twisted, soared, and bounded around the room to excite the crowd, who joined in by chanting and clapping.

Servants trailed behind and draped wreaths of sweet lilies around the necks of every woman and man. Other servants placed perfumed cones of tallow, fragranced with dusty myrrh, upon each head.

Lot laughed good-naturedly. "What is this?" He reached up and touched the greasy, pointed cone.

"The heat of your body melts the tallow as the evening wears on, and the woody scent of myrrh shall enter your nose," Tameri answered. "Pharaoh provides favors to all his guests, along with the best food and drink." She inhaled the intense fragrance from the garland and smiled. "Our people love a good time, and no expense is spared at a feast."

"You may remove the cone, my lords," I said to Abram and Lot. "It will melt into our wigs and release the perfume. But they are made of ox fat and will damage your turban and be unpleasant upon your scalp."

Tameri rolled her eyes.

Abram removed his cone, as did I, but Lot left his on his head.

Tameri leaned close to him. "Well done, my lord," she gushed, "now tell me, what was it like sailing here from the delta amid so many boats?"

"It was an experience I shall never forget," Lot said. He spoke our language almost as fluently as Abram and Sarai. "Music from the …" He mimicked a wind instrument with his fingers.

"Flute," Tameri said.

Lot nodded his head. "Flute, yes. We call it an *embubu*. It was our constant companion. At night, the boats moored together, and your people filled the air with incense, music, and singing."

"Music is a big part of our lives, and we always seek to enjoy ourselves," Tameri mumbled around a mouthful of grapes. "The gods used music to establish order out of chaos at creation. It is highly valued in our culture and used to thank the gods for giving us life."

"Music is a part of our daily life as well," Lot continued. "But your people immersed themselves in it so much it was ... frenzied."

"I guarantee," Tameri said, "it was far more carefully orchestrated than it might appear to the foreign eye."

A male servant brought a platter laden with savory minced beef pastries. He smiled nervously and served the crown prince first, as he held the highest rank at the table. Merikare took two pastries, ripped one in two, and stuffed half into his mouth. He nearly consumed both before the servant served everyone else. It was a show of blatant disregard for our guests and the high vizier. Not even the king would behave in such away.

I tucked my arms into my sides and twisted the amulet around my wrist, unable to meet anyone's eyes. Thankfully, Lot continued his conversation with Tameri, and everyone appeared to ignore the slight.

"Many of your people danced and removed their garments." Lot's ears reddened. "Our dances have a different purpose, and we always remain clothed."

My brother guffawed loudly, and chopped pastry meat tumbled from his mouth and onto the table. Servants appeared seemingly out of nowhere and cleaned up after him.

I mused on the image. How many times over the years had I watched others clean up my brother's messes? My memories were full of people he had offended or harmed being paid off by the high vizier. Merikare would take anything from anybody, and Rensi was always there to replace it or pay for the damages. The high vizier had even arranged several marriages for peasant girls my brother had taken advantage of. He had sent expensive gifts to nomarchs and nobles who had been insulted or snubbed by the future king. Merikare had defiled others, caused fear, quarreled openly with the high priest, remained deaf to the pleas of our mother, trespassed, and violently attacked fellahin who came too near to him.

And yet, the gods and Pharaoh preferred him to me.

Dread stirred in me again, knowing I would soon be his to do with as he pleased. And there was nothing to be done about it. I shuddered as gooseflesh covered my arms, but I determined to put aside the disgusting thought for now.

Lot seemed to be enjoying his visit with us. His quick wit matched Tameri's and had a bawdy edge to it that surprised me but delighted the high vizier's wife. His ears colored, and he rubbed the back of his neck when naked servants and dancing girls appeared. But he did not turn his eyes away as Abram did.

Merikare noticed Abram when he did this. "At least your nephew appears to like the ways of our people."

I held my breath.

"Your land has many things to admire and to experience, and it humbles all in our tribe," Abram replied soberly.

I exhaled as a pair of lofty copper trumpets echoed across the Great Festival Hall. They signaled our father's arrival, and even Merikare had to observe protocol when it involved the king.

We all stood.

Silence rested upon us as Sarai entered behind Pharaoh, clad in a full-length pleated, transparent linen dress. Large gold earrings dangled from her ears, and a delicate gold collar filled with precious stones adorned her neck. The black, plaited wig on her head and kohl eyeliner stated that she was Egyptian now.

Abram's intense brown eyes lost all of their light as they fell on his sister. His shoulders stooped, and his hands clenched into fists. She lifted her chin and returned his regard with flinty, hard eyes. Her face appeared so bitter, my lips puckered as though I'd tasted something sour. I could not believe this was the same woman I had spent the afternoon with. Abram lowered his head and turned away.

Alarmed, I glanced at Merikare, but his attention diverted to Imi, who sat at a nearby table. I'd noticed her when I first took my seat but ignored her. Now, I was almost thankful for her attendance. I needed a moment to sort out the feeling in my bones. *What am I missing?*

The haunting sounds of a harp drifted through the air, and we sat again as musicians assembled near the rear of the hall. Flutes and drums joined in and altered the music into a light and lively song. Beautiful dancing girls appeared before us, temple dancers, the finest in Egypt. They leaped and swayed as though they had double joy in their hearts. A thin white belt sat low on their hips, and a menat necklace—a heavily beaded neckpiece shaken in dance—were all they wore as they interchanged slow, elegant steps with wild acrobatic movement.

Abram averted his eyes. Lot's remained on the girls, his ears now bright red, even as the dancers trailed away.

The music continued as lovely servant girls served grape leaves filled with lamb and fresh mint from gold salvers. They too, were scantily attired with only thin gold ornaments around their throat and waist. Abram turned his handsome face away again when they approached our table.

Lot stared.

I caught Abram's head turn away from the corner of my eye, and he shifted from side to side, appearing uncomfortable. Did he consider nudity to be distasteful? Nakedness, like sex, was just another aspect of life and had no trace of immorality attached to it. That was the way of it in Egypt.

Next came trays of my favorite dish, fish kufta, made with coriander and cinnamon. Plates of leeks, cucumbers, and chickpeas quickly followed, and we passed those around. Near our table hovered the tall, effeminate manservant that always glowed like he sipped as much wine as he served. He stood ready and refilled our cups so they were never empty.

I had barely eaten today, and the smell of all this food made my stomach rumble. Yet, despite being hungrier than I'd been in too long to remember, I found it challenging to eat in front of Abram. It was as though I had an unknown malady.

My laughter sounded shaky, and I smiled at nothing. I stared at him when he spoke, barely blinking, as my heart fluttered and seemed to keep beat with the music.

Abram appeared ill at ease, making my awkwardness feel blaring.

I could sense Tameri's beady eyes scrutinizing me and wondered if others saw this strange affliction in me. I silently hoped that she would be wise and not say anything in front of Merikare.

The thought made me feel foolish.

Abram was older than my father. I kept reminding myself of that. But something about him drew me in. He was a man of mystery and power, and he looked at me as if he really saw me. Almost as though I were something special.

You're behaving like a common daughter, not the daughter of a king, is what my mother would say. And somehow, her voice came through.

I took a deep breath, sat up straight, and tried my best to assume the role of a princess of Egypt. I had recognized years ago the difference in this role from when I was free to be myself. Like all royals, I had learned when to use it and when I could rest from it.

I needed it now.

Chapter Seventeen

I HADN'T SAID TWO WORDS TO Abram since the feast began, but I was determined to do so now.

"This festival is for the opening of our new year." The words came out too rushed. I took a breath. "We call it Wepet Renpet." He leaned toward me as if to hear better. My heart pounded. "Sopdet is the deity, the star that tells us when the inundation is upon us. When Sopdet rises, so does the Nile. She vanished from the eastern horizon nearly seventy days ago, in late spring."

Abram nodded. "We saw her appear before sunrise this morning, burning brighter than all other stars." He smiled, and it burned brighter than all other smiles.

"Everyone on the boats stayed up all night and watched for her," Lot added. "As the night drew on, it became deathly quiet until the first twinkle. Then the party erupted, and the music and dancing began again until sunrise."

"That's because Wepet Renpet is also regarded as a dangerous time," Merikare added, seizing the conversation. He seemed to sway as he spoke. "The sun god Ra grows weak over the course of the year and becomes vulnerable to attack from his enemies. If he were defeated last night, it would have been the end of the world. So, they celebrated the continuation of life with the rising of the sun." He lifted his glass with a gesture of merriment and took a long drink. Everyone at the table joined him. I brought my glass to my lips but did not drink.

"But I believe," Merikare went on, with raised eyebrows and a silly grin, "Wepet Renpet is just another excuse for drunkenness. We consume more beer and wine during this holiday than we do during the rest of the year."

Lot laughed heartily, raised his glass, and took another large swig.

"This is also when the goddess, Sekhmet, wanders the earth with twelve demonic murderers," Merikare continued. I tightened, recognizing the menace in his voice. "Demons who travel all over Egypt and shoot arrows from their mouths. They cause chaos and disorder wherever they wander. To protect ourselves, we wear these charms around our necks." He lifted the heavy gold amulet he wore. "This ensures I receive Sekhmet's protection instead of her wrath."

My neck and jaw stiffened. Merikare tormented my heart with his voice. He often snatched a conversation and kept it for himself. Usually, this didn't bother me, but tonight, I wanted to talk to Abram.

"I've heard the region of Sumer—where the city of Ur is—lies between two rivers," my brother said. "And that the rivers are wild and untrained and flood whenever they wish."

"They can," injected Lot. "The rivers can change their course when they rise too high, as easily as a woman changes her mind. That's when they become the most dangerous."

"The rivers or the woman?" Merikare laughed at his own jest.

"Both," said Lot and laughed with him. "But the rivers most of all. They have been known to sweep away entire villages."

"A lot of trouble can come to a king from that." Merikare grinned. "People always blame the royal family. Which is why we blame the gods." He lifted his cup and drank.

Lot spoke of death and destruction, and my brother beamed as if someone told him a jape only he understood. *He's a drunken fool, and Lot is not far behind.*

"The two rivers are the Euphrates on the west and the Tigris on the east," Abram said as though he talked to children. "Sumer is bordered to the north by mountains, so the rivers swell from melting snow. In the past, they were completely unpredictable and violent. But canals were built to create arable land out of swamps and sand. Like waterways to the desert." He looked at me and smiled, and my heart quickened. "It helped control the floods, but water will always take the course it wants to take," he said easily to Merikare. "I'm sure you've found that to be true in Egypt too."

"We have." Merikare's tone was undeniably condescending. "But the gods themselves fill the Nile, mysteriously, from water that issues forth from the darkness. We are a favored people."

"Meti told me stories of snow during our studies when I was a child," I said to Abram. "But it seemed more myth and magic than something from the real world." I suddenly found myself feeling remarkably lighthearted. "You seem too discerning of a man to put stock in fables like snow. How can you claim it fills your rivers?"

"O, it is not a fable, Princess. I have watched snow falling many times in my life." Abram smiled and nodded. "I clearly remember the first time the soft and silent flakes floated from the sky and landed gently on my skin. It is one of the most beautiful things the Lord has ever made."

My eyes widened and I glanced at Merikare, who shifted his attention to Imi. Thankfully, he missed Abram's remark about his lord.

I had never met anyone who had first-hand knowledge of the cold, white creation. I demanded a sample years ago, but no one could provide one for me. Since my imagination could not grasp it, I decided it was lore and not logic. But now, even with a witness, all I thought of was Abram's words that it was *soft and silent, gentle on his skin.* Strangely, the story of the cold snow caused a flood of warmth in me.

Abram reached for his cup and accidentally brushed my hand. His touch caused me to recall myself as a red-hot blush spread across my face. He didn't appear to notice the contact or the blush.

There was a long moment of silence. Eventually, I spoke up. "I would love to travel and see such things with my own eyes."

Tameri snorted. "Surely, you don't." She looked at Abram.

"Egyptians rarely travel. We are denied entrance to the afterlife if we die away from home and cannot be buried properly." She shuddered. "It is too great a risk. Even to see something as inexplicable as snow."

I noticed for the first time that Rensi had yet to speak. The high vizier sat unusually quiet, his thoughts clearly far away from the talk of flooding rivers and snow.

But I was more interested in Abram's adventures than Rensi's silence.

How exhilarating it would be to see such things, to make one's way across the world and wake every morning in some new place. Especially with Abram.

My breath hitched.

It was folly to hope for such things and dangerous for a betrothed princess to even dream of them. I would never leave this land.

Not for snow.

Not even for Abram.

But somehow, my thoughts were at odds with the longing in my heart.

Tameri gave another snort. "Crown Prince Merikare, I see you invited your lovely Imi to this royal celebration." She looked at me, but I avoided her gaze.

I still had not spoken with Merikare about his first wife.

Imi looked as regal as any of us. A thin gold crown encircled a mass of intricate dark braids in the wig she wore, and her long, draped dress of white linen with vertical and horizontal pleats was a style reserved exclusively for royals. She truly stood out as someone quite special. If Sarai's beauty had not been so astonishing, all the talk would have been about Imi.

I tried to ignore the many furtive glances between her and my brother. I determined not to be bothered by it.

The servants returned with the next course, and Lot eagerly helped himself to grilled antelope seasoned with cumin and coriander. I served Abram a slice and took one for myself.

Cubed lemon lamb with rice and almonds followed. I served Abram again and then myself. Salvers filled with several types of bread and goat cheese came next, with bowls full of ghee and honey.

Food fit for the gods.

I pushed it around my plate and barely touched it.

Hyrcanos, one of Pharaoh's chief advisors, approached the king. He bowed his tall, thin frame and then announced, "I have found a special attraction for the night. May I have your permission, Your Majesty, to present little people with celestial gifts to help us celebrate the new year?"

Pharaoh nodded.

Tamari scowled.

Hyrcanos was a young man but the closest in rank to Rensi. There was talk that he desired the role of high vizier. I knew his ambition menaced Tameri, but it didn't seem to bother Rensi.

Hyrcanos was present when Sarai was found and had been adamant that only the king should have her. He returned from the delta early with Rensi and described Sarai's wondrous beauty to Pharaoh in a poem. I looked at Sarai and thought of his words.

How splendid and beautiful is the aspect of her face,
And how supple is the hair on her head.
How lovely are her eyes and pleasant her nose.
And all the radiance of her face ...

I tried but could not recall all of it. But I remembered the ending.

Neither virgins nor brides entering the bridal chamber exceed her charms.

Her beauty is supreme over all women.

Yet with all this comeliness, she possesses great presence and wisdom.

I wondered what else she possessed, or more correctly, what possessed her. Her god inhabited my dreams, I had little doubt now, and his magic was strong. Suspicions tormented me, but the affection in my heart for her brother seemed to keep my tongue silent, as though the *presence* possessed it too.

Hyrcanos clapped loudly, and a troupe of diminutive dancers took the floor.

"We believe that whoever sees dancing dwarfs will have a prosperous and healthy life," I explained to Abram and Lot. "They are from the land of spirits and express their spiritual powers through their movements. We hold them in very high esteem."

"The king will be pleased with the nobleman Hyrcanos, and heap praise and honor upon him," added Merikare.

"We met Hyrcanos in Zoan," Abram said. "He is a determined young man."

"He is ruthless," snarled Tameri.

Rensi placed an arm on his wife to silence her but said nothing.

The dancers moved slowly, in perfect symmetry, as musicians gave rhythm to their steps with wooden clappers. It was somber, almost a religious ritual. A gifted singer joined in while two women added to the dramatic dance by creating a conquest scene. One knelt on the ground representing a defeated enemy king, and another stood beside her, representing Pharaoh. She grabbed the enemy by the hair in one hand and threatened her with a club held in the other.

The performance finished, and everyone took to their feet and erupted in applause and shouts of joy. The audience threw flowers toward the troupe as they bowed respectfully to the royal and noble crowd and then dashed from the room.

Tameri pouted through the entire presentation.

Instantly, the effeminate manservant returned and filled our cups. More food arrived without limit, fruit-filled honey cakes, crocodile-shaped date loaves, and Tameri's favorite, Tigernut Sweets. I watched her reach out and pick up one with each hand.

"You have traveled far, Abram of Ur," I said, drawing him back into conversation. Lot distracted Merikare, allowing us to speak alone. "What made you leave your home by the two rivers and delivered you to Egypt?"

Abram's eyes became passionate and powerful. "My God appeared to me and told me to leave. He said, 'Get out of your country to a land that I will show you. You will become a great nation and be a blessing to all the families of the earth.' He also promised that he would bless those who bless me and curse those who curse me. So, with a divine promise of four things, seed, land, a nation, and blessing, I journeyed from the other side of the two rivers and ended up here."

My breathing stopped. I was wholly unprepared. Never had I heard anyone speak with such inner conviction and external authority.

I peered around, but no one except me heard the words that had come from Abram's mouth.

Having Abram near me suddenly mattered more than anything. I had so many questions. I needed to determine if the god who appeared to him in Ur, now appeared to me.

Chapter Eighteen

I GLANCED UP AS MERIKARE SLID his pillow seat around the table to engage in conversation with Lot. At first, my brother seemed genuinely interested in Abram's nephew, until I realized Merikare had positioned himself where his eyes could fully claim Imi. Oddly, nothing disagreeable rose within me. I didn't care in the least.

Perhaps I'm foolish not to care more.

I gave Abram a warning look to keep our exchange unnoticeable. "How did this god appear to you?" I whispered. "In a vision or a dream?"

"He spoke to me as a man speaks to his friend. He called me by name with a voice as clear to me as yours."

Whatever I had been expecting, that wasn't it. I had never heard such a thing before. *A god speaking to a man as a friend?* I stared at him, unblinking, and recalled the being in my dream. He had called *me* by name and had appeared as a *man.* My thoughts froze, and it took a moment to gather them. "Where is this unseen god that has spoken to you?" I finally said. "Sarai says he is invisible."

"His glory fills heaven and earth which He created." Abram whispered, but his eyes flashed a bit of mischief. Speaking about his god made him bold ... too bold.

I twisted the tight amulet I wore. "If *your* god created the heavens and earth." My voice stayed low. "Please be careful. This conversation borders on treacherous ground." Abram watched me closely. "If *your* god created the heavens and earth, that would empty the sun and moon of divinity. They could not be gods. If we create something, then it is separate from us. We are two, not one."

He looked at me with approval, and my heart soared. "You are clever, Princess Hagar," he said appreciatively. "Yes, it separates us. But are we not still a part of it? Are you not a relation to your mother and father even though you are a creation of the two of them?" His face turned serious. "We worshipped the moon as if it were a god. But I now see the moon this way, that it is not divine, but a symbol of the divinity that created it. I look on it and see evidence of the very presence of the one true God."

My eyes bore into his deep brown pools, and I wondered if I could simply fall into their warmth. "When I look upon the moon, I see it this way," I said. "I want to pass into it, to join with it, and become a part of it. But we are at such a distance, we must remain separated." *Am I still talking about the moon?*

"Princess, it does not have to be as you speak. Inside every one of us is a longing to be reunited with something outside of ourselves. I have been reunited with my Maker. I wish for all of mankind to do so as well."

Somehow, deep in my bones, I knew he spoke the truth. I leaned closer to him. "Abram, tell me more about what you have learned about your god."

A kind smile filled his face and made him appear even more extraordinary. His eyes probed mine, and for a moment, he remained near enough, I could feel his heat. Then he leaned backward and stroked his beard as if the action took him back in time. "Long ago, I rested on my bed and slept. Great distress filled my heart, and I wept while sleeping. My soul grieved to know the truth about God." His eyes widened. "Then I heard a voice from the heavens ask me, 'What help or profit have you from the idols you bow to and worship? They are forms without spirit and cannot hear. They mislead the hearts of men.' As I said, His voice was as clear to me that night as yours is on this night. So, I arose from my bed, and He kept speaking to me. 'Teach your people that worshipping idols will not help them. Trust only in me, the living, eternal God, and I promise to make my presence known to all.'"

I sensed something and sucked in my breath. Gooseflesh once again covered my skin. The *presence* that haunted me since Sarai arrived was in the room.

I looked up and met Rensi's eyes, wide as the gold plates we ate from.

He discerned it too.

"He is here," I whispered breathlessly.

"He is always here," said Abram.

I brought my fingertips to my cheeks. "But he flees so quickly. Why doesn't he stay?"

"He never leaves, Princess Hagar. Even when you can't feel Him, trust me. I tell you the truth. He is still with us."

"Sarai told me the story of how the rest of your family came to know your one god." I went over the daring event in my mind. "You destroyed all of your father's idols?"

"Indeed." He let slip a small chuckle. "I shattered all of them but the largest one and blamed him for committing the crime. My father admitted that the idols had no life or power and could not have done so. He could not answer when I asked him, 'Then why do you worship that which hears not, sees not, and cannot benefit you in anything?'" Abram stroked his beard again. "At first, he threatened to stone me for rejecting his gods. But then he admitted that he only served them because his father did. That very day, he turned his face away from idolatry and toward the one true God."

While he spoke, I tried not to think about how handsome he looked. His long, groomed beard reached over his collar to his purple robe, and a tuft of dark, wavy hair had slipped the bounds of his brightly colored turban. I wondered why it was not gray like the hair on his face. It made me curious to explore him more and then embarrassed to be attracted to someone so much older.

Abram tilted his head as though he wondered what I was thinking and added, "The sun goes down, and then it rises. The same is true of the moon. The winds go south and then turn and go north. All the rivers I have ever seen spill into the sea. Yet the sea is never full. In my heart, I have always known that one God divinely created it all."

He paused, and we both took a sip of wine. His eyes looked a lifetime away.

"My father, Terah, was Chief Minister of Ur, a position like your high vizier." He nodded toward Rensi. "Alongside our house, he had a workshop where he fashioned idols out of wood, stone, silver, and gold." He took a breath, and I did the same, conscious of my need for air. "Always a line of people stood outside our door, people coming to offer sacrifices to these idols or to buy them if they could afford it. His business thrived." Abram pulled at an errant thread in his cloak. "I often sat and watched my father create the idols. I could not, in my young mind, figure out why he was not a god since he created all the other gods." He paused for a servant to refill our cups.

I didn't recall emptying mine and believed his words made me lightheaded. "As a child," I whispered, "I saw our high priest mend one of the idols. I also wondered why they didn't bow to him for creating them."

"Did that not give you the fleeting sense that there is something more wonderful out there?"

"No," I said truthfully. "It confused me."

"It confused you because your child's heart could not accept as truth that stone figures are gods. That is why I spread the knowledge of the one and only God in the heavens. I am the-one-on-the-other-side, or *The Hebrew*, in our language. Because the world is on one side worshipping idols, and I am on the other worshipping the true God."

I cocked a brow. "Hebrew. That is a good name." I smiled as though we held a secret together.

Merikare cleared his throat from beside me. "It is easy to see your sister, Sarai, is a woman of worth," he said.

I recoiled. I did not know how long he had been there.

"Yes, all of Egypt shines with the beauty of Sarai," Merikare continued. "Her face is more radiant than the sun. And we worship the sun." His mouth twitched. "I do not wish to be enraged against a man unjustly, Abram. Especially one who has found favor with the king. But you are still required to do things according to the laws of Egypt while you are in Egypt."

My insides cowered. Merikare had heard more of our conversation than was safe. I watched him carefully.

"I grieve in my heart because I believe the ways of our gods have been violated." Merikare kept his eyes on mine as he ripped the leg off a fattened fowl and tore its flesh with his teeth.

"I know my idea of one God is unique and quite different from the idea of multiple gods." The words wavered in the air for a moment. "I find it difficult to withhold the truth from a ripening mind and heart like Hagar's. But I am a peace-loving man and do not wish to cause you strife."

"You risk being tossed in the Nile to become food for the crocodiles when you speak against the gods of Egypt," Merikare replied testily and wiped his greasy mouth with the back of his hand.

"Your father has granted me permission to enter into conversation on any subject with the most learned among your people," Abram answered. "Surely that would include Princess Hagar. Is there any more learned amongst you?"

A smile escaped me, utterly against my will.

Anger flared across Merikare's face. "This is not conversation appropriate for the malleable mind of any woman. Pharaoh is half man and half god and worshipped as such. He would be insulted to hear our beliefs challenged in his own home." His eyes fell on mine again. "My learned sister would be wise to remember that."

I sighed deeply. "My heart has not abandoned our gods, Merikare. But each man's heart is for himself. Can you compel another to eat or sleep? How can you force a heart to change what it hopes for? What it believes is truth?" I repeated the words Sarai had said to me. Then I turned to Abram. "You need to be fiercely awake about your conversations and actions while you are in Egypt. We would not want anything unfortunate to happen to you."

Rensi found his voice. "Abram, we are grateful that you have been led to our door. A man as wise and knowledgeable as you can only improve Egypt."

"Too many foreign elements have sifted into the delta and gained access to our country if you ask me," Tameri snarled. "What good can come from that?" She shrugged. "Although, I suppose if you had not settled in Egypt, Abram, Sarai would not be among us now."

I frowned as the words fell from her mouth. Pharaoh taking Sarai into his harem had caused Abram grief. I looked at him apologetically.

But his eyes were on his sister.

And the whole earth tilted when it should have remained flat.

What I saw in his eyes was what I wished for when he looked at me. *O, what maiden would not want that gaze from her beloved?* My brow furrowed as an icy foreboding shuddered in my bones.

Something was amiss.

Chapter Nineteen

I SAT STUNNED, UNABLE TO HEAR anything other than the pounding of my heart as I struggled to understand the way Abram looked at Sarai. I picked up a pastry filled with sweet figs and walnuts and nibbled. *O, gods of Egypt. What did I see?* I lifted my eyes, fearing everyone watched me. But no one looked openly or craned their necks to observe my behavior.

Rensi engaged Abram in conversation, and it sounded normal, like friendly arguing, the way men talked when they discussed nearly any subject. Lot nodded periodically, pretending to listen to them, but his eyes wandered the room and rested on a beautiful servant girl. Tameri's attention remained on the food in front of her. Merikare's gaze was fixed on Imi.

I smiled amiably and leaned toward my brother. "We've not had a moment to speak about your new wife, Merikare. She is quite lovely."

He eyed me warily.

"Tell me, how did Imi rise so quickly from the streets of Zoan to the palace of the king of Egypt? I haven't heard how you discovered such a treasure."

"If you really want to know, I suppose I rescued her." His expression relaxed. "I was walking through the marketplace and saw a great crowd gathering. I pushed into their midst and found them watching women spinning flax into thread. It seemed odd that men would congregate for something so commonplace. And then I saw her. One young woman spinning flax so fast everyone cheered her on." He blinked. Smiled faintly. "She was the most beautiful girl I had ever laid eyes on. She looked up at me and sent my heart to a place it had never been before."

Merikare took a sip of wine, and my eyes secretly flicked to Abram and back again. A yearning moved in me, along with a sense of emptiness and sadness. My brother would take the crown and everything else our father had to offer and to add to the injury, he was free to experience love.

"I determined to have her," Merikare continued. "'What can I give you for your daughter that spins so quickly?' I asked her mother. 'Buy me a loom to make cloth, and you may have her,' she replied. I dispatched a servant to do just that and delivered the loom that very day." He paused for another sip of wine. "I intend to gladden her heart and give her everything, Hagar. Her own chambers and servants, and a carefully tended garden filled with fragrant flowers shaded by climbing vines. That is what I promised her. Anything and everything that will delight her."

"For the price of a loom, you found true love?"

Merikare shrugged. "I do not know about that. But when I see her, I feel, my heart feels ... revived." He looked at me fully. For a fleeting moment, I experienced a connection to him I'd not felt since we were children. "Is that love, sister?"

"What would I know about love?" My eyes flicked toward Abram again. I was so drawn to him, and he was a stranger really—I hardly knew him. But my heart cried out with something wild and irrational, as though it awakened for the first time. Was this what made the crown prince abandon his senses and take such a huge risk for a lowborn girl? Merikare could have lost favor with our father, just asking to make her a wife. The king could have insisted she become a concubine without title or position. He could have claimed Imi for himself or traded her to a noble for a favor. But my brother *fought* for her. "Life would be less uncertain in the Royal House of Women if she didn't come to us as your wife, Merikare. Why did you insist on that?"

"I don't concern myself with matters of the women's quarters, Hagar," he barked. "Father taught us not to distinguish between a nobleman and a poor man. 'Take to yourself a man because of the work of his hands' were his exact words. I simply applied our father's principles to a woman and used that argument with him." Merikare glanced toward Imi. "Besides, she wouldn't share her young, ripe fruit with me unless I promised to make her my wife. She said she'd rather serve in the palace as a slave for the rest of her life."

My face clouded. *That's all it took to snare you, brother? Clever girl.* "I hope she was worth it."

"Sweet as a draught of honey. When I entered the water, I plunged right into the flood, and my eager heart carried me swiftly over the waves." Merikare laughed a belly full.

My own belly roiled, and our brief moment of connection was over. *And you are the one the gods chose to be our next king over me?*

Merikare laid a hand on my thigh and whispered in my ear. "I swim as surely as I walk on solid ground."

I removed his hand and noticed a wine stain on his white shendyt. His stupid grin irked me, and I wanted to slap him as I had done Zadah. "There are many perils in the river, dear brother, and it would be wise to avert as many as possible. You never know what lurks below the surface."

I expected a sneer or some contemptuous remark. Instead, he sat up straight and fought for the lowborn girl again. "I could easily forget the blasphemous conversation you had with Abram if you would extend kindness to Imi in the harem."

It was nearly unbearable. "As you said, our king does not restrict his favors to the rich and wellborn." I attempted levity I did not feel. "I could do the same. As long as she is clear on her place." I kept my eyes on his. "And I am clear on that too. What are your intentions, dear brother, regarding the position of your wives when you become king?"

His jaw clenched, and his eyes narrowed as he looked at me as dismissively as he would a servant. The way he had since we were children. "I intend to love many wives with passion. I will soothe their bodies and fill their bellies." He placed his hand on my thigh again.

With a jerk, I pushed his hand away. "Do not be so greedy, brother. Even a king should not covet more than his fair share."

I tried to keep my voice gentle. "Did you ever consider that your family should have begun with me? We've been betrothed since the day we were born." I searched his face. "You always bring things from afar for our younger brothers and sisters and seek to make them happy. Have you ever pondered anything that might delight *my* heart?"

Merikare's laugh took on the sharp edge of a flint knife. "You will have your moment, dear sister. But I am royal blood and food to be shared. I will have more sons and daughters than any pharaoh before me." He jutted his chin toward his beautiful prize from Zoan. "Imi already carries my first."

It was as though the full force of a slap landed on my face.

"Merikare, is that true? Or do you say such things to displease me?" I crossed my arms and glared at him.

"Princess Hagar," a soft voice said from behind me.

I turned to see Dendera, and a full fury rose within me. "How dare you interrupt at such a time as this."

"I am so sorry." Her face was pale as bleached linen, and her hands shook uncontrollably. "We weren't sure if we should disturb you, but we thought you might want to know. Again, I am so sorry." She glanced at Merikare for the briefest of seconds and looked over her shoulder as if to run.

"So, what is it?"

"It is Zadah."

"Zadah?" I snapped. "What has she done now?"

Dendera closed her eyes and swallowed hard. Once. Twice. "She is dead, Princess."

"*Dead*?" Surely, I heard wrong. The voices in the room must have absorbed what Dendera said.

"She is dead," Dendera repeated. "The river has become her tomb."

Chapter Twenty

KIYA STOOD NEAR THE TUB, DRENCHED in blood and river water. She clutched my silver bucket and sobbed. Her body quaked with violent spasms while water from the bucket spattered the floor.

I remained by the door, my mouth agape and silent, staring but not seeing. Bitter dread washed over me, and I believed I would drown in it. I had to enter the room, take a step into the face of the misty shadow of death that I alone had cast. I jumped at a burst of children's laughter in the distance. It jarred my core until the last echo of it died away.

"We were on the riverbank for only a moment," Kiya said. Her voice trembled as fiercely as her body. More river water splashed the floor. "Zadah was terrified, but she did it anyway. She obeyed you. But when she leaned forward into the water, the crocodile snatched her. He came out of nowhere. And snatched her." Deep and unrestrained moans followed her words.

I stood there, frozen, and watched Dendera rush to her and pry the bucket from her hands. Kiya offered resistance at first, her shoulders curled over her chest as she gripped the handle of the vexatious vessel. But a few gentle tugs caused her to relent, and she released her hold.

"I could see her hand." Kiya looked at me, her eyes crested on the verge of anguish and insanity. "Your silver bucket still in it, she wouldn't let it go, even as the beast whirled round and round with little Zadah between its jaws."

I took a few hesitant steps toward her.

"Round and round he went in the water with only her feet and one arm hanging out of his dreadful mouth." Her voice sunk almost to a whisper. "He shook so hard that her arm and the bucket landed on the shore. That is all that is left of her. One arm and the sandals she slipped off before he stole her from us."

The sandals sat by the tub—so small a child could wear them—looking empty, sad, and alone.

Dendera placed the silver bucket on a low table by my feet. "Kiya brought the arm too," she whispered. "I wrapped it in linen and had it taken to the *ibu* for purification."

I looked at the bucket and nearly retched at the sight of bloody water. I gripped a nearby chair to steady myself.

Kiya continued, half-crazed, her face pale, her breathing shallow. "Even though there was only an arm left of her on the shore, I had to force the fingers from the handle." She shivered and clutched herself tightly. "The grip on it remained so tight. Even through the death roll. But I brought it for you full." She looked at me again, but this time with an odd smile and a vacant gaze. "For your bath. As you commanded."

"No," I shook my head. "No, no, no." Tears welled in my eyes. How could I have let this happen?

Both of my mother's hands were on my shoulders. I had not noticed her enter the room. I looked up and met her eyes. Tears streamed down my face, and I began to shake.

"Dendera, take Kiya to my chambers," my mother said. "The Overseer of the Royal Harem waits for you and will attend to you both this evening."

Through a watery haze, I watched Dendera bow low before my mother and then wrap her arms around Kiya. They moved past me crying, so bent they appeared years older than they were. My eyes followed them out the door.

Mother spoke to me, but I couldn't understand a word she said. She turned me around into her arms just as my legs buckled, and I collapsed to the ground.

"I did this to her," I cried, the flesh of my knees aching from the stone floor.

She knelt and held me tight.

"I put her in that crocodile's mouth. What a wretch I am."

Mother lifted me and led me to my bedchamber. I could smell sweet wine on her warm breath. "This is a deep wound,

Hagar, and will take time to heal." The Great Royal Wife's words were calm but concerned as she helped me abed. She settled in next to me, and I rolled over and laid my head on her lap. She tenderly stroked my hair. "Whenever a crocodile enters, grief arises. But you must use this to become a better sovereign." She paused, but her stroking continued. "And a better woman. We rule the people because the gods have deemed us worthy of doing so. But none of us are perfect in conduct. Not one of us is free from evil. That I can promise you."

"I was cross with her, Mother. I even laid a hand on her out of anger. But it had nothing to do with her. Zadah was devoted to me, and I attacked her because she was weak and because I could." My voice sounded cold. Hollow.

"We must strive to rule in rightness, daughter. But unfortunately, some things can only be learned by experience. Controlling your anger is one of those. Death is another." Her strokes paused, and she cleared her throat.

"I have known death." I sat up and faced her. "How many of my infant siblings have I seen placed in a tomb? And even Montu, your own son, who passed so suddenly in his tenth year? I have known death, but I have never *caused* death before."

Mother's eyes made me wish I'd not mentioned Montu's name. She exhaled. "Hagar, listen to me. A crocodile snatched Zadah's life. You did not kill her."

A crocodile. My black dreams were full of them. Was I forewarned about this impending danger and didn't listen? Could I have avoided this?

No. Crocodiles symbolized high officials because of their incredible strength and power. Zadah had neither. It had nothing to do with my vision, but was still my fault. No different than if I had torn her apart myself.

I pictured her before me. So faithful. Always loyal. Quick to protect me, even though I should have been the one protecting her. "She was snapped in two before her time, by my hands," I said as I lifted them and stared as though they dripped with blood.

Mother responded instantly. "Don't say such things, my daughter." She grabbed my hands in hers. "The river is teeming with danger. Yet, people bathe in it every day and take their ease on its shores. Occasionally someone is lost to it." She held my hands firm and looked deep into my eyes. "We all have an appointed time when death will find us. Today, death found Zadah because it was her time."

"She was so committed to me, and funny, and passionate …" I collapsed into Mother's lap and sobbed deeply, lost in the darkness of misery.

Mother held me in her arms and rocked. Gold beads woven into her wig chimed faintly as she swayed. She let me cry until the tears subsided, and the great sobs lost their vigor.

Mother gently wiped my face with her fingers as she had done many times in my life. Always able to wipe away every hurt or pain I experienced. But I knew no amount of rubbing would erase this one. It would smear and spread and never be expunged because something about death always remained behind with the living—a ghostly sense of unreality.

When Montu died, Mother cried out in madness. For a long season, she mourned the affable young prince who held so much promise and whom everyone loved and adored. Born only a year after Merikare and me, Montu had a crooked smile that lit up the world. His generous laugh filled the harem with joy. He loved to tease and had a sense of humor that tickled and entertained everyone. I'd even caught a slight smile on the lips of one of the palace guards as Montu passed and uttered something in jest. How I wished I could remember what he had said.

His end came fast and much too early. All the potential he was created for snuffed out quick and easy as a candlewick. The Great Royal Wife could not be comforted. At times it seemed the bashing weight of profound grief would prove too much for her to bear. She still thought about him daily—she said so many times. Her maternal happiness suffered even after all these years.

I shuddered, thinking about what it would be like to die. To never feel, or see, or think. To lay ice cold and alone in a tomb. I started to cry again.

"Bewail your young servant, Hagar." Mother hugged me tightly. "And always keep the silver bucket near you. When it tarnishes, polish it yourself. And remember Zadah when you see your reflection in it."

I bit my lip. My fresh tears had been for me and not Zadah. *How dare I cry for myself?* My eyes wavered to the silver bucket that Dendera had moved near my bed. I cried again, but this time for Zadah, and for her lonely arm, all we had left to bury.

"She lost her life to teach you a lesson. Never forget it, so your future conduct may be blameless."

Her words pierced my shattered heart. "Mother, I knew she was terrified of the river. Since we were small children, she woke in the night crying out in terror of the Nile. And of crocodiles snatching life away. She could never fully remember the dream in the morning, but she remembered crocodiles eating flesh." My voice cracked with grief. "Nothing in my dark vision disturbed her as much as hearing I saw crocodiles in it. Then I personally delivered her to the wild beast of her nightmares."

"One of the hardest things as a parent is to see your children suffer." Mother sighed. "If only I could take this from you and carry it myself."

"How did Zadah come to live in the harem? I remember her being here my entire life. But I don't know where she came from or how she came to be bound to me."

"I brought her to you when you were both little girls," Mother said. "She was such a tiny thing. You treated her like a doll. You dressed her, and fed her, and played school with her, trying to teach her what you learned from Meti."

"I remember that. Zadah was a good pretend student, but never a real one. She didn't have a head for such things." A sob caught in my throat. "She grew up to become fiercely devoted to me. I grew up to never really consider her much." My voice dropped low. "Do you know anything about Zadah's parents?"

Mother hesitated. I wasn't sure if she had to find the memory or was reluctant to share it.

"Zadah's parents?" I said again.

Mother stretched and leaned against the wall. I settled next to her. "Your father was the crown prince at that time. It was just before his father died. We had several years when the Nile failed us and did not inundate and fertilize the land. Egypt was in turmoil as there were few healthy crops, and famine was upon us." She shook her head. "Things were about to become disastrous. It was essential for the farming communities, in all the nomes, to work together so no one would starve. But there was one nomarch who used this difficult time to try to leave the central government. He had decided to rule on his own."

"Meti has told me of this time, Mother," I said. "I did not know it had anything to do with Zadah."

"Her fate was tied to the ambitions of a single proud man because if he were allowed to leave, others would follow. That would have weakened us and made us easy prey for Waset. Your grandfather sent your father to do whatever was necessary to bring them back into the fold. Force had to be used." Mother paused. "Zadah's father fought for the nomarch against the crown. Like all the other traitors, he and his wife were beaten violently with clubs, then tied up and thrown into the Nile. The crocodiles feasted that day." She bent her head toward me. "While everyone else fled, one small girl remained at the edge of the river as it filled with blood and cried out for her mother. A soldier picked her up to toss her into the Nile too. But your father stopped him. He brought her home and had me deliver Zadah to you."

There were no words.

No wonder Zadah's eyes always carried a hint of sadness in them. And her dreams were not dreams at all but memories in the form of night terrors. There had been frequent episodes, when we were children, where she'd thrash around in bed, then sit up crying and screaming. She would be wet with sweat, breathing hard, and appeared awake, but was always unaware that I was there. My nurse wanted her taken away from me. But I was a stubborn child and refused to let them move her. I held her and petted her—much the way I did with Bastet—until she went back to sleep. In the morning, she could not recall the dream but always said a crocodile visited her in the night.

Chapter Twenty-One

"FORGIVE MY INTRUSION, GREAT ROYAL WIFE." Tameri swept in and addressed my mother with a bow.

I stirred but did not rise.

My head throbbed, and the light aggravated my eyes as I slowly opened them. The room was unbearably hot, my skin damp and clammy, my mouth dry. I realized morning had passed, and the afternoon brought a sharp temperature rise. Yet Mother remained next to me.

I scanned the room as though in an unfamiliar land. Something was very different. My eyes landed on the silver bucket, and the full memory of Zadah's loss swept my body.

"I have been sent by the great man, the high vizier Rensi—my noble husband—with a message for you both." Tameri talked, but what was she saying? "Do not fear, mistresses, but neither must you take lightly the news I bring you." Her shallow face appeared unusually grave.

I sat up groggily, still tangled in Mother's arms. I stared at Tameri. Her shrill voice caused my head to pound even more, as though someone beat on the door. I was tired, and my spirit too broken, to do anything but take from her whatever she was about to set before me.

"Give us his message then, Tameri," Mother said.

"Give it to us as he said it," I added wearily.

Tameri's shrill voice dropped to a whisper. "A wall of sand has appeared in the distant sky. It will soon be upon us. The high priest has forecasted evil from this storm and expects it to occupy the land as savagely as a foreign army."

"Keep to the truth, Tameri," I snapped. "Do not exceed it."

"Princess Hagar, do not malign me. My words are as they came from my good husband's mouth."

"Where is Pharaoh, Tameri?" Mother asked.

"On the roof of the temple with Rensi, Meti, and the crown

prince. They can see the entire city and beyond from there." Her voice trembled, and her small rodent-like eyes twitched rapidly in their sockets. "They are trying to determine how much time we have to prepare."

My stomach turned. I did not want to deal with this today and preferred to wallow here in my misery. But Tameri's words sounded familiar, causing me to recall the scene vividly from my vision. The desert sand rose, roared, and rolled toward me like an angry wave. Every hair on my body stood straight as a powerful *presence* provoked my heart.

I found it unnerving that neither my mother nor Tameri appeared alarmed. Mother simply unwrapped her arms from around me and stood and stretched. "We shall need a few moments to dress," she said.

"I went to your chambers first," Tameri said to her. "I told your servants to come quickly."

As she spoke the words, Kiya and Dendera appeared with a washbasin of water and fresh clothes for me. Bunefer—Mother's most trusted servant—entered behind them to attend the Great Royal Wife.

I rolled on my belly and covered my head with my arms. The *presence* that disrupted my heart was gone, but Abram told me it remained near even when we couldn't feel it. That unnerved me even more.

"You must rise, Hagar, and attend to your duties," Mother said. "We must see for ourselves what is about to ensnare us." Her words were firm, and I peeked at her. Bunefer efficiently slid a clean linen sheath over her head, adjusted her crown on a plaited wig, and touched up the black kohl around her eyes.

Tameri shrieked at me. "Yes, rise, Hagar, you must not be lazy now."

"Tameri," Mother said, slightly taken aback, as I stared at the high vizier's wife with distaste and wished for a big stick to beat her with. Then my eyes fell on the silver bucket again, my throat thickened, and my heart dropped hard.

Reluctantly, I allowed my servants to make me

presentable. Dendera quickly swept my hair under a wig and buzzed around me with Kiya, reconstructing the damaged princess who brought tragedy to them.

Noise stirred outside my door. Anxious voices and the scraping of sandals running in the hall. The news had roused the palace.

A wisp of fragrant smoke rose from lit incense near the table the silver bucket sat on. I followed it with my eyes as it drifted to the ceiling while Dendera tried to outline them with makeup. She paused a moment, forced her fingers to stop shaking, and then began again with the black kohl.

In no time at all, the Great Royal Wife's feet turned to depart.

Yet I stood still. Numb. Afraid of what I would see from the roof of the temple.

"Daughter." Her eyes traveled the length of me, making sure I had been adequately prepared. "We have no time to waste. The high vizier would not have summoned us at such a time as this if it were not urgent."

"I am right behind you," I assured her.

Mother moved with the swiftness of one of the cheetahs my father kept leashed and used for hunting. Like the spotted cats, her thin, agile body seemed suited for short bursts of high speed. I struggled to keep up with her as she made her way out of the palace, through the temple's massive pylon gateway, and effortlessly scaled the stairs to the roof.

Tameri had fallen far behind us.

We reached the top where Father, Meti, Merikare, and Rensi peered over the west wall. Across a sea of shrubs and sand, an enormous mountain of churning earth rushed toward us, gray, orange, and ominous, powered by a violent and hideous wind.

"We have come to our end," I muttered, and my mouth remained open. I clutched my chest and looked to the opposite side of the Nile, where the sky to the east shone bright blue, clear, and beautiful. As though nothing was amiss.

Meti held his stomach and rocked in place, his eyes bloodshot and weary. I could tell the high priest had been up all night. "I have examined all the sacred writings that hold the history of the winds. This outpouring of fury has never been seen," he said. "I have pleaded with the gods for a sign of what is to come, but they are silent." He cast a glance toward me. "I only know that Set, the god of the winds and storms, is furious. His rage causes my bones to tremble."

"This looks like the anger of *all* the gods descending upon us," Merikare said and shook his head. "Will only our blood quench their thirst?"

"How long ..." I swallowed. "When did you first notice ... how is this different ..." I couldn't get words or my thoughts straight.

"Sailors sleeping on their boats noticed the western sky blotted out late last night," Meti answered. "We didn't get a good look until the sun rose."

"It's *hovering*," Rensi said. "Hanging there as though it has a mind of its own, waiting for the perfect moment to attack."

"This wind will have its way with us," Meti added. "But its aim is clear. We are its mark and running out of time."

"With no cliffs, valleys, or bodies of water to hinder its progress, it will sweep across Henen-nesut and leave us all gasping for breath," Rensi said. He paused as Tameri finally joined us, edged her way beside her husband, and took his hand. "Pharaoh, there will be no shortage of the dead."

"Since the homes are nothing more than dried mud and straw, they will easily be reduced to rubble." The King of Egypt spoke matter-of-factly. "The city is also filled with citizens who live in villages outside our walls who came to celebrate Wepet Renpet, which may be a blessing in disguise. None of them would survive if left to fend off the storm on their own."

"And what of the many who followed Merikare home?" I

said stiffly.

My brother shrugged. "As you can see ... most of them have already fled."

Indeed. The Nile was nearly empty of all the boats that had filled the river the day before. I searched for the royal barge, but it was no longer in the harbor and nowhere within my sight on the river.

"Your boat, Father?" I cocked my head a little to the side, but I believed I already knew the answer. In my grief regarding Zadah, I had forgotten all about Abram. And now he had gone, never to be seen again, taking my whole heart with him.

"Abram and Lot set out shortly after you left the banquet. It was as though their leaving signaled the arrival of this tempest," Pharaoh said solemnly. "Only their god can save them now."

I twisted the amulet on my wrist. *There is more truth in your words than you know, Father. Perhaps only their god can save us too.* I took a deep breath to calm myself.

I followed my father's eyes to scores of hastily built trinkets and food stalls that had been constructed all over the city for Wepet Renpet. The tent-like structures were where the common people from the villages worked and slept during the holiday. Made from four poles with animal hide stretched atop for cover—from the sun during the day and the dew at night—they would be easy prey for this storm.

"My people will need shelter," the king said without looking up, his voice tense. "We'll open the doors of the palace and make it available as a refuge for them and their livestock. Lesser storms have blinded some of my toughest soldiers. This one will take more than eyes." He sighed deeply. "You are right, Rensi, this may consume many lives."

"Surely you don't intend to open the palace to that rabble," Tameri said. "All those peasants running around like packs of dogs." She tsked several times. "The great do not mingle with people of such low birth."

I sucked in my breath. Tameri would speak to my father in

such a way?

Rensi dropped his wife's hand. "Enough, Tameri. Are you the master here? You are the bull of heaven. Would you leave them for the gods to feed on?"

"The gods may eat their entrails for all I care." She gave an impertinent shake of her beaded and plaited wig. "Who knows how long this storm will last? And it's safe to say it may take a season to recover. If we feed them too, we'll have nothing left for our bellies and the bellies of our noble children."

"What evil speech is this?" Rensi snapped. "The dignity of our house will not be taken by you. And my patience with your tongue will not last an eternity. You forget yourself and where you were raised from. Your parents were barely above the servants in this palace." He made a disgusted noise and looked away.

"But they were above the servants. And our king's father saw my great worth and educated me with his own children." Tameri held her head high. "That counts for something."

"No one will lack sanctuary from this storm, Tameri," Pharaoh declared in a stiff voice. "Today, master and servant shall fare alike. They will live on what we live on and be welcome in my home. I will not have their blood on my hands. If royal and noble stomachs suffer … so be it."

Tameri started to say something, but Rensi turned his face toward her. Even I could feel his sullen stare. She appeared to think better of complaining further and favored us with one of her mocking bows before walking away.

"Your Majesty," said Rensi, a note of strain in his voice, "I'm sorry …"

"Do not speak on this, my friend. Tameri has been hot-tempered since we played together as children. To scorn her will not make her agree with you." My father stared at the oncoming storm. "I need all of you in accord with my desires and bring about what I decree. This is a time for action. All living things must be brought indoors, from the mightiest lord to the lowliest orphan. Every cow, lamb, and fowl—bring them all to the palace. See now that these things are done, even though they have never been done before."

I looked up at the nasty cloud of destruction blowing toward us. Familiar shapes seemed to appear swirling in the madness. I believed I saw crocodiles, hippopotami, scorpions, and snakes lashing out of the dark. I gasped. These were dangerous animals, and I knew their presence was a harbinger of dire misfortune.

Indeed, the sand had risen and roared.

I slid my arms around my mother. Hers naturally embraced me. And, like Meti's, our bones trembled.

Chapter Twenty-Two

NOW IT UNFOLDED.

Clouds of swirling earth and debris tarnished the sun, while heat-trapping dust caused the temperature to soar. The air stank of the rancid odor of animal feces and sweat. My mouth felt dry and mealy, my nose congested as choking sand tore through the palace courtyard swarming with people. Some bent over, their backs strapped with belongings, while others herded restless animals or pushed carts full of furniture, food, and children. Panic filled the air as sure as the sand clouted my face.

I had left the roof and followed Meti to the library in the temple to help secure our ancient and sacred scrolls. But I found myself glancing through many of them while priests scurried around me. They carried armfuls, safeguarding them in storage chests made of wood and secured with rope and a clay seal. Many of the old texts held prayers and spells written by priests and magicians to call upon the gods. Others were historical and recorded the battles of the pharaohs, but I had realized as a young student of Meti's that they curiously only chronicled the ones they won. There seemed to be no record of their defeats.

One of the scrolls, so ancient it nearly crumbled in my hands, had a prayer from the first dynasty's high priest to *the one true god*. The priest called him Amun-Ra, and *his friend,* and said he knew no other gods lived besides him. I swallowed against the dryness in my throat and sat at a low table to read more of the prayer. Lingering over it, I must have drifted off because my black dream came upon me again.

I saw myself standing barefoot in the shade of the mighty wooden ankh in the middle of a dry Nile. My head bowed, my long, dark hair flowed free in spirals down my back.

The same man stood near me, and his face blazed like the

sun as before. And as before, the breath of life was in him. He spoke the same words. "You have found grace in my sight. My face is toward you, and my heart is inclined to you. My word will live in you."

I woke with Meti gently nudging me and remembered the last thing the man in the dream said. "Consider me, Hagar, Princess of Egypt."

"Lo, Hagar," Meti was saying softly. "You have stayed too long. Go now, to the palace, while you still have a chance."

My head laid on the table in a pool of perspiration, and my limbs shook. But I found my legs and nodded at Meti. "Will you come too?"

"No, no, no. My place is here." He smiled nervously. "But you need to go." He handed me a linen shawl to cover my face and nudged me toward the door. "Quickly, Hagar."

Now, I desperately tried to fight my way back to the palace through the crowded courtyard. Time seemed to slow as I pushed against the forces of nature and the swarm of terrified people. Dust and sand struck me, relentlessly beating my face and body, filling every nook and cranny. I stopped a moment and bore the rapid pulse of the storm. Had I become the mouthpiece to this gloomy forecast?

As I stood, jostled back and forth by the crowd, a sensation of perfect peace washed over me. I heard the words, "I am with you," audibly, as though a friend whispered them in my ear.

My dream was not a threat.

It was an invitation.

"I believe in you," I whispered. "You are the god of wonders and the god of my dreams."

My spirit was no longer vexed, as I believed the God of Abram spoke to me as a friend too.

His name. It dawned on me that I had no idea what to call him. Sarai never breathed it, never spoke it. If he had a name, she declared, it was too holy to utter out loud. She referred to him only as "the God of Abram" or "El," which meant "god" in her language. The El of Abram.

Perhaps that would be my purpose. To be the one who found a name that generations could utter from their lips. A god who called the winds, and withered the hand of a king, deserved a name that could be spoken.

Of that, I was confident.

Someone shoved me so hard I might have fallen, but beefy fingers grabbed me and kept me on my feet. I glanced up and saw they belonged to a living mummy. If not for his round belly, I would not have recognized Rensi wrapped in layers and layers of linen gauze.

It made me smile. "O, High Vizier, I am glad to see your face, at least what I can of it. You look like the walking dead."

"If this day drags me toward death, at least I am dressed for it," he jested as he pulled the linen from his face. "Why are you just standing here, Hagar? You could get trampled. Why aren't you in the palace?"

"I was in the temple with Meti, helping to secure the library of papyri," I shouted as sand and people assaulted us from every direction.

Another blast of dust filled my eyes, nose, and mouth and caused me to cough. I pulled the shawl I had draped over my head tight and wrapped its ends around my face.

Rensi tightened his arm around me. "We need to get inside now. I fear this horde may become more dangerous than the storm if madness overtakes them."

"They are all so frightened, my heart weeps for them," I said, breathless.

"My heart weeps for me. I am frightened too."

"Another heart would bend, Rensi, but your heart is strong in distress. It is a comfort to me."

"My heart is not skilled in hardship, Princess." He ran his hand across his bald head, now covered in linen gauze. "If I knew where to find the god in your dream, I don't know if I would serve him or what I would do."

"Serve Pharaoh, serve the gods of Egypt, and serve me by not listening to my nightmare." I smiled, thinking about the moment peace had covered me. "I am afraid I've misled you. I can't explain it now, but the dream was not a threat, Rensi. Sarai is not a threat. We must, and we will find a way to honor and appease this God of Abram. I promise you that." Strangely, I sounded in high spirits, awake, and rejuvenated, despite having had little sleep.

Rensi looked at me as though I were mad. He led me beneath large awnings by the palace doors, placed above courtyard columns to provide shade from the sun. They supplied a brief respite from the wind and sand, and we stopped shouting at each other.

"Before the Festival of Heaven and Earth, your father mentioned to me how he looked forward to his evening with his new bride." Rensi's voice contained quiet alarm. "He collapsed before my eyes and complained of a pain in his back that was intolerable." Rensi removed more of the gauze from his face, and I could see the concern in his eyes. "When he said he would have to delay his pleasure with Sarai, the pain ceased. A sense of foreboding overwhelmed me."

"I remember you being strangely quiet that night."

He nodded. "After the banquet …" His eyes softened. "I am sorry for your loss, by the way. I know Zadah was a favorite of yours. It is tragic to see a young life snuffed out so violently."

My heart ached afresh. "Thank you, Rensi. It is hard to bear. She had been with me since we were both quite small."

He patted my shoulder with a linen-clad hand.

"You were saying, after the banquet …"

"After the banquet, the king changed his mind and reached for Sarai to lead her to his bedchamber. Again, his hand froze and withered. Yet no one seemed to notice but me. Yes, I had guzzled copious amounts of beer, but I still know what I saw." Rensi gave a massive shrug. "What kind of magic is that, Hagar? Your father's motionless, withered hand remained in the air until the very moment Meti arrived and alerted us that something was amiss in the skies." His voice grew more serious. "I do see her as a threat, and I feel threatened, Princess. By a power I know nothing about. I am very concerned for our king."

I turned away from him and could not answer. I had been so sure I was beginning to understand this new god. Had I been that wrong? I remembered the menacing feeling in my spirit when I saw Abram cast his eyes upon Sarai.

That had mystified things.

But what about the peace I just felt? I twisted my silver amulet. Grit penetrated the tight space between the cuff and my skin, and it chafed my spirit as plainly as it chafed my wrist.

We heard shouting right above us and looked up to see Merikare. He stood in the Window of Appearance, the formal balcony that faced the palace forecourt. It provided a perfect place for a king to stand and show himself to his subjects. Our little sister, Ana, stood next to him, holding his hand.

"Everyone must get inside," Merikare barked to the crushing flow of citizens around us. "We must close the doors *now.*"

Ana shouted, and I assumed she mimicked his words as she did his manner, but the pressing crowd and thrashing wind muted her tiny voice.

The pushing increased, and each face in the swarm looked more desperate and panicked than the last. No one wanted the doors to shut and be caught outside in the raging, whirling sand.

Rensi started to move, but I raised my hand. "Wait." I wanted a moment to observe my brother commanding the people of Egypt. He seemed every bit a man of authority. "He says, 'go,'" I muttered, "and the people and servants go. He says 'come,' and the people and servants come."

"His words are urgent, but his manner is cool and free of haste," Rensi said. "One would believe he knows what to expect and what the outcome will be. That everything will be all right in the end. Exactly what a leader needs to portray."

"I begrudgingly have to admit he appears to be doing a

fine job," I said, my mouth tightening. I wished for a cup of wine. Nothing made me need a drink more than seeing Merikare appear competent.

"The threat of death and destruction seems to make it easy to forget our grievances against one another," Rensi said. Then he laughed. "At least until the sun shines again." He urged me toward the entrance of the palace.

"Secure all open spaces," Merikare instructed, Ana now in his arms. "Keep moving. We have to close the doors."

Rensi pulled me along until we crossed the palace threshold. I shrugged off the shawl draped around my head and folded it over my arm.

The high vizier mumbled something about being needed elsewhere. He bowed as I bid him farewell and watched him walk away, hastily removing the gauze swathing him.

Chapter Twenty-Three

I JUMPED AS SOMEONE PRESSED A basket into my arms.

Imi.

I looked at a beautifully woven rush and leather basket filled with dates.

"And where did you disappear to?" Imi hissed. Her eyes no longer avoided mine as they had at the temple, nor did her delicately shaped mouth smile sweetly. The heavy floral scent of her perfume closed the gap between us. "My husband, the crown prince, appointed me the task of the overseer of mothers and children seeking shelter. For now, distribute these dates as they come through the door. There are more baskets by the entry, so make sure every child gets a handful." She stopped and looked me over. "Is that how a princess is supposed to present herself to the people?" She shook her head. "Never mind. I will have another job for you after the doors are secured."

My cheeks blazed, but I just nodded awkwardly and held my tongue. Imi spoke to me like a dog on the street, and I wanted nothing more than to issue an insult. But when I opened my mouth, Zadah and my silver bucket flashed in my mind. I thought about the reflection of the woman I would see when I looked at it again. That silver bucket was an all-too-real reminder of the consequences of anger. My back stiffened. *But how dare she assume authority over me.*

I took a deep breath.

Imi performed a beneficent deed. Should I attack her to prove she was not my equal? That it was my father's ground she stood on? If I vented now, would it relieve my heart? *Let her alone. So your conduct may be blameless.* My mother's words.

Merikare walked down the stairway from the Window of Appearance, still holding Ana. The air around them cast garish yellow pools of light from sand that already seeped in. Imi looked up at him in such an intimate way that I could imagine the two of them engaged in passion. I cringed.

"He does justice for the people and the king," she gushed. "And is a gift from the gods." She ripped her gaze from him and sneered at me. "He has promised me everything."

Everything? I wondered what that meant to her—and me. Did that promise entail the power and position of the Great Royal Wife? Was Merikare pledging her the rank that had been mine from birth?

I risked a glimpse at her face, and her self-important eyes didn't surprise me, but my displeasure at hearing her words did. I was astonished by the twinge of jealousy that leapt in my heart. *Am I envious of Imi?* I glanced at Merikare. My nose wrinkled and I recoiled. It had nothing to do with him. Or the threat to my status.

I wanted to look at a man like that—at Abram—and know when he looked at me that I was his favorite. That I was special to him. I wanted to hear him promise me everything. Imi's man was near to her. I would never see mine again. *What a thought. Abram mine? He never was and never will be.*

I shook my head that such a silly notion even passed through it. Besides, in this storm, he could end up at the bottom of the Nile. My chest tightened. *Don't think like that.* I clutched the silver amulet around my wrist and took another deep breath to calm myself.

My eyes flitted around the room and landed on Merikare again. He briefly stopped to set Ana down. A kiss on his cheek and a wave, and she rushed off. His eyes followed her briefly, and I flinched at the tenderness in them. Never had he regarded me that way.

Merikare quickly turned his attention to the distribution of bread and jars of beer given to each citizen who entered— provisions to help them through the storm. He directed a few men to storerooms for their livestock and belongings and explained that from there, someone would lead them to where they could camp for the duration. They bowed low before him, so grateful. His face glowed in the hazy light.

A bitter tang entered my mouth, seeing our people fawn over him. They looked to him as the one in command, and he appeared mature and capable. No one was more surprised than me. It was a side of him I had never seen before. In my eyes, he had always been a self-centered drunk and fool.

A small boy with a dirty face looked up at me.

"Here, little one." I reached into the basket Imi had pushed on me. I gave him a handful of dates and scanned the room to see where my brother had wandered.

I looked down again.

The little face still looked up.

I stared back for a moment then tousled his hair. "Is this one yours too?" I said to a young woman standing near. She looked gaunt and haggard and held an infant in her arms. Four other children clung to her legs. I held up my basket, and they warily released their grip on her as I placed dates into each of their hands.

Imi's commands echoed in my ear: *Distribute these dates as they come through the door. Make sure every child gets a handful. I will have another job for you.* My back stiffened again. I wasn't ready to yield or take orders from Imi. Perhaps it was her, and not me, who ruled alongside Merikare during this time of crisis. But I would not be treated like a servant by anyone.

"May I escort the weaned ones to the harem?" I asked the young mother. "We are using it to house the older children through the storm. The king's family is caring for them there."

"O, how good is what comes from your mouth," she said as tears welled. "Their father is in service to Pharaoh, and we've been separated from my mother in this crowd. Please, tell the royal women it is no minor thing they are doing."

I walked toward Imi, carrying my nearly empty basket of dates. "Imi. I have tasks of my own to perform," I said sweetly. "I'm afraid you have to find another for this job." I narrowed my eyes and held the basket out. "Take your dates."

Her eyes bulged cold and hard. I flinched involuntarily as her hand lashed out and knocked the basket to the floor.

Children scurried to pick up the few spilled dates. An old man accidentally stepped on one, and it squashed under his sandal like a dung beetle.

"I have given you a task." Imi gritted her teeth, her tone unreasonable and childish. "I expect you to do it. The future king of Egypt has given me that authority."

I returned her cold stare and caught something behind her eyes. She seemed spiteful but also fearful. "You forget yourself, Imi. And your rank. Because of the circumstances, I will disregard it this one time." I turned my back to her and smiled at the children under my charge. "Do any of you know how to play Senet?" I said and gathered them to me. The weight of Imi's eyes pulled on me until I glanced back. She scowled and stalked away. A lump rose in my throat, but I wasn't sure what caused it, guilt or concern. This was a different woman than the one who helped me at the temple.

A soft tug on my arm brought my attention back to the children. The oldest girl, not more than nine or ten, had a long oval face and ears like a mouse that overwhelmed her wee body. "Yes, we know how to play," she whispered, then flushed a deep shade of red and lowered her dark eyes to the floor.

She and her siblings took tiny steps first, keeping their eyes on their mother, but followed me nonetheless as I herded them toward the harem. "I have the finest Senet boards in all of Egypt," I said and laid my hand on her shoulder. "They are made of ebony and ivory and even have a special drawer for the counters. I have spinning tops, and wooden dolls, and a little hippopotamus on wheels. You can play with them all."

Her tense shoulders relaxed under my touch. Even her siblings looked more interested in me now and picked up their pace.

I laughed when we entered my chambers. Children were

everywhere, along with the pungent scent of youthful sweat. Naked little boys and girls jumped on my bed and couches, others snacked on dates and grapes, a few splashed in my tub, and a small girl played with Sarai's long hair. It had the feel of wild disorder, but in the midst of it all, Sarai appeared blissfully content. She looked like a shining star on a dark morning.

The difference between our two newest additions to the harem, Imi and Sarai, staggered me. One brought to marry a prince, one to marry a king. Sarai overflowed with affection and warmth for my people. Imi walked past without seeing them.

"Sarai, where did you find all of these fledglings? You've accumulated more royal companions in one day than I have in all my years," I jested.

She smiled. "There is plenty of room for more. I've been telling them stories, but I am the one being entertained. These little ones speak phrases that are strange to my ears. They seem to have a dialect of their own."

Kiya and Dendera quickly gathered the children I arrived with. "Pull out my Senet boards for them," I said.

Kiya nodded as she steered them away.

I made my way through the rowdy sea of youngsters and sat next to Sarai.

"Tell me, Hagar, how are your people faring?" she whispered.

"Merikare has kept order remarkably well." I rolled my eyes. "There is no chaos in the halls, but I admit I'm worried. With the force of this storm, whole towns and villages will disappear. Many will be lost despite our efforts. Meti said Egypt has never seen such wrath from the gods."

"Your gods can only rage if my God allows it to be so," she said. "Disquieting thoughts fill my head, and there is much sorrow in my heart because of it."

"Perhaps it is not your god at all. Our god, Set, is the master of the wind. And Meti is sure it is Set's spirit that has called the winds to assault us." I gripped my silver amulet. "Unless you are saying your god commanded him to prevail upon us like this."

"Have you felt Set's spirit before?"

I stared at the floor witlessly. *No, but I would never admit that to you.* "Why do you not fear for your brother and your nephew?" I looked up at her. "They may still be on the Nile and will be crushed like moths in this wind."

"God revealed to me they are not in danger. Nor are the tents of my tribe in harm's way. If you visit their dwelling place after the storm, nothing will be amiss."

I tilted my head to the side. "How did your god speak to you? How could an invisible being make known to you the fate of your kin?"

"I approached El with reverence this morning and asked if their lives would end in this tempest, and my people removed from the earth. But He filled me with peace and hope beyond anything I can explain. Beyond anything I understand." Her eyes flashed upward. "I know they are safe."

She seemed so confident. I wanted to believe it too because it made my heart glad. *O, Abram. I want you to live.*

Sarai looked away. "I chastised myself for even asking such a thing. I know who my Lord is. But I panicked and needed to see El's light amid my distress." She turned back to me with a half-smile. "I should not question the promises made to us."

Promises. Abram said there were four of them—seed, land, a nation, and blessing. I opened my mouth to ask Sarai why she didn't feel abandoned by her god since he delivered her into the hands of Egypt, when Tameri entered the room.

"I loathe my life," the wife of the high vizier declared as she stood in the doorway and scornfully surveyed the new occupants. "It reeks in here." She held her nose. "How are we supposed to endure until this rabble can be tossed back into the street where they belong?"

The children stopped what they were doing for the briefest

moment and stared at the sneering intruder. A few cast large eyes at me.

I stood. "These are special guests of the royal household, noblewoman Tameri. I don't know what rabble you speak of." I smiled, and the children happily went back to what they were doing.

Sarai went to her. "Don't complain, dear Tameri," she said, keeping her voice low. "And do not oppress these little ones. Come in and help us. Your heart will be lighter for it."

Tameri softened a little.

But I couldn't keep quiet. "And that heart will be weighed one day against your past deeds, Tameri." I was unable to mask the sarcasm in my voice. "Kindness today may balance the scales in your favor. Besides, any help you offer would not go unmentioned to Pharaoh."

Tameri placed her hands on her hips while her foot tapped away at the floor. She raised her eyebrows and looked around the room with pursed lips. I believed she tried to decide if Pharaoh's favor would be worth the sacrifice. "I am, after all, the wife of the high vizier. I will stay. Even the gods can see you need my help. Moreover, someone needs to be sure these youths do not indulge too much on Pharaoh's good graces."

A heavy sigh slipped from my lips. *Perhaps I will survive the wind and the heat, but enduring you, Tameri, may end me,* I thought, but said instead, "Are you certain your children do not need their mother during this frightening time?" My tone was so sweet one would think honey flowed out of my mouth.

"My husband, the high vizier, insisted that it would enrich our boys to assist Merikare. Our girls he dispersed throughout the palace to help where needed. My baby has his nurse with him. My husband and children are fine without me, Princess." Tameri's shoulders slumped and she stared at her hands. "Rensi believed Sarai would best use my generous spirit and kind nature."

"And he was right," Sarai said gently, but I noticed a flash of the flinty eyes she had given Abram at Wepet Renpet. She offered support and affection to the high vizier's wife, but it was as though I caught her in an act. She seemed insincere in her affection toward Tameri.

I was surprised by how ... well ... by how surprised I was by that.

I wasn't sure what to say. For a moment, I felt sorry for Tameri. She was clearly hurt that she was not needed by those she loved. I would mention it to Rensi.

Two little girls sidled up to Sarai and she embraced them.

"Sarai," Tameri squawked. "Should you be *touching* them?"

And just that quick, my compassion toward Tameri fled.

My Senet boards had been set up in a corner, and I sat to play with the older children. They behaved remarkably well, and each politely took a turn playing the complex game with me. I reflected that I had never spent much time with games growing up. Instead, I preferred to study and read. I would read anything, including the ancient hieroglyphs on the temple walls. Or practice writing all of the hundreds of signs that made up the Egyptian language. The simple joys of childhood never held any interest for me.

I left the game and handed out wooden dolls with hair made of clay beads attached with twine. I owned many of them, and they were all like new. As a child, I received them graciously when others in court gifted them to me. But I never played with them. Now, eager little girls reached out, took them in their arms, and hugged them tightly. My heart warmed knowing my dolls finally found loving mothers.

As the day pressed on, the temperature continued to rise. The heat made pastimes like leapfrog and tug-of-war impossible. No one jumped on my bed or couches anymore. Tameri and many of the children napped. Others played quiet games and enjoyed the cakes, figs, and pomegranates my girls served. Overall, their spirits remained high like the souls of children did.

They'd not yet grasped how desperate their situation was.

Chapter Twenty-Four

"I GIVE UP," I SAID, SETTING aside a cup of wine. Nasty, buzzing flies, blown in with the wind, now covered everything. I couldn't sip without them rimming my cup with their greedy, filthy mouths. I sank my head into my hands and listened to the ragged, wheezy breathing of the children in our charge. We covered their faces with linen—wrapped them up like Rensi, so they all looked like living mummies—but we couldn't do enough to avoid the fine red sand that found its way in despite our best efforts.

I wondered if I had already seen my last sunset. My heart raced as I thought about the way it reflected off the Nile. I thought of the floating clouds that added so much color and the balanced way the sun dropped and the moon rose. Was I craven for thinking about death? I shook my head, lost, and had to bite down on my lip to keep from screaming.

Then Sarai began to sing in her native tongue. It was a simple song with a simple melody, a cradlesong, meant to soothe children at bedtime. I hummed along with her and heard the gentle strumming of a lyre. Dendera, her dark brown eyes closed peacefully, picked up the mellow tune and accompanied Sarai on the instrument. I had no idea what words Sarai sang, but they were gentle and calming, and I was grateful.

More lyres joined in throughout the harem, and I even heard the soft exhale of several flutes. Sarai finished her song, and someone started another. When that song ended, someone began another. As the wind grew more robust, the music grew louder. The children relaxed. Some fell asleep. Even my heart calmed, and I smiled, believing my people could endure anything.

The music continued for a while, but the voices began to crack, and some coughed. Soon the singing stopped, and one by one, the lyres and flutes became silent as well. The effort was admirable but impossible to maintain when we could not breathe deeply, and weariness penetrated the bones.

"O, no, don't." I stared hopelessly as the reed mats that covered the doors and windows heaved in and out. The wind and sand scoffed at our efforts to obstruct their path. They would toss the mats aside before too long. I stood and looked around. "We need more shelter."

Kiya and Dendera labored to rise and trudged to my storage closet. They returned with bolts of fabric. Everyone, even the smallest children, helped slog through the task of constructing a large, tent-like structure. We swiped at flies and worked in silence. Before long, we gathered beneath it, uncomfortably close to each other, making the heat even more unbearable.

Bastet appeared out of nowhere. I had no idea where she'd been hiding. She nestled beside me and warily watched two little girls who snuggled together on my other side. The girls sat up, and one of them reached for her, but Bastet hissed and bared her teeth and claws. The girls looked at me wide-eyed. "You'd be wise to leave her alone just now," I whispered. "She's frightened too." I swatted at a horde of flies on the sand-laden fur of my cat, but they avoided the blow and instantly reappeared.

Tameri cursed the wind and the gods under her breath, deep and mournful, sending chills through my soul.

Sarai hummed softly.

Halima—one of the children I had brought to the harem—chose Sarai to snuggle close to. "Sarai, are you not fearful?" she said, shaking her silky black hair, now gray from dust.

Sarai put an arm around Halima and pulled her close. Her own crowning glory, thick sable hair, was also covered in dust. But she still looked radiant. All the sand on earth could not conceal her bewildering beauty. "Beyond a doubt, I am fearful when I feel the venom of that wind. But then I remember the one who watches over me. And that's where I find peace and comfort."

"How?" said Halima. "I am very afraid."

"Because I know my God loves me very much." Sarai opened her mouth and then paused a moment. I could see the tightness around her eyes, the barely suppressed unease she fought hard to contain. "He is here to protect me or take me unto Himself forever. Either way, it is God's will."

"Does he love me too?"

"O, yes, little one. He loves you very much."

Halima smiled. "How do you know?"

I shot Sarai a look of warning—which I was sure she saw but chose to ignore.

"In the beginning, God breathed life into a man and woman named Adam and Eve. And the first thing they saw was the very face of God. Can you imagine that?"

Halima shook her head, her eyes large now.

"God told them He made them in His image and that He loved them. Because of that love, I know He will protect and take care of us."

"Sarai," I said. "You really should consider your words." I nodded toward Tameri, who sat in a stupor.

She smiled at me as though she knew she crossed a dangerous threshold but did not care. "I trust God, Halima. His *presence* is with us, and I would grieve if it were not so."

"Are you saying there is a spirit here?" Halima said, her eyebrows raised.

"Yes, Halima. The Lord himself is encamped in this very room. I find great comfort in that."

"Can I too?"

"O, Sarai," I whispered.

"I know I risk much speaking of El, Princess," Sarai said, "but I cannot deny Him."

Tameri stirred from her trance. "What magic is this you speak of, Sarai? Sometimes I wonder about the soundness of your mind."

"Tameri, do not cast my words away too quickly," Sarai

said. "One day, you may be prepared to hear and understand them."

I tensed and held my breath.

"Well, today is not that day," Tameri answered sharply and turned her back to us.

Sarai shrugged.

Tameri had not been short with her before. I hoped her awe of Sarai would keep her lips closed.

Bastet growled low and deep. "You'll be fine," I murmured and scratched behind her ears. She hissed but settled with the comfort of my touch.

Halima laid her head in Sarai's lap and stared up at her. "Will your god dwell with our gods in the temple? Will we make him a body of stone or bronze?"

Sarai stroked her hair. "I promise, Halima, El does not need a body of stone or bronze. He can be at any place at any time. When you cast your eyes upon a calm pool and see the reflection of yourself, that is how it is with God. When He casts his eyes upon you, El sees Himself. The living God who created the whole world, who placed the sun and moon and stars into the heavens, sees His reflection when looking at your beautiful face."

"I have never heard such things before," Halima murmured and closed her eyes, a peaceful smile on her face.

"You are giving me a knot in my stomach so hard it hurts," I whispered. "What will we do when Halima tells her parents what you have said?"

"We?" The corners of Sarai's lips turned up. "Are we in this together now?"

"I am not ready to die next to you, Sarai," I said flatly. I reached for a cup of wine on the other side of Bastet, swatted the flies that covered the rim, and took a sip. I spat it out and heaved up sand and drowned flies. "Perhaps I will die next to you after all. We won't last long without something to drink."

"We will be uncomfortable for a while, but we will survive this, Hagar," Sarai said. "I have judged my God to be faithful to the promises He made to me."

I sighed loudly, wanting to believe her, leaned my head back, and closed my puffy, heavy eyes. They burned and itched, and I found it challenging to resist rubbing them. Everyone seemed to slip into a restless sleep, so I too, would try to rest.

Something crashed outside and woke me along with all the children. They sat up and screamed. It sounded like the high wall that enclosed my garden had given way. Bricks pummeled the harem as though they tried to break through the barrier between us. The hair lifted on my nape and arms. I could not recall a time in my life when I felt more disoriented and afraid.

"We are all right, little ones," I said in a feeble attempt to reassure them.

Bastet did not believe me and dashed away.

Sarai and my servants joined in to soothe the children, who slid as close to the adults as they could. We rocked and shushed them, promising we were all right now.

Tameri's large lips and chin trembled as her bulging eyes stared at me. She pressed herself against the wall and held a little boy as though he were a shield.

"The gods have woken us because it is time for me to tell you a story." I tried to appear calm. "I will tell you the story of Osiris and Isis and their son, Horus."

Little heads turned toward me.

I yawned and stretched as if nothing was amiss. Then I began in that singsong way one tells stories to children. "Who is the most powerful god in Egypt?"

"Amun-Ra," a few replied in unison.

"And Amun-Ra was father to?"

"Osiris and Set," more of them answered.

"Osiris is the husband of …?"

"Isis." I had all of them now.

"You are good at this," I gushed. "Isis and Osiris had a son together and named him?"

"Horus," they squealed.

I looked at Sarai.

To my surprise, a smile flickered on Sarai's lips as though I amused her. She lowered her head and turned her face from me.

The children shuffled close to me. One tiny girl wiggled her way in and snuggled close. She laid her head on my lap and sucked her thumb while I stroked her dust-covered hair. "Well done," I said. "Osiris was killed by his brother, Set, the god of the winds because he wanted Osiris's throne."

Startled, the little girl in my lap sat up. "Is Set going to kill us?"

The other children grew quiet and looked around at each other. Sarai turned her face toward me again.

"Does Set want your father's throne?" the little girl said in an unsteady voice.

What was I thinking, telling this story now? "No, no, no. Set does not want our lives." I peered into the little girl's wide-open stare. She had no more than five or six years upon her, but lines already crossed her forehead. I saw a lot of myself in her—she was a thinker too. "What is your name, little one?"

She released her palms from the side of her head. "I am Fukayna." She jutted her thumb back into her mouth.

"Your name means 'intelligent,' and I can see that in you, Fukayna," I said.

She smiled around her thumb.

I looked about at all the children. "Set does not need my father's throne. He has his own throne."

Fukayna's thumb popped out of her mouth. "The one he killed Osiris for, right?"

I wanted to stick the thumb back into her mouth and demand it remain there. Instead, I gently pressed her head back onto my lap and stroked her hair. The thumb found her mouth by itself. "Osiris went to the underworld and is now the merciful lord of the dead ..." The word hung too long in the air. I took a deep breath. "But Isis was able to resurrect him for a short time with a magic spell. That is when Isis conceived Horus, who now rules the sky."

"The sun is his right eye, and the moon is his left," the children chanted. It was part of a hymn they would have heard all of their short lives.

My thoughts drifted. *Abram watched the sun and moon and noticed the sun gave way to the moon, and the moon gave way to the sun.* "There must be a power above and beyond the gods we worship," he reasoned. *Why does his logic ring so true in my soul?*

Fukayna tugged my arm.

I shook myself out of my reverie and noticed Sarai's eyes upon me.

"What is it, Hagar?"

"Nothing," I said. But it wasn't. My heart pounded in my chest as Meti's warning rebounded in my mind. *"Beware of loosening the cords of your soul, my dear girl."* Was it too late?

I caressed Fukayna's hair, and she closed her eyes. A few moments later, her mouth fell open and her wrinkled thumb slipped out. Her breathing was irregular, but she slept.

Sarai gently disentangled herself from the small limbs that clung to her like tendrils. The children had fallen back to sleep and didn't stir as she moved them. Quietly, she made her way toward me and took Bastet's abandoned seat.

We both looked at Tameri, who snored loudly now.

"Hagar. Talk to me," Sarai whispered in my ear, her soft breath warm on my cheek.

"Perhaps I can't comprehend such a mystery as your god after all." My chest crushed my heart. "What if he's just revealed a glimpse of himself to me? Then what scholar could explain his magic? Or deny his authority over our gods? What scribe could find the perfect words to describe all that he is?"

Sarai drew a quick breath. "O, my dear girl," she said and became suddenly still.

"My father is worshipped as a god on earth," I continued. "The fate of our nation rests upon it." I looked down at my fingers. "Yet he does not seem to realize that a new god has come. A god that has eclipsed the king and the gods of Egypt." I didn't know if I spoke to Sarai any longer or myself. "It's like my mind is seeing the shadow side of all that I have ever believed. Of lies I have accepted and myths that are not true." I looked up. "Who am I really? I know I am not what the world wants me to be." My voice cracked. "I thought I could harness the power of your god and place him beside the stone gods in our temple." As I looked full into Sarai's face, she glowed. "What is your god doing to me? I have never been this vexed in my spirit." I shivered. "The cords of my soul are completely undone."

Sarai folded her arms. "We call it 'the dark night of the soul.' A time of searching, but not yet finding. You are grieving, Hagar, losing what you've always believed. It is like death, as though you have lost someone very close to you. But this anguish is necessary to shed that which is false and experience forgiveness."

I started, jerking my head backward. "Sarai, what was that?"

Her eyebrows rose. "What Hagar? I don't hear anything."

"Indeed."

The wind had calmed, and the world was quiet.

Chapter Twenty-Five

WE LINGERED FOR A MOMENT AND smiled wide at each other. "Wake up! Wake up!" we shouted.

The children lifted their heads and looked confused. Some stared at us as though we'd finally gone mad.

Their expressions made me laugh. "What do you hear?"

The silence closed around us, light and loud and wonderful. Tameri opened and shut her mouth, for once, unable to find words. We pushed away our linen tent, thick with dust that poured to the ground and covered us with another layer of dirt.

No one cared.

We were hot and sticky, crusty and miserable, but alive.

We rushed to pull back the reed mats that covered the windows and doorways, which, miraculously, had stayed in place after all. Cool morning air greeted us. And, it turned out, I wasn't quite grown up yet. Like all the children in the room, I jumped up and down and squealed. Tameri turned, and without a word, rushed out the door.

The older children freed their faces from the linens and hurried to unwrap the younger. Kiya and Dendera wiped debris from my tub, and Sarai and I helped them hoist jars of water—heavy with sand—and hurried to pour the restoring liquid into it. We waited for the sand to settle on the bottom, and everyone took a drink. Thirst quenched, we took a turn around the tub washing and splashing our faces and hands and each other. We weren't completely clean, but it invigorated the spirit and had to do for now.

The children were restless and ready to be reunited with their families but waited patiently for my servant girls to wipe down the board games and dolls. We wanted to make sure each child had something to take home.

Home. I knew it would not be *home.* This storm would

have made rubbish out of the best of them.

I gripped one of Fukayna's small hands in mine. She sucked the thumb of the other, and a doll dangled from the crook of her arm. She looked up at me with trusting brown eyes, and a tender smile touched the edges of my mouth. "Come, children. Follow us. Let's go find your mothers and fathers."

There was a simple cheer, and I set off with Sarai and my servant girls, ushering our charges back to the entry of the palace. Along the way, we weaved through an abundance of people who danced and sang grateful hymns to the gods. Their dark skin, crusted with dirt, made them pallid. But no one cared. They had been forgiven their sins and granted continued life. Cups of beer passed from one dirty hand to the next, and their grins and throaty laughter were contagious.

Everyone shared in the happiness.

We managed to find the anxious parents gathered around waiting, where we had left them the day before. They looked worn and weary but thanked us profusely and clasped their wriggling young close to them. Fukayna found her way into her mother's arms, grabbed her around the neck with one hand, and continued to suck the thumb of the other. Her mother's face burrowed into the little girl's hair while Fukayna smiled at me and waved goodbye with four free fingers like a small wing flapping.

A heavy weight bore down on my soul as I waved back. I shook my shoulders but could not lift it off. The joy around me, the relief from surviving a brush with death, was fleeting. We had yet to see what, if anything, the storm left for us beyond the palace. I looked outside toward the forecourt and knew what I had to do. I mumbled something to Sarai and my servants, I can't remember what, and began the long trek back to the temple roof.

I pushed determinedly through crowds of elated people and ignored the gravel that slid through my sandals and rubbed between my toes. I made my way past the sacred alabaster washbasins, now drowned in sand, and the pair of massive, dark gray statues of Pharaoh and the Great Royal Wife. My parents were half-buried but had not toppled from their pedestals. The mottled rose obelisks that flanked them pointed up to a clear blue sky.

Breathless, I passed through the temple gates, the thick walls pockmarked and stripped of white paint. A gasp released from my lips. Not one exotic, fragrant tree, nor any of the sweet blooming flowers, not even the T-shaped pond, survived. The famous gardens lay flattened, covered with heap after heap of sand.

As though it had never been.

It was a harbinger of what I would see next, and the truth was, I was afraid to go further. But there was no other choice.

I found my breath, and firm-footed, slowly climbed the steps to the roof to see what remained of Henen-nesut. My father, Rensi, Meti, and Merikare, already there, looked at me, but no one uttered a word. Meti closed his eyes and ran a hand over his face. The others remained very still. My pace slowed as I edged my way near them and gazed out to survey our city. I shuffled back a step. Naught would have prepared me for what I now cast my eyes upon—an entire town uprooted and utterly laid waste.

Nothing had been spared, from the humble huts of the common to the beautiful, whitewashed homes of the wealthy. Everything was torn apart and reduced to mountains of rubble. The stalls in the market, the workshops, businesses, and all public areas—wholly leveled. Beyond the edges of Henen-nesut, past its fifteen-cubit thick walls, we could not see one small farming settlement or hamlet. I shuddered, realizing if it had not been for Wepet Renpet, none of those people would have been in the city and able to shelter in the palace. Their remains would be buried forever under the sand.

A benevolent act by a caring god no matter what god it was that saved them.

I looked toward the Nile—it was the reason I came to

examine the destruction with my own eyes—and the blood in my legs turned cold. Rensi reached to steady me. The river of Egypt had gone dry—there was not a drop of water in it. If one desired, one could cross the Nile on foot.

Exactly as I saw it in my dreams.

A few barges rested on their flat bottoms in eerie slumber. Twisted planks from narrow sterns and prows, the skeletal remains of any ships left in the harbor, stuck out of mounds of sand here and there. The new landscape was dotted with what I assumed would be a variety of animals—*bloated and bloodless* since the sun grew hotter now. Sweat trickled down my back and dampened my kalasiris. It stuck to me as the heat became intolerable.

But I could not turn away.

Gone.

Everything was gone. What an impossible idea to grasp.

We watched as our citizens poured out of the palace and now saw the magnitude of the storm. Only a sea of sand and ruins stretched out before them. Grown men crumpled to the ground, women sobbed, and children stumbled as if drunk.

A bit of wind blew up the dust and stung my eyes, along with the threat of tears. The breeze also carried the swirling stench of choking death and earth, devastation and decay. It pricked my nose, and I knew it would stay with me my entire life.

"A fearsome thing for our people," Rensi observed. Old habit made him wipe his bald head. "They went from being thankful for being saved to being stricken with dread for their future."

"This is a very dark spell," Meti lamented, his breathing labored. He looked unwell, and I could almost see his bones through his thin skin. "An old curse, full of loathing. We have been brought low."

"Low, but it will not break us," Pharaoh said. Fine sand still covered his eyes, nose, and mouth. "Considering how violent this storm was, so many have been spared because of the festival. I think the people will soon realize how fortunate they are. They are alive. We can rebuild what was lost."

"However, one glimpse of our life-giving river ..." Meti trailed off. "That is something else. That is death. An abysmal fate cast upon us. Even the most courageous among us will falter."

Rensi turned his head toward the high priest. "Meti, do not heap too many joys upon us at once. We are already weary-hearted, and wailing saves no man."

Meti gave him a sideways glance. "You are right, my friend. There is nothing gone that cannot be replaced. Forgive an old man who, for a moment, lost his faith and his strength."

Merikare cleared his throat. "The cleanup will be an enormous task," he said, loudly stating the obvious. "We can clear the debris, but we can't rebuild without mud from the Nile to mix with straw for bricks. The inundation was upon us. Without it—" The words halted in his mouth.

Rensi finished. "We will not have rich soil to grow crops." He turned away as though he needed to gather his thoughts.

"We cannot fish," Merikare said.

"We cannot drink," I said.

Merikare turned toward the king. "We may need to leave this desert for better land."

"And where would we go?" Pharaoh said.

"We don't know how far this curse spread," Meti added, then coughed, spat, and lifted his head. "Do you hear that?"

The sound of urgent voices below made us stop and look down.

"O, those servants of our holy city," Meti praised.

Beneath the limestone walls of the temple, an assault on the wreckage had begun. The people of Henen-nesut did not need a taskmaster. They knew what must be done and had set upon the work with zeal. Carts rolled out of the palace, and men, women, and children bent their backs to fill them with the dry, dead bones of the city. We heard shouts, a few instructions here and there, and the press of people grew thicker, the shouts louder and more urgent. Bakers, brewers, craftsmen, fellahin, scribes, and soldiers joined together and began to clear the ruins. No matter their station, everyone heeded the call and went to work even though the day had turned too hot to breathe.

"Perhaps they will restore it all, better than it was before," I said after a long silence. "But the task has an impossible end if the Nile does not flow. Perhaps we should consider the delta if we need to leave. Sarai is certain the storm avoided Zoan, and her tribe is safe there."

All four men turned and looked at me.

I didn't think they were even listening. I was musing really, thinking to myself, but I said it aloud, and they heard me.

Rensi shook his head and frowned. Meti pursed his lips but said nothing. Pharaoh slanted his head and raised his eyebrows as if determining if my words were good or bad. But Merikare barked a laugh and rolled his eyes. "Hagar, what comes out of your mouth?"

My face burned as I stared at his scornful expression.

"How could Sarai be certain about the fate of her people?" Meti said, his body rigid.

I rubbed my arms. "I meant she *hoped* her people … are safe. It makes sense, with all the tributaries, water must be flowing from one of them."

Meti pressed. "But you said she was *certain.*"

I breathed in sharply. *What have I done?*

"Upstream?" Merikare scoffed, but I was grateful for the intrusion. "The Nile flows from the south to the north, my *learned* sister. If there is water in the delta, it will dry up quickly too."

"There is no need for such talk, Merikare," Father said. "But you are right. The river is blocked below us."

"If we go anywhere," Merikare said, giving me a condescending smile, "it must be south."

"We cannot go south," Rensi said. "We would be at the

mercy of the King of Waset ... or worse, the Kushites. They would crush us in our weakened state and make slaves of us all."

"We can't cross the desert, to go north or south, with all of these people and no water anyway." Pharaoh crossed his arms over his broad chest. "That has always been clear to me."

We all turned back to the mass of people below us. Many carts had already been filled and were being hauled outside our city gates, which still stood, but only as fragments of what they once had been. Men emptied the carts, and women and children searched the rubble for usable mud bricks, reclaiming anything they could.

"It is also clear that Hagar foresaw this disastrous occurrence in her dream," reminded Meti. "You were wise to act upon it, Pharaoh." A sudden agonizing cough bent Meti over. Rensi moved to help him, but the high priest waved him off.

I twisted the silver cuff on my wrist and waited until Meti recovered. Everything swam unsteadily around me, knowing the high priest had shared my dream with Pharaoh. I had gone to Meti after the first occurrence and nearly every episode after. "What did you do, Father?" I said, hiding my alarm, having no idea what words would come from his mouth.

Merikare jerked his head back. "Yes, what did you do? And how could such a project remain secret from me?"

I stood a little straighter.

Merikare had not been included in Father's confidence either.

Pharaoh nodded at Rensi to answer.

"The annex toward the south ... the ruse was not to keep a secret from you, Merikare," he said. "It was to keep panic from our people. The fewer who knew our affairs, the easier it was to keep it quiet."

Merikare glared at the high vizier with cold, hard eyes. "You think I would not have kept my father's secret?"

Pharaoh gave Merikare a sharp look. "The high vizier

carried out my desires as I commanded him." He turned to me and his face transformed into a warm smile. "Meti told me of the black dreams you were having. He believed the gods were speaking to you and gave you a prophetic vision. My spirit became troubled by it. I ordered our grain to be stored safely and for scores of deep water basins to be excavated and flooded. We protected them with layers of palm branches and animal skins. My men tell me it worked."

Rensi also smiled at me. "We have water and grain to sustain us ... for a time."

"But if the dream had not come upon you ..." Pharaoh shook his head. "If the god you saw did not tell us what was coming, the outcome would have been disastrous. The scarcity of food and water upon the land would have been the end of us." A slight change in Pharaoh's eyebrows and a bit of wrinkling around his eyes made me think I saw a look of admiration on his face. "You saved us, Hagar."

I wanted to hug and kiss him. No other compliment in my life meant more. Those few words gave me vindication for all my hard work and efforts to please him. Yes, those words could live inside me forever.

I fell face down before my king. I didn't know how else to answer him. "Life, health, and strength be to you." I looked up at him. "Thank you, Father."

He smiled again and bid me rise.

Merikare stepped backward and shrugged. "But it was only a nightmare. Surely, Father, you can't tell me you *believed* her foolishness." He looked around for support but found none. "I dream too. But my dreams are filled with adventure and desirable women." He laughed while Meti and Rensi bristled.

"Go softly, my son. It is a foolish ruler that would ignore a message from the gods," Pharaoh said firmly. "Our ability to divine the future based on her dream may have enabled us to survive this disaster. I am certain that is why it came upon her. To help us survive. Because I believed and acted, we may live through this." His eyes bore into the crown prince's. "My heart is relying on you, Merikare. All kings before me have understood the significance of dreams. I too have resolved problems, made decisions, and even waged battles based on the high priest interpreting my visions."

Merikare seemed dismayed. "*Your* dreams, my pharaoh," he threw back. "But this dream did not come upon a king. It was the fantasies of a *girl*." He turned toward Meti. "You said this is a dark spell, High Priest. Perhaps Hagar had something to do with creating this curse. Has that thought entered the mind of anyone else? Or am I really to believe my sister can dream what the gods will bring to pass and I cannot?"

Meti started to answer, but my father raised his hand to silence him, his face full of dark clouds. "Never question the source. That is essential. *She* is essential. Her dream was true, and our people may not perish because of it. How many times have you heard me say that the tiniest light pierces the darkness, Merikare? Her vision was that light. Anyone who would take my throne would be wise to remember that."

Merikare blanched but stayed silent.

Her dream was true. Father's words were all that echoed in my mind and heart. Lightheaded, I remembered the god who appeared to me as a man in my vision. *"Consider me, Hagar,"* he had said. I turned away from my brother and gazed toward the dry Nile. *But who are you?* I thought. *How can I consider what I do not know? What my mind cannot understand?*

I looked down, and my eyes caught a young boy poking a stick into a large pile of sand. I stared at the child and his intense curiosity to see what was beneath the sand. And at that moment, I knew what I had to do.

Chapter Twenty-Six

PHARAOH TOOK ANOTHER LONG LOOK AT his city, his countenance regal but grim. He and Meti turned to leave, and as they did, Father stopped and placed a hand on my head and patted me. Like a pet. It was awkward—I admitted that in my heart—but I would take what I could get. I smiled warmly at him.

Merikare scowled at Rensi and then aimed it at me. I gazed at him coldly. A final smirk from him, and that was all. Thankfully he headed off too, down the steep, narrow stairs and away.

I stood there vacillating, feeling the affection from my father and the malice from my brother.

Rensi touched my arm and roused me from my bewildering. "Lo, Hagar. You need to keep a watchful eye on your brother. A rightful king must be able to bridge the dream world between the gods and his people. You can do that, but he cannot. You have become more of a threat to him now."

"O, High Vizier. Surely, he can't despise me that much. Or see me as a menace. In my opinion, he thinks of me as nothing more than a nuisance if he thinks of me at all."

"How can you say that after what just happened? I now know my time as high vizier is tied only to the days of your father."

"I admit I had not lost as much of Father's favor as I believed. But Merikare is still my brother. And my betrothed. We will always be connected, no matter how deep the divide between us. Besides, it's not as though he is capable of evil. My only question is if he is simply capable."

Rensi glanced over his shoulder toward the stairway. "I don't know what he is capable of. If it's not evil, it is very close to it. He has a way of drawing in and manipulating the wrong sort of people. Dangerous people."

My mind flashed to Merikare's royal companions—*two wild dogs gnawing flesh off bones*—and my heart thumped a little harder in my chest.

Rensi shook his head, very somber. "How your father can be so taken in by him, I don't understand. But I fear a reckoning between the two of you is coming. And don't ever make the mistake of thinking he cares at all for your feelings. He will do anything he wants to you because, I swear, he does not care. And that makes it easy for him and perilous for you. If only your father would change his opinion of a shared kingship. I believe it would end up saving both of us in the end."

I looked at Rensi hopefully. "Do you think it possible?"

"No," he said as though it hurt to say it aloud. "And it is a shame. A terrible shame." Then he changed the subject. "How did Sarai know her tribe is safe?"

I gave an uneasy laugh. "She claims her god *spoke* to her and filled her heart with peace. She is quite sure their tents have not been disturbed. Nor, she believes, have any lives in her tribe been lost."

"Hagar, you have heard his voice and felt his *presence.* Do you doubt her?"

"Not at all, Rensi. And I am that glad about it for Abram's sake. But have you ever seen a god wield this kind of power? Withering our king's hand when he moves toward Sarai is nothing compared to what has happened to our city." I twisted the amulet on my wrist. "Could this be divine protection of *her*?"

Rensi's face paled. "The storm started when her brother departed, *without* her. As though Sarai staying caught us in this trap." Rensi rubbed his hands as though he washed them with air. "But for what purpose would she need protection? Have we not been most kind? Unless you know something that I don't."

"No. Nothing I can think of now. Sarai has made herself loved in the harem. There is no harm in Henen-nesut for her that I can foresee. As long as she keeps her god in her heart and away from her lips."

I peered over the side again. The young boy with the stick was still there, poking the sand. But now, three young companions had joined him. Sunlight flashed off whatever they were trying to unearth, something metal.

"Pharaoh has given her more than any woman has ever received from him. Including the Land of Goshen for her tribe to live on and be safe. He made her brother rich beyond his dreams. Beyond my dreams."

I tilted my head, trying to discern what the children had found. "So, what have we done that could cause such wrath to fall upon us?"

"O, Hagar, pay attention to me." He glanced down at the children. "It's a metal *Mehen* table. They play the game of snakes on it."

I pulled my eyes from the children and realized the high vizier looked at me with profound disdain. "I'm sorry, Rensi."

"I'm very concerned, Princess. I have no answers, and I'm rarely in that situation. You had the dream that occurred again and again and now has come true."

"But I have no answers either. I'm not yet certain if the god I saw is her god."

"I find it hard to doubt it."

The conversation stilled. I clutched the balcony wall and watched the work below, the air hazy now from agitated dust. A cart, heavy with rubble, bobbed forward pulled by four onagers. Two men walked beside them, furiously whipping the stubborn, donkey-like animals to keep them moving.

"Tell me, Rensi. Why have you not told our king what you see when he reaches for Sarai? Or our suspicion regarding a new god that has entered Egypt?"

"I have tried. But the words cannot find their way out of my mouth. Sometimes I want to shout to my own voice, 'Where are you?' It's as though an unnatural hex has silenced me." He shifted from foot to foot and shrugged. "Do you believe this god has never been here before? I find it hard to think so. It's more like he came, but we turned our face from him, and he departed. Now he has returned and makes himself known in a way that we cannot ignore."

"I don't know. You are ahead of me in discernment. But I found an ancient prayer in the temple when we were securing the library. The high priest of the first dynasty wrote it. He spoke to Amun-Ra as Sarai speaks to her god. That priest claimed there was only one god too. I had never considered that he had been here before, but now I think you could be right." I shaded my eyes with my hand and looked up at the sky. "There are no birds, Rensi." I paused and scanned the vast deep blue above me. "Not one." My voice sounded wet and thick, and I realized I trembled. I turned toward my potbellied friend. "It is near noontide. You know where I must go."

Rensi leaned forward as if to concentrate his attention on the progress of the people below us. After a moment, he looked up. "I am going with you."

"Yes. I'd like that."

He placed his hand on my elbow, his fingers clammy from sweat, and led me to the stairs. He dropped his grip as we made our way down the tight passage. We passed through the decimated gardens—again, my heart plunged at the sight of it—and out the back gateway that led to where our city once stood. People whirred around me, and I wished for a thin linen shawl to wrap around my face to hide it. But I quickly realized it wasn't necessary. No one paid any attention to the high vizier or me. They all clustered around empty carts and filled them as they dismantled each pile the storm left behind. They worked together to save each other.

I slid my arm through Rensi's, and we stole, unnoticed, through the residents of Henen-nesut. Except for Fukayna, who I spied in the distance. She saw me too. Still in her mother's arms, thumb in mouth, her four little fingers flapped like a wing at me again. I smiled and waved back.

We left the city behind us and walked across dried

marshes where papyrus grass, once twice my size, now lay on its side. We stepped gingerly through a maze of *bloated and bloodless* carcasses—just as I had seen in my dream—of large perch, catfish, mudfish, turtles, snakes, and eels. We passed a dead hippopotamus and countless dead crocodiles swelling in the heat of the day. I could not help but wonder if one of them had snatched Zadah from me.

We covered our noses, gagged, and coughed, the air rank with the smell of death. We tried not to breathe as we pushed on in silence.

We did not stop until we stood in the middle of where the Nile once flowed. Neither of us spoke. I reached down and removed my sandals. Rensi did the same. I looked up, but the sun blinded me, so I closed my eyes and waited, even though it burned my face.

I wanted to say something to the god in my dream, to recite a hymn, like those written on sheets of papyrus and kept safe in the temple. But those were enumerations of the powers and attributes of the gods we knew. And I knew nothing of this god.

What did one say to a mystery? *Nothing,* I decided and stayed silent. It was the only thing I could think to do.

After a time, I opened my eyes and looked around. But there were no strange events in the skies, no portents in the sun. I wanted to shout, "I am here. Where are you?" No shadow fell upon me, not even the palest hint of one. I thought about our symbol of eternal life that hung in the sky, *this* sky, in my dream. I thought of the specific words the god I saw spoke to me and how he seemed to know me, almost intimately. Even though I could not look upon his face, I felt him *smiling.* I was sure of it. He was smiling at me. It made my heart happy and was the one thing I never shared with anyone, not even Rensi.

But now, my heart ached in turmoil.

I stared at Rensi's bewildered expression and his upturned palms and scrunched up shoulders. The sun glinted off his bald head in the middle of that desolate landscape of dead things.

How can he not be here? The sky was scorching blue and clear, not something of wonder, a miracle, or a *god* visiting *me* from heaven.

It could have been anyone's dream, but it was mine. *So why hide from me now?*

Noontide passed. We stood as long as we could, perplexed and barefoot on hard, dry, hot silt. "I swear it," I said. "After all we have been through ... seeing the river dry with my own eyes as it was in my dream ... and everything else that came true just as I saw it. I thought he would be here. I was certain he would be here and explain it all, how I'm to *consider* him. What it means that his words would live in me."

"Perhaps we should have brought an offering like the king gives the gods of Egypt? Or maybe we should have brought the high priest to consecrate this place."

"I can't imagine what Meti would say if he knew we were here."

Rensi nodded. "You're right. He wouldn't like it. There is no need to trouble him with this."

"Although, you'd think he would have wanted to come."

"He's still looking for the god of your dream in the temple. They are so intertwined with the kingship, you know it's blasphemy to allow any other god a position among them."

The sand became unbearably hot, so we put our sandals on.

"If I had encountered him here today, Rensi, I was prepared to offer him my whole self and surrender all. That was to be my offering to him." Tears welled in my eyes, and I fought to keep them as dry as the desert around me. "I planned to sit here before his presence and agree to follow him obediently. Now I don't know where to turn or what to do." Again, tears welled. *What is wrong with me? When did I become so soppy? Tearing up at everything.*

We stopped speaking and moving. Almost not even breathing. We stood so long my lips began to crack. I knew we had to go, to get out of the sun and find something to drink. I couldn't wait to take large gulps of water.

I looked back up at the empty sky and felt my breath hitch.

Then I took Rensi by the arm. He looked at me as though he had just woken and shook his head. We set off, back through the stinking carcasses. I looked at each of the crocodiles again and thought of Zadah. We zigzagged through them, avoiding contact with rotting flesh, but we couldn't avoid the smell. It overwhelmed and stuck to us like perfume. Covering our noses offered little relief, so we pushed on as fast as we could. We were sapped of energy and resolve. Hot and thirsty. Baffled and disappointed.

But I was also surprised to feel relief in my heart.

My servants had made tremendous progress in my chambers. The cloth used as a tent was gone, and all the sand swept away. I stood a moment and watched as they bustled around until Dendera caught my eye and cleared her throat. Kiya spun toward me, wrinkled her nose, and looked at me oddly.

"I know I must smell of death," I said. "Is it possible to bathe? And I'm quite thirsty."

Dendera pressed a cup of water into my hand. I drank deeply. She filled it again, and I drained that one too. She served it once more and hurried back to help Kiya. Jars of water already sat next to the tub—my need anticipated before I arrived—and they poured it as quickly as they could. Kiya helped me shed my filthy clothes, holding her breath the entire time. I slipped into the restoring water. But I sensed something more disturbed the girls than my disheveled appearance and malodorous scent.

The grim look on their faces foretold difficult news.

I resisted as long as I could. "Will your words be good or bad to my heart?" I finally asked.

This startled Kiya. "We do not know, Princess." Her voice was hushed. "We cannot judge how you will take it."

"Then you should be quick to find out."

Zadah would never have hesitated to give me news. She had been the mouthpiece for my servants, and they all seemed content with that arrangement. Now Kiya assumed the role, but I knew she did not like the position from her sidelong glances at Dendera,.

"What you tell me will not be taken out on you," I said, trying to ease her. "You know that, don't you, Kiya?"

She smiled at me, but the smile faded swiftly. "Your chambers are to be divided and shared, for now. For a little while."

"I know Sarai will have to stay longer," I said. "I am fine with that. The city will take time to rebuild. Our resources must go to those in dire need, even if it causes us discomfort. We will bear what we must."

She went silent again.

They had set the table for my midday meal, and I was quite hungry. So I made the bath quick, and the girls helped me dress simply. I eyed the table the entire time. A fried fava bean cake, rolled in sesame seeds, was the first thing in my mouth. Two more followed quickly. I picked up a bunch of red grapes, and instead of selecting them one by one from their stems, I pulled off several and stuffed them in my mouth. *O, the juicy sweetness.*

Dendera continued to work, the soft thud of her busy feet bustling around the room. Kiya remained beside me with her head bowed.

"Is that not all, Kiya?" I said, exceedingly courteous. I felt much better now—perhaps that was why she waited.

"No, Princess," she said.

"You would serve me well if you would tell me what it is that is troubling you so."

"The crown prince came to visit earlier, around noontide. We did not know where you had gone." Kiya looked at Dendera, who kept her head down. "These tidings should not come from the mouth of a servant." She shifted from one foot to another. Her thin, willowy frame bent as though the weight of the world hung on it. She looked mournful, almost despondent, as though she longed for rescue from an awful fate. "Prince Merikare has a marriage settlement with Imi. A scribe has already drawn up the contract, and he intends to establish a common household with her. She now has the title of 'The First Wife of the Crown Prince,' which makes her a princess."

Princess Imi. The red grapes soured in my mouth. "I know all this, Kiya. You need not worry on that account any longer. She still does not usurp my position in the royal family." *Yet.*

Kiya leaned forward and lowered her voice. "She will be sharing these rooms with you. Prince Merikare said this is where he desires his household to begin."

My body tensed, and heat flushed through me. "There is more?"

She nodded. "Prince Merikare has given Dendera to be in service to Princess Imi."

Dendera paused, and I turned my gaze to her long enough to see the tears and anxiety that ruined her face.

"I see." I wanted to tell them that it was all right. But it wasn't. And I couldn't pretend. I knew Merikare had a variety of motives in this, and none of them were noble. "I thought my brother had already provided a room and servants for Imi in the harem."

"He did, Princess Hagar," said Kiya, "but she prefers your rooms and your servants."

A dark fog wrapped around my head. I stared at a tear that slid down Kiya's hollow cheek to her chin, wavered a moment, and fell to the floor. *A reckoning. That's what Rensi had said. And so soon. Dear brother, why do you torment me so? You are like a sickness to my soul.*

"You are right, Kiya. This is news the crown prince should have waited to discuss with me privately. He should not have burdened you with it. I am sorry for that."

Sarai slipped in from the garden carrying an armload of

dirty, dusting feathers. She was as soiled as they were but still looked stunning.

"Have you joined the ranks of the palace gardeners?" I asked her.

She smiled kindly, and her face glowed. "I have always enjoyed working with plants and do not mind dirty hands. It seemed a good place for me to help in the cleanup. The flowers are lost, but the roots can be dug up and saved." Dendera filled a water basin for Sarai. She thanked her and began to wash. "The girls have told you of Merikare's visit?" she said and paused to examine my reaction.

"They have."

"Did they tell you the little princess is resting on your bed?"

I looked at Kiya, whose cheeks burned like a flame. "They have not."

Chapter Twenty-Seven

"SHE'S IN MY BED?" I LOOKED toward the door that led to my private refuge and then glared at Kiya for an answer. "Do I matter so little to you in my own home? Is it as though I no longer exist in Egypt?" I stopped right there.

Kiya's tears brimmed then flooded.

I looked away from her, my throat thick. *It's not her fault.* I tossed the small bunch of red grapes in my hand onto the table. My head and stomach ached, strung as tight as twisted rope.

Dendera and Kiya huddled together, weeping. Merikare snared them in his net as surely as he trapped me.

"I'm sorry, Kiya. I should not yell at you. But I prefer that I don't learn things in bits and pieces."

She bobbed her head.

"What is to be done about it?" Sarai rubbed her hands irritably with a linen cloth. "Perhaps I should take this to Pharaoh myself. He will listen to me."

"To my father?"

"Yes. Directly to your father. Let me tell him of your brother's unpleasant visit and the burden he is imposing on you." She crossed her arms as though creating a barrier between Imi and me. "You know Pharaoh will do anything I ask. I'm not going to let that harsh little girl hurt you, Hagar. I could send a missive to my tribe and have a few discreet men sent to her village in Zoan to uncover any secrets Imi may have hidden there. We may need them in the future."

"Rensi uncovered all he could about Imi before he brought the marriage proposal to my father. She was an unfortunate girl from a poor family, but he found nothing alarming."

"Forgive me, but the high vizier missed her connection to royal blood. Perhaps I could discover more. Something we could use to overthrow her if she rises too high in the harem."

"Are we planning a takeover?"

"O, no, Princess. That would be dreadfully dangerous, even for me. I'm just trying to protect you."

I considered Sarai a moment. She baffled me. Sometimes she seemed secure in her skin, and sometimes she appeared as anxious as a rabbit. But in a crisis, there was no fear in her. She performed very well, and I found her trustworthy. I believed in her devotion to me.

I shook my head. "I'm afraid my brother has bested me today, Sarai. He knows I will not burden my noble parents with trifles when they have more vexing problems." Bastet rubbed against my ankles, and I reached down to pick her up. She purred as I scratched under her neck and behind her ears. "How can I complain while our land is in distress? I am not the only one whose life has been turned upside down." I pinched off a piece of fava cake and gave it to Bastet. "However, I am distressed the crown prince would take time to deal with matters of the harem when life and death plague his realm. I admit my thoughts scramble to understand that."

Sarai took a seat next to me. "Hagar, I believe Imi is with child," she said. "At the banquet, I noticed her thick waist and swollen breasts. And her hands frequently touched her belly. I've observed pregnant women my entire life. I'm quite certain the little princess is expecting."

Kiya gasped and grabbed Dendera's arm. Their stark eyes stared at me in disbelief, as though Sarai told us the world had come to an end.

But now they knew. And I was glad I didn't have to say the words to them.

I took the moment to compose myself. "I know. Merikare told me. He plans to have more children than all pharaohs before him." I grinned half-heartedly to bolster an act of indifference. Bastet licked crumbs and oil from my fingers with her rough tongue. I watched her for a moment and then looked up when Tameri's flowery perfume entered the room before she did.

"Swifter than the ill wind that came upon us," she said, her voice shrill.

My jaw tightened. "Tameri. What are you about?"

"The rumors." She smirked. "They are blowing through the harem wilder than the wicked sandstorm that brought us low." She seated herself without invitation. "I am ravenous," she said and stuffed an entire fava cake into her mouth. "All I could get at home was dried grapes and cold roasted ox." Kiya rushed over and poured a cup of wine for the high vizier's wife. "When I complained to my noble husband, he said, 'The whole land has perished, and you have not yet gone hungry.' He showed no sympathy." She snatched the cluster of grapes I had tossed. "I knew your table would be more appealing."

"Let me fix a plate for you, dear Tameri," Sarai said, a touch of disdain in her voice, "while you tell us how your children fared through the storm."

"They are all fine, the gods be praised," she mumbled, her mouth full. "But as soon as my servants told me Imi and her sister had been installed in your chambers, oho Hagar, I knew I must see how you were coping." She drained her cup of wine.

Kiya edged between us, ready to fill it again.

"Her *sister?*" I spat and looked at Kiya. "Surely, Tameri, you jest at my expense."

Kiya's head drooped to her chest. "There is a sister too," she whispered.

I inhaled deeply and released it while Kiya stood still beside me. Then I reached up and squeezed her arm. "No worries, Kiya. But nothing more in bits and pieces. Please."

She lifted her head and nodded.

"I've met that sister of Imi's, and her tone is a little too severe for my liking," Tameri said. "Only weeks ago, they were two little street waifs. And now they threaten the entire order of the royal harem."

"Is she older or younger?" I didn't know why it mattered.

"Younger," Tameri said. "And they seem to be very close. I imagine that's why she didn't leave her behind."

"You didn't know about Imi's sister?" Sarai said with raised eyebrows. "She sailed here with us on the royal boat. They tried to keep their relationship secret, but women whisper."

I shook my head and sighed. "I do not know how I missed it."

"You never pay attention to the affairs of the harem," Tameri said.

Zadah did that for me.

"But this is one you may have missed anyway." Tameri smacked her lips. "Merikare and Imi tried to keep it between them. Imi wanted it that way until she knew her place here. But, as Sarai said, women whisper."

"It seems there is nothing Merikare will not do for Imi." I stroked Bastet, trying to appear unruffled. "Princess Imi. She is a princess now. I must remember."

"O, no doubt at all that she will remind you," Sarai said and nudged a plate she filled in front of Tameri.

"Yes," Kiya whispered. "She will remind you. And she is tyrannical about it too."

I looked up and smiled, glad she'd found her voice.

"She's cast a spell on the crown prince," Tameri whispered. "And to think, their mother only asked for two looms for two daughters. The fool. She sold a royal bride to the future pharaoh for a pittance." Her hyena laugh filled all the empty spaces in the room.

The sounds of stirring turned our eyes to my bedroom door, but no one emerged. We now heard low talk and laughter. I shot Tameri a warning glance and lifted a finger to my pressed lips.

"Dendera!" Imi shouted from behind the closed door.

My servants looked at me, their eyes wide. I waved a hand at Dendera, angrier than I meant, and she rushed off to see what her new mistress needed.

Tameri shook her head. "The sun has not risen a score since those girls slept on a thin rug spread on a dirt floor. Now they recline on the bed of a princess and call for your servants as though they were born to it."

Sarai leaned over and tried to pet Bastet. The cat deftly evaded her touch. Sarai offered her a small piece of roasted fowl. Bastet sniffed at it, appeared to think on it for a moment while Sarai patiently waited, then seized it from her hand. She jumped from my lap to go off and enjoy the prize alone.

"You're handling this admirably, Hagar," Sarai said. "Not long ago, your world looked very different than it does today. In so many ways."

"That is true," Tameri added as she lifted her wine cup to her lips.

I fingered the hem of my kalasiris. If they only knew the bitter words that filled my thoughts. "I admit, for the first time, I see my foundation is built on nothing more than shifting sand. But I will not be overtaken by my troubles. Not while a dry riverbed determines the fate of my people. If the Nile does not flow again, we are all finished."

"So Imi's child does not threaten you?" Sarai asked.

It's likely quite threatening, yet I will never reveal that to anyone.

Tameri stiffened. "Imi is expecting?" She slammed her hands on the table. "How long would you keep that from me? Does my good husband, the high vizier, know this? How did this happen?"

"You know how these things happen," I taunted. "I've heard you describe it in detail."

"This is no time to jest, Princess," Tameri said with more than a touch of impatience. "This is not bastard stock. If she has a son, she is one step away from wielding real power."

"We've been over this before. The line of succession is to come through me. No matter what."

"But what if you fail to produce a son?"

"Then it leaves no question of succession. The eldest son of the First Wife will become king."

"She will hold it over you to the end of time." Tameri

looked miserable. "She will hold it over all of us."

"We don't know what the future possesses, Tameri. I am sure my father's desires will be respected, and I'll have an heir and a spare, and many more children besides." I didn't believe a word of it. And neither did anyone else. My head throbbed, and perspiration gathered on my forehead. The walls in my expansive chambers closed in on me, and I wanted to flee.

"I do hope you have many sons, Hagar. But this life in her womb ensures her influence will be far-reaching, forever." Tameri's voice screeched too much for my liking. "Please remember, I'll always be your friend and confidant. If there is ever anything I can do to assist you in any way—"

"Perhaps, dear noblewoman, your help is needed here already." A smile crossed my face. "You are the one person in the kingdom I can count on to express to the sisters how welcome they truly are in my chambers." Lightness took hold in my chest. "Since you are the wife of the high vizier, I think you should become a second mother to them. They have never lived at court before and will need a firm, guiding hand to teach them the ways of the royal."

Sarai's eyes smiled with mischief. "I benefited abundantly from your tutelage, Tameri. I can only imagine how much they will learn if you spend time with them."

"Lots and lots of time," I added.

Tameri paused a moment, then nodded. "You are both right. There is none better to instruct those two than me." She filled her mouth with fava cake.

"Impart all manner of wisdom to them, as you did with me," Sarai said.

"And more," I said. "Do not leave any little thing out. And do not let them deny you this honor if they protest." I stifled a giggle. "Remind them that Merikare will be king one day, but our father is still alive. His majesty has found your husband the worthiest in the land, and it is a great privilege for them to have your attention. My father's heart will be filled with you when he hears of your service." I stood. "I must go out for a time.

But noble wife of the high vizier, I leave my chambers in your capable hands." My eyes rested on Sarai. "Will you walk with me?"

Sarai pushed herself to her feet. "Of course."

Tameri wiped her face with a piece of linen and also stood. "Princess Hagar, attend to whatever duties you must. There is no need for you to trouble yourself here. I will not leave the side of Merikare's favorite or her sister until I am certain they know how to conduct themselves at court." She belched and then commanded, "Kiya! Prepare a bed for me, between the sisters." She looked at me. "They have much to learn, and who knows how long until my business is concluded? This could take days."

"Or weeks," Sarai said.

"Or maybe months or years, dear Tameri," I said and watched her stride toward my bedroom, her shoulders as rigid as her will. "They are now in the best of hands." I turned away and pressed a fist to my lips to confine a laugh.

"I hope you have found peace," Sarai whispered.

Tameri opened my bedroom door and bellowed, "I am the wife of Rensi, the high vizier, and I have been instructed to govern you in all matters. Do not worry, young ones. I will not leave your side from now on."

"If Merikare bested you, Hagar," Sarai said, "it was only for a moment."

I bowed my thanks, and then my face turned serious. "Follow me. You need to see something. And we need to talk."

Chapter Twenty-Eight

I PAUSED AT THE FOOT OF the narrow stairs that led to the temple roof. Sarai had not left the harem since the storm ceased. She'd not laid eyes on the broken city the great wind left behind. I wondered how she would take it, but I knew there would be no answer until we reached the top.

Sarai walked around the roof, taking in the tragic scene and the devastation as far as the eye could see. She looked to where the Nile once flowed. "I have no words," was all she could summon as stirred earth, ash, and plumes of incense settled on us like a cloud.

Below, no carts lay idle, and my people moved in an organized flow. The amount of debris piled so high, it seemed there would be no end to their labor. Simple stalls—four poles with animal hides stretched atop—had been set up with water, beer, and bread. But like the bee that eats while it works, so did the people of Henen-nesut. They would not rest until the sun went down.

"If I had not seen this, my mind could not have grasped the magnitude." She turned to me. "I am so sorry, Hagar. For you and your people. I mourn for them."

"Is this the act of your god? If it is, it's a shockingly cruel one. What type of god would let this happen?" I crossed my arms. "I would like to speak to that god about justice. My people do not deserve this."

"I do not know for certain, Hagar. However, if this is a divine act, I still would not charge my God with wrong," she insisted with empathy in her voice. "Wouldn't we be foolish women to accept only what is good from God and not misfortune? There will always be days when the sun shines brightly and days when all turns to darkness. But there will never be a time that we should consider cursing God, for He is merciful."

I thought about the new year festival and all the lives saved because everyone had come into the city to celebrate. The timing *was* merciful.

A single ibis soared by, so close I could almost touch its featherless head and black, scaly neck. The whirring rush of light air from its wings felt cool on my face. "There wasn't one bird in the sky this morning," I squealed. "O, Sarai, surely this is a sign. A good sign. The ibis is sacred and the form our god Thoth takes. Seeing one gives me hope. It will give my people hope."

The large bird had long legs and a thin, descending curved beak that looked like a crescent moon. White feathers covered most of its body, except for black plumes on its lower back. It made a croaking sound and landed on the roof of the temple, not far from us.

Sarai spoke gently. "Thoth. Your god of wisdom and writing. I have seen the stone reliefs of him. A man with the head of the ibis holding a writing palate."

I nodded. "He is the god of the scribes. Meti often recited a saying attributed to Thoth when teaching Merikare and me to read and write. 'I'll make you love scribedom more than your mother. I'll make its beauties stand before you. It is the greatest of callings—there is none like it in the land.'"

The rumble of carts slowed below us. A chorus of excited shouts rang out as the good omen was spotted. Everyone stopped, shaded their eyes from the sun, and looked up at the glorious bird.

"But more importantly, especially at a time such as this, Thoth is the herald of the inundation."

"He appears before the flood?"

"Yes. It is his honor. Ra, the sun god, appointed him over this region because he successfully restored Ra to his daughter, Tefnut."

"I don't think I know that story."

"Amun-Ra and Tefnut had a terrible fight, and she fled south to Kush, taking all the precious water of Egypt with her.

The land quickly dried up." I looked at my ruined city. "Chaos followed."

Sarai seemed to contemplate my words. "How was the land restored?"

"Thoth took on the form of the ibis. Just like that one." We looked at the large bird as he stretched his widespread wings and flew toward the palace. "Thoth followed Tefnut to Kush and told her stories spun to portray how hopeless Egypt had become without her. He made her believe the people would do anything for her if she returned. She relented and made a triumphant homecoming by bringing back moisture and water."

"It makes me think your land has seen this before, Hagar. Myths are often woven with a thread of truth in them." Sarai's words were matter-of-fact. "There is nothing in the world that has not already happened."

"I don't know about that."

"No, my dear girl. I suppose you wouldn't." My back stiffened.

"I didn't mean it as an insult, Hagar. You are just so young still."

I turned, stepping a few paces toward the stairs.

"Wait. Please."

I stopped and faced her, one hand on my silver amulet, turning it back and forth. "I didn't expect you to treat me as one incapable of understanding a thing or two."

"I meant nothing like that. I have developed a great respect for your intelligence and intuition in the short time I've been here. Perhaps my true meaning was lost in translation." Sarai tilted her exquisite face to the side and raised her eyebrows. "Princess, you brought me here. I sense you had a reason other than discussing the legends of Egypt."

I met Sarai's gaze and considered what to do. I could withdraw. Return to the harem without answers. Or I could stay the path and finish what I brought her here for. I released the silver amulet on my wrist and took a deep breath. "I know you are a woman with profound understanding. Especially of things that can't easily be explained. I want you to hear my words and interpret what I tell you." My hand went back to the amulet. "A vision of the night was given to me. A gift, some have called it. It came upon me time and time again before your arrival."

Sarai clasped her hands together, low and in front. "It is not possible to live in your father's harem without hearing some version of this dream. Tell it to me from your lips. I will see if some explanation comes to me."

"It began as a dream. But awake, I find this nightmare." I bitterly pointed toward the grotesque garden of ruins that once was Henen-nesut.

"Sometimes, a voice whispers in our hearts," she said. "but we pretend not to hear it. So, we need the words shouted at our face."

I looked at her, perplexed, and heard Rensi's words. *"Do you believe this god has never been here before? It's more like he came, but we turned our face from him. Now he returns and makes himself known."* But I said nothing to her about that.

The sun dropped closer to the horizon, but the day still smoldered in heat. The sweet, woody fragrance of frankincense and myrrh swirled restlessly around us from massive quantities of incense burning around the temple below. I met her gaze again, pondered the risk, and decided to hold back.

But then she laid a hand on my arm, and every detail of my black revelation rushed from my mouth.

Sarai listened intently and asked occasional questions. "You saw the Nile dry, days before this happened?"

"Weeks before."

"You said you could smell the air. What could you feel? When you looked up and saw what appeared to be a man next to you, what did you feel when he called you by name?"

"Fear and awe mingled in my heart. There was someone or something there larger than me, larger than life itself. All of it was so real, and now most of it has come to pass."

"Most of it? Except what part, Hagar? What happened

today when you went and stood in the middle of the Nile at noontide?"

My body went cold. "How did you know I went? No one knew except Rensi."

"It is where I would have gone," Sarai confessed. "How could you not? Your vision was detailed and precise. The river is dry, just as you visualized." Her breathy voice quivered. "But there was no one there."

"No."

Her eyes closed briefly.

"There was nothing in the middle of the Nile today. Except for death." My shoulders dropped. "I thought he would be there. In the same place I saw him in my dream."

"I am sorry, Hagar."

I waved my hand before me. "I thought he would be there and tell me how to fix this."

"It is not your responsibility to mend this. It is beyond everyone's control, even your father's."

"Do you think it is your god I see in my dreams?"

"Yes. I believe it is."

"Then why didn't he meet me in the dry riverbed and tell me what to do? Why does he reveal himself only when I'm sleeping? Why did he reveal himself to me at all?"

"His purpose and plan is for all to know Him. So we can work with Him and not against Him. But God is a being of infinite greatness and goodness and glory. Our nature is so estranged from Him that much is required for us to reach Him in our fallen state. Our whole heart, our every desire, must rest only on Him. Even if it is in only some small measure. He is that gracious for us to know and receive—"

"Stop." I held up my hand. "I have wrestled with this for longer than I can recall. I am a princess of Egypt, and for the first time in my life, I realize how powerless I am. I have no actual control over anything. I walked out into a wash full of rotting corpses today to give him my whole heart. That's what I had prepared to do. To promise to serve only him, even if it cost me my life. But how do you offer everything to someone who isn't there?"

Sarai drew in a breath. "I promise you. El passed by where you stood. He was there. But you didn't need to go so far to find Him. One day your spiritual eyes will open, and you will see El's reflection in everything and know He is everywhere."

"Why would he choose me to be his vessel of prophecy if my spiritual eyes are not open to him?"

"O, Hagar. I believe El singled you out because you have a seeker's heart." Sarai leaned toward me. "God has put eternity in all of our hearts. He wrote his eternal truth there to remind us of His *presence* and bind us to Himself since the beginning of time. And all we have to do is seek Him to find Him. How many people do you think would risk their life in Egypt to do that?"

"Little to none."

"And that is no different than we found in Sumer."

"But seek him where? What sacrifice does he need for me to get to him? To get to wherever it is he resides? Tell me what to do. For the sake of my people."

She took my hands. "You cannot get there, Princess. His cavern is not found on the earth. He comes to us. You can abide with El right here." She whispered as if she were telling me a great secret that no one else could know.

"Perhaps this is a mystery beyond my understanding after all." I pulled my hands from her and turned away. "Why would he choose me and then not show himself to me?"

"I don't know why El chooses to do one thing and not another. But I believe He has been showing himself to you for some time. And now He finally has your full consideration. Why else would you go looking for Him?"

"My curiosity was aroused, and I needed answers only he could give. Now I am disappointed and confused."

"He doesn't need to hear your questions, Hagar. He knows them before you ask. He wants you to decide if you will listen to Him. If you will acknowledge the *presence* I know you feel." One of the straps on her linen dress slipped off her shoulder. She paused long enough to slide it back into place. "I believe God is like this."

She had my full attention.

"I've tried to get your cat, Bastet, to take to me. But she is wary. I've tried to entice her to come to me with treats and sweet-talking. She comes close, but never within reach, always evading my touch. Often, she stops just short of me, looks around, stretches, and purrs. Like she wants to give in. But I have not quite won her trust yet. I could grab hold of her and inflict my will upon her. But she is in my heart, and I want her to trust me. I will not give up. And I will not force her. When she is ready, she will cross over into my arms, by her own free will. I will be patient and wait for her." She took a breath. "That is what love does. That is what El is doing for you. He is waiting for you to come to Him. He will not reach out and take you by force. He will be patient until you come of your own free will."

I recalled how it felt beneath the shadow of the ankh in my dream. I had trembled in fear and wanted to flee but was rooted in place. There was a great god before me, not of stone, but one breathing and alive. He called me by name and asked me to consider him. Again, I realized his words were an invitation, not a threat. I remembered Sarai offering roasted fowl to Bastet and the cat taking it but not jumping into her arms. Bastet took the gift but did not accept the invitation that was also offered.

Was that what I was doing?

"How did you come to know this god of yours?" I regarded Sarai with fresh eyes. "I know the account up to the point where your whole family bowed before one god, but how did he enter your heart? How did your relationship with your god begin? When did he fill you with such light?"

Sarai hung her head. "You are wise for one so young. If there is any light in me, it must come from God Himself. I have no light of my own, because I have utterly given myself up to sin. I'm intoxicated with it."

I stayed silent as Sarai wrung her hands and looked out onto the rubble of the city.

"This has taken me to the depths of my soul in mourning." She sighed heavily and turned back to me. "But you are right. Our union with God is relational and personal. We individually yield our will for His. For me, it began with a sense of wanting something that I knew was beyond my ability to control. I wanted a child of my flesh. I was blinded to my need for God when my life went well. But when my years of childbearing passed before me, I sensed my powerlessness. I was alone in my pain and felt like a worthless outcast in my tribe."

"Our culture is the same. Only the number of sons we deliver estimates our worth as women. So why did you never marry, Sarai? You are more beautiful than even the first woman created by the gods. Surely many men before my father have wanted you."

Sarai blushed and hung her head again. "It is not a story I can tell you, Hagar. I don't know if it will ever be told." She shook her head. "But it is not mine to speak of."

I laid my hand on her arm. "I'm sorry, Sarai. I see it brings you great suffering. I will not ask again."

She wiped a tear from her cheek. "It would be easy for me to be a bitter and angry woman. I have fought the inclination for a long time, even after our family found God and worshiped Him only. Then, God, Himself came to me, and I knew He loved me." She looked at me through wet eyes and smiled. "I asked for one gift, a child. Then I realized He had already blessed me with so many other gifts that I could not number them. I found myself weeping before God, realizing He refused my small request and instead gave me something greater. My faith soothed my hurt and healed my anger."

I left her words in my heart for a moment. I wasn't quite sure how to respond to what she told me about her journey with her god. I stayed silent and walked to the edge of the roof, where I could better see the sun sink lower.

Along the horizon, pink wisps of color mixed with the

clear blue desert sky. My chest squeezed at its beauty. "It's incredible that something so pleasing to the eye could come after the terrible storm we have just been through."

Sarai took a few steps and stood beside me. "When you look into the distance like that, you look as though you are about to take flight. As though you could spread wings and fly away like the ibis."

"You have no idea how many times I have wished for wings so I could do so. I have watched flocks of birds fly overhead and desired to go wherever they were headed without a care as to where that would be."

"That's why the name Hagar suits you. It translates to 'flight' in my language."

"It does? I like that. It means 'reward' in Egyptian. My mother said Merikare was our father's gift, but I was her reward." I turned back toward the sunset. "I do admit. It is hard to look at that sky and not sense the presence of something divine. And harder to not want to fly off into it."

"I see nature as the first words that El ever spoke," Sarai said. "His *presence* fills the earth, Hagar. In a sunset like this, in the scent of a flower, in the twinkling of the stars. Even in the cry of a child," she added as a baby fussed in the distance. "Feeling His spirit is the most natural thing I have ever done. And it all began when I willingly bent my will toward His."

"Your words please me, and your counsel helps. But I still don't grasp all of that, Sarai."

"We all have a choice, Hagar." She smiled as she said it. "We can be on the journey with him. Or not. Only you can decide."

"All I know is that I have gazed on the silent figures in our temple all of my life." I twisted the silver amulet with the bloodred stones that kept me tethered to the gods of Egypt. "But in my dream, your god gazed upon me."

"That is where we all begin. Acknowledging the *presence* behind all that is."

I grasped my amulet and held it firm. "It may be as you

say, Sarai. And I will consider it. But I have begged my gods to forgive me if I am wrong."

"You sought the true God where you saw Him in your dream, in the middle of the dried-up Nile. You thought you were ready to offer your life to Him. But you weren't prepared to give everything. I believe El saw that in your heart."

I pressed my lips together. I had nothing more to say. The sun vanished beneath the palace walls and a shining silver moon rose to replace it. The work below stopped as the weary laborers settled in for the night. I knew their backs and arms must be cramped and spent after doing more today than seemed humanly possible. They pitched makeshift tents, built small fires, and began to cook meager meals. I stood still as stone and listened to the songs they began to sing and the soft rush of the flutes that accompanied them. O, my people. They would rise tomorrow to do it all over again, but tonight they would sip beer and sing.

"We need to get back before it's too dark to find our way," I said.

We turned to depart, but excited cries drew us back to the edge. I cocked my head and tried to discern the urgent words yelled below us. The people were no longer settled for the night but running around lighting torches. Hurriedly, a long, snakelike procession was being formed and headed out of the city.

"Be steady and follow me, Sarai," I said as I ran for the stairs. "We need to see what waits for us in the muddy shallows now."

Chapter Twenty-Nine

"WHAT NEWS IS THERE?" I PRESSED two young men who looked to be my age.

Short, springy coils of black hair glinted with sweat in the torchlight. Their wide cheekbones and thick noses set off dark, hope-filled eyes. Both fellahin, possibly brothers, heavily built and equipped with farming tools like warriors setting out to battle.

"Pharaoh sent an expedition south to see where the river stopped," one said without stopping.

"Yes, this morning. We know that," I said, striding beside him.

He halted long enough to adjust the mattock that rested on one of his rugged shoulders and took a good look at Sarai and me. He gaped at us as though he tried to discern who addressed him.

I smiled patiently at him.

"The men found the barrier that caused the river to dry up. A massive dam of carcasses and hills of sand, and who knows what else, not even half a day from here on foot. We march tonight and come dawn, we'll remove the obstruction that blocks the Nile." He grinned. "Start watching for the waters of our lifeblood to flow again soon."

I gasped and felt breathless and light. "I will, I promise."

He set off again.

"We will smite this foe and be home in time to see the inundation," he added with great confidence before he double-stepped to catch up with his companion. "Did you see the ibis?" he shouted over his shoulder. "Thoth came to herald the good news."

He adjusted the mattock again and turned his head back toward us once more, still trying to figure us out. He would doubtless be abashed to know he had just spoken to royalty.

"Isn't that wonderful," I said. "Our river will flow again soon." And, as I promised the young fellah, I resolved to watch for it. My hand went to the silver amulet and I twisted it a time or two. "There will be battles left to fight, but now we know where the enemy musters."

The high mood rushed our happy feet to the palace courtyard. We stood for a long moment. The black shroud of impending doom had been lifted and laughter hung in the air. Servants and nobles alike danced and sang songs of praise to the great one, Thoth, who showed himself in the form of the ibis and saved Egypt again.

My smile could not be contained.

"Why, Princess Hagar, you have no wine to drink," shouted an old woman, dark and large with several missing teeth. She pushed a cup into my hand. I recognized her but couldn't remember from where.

I sipped the young wine and closed my eyes in delight. Had I ever tasted anything more pleasing? I opened my eyes and offered the cup to Sarai. She took a sip and handed it back to the old woman with profound thanks.

A friend of my old wet nurse. That's who she is. I shook my head. *No. That's not it.*

"Did you see the ibis?" was repeated over and over by hoarse voices all around us, strained from yelling. "It is a good omen. Thoth has saved us again."

"Have you ever felt such relief from so many?" I asked Sarai.

"No." She laughed. "And I must say I feel it as much as they do."

"A short time ago, we believed we would die of thirst and starvation, and our bones would perish in the dirt," said the old woman. I noticed her remaining teeth were worn from years of chewing bread. Grit from the stones used to grind flour always ended up in bread and caused the erosion. "Remember this happiness when you return to your chambers."

"What?" I said.

She looped her arm around my elbow and drew close. "We've been looking for you." She smelled like soap made from clay and olive oil, clean and earthy. "You should hurry back to the women's quarters. Your servants need you."

"Bak-mut," I said as I now recognized one of our cooks and closest friend of Bunefer, my mother's most trusted servant. "Are they not well?"

"Their health is not in danger. And I am just a messenger. Bunefer sent me to watch for you here. She couldn't disturb your royal mother with it at this time. But she told me to warn you that the spider in your room is spinning a poisonous web."

"Thank you," I muttered and bolted away with Sarai right behind me. We didn't stop until we stood panting in front of my chambers.

I opened the door.

The room had a gentle, soft glow from candlelight. The warm air held a strong aroma of rose and myrrh and the heavy fragrance of lily and cinnamon.

Imi reclined on my couch with a cup of wine in her hands. My beautiful alabaster bottles of perfume were opened and surrounding her. Dendera stood over the new princess and fanned her with an ostrich feather. She looked pitiful, her profile swollen with misery.

Only a few heartbeats ago, joy filled my soul. Now, my temples throbbed, my orderly mind clouded with rage, and perspiration dripped from the edges of my wig. I took a deep breath and held it. Then I folded my arms across my chest. "Have we anointed the entire room with my perfume? Surely it would be better to sell the costly fragrances and give the money to the poor than to waste it all for a moment's pleasure."

Imi sat up and met my gaze with cold eyes.

She was someone I had to deal with now, even if it caused my world to crumble around me. "With all the damage done to the palace, I'm certain we can find a better use for Dendera than your comfort, Imi."

Something disrupted the stillness near my dining table. "*Princess* Imi," said a snappish voice I was not familiar with. "You are speaking to the wife of the crown prince and the mother of his first heir." The voice came from a girl with the same large, sleepy eyes, square face, and long hair as Imi—the sister. Her mouth showed an unfortunate overbite, her lower jaw too far behind the upper jaw, causing her top teeth to rest firmly on her bottom lip.

My heart found solace in it.

Tameri, also seated at my dining table, sprang to her feet. "Amisi, you do not address royalty unless they address you first. This is Princess Hagar. And no one ranks higher than her or is more highly thought of in the harem, except her royal mother. Now bow and show respect before she has you cast into a pit for carrion to feast on."

I glanced at Tameri. *Did she just praise me?*

Amisi looked at Imi, then looked at me, and cautiously relented. She placed her forehead on the limestone floor in front of my feet.

Imi raised her hand, and Dendera stopped waving the large feathered plume. She stood and addressed me as an equal, but her mouth twitched and gave her nerves away. "I am glad you have returned," she said, her voice stiff and unemotional. "First, we do not require the expertise of the wife of the high vizier. My royal husband provided us instruction in palace etiquette on the voyage from Zoan. We have observed how the wealthy live and behave our entire lives. Trust me when I say that it is not a difficult life to ease into." She lifted her wine cup toward Dendera, who ran to a decanter. "This is my sister, Amisi. I hope you will show her the same consideration that you will show me as Merikare's First Wife."

"You may trust me when I say that I will." I raised my hand to stop Dendera from refilling Imi's cup.

The room went as silent as the tomb of any deceased pharaoh must be. Sarai was behind me when we entered, but she now stood beside me, grounded, serene, and valiant.

Tameri sat again and whimpered as though wounded. "O, my head, my head. It aches. I have done only a good deed today. These girls owe me gratitude, not ridicule." She picked up some tidbit from the table and stuffed it in her mouth.

Kiya, who I had not noticed until now, my mind in a haze, slipped into a corner of the room. Dendera sat the decanter on the table beside Imi and joined her. They hunched together. My heart ached to see the shakiness in their limbs. I was sorry Imi caught them in the middle of this.

Amisi remained stretched out on her belly on the floor at my feet. I made no effort to release her.

"Imi, I am glad you are finding our life so effortless to ease into," I said with an amiability I did not feel. "But I disagree that you and your sister are ready for court. I must insist that Tameri stay on until you are. Your sister addressed a member of the royal family without permission. I am a congenial princess, but many in my family would not be as forgiving as I." Sour honey gushed from my mouth. "I could not live with myself if she were to insult the wrong royal and pay for it with lashes from a whip." I paused long enough to let the sisters understand the depths they were in. "Furthermore …" My jaw clenched, and the honey stopped. "If you take Dendera from me, I will require that your sister replace her."

Imi gasped.

"Unless you are keen to be housed elsewhere and find your own servants to assist you." I stopped long enough for them to think on that too, and then strolled toward my dining table set for the evening meal. Which I found picked over by the intruding sisters, and no doubt by Tameri. My servants saw the displeasure on my face and hurried to clear the table. Kiya started for the door to replenish the plates of food. "Kiya," I said, "take Amisi with you and help her to understand her new role as servant to a princess of Egypt." Kiya's eyes were as wide as the plates she held in her hands. "When you return, give her the appropriate attire of her new station and return her fine linens to her sister." She nodded in understanding. "Amisi, you may rise."

Amisi stood and gazed at me. There was no fear on her face. She turned toward Imi and snorted. Snorted!

Imi looked aghast and nodded toward Kiya. "Go with her. For now."

Amisi rolled her eyes and sauntered out as if she strolled through a garden.

Her brazenness turned my blood cold.

"Why do you care which slaves I choose to serve me? They are nothing more than tools that speak. Barely even human," Imi hissed.

It took a moment to realize I'd heard her correctly. I shook my head in disbelief. "I assure you, Imi, that is not the belief of this palace or the law of the land. If you mistreat a servant in my father's kingdom, you are breaking the law."

"And it does not go well for even royal women who break the law," Tameri added. "You could lose a nose, or an ear, or feel one hundred strokes of the cane on your back."

"You jest," Imi said. "I am not a fool."

"I assure you we do not," I spoke with grim firmness.

Imi looked afraid, but only for a moment. Her large brown eyes turned hard, and she gritted her perfect teeth in willful defiance. "I will find my royal husband and return with him. I'll let him choose who serves me. And only he will decide if my treatment of them rises to a crime in Egypt." She turned to leave, but not before snapping her fingers at Dendera.

Dendera looked in my direction. Her face showed the same unhappiness crawling under my skin. I nodded at her, and she followed Imi out with a slow, pathetic walk.

I sighed heavily, thinking about the coming confrontation with Merikare.

"You can relax, Hagar," Tameri said. "I may have forgotten to pass on a message to our little jewel about the crown prince. I promise you will not see your brother tonight."

I tilted my head toward Tameri. I found her new attitude toward me as refreshing as the north wind.

Chapter Thirty

I STOOD STILL AS A STONE, trying to determine if I'd done the right thing. This was my home. My belongings. What right did anyone else have to them? But there was so much suffering in the land. Many people had lost everything except what they carried into the palace with their own two hands. Who was I to cling to so much? Perhaps I should have handled it differently. Ignored it. Ignored her. But how do you overlook that which causes turmoil in your very existence?

"My noble husband, Rensi, the high vizier, sent a message that he and the crown prince traveled south to oversee the removal of the obstruction that blocks the river." Tameri sat at the dining table, leaning back in a chair with a wobbly leg. "I'm afraid I forgot to mention it to Imi." The corners of her mouth raised. "Your royal brother will not be available to her—for some time."

I caught a glimpse of my silver bucket through the open door of my bedroom. Grief settled in my throat and I turned away from it. "Was I too hard on them?" I said, my tongue thick. "I can't imagine what life was like for them up to now. What miseries they have faced."

Tameri shook her head. "There is nothing worse than the poor being lifted to a high position," she said matter-of-factly. "You have given them a gift of tears. You are wise to tread on their pride now while they can still be fashioned into women we can live with."

"Bad manners are found in all walks of life," Sarai said. "Their situation is rare, being raised up overnight and now fighting for position here. But Tameri is right. It is good for them to cry now, where they are safe. Others in the palace may not forbear their disrespect with the restraint you have shown. They may one day realize what you are doing for them and even appreciate your guidance."

"Well, they don't appreciate mine," Tameri said. "I warned them to stop, over and over, as they emptied your priceless bottles of perfume into their bathwater. They bathed in it. This place stunk like a house of sacred prostitutes." Her nose wrinkled. "It still does. They even cursed me when I tried to stop them going through your fine linens and jewels. I've never heard such gutter talk before. O, the foul insults they cast on me."

I looked at her fully. "My linens and jewelry?"

"And your makeup and wigs. They even tried on your royal crowns." Her chin dipped. "I warned them but they would not listen to this noblewoman. I would be wary of them, Princess. They are on an eager quest to fill all the desires of their hearts."

"There are no words." My fists clenched. "They behave as if they are above the royal family. No one has ever treated me with such disrespect. And it terrifies me for anyone charged with serving them. If they disregard a princess, how will they treat those they believe are tools that speak?"

"As I said, they certainly showed no regard for me, a noblewoman of stature, wife of Rensi, the high vizier. It is a matter for concern."

"It's likely, Hagar," Sarai said, "that Imi offends others to feel better about herself. Especially when she feels vulnerable or threatened in some way."

"O, no." Tameri was fixed. "She believes she is more important than everyone. And more deserving. The existing power structure does not please the little princess. She means to bring you low, Hagar."

Sarai and I exchanged a glance. Tameri's previous behavior toward me had not been much different than Imi's. But she seemed blissfully oblivious to it. I pressed my hand against the table. "What reason could Imi possibly have to challenge me in such a way?"

"I don't think she needs a reason. And while you were

gone, Amisi freely referred to her sister as the Great Royal Wife."

The air in the room became suffocating. "She can never reach that title. Royal blood runs through females, not males. And Merikare must marry a royal princess to become pharaoh. Only a daughter of the king can be a royal princess, and only a royal princess can become the Great Royal Wife. Does she not know that if it were not me, one of my half-sisters would assume the role?"

Tameri shrugged. "She knows it's only a matter of convincing Merikare not to consummate a marriage with you, or whichever royal princess he marries. That way, if she produces a male heir, she obtains the title of Mother of the Future Pharaoh and the semi-divine status it carries. They seem to have it all figured out."

"That still would not give her the title of Great Royal Wife," I said. "She will never be the most powerful woman in Egypt."

Tameri's back straightened, and she pulled in a deep breath. "If the royal princess dies, naturally, or mysteriously, without bearing an heir ... Imi believes she could become the Great Royal Wife. She told Amisi that it had happened before. I heard it with my own ears."

A nervous laugh rose in my throat. "It is a far leap from using my makeup to planning my murder. And if the sisters know such history, they are already better students of Egypt than I am. I've never heard of it." *But why would such things unfold so easily from Imi's lips?*

"Imi will find a way to power any way she can," Tameri said without a doubt. "After you and Merikare wed, I would not let a thing pass my lips that has not been tasted by the one who serves it."

"A thought that makes one shiver," I said.

Kiya returned carrying a salver filled with flatbread, chickpeas and boiled beef with leeks. She seemed jumpy and avoided my eyes as she placed the food on the table. Tameri sat up straight. Her tongue darted between her lips as the scent of beef settled on us.

Amisi was not with Kiya.

"Kiya. Do I have to ask?" I prompted.

She shook her head. "No, Princess Hagar. The wife of Crown Prince Merikare has found new housing with the Great Royal Wife. She will return Dendera to your service and reclaims her sister." Now she looked abashed. "The Great Royal Wife has asked that you come to her chambers to settle this dispute as soon as you have finished your evening meal."

Tameri raised her eyebrows.

"Imi involved my mother?" My voice, barely a whisper. "I feel ensnared in something I don't understand, and I can't free myself from it." I twisted the amulet around my wrist as I walked to the door. "I will eat when I return."

"Princess," Tameri said eagerly. "I believe I should be in attendance since you have given me charge over the sisters. And don't worry. No matter what grievances they have taken to your royal mother, I will stand with you against them."

There was no point denying Tameri this audience with my mother. Her tongue would wag throughout the harem anyway. And it would be better if the tales she spread had truth in them.

"I have no desire to be against them, Tameri. You may come if you wish. I know the Great Royal Wife values your good opinion in all things."

The chambers of the Great Royal Wife were nearly as luxurious as the kings. A columned entry led to where she sat on a great throne made from acacia wood and covered with sheets of gold. Mother wore a tightly fitted dress of colorfully embroidered linen and an exorbitantly decorated gold collar around her neck. A tightly plaited wig sat on her head with the red crown of Lower Egypt. She held, crossed in her hands, the crook and flail, the symbols of kingship. The crook represented the shepherd, or the one who cares for the people. The flail symbolized punishment deemed necessary to sustain order in society. This told me Father left the city with the rest of the men, and Mother now acted as regent.

Imi had brought our quarrel before the sitting pharaoh.

A man was on his knees before my mother. Meti stood at her right side, indicating this was official business. But when the Great Royal Wife saw me, she asked the men to give her a few moments, and as soon as they departed, she lay the crook and flail in her lap.

Tameri and I approached and bowed, touching the floor with our foreheads. "Life, health, and strength be to thee, Great Royal Wife," we said in unison, observing all formalities.

"Dear royal daughter, dear noblewoman Tameri, please stand and come sit beside me," my mother said. "I am pleased you have come, wife of Rensi, the high vizier. This matter very much concerns you too."

Bunefer stood in a corner and nodded at two servants who appeared with large luxurious pillows and placed them on each side of the throne. I sat on my mother's right, and Tameri took a seat on her left.

Imi, her pretty face puffy and her lashes still wet from crying, sat with Amisi on a small couch, wine cups in their hand, chins in the air. They looked relaxed in the presence of the Great Royal Wife, as though they had spent their entire lives lounging in front of kings.

Amisi gave me a stiff smile.

Does she fear anything?

"I understand there is discord in the palace between my royal daughter and the wife of my royal son. I have heard the complaints of both Princess Imi and her sister, Amisi."

"O, Mother, listen now to our side," I said.

"There is no need, Princess Hagar. I have made my decision based on all I have already discerned."

My heart sank. *Where is the justice in that?* My eyes clouded with tears, but my mouth stayed closed.

"Princess Imi and Amisi," said the Great Royal Wife.

They both stood and moved in front of the throne. "Hagar is the daughter the gods fashioned for me, and it is she who will one day be the Great Royal Wife of the pharaoh of Egypt. There is no doubt that she will be remembered as one of the greatest sovereigns ever to rule our country."

Imi flinched, and a bright red flush of color swept across the cheeks of both sisters.

"You will not covet her position or belongings," Mother said firmly. "You will stay with me until we can prepare a room for you. That may take some time, but we will make the best of it. The noblewoman Tameri will remain as your guardian. She will teach you, Imi, how to be a proper princess. Since the beginning of time, men have wrongly believed that the most attractive women tend to be the fertile ones. And we all know that men must prove they are masculine by fathering many children."

Mother paused a moment and took a gentle breath. I could see the anger she fought to suppress in the tightness around her eyes.

"We cannot change our men. Prince Merikare has chosen you as his first wife, and my good husband allowed this to happen." She glanced at me, a shared understanding between mother and child. "Sometimes he goes too far to please our son. And only the gods know what you have done to capture the crown prince as you have." She shook her head and sighed. "You will meet with the noblewoman Tameri daily. She will instruct you in all things, such as how to be well mannered, polite, and above all, respectful."

I couldn't believe it, but Amisi opened her mouth. "But Your Majesty, Merikare provided this instruction on the—"

My mother's eyes widened, and she raised a hand to silence her. "Do not address a royal without permission. And never give opinions unless asked." She had raised her voice. Now she drew in a breath and lowered it. "Amisi, you must learn to think before you speak. You may follow Princess Imi and the noblewoman Tameri while she is instructing your sister. If the noblewoman reports that your behavior is favorable, I will look for a suitable match for you among the noblemen. If the report is not favorable, I will place you in service to one of my husband's minor wives." She cocked a brow and my heart smiled. "The first lesson you will learn is that you must be obedient to Pharaoh and the Great Royal Wife in all things."

"Yes, Your Majesty." Amisi prostrated herself before my mother.

"Rise, Amisi," Mother said.

She stood and kept her mouth quiet, but I saw fire, not fear in her eyes.

"Princess Imi, never become arrogant in your role here. You will only create enemies, and people will not respect you. If you are helpful and become a delight in the harem, you may make friends and win their favor. Learn as much as you can. We will provide an education for you with the priests. Believe it or not, knowledge will be your most important asset." Her lips formed a hint of a smile. "Not that pretty face."

Imi bowed. "Yes, Your Majesty."

Mother turned to me. "Kiss me goodnight, daughter, and go enjoy your dinner. I know you must have sacrificed your repast to come to me so swiftly."

I kissed the Great Royal Wife on both cheeks and returned to my chambers to the most enjoyable meal I'd had in years.

Chapter Thirty-One

MOTHER AND I SAT ON EBONY and gold stools at a low table on the royal quay to take our midday meal. I inhaled the scent of fresh, warm flatbread and dipped it into mashed chickpeas blended with olive oil and garlic. I dropped the bread before it reached my mouth. "A kingfisher, Mother—he snatched a water snake."

The bird had moved swiftly and seized the belly crawler as it slithered through the reeds along the bank of the Nile. But the snake's next move was deadly. It wrapped itself around the bird's neck and forced it underwater before it could take flight. Mother and I stood and clutched each other, unable to do anything but gape at the epic battle of survival.

The kingfisher thrashed and squawked, desperate to break the surface and breathe. It nearly made it. But the elongated, legless prey it hunted coiled completely around the hapless bird until both disappeared.

"No," Mother and I shouted.

Then the brightly colored kingfisher emerged, having somehow broken free from the snake's grasp. It landed on a low branch and shook the water from its wings and tail before flying away. We squealed in delight and hugged, agreeing that neither of us had ever seen such a thing before.

When the men departed south, the Great Royal Wife and I began meeting daily along the riverbank at midday. We discussed her many duties as regent, and as I had promised that young fellah, watched the slow return of the Nile's waters. The most pressing issue she faced was rebuilding our city, followed by rationing the water and grain my father stored before the storm. I helped as much as possible.

Pharaoh and Merikare had returned a fortnight before, but Mother and I continued to meet. It was so pleasant there—we could feel the breeze of the north wind, enjoy new sightings of wildlife, and see the green returning to the riverbanks. But those rare moments were most precious to me because I had my mother all to myself.

She smiled a flash of white teeth. "Before you arrived, Hagar, a small flock of red-bellied ibis waded right there, in the water, swinging their heads side to side foraging for food. I watched them as though awestruck." She shook her head. "I have lived many years looking at our natural surroundings through a blind man's eyes. Not giving nature much thought, and rarely taking time to consider its beauty."

I nodded in understanding. No one would be ambivalent toward life on the river again or the sight of flowing water. Not even the most hardened among us.

The best part, though, was that the rising river finally washed away the horrific scent of decaying flesh. We were beyond grateful on that account. The sun had turned all stranded carcasses into disgusting rot. Putrid air assaulted us for weeks, gagged us, and made our eyes burn and water. No one could hold food in their belly for long.

But now, we could smell bread baking, sweet perfume, and musky incense.

"Yesterday, I saw the first sighting of a black crocodile." I shuddered. "He moved along the river in a very easygoing way, then, in one attempt, took the life of a small gazelle that stopped to drink. I watched the gazelle struggle as the beast held it in its jaws and rolled over and over in the water until it struggled no more. Then the crocodile twisted and turned, and ripped it apart, limb by limb." My voice cracked. "I thought of Zadah the whole time." I bit my lip to stop its quivering.

We both took a sip of pomegranate wine and sat silent for a moment.

"You have to stop torturing yourself, Hagar. A premature grave is the fate of many." Mother sighed dismally. "The joy we feel as the river returns to us is filled with heartache too. Demolishing the dam proved treacherous, and many men met an early death there. Scores of fathers, sons, and husbands will not return home. Crocodiles have taken some, a hippopotamus attacked one, and others have died from snakebites. And countless more have drowned."

"I'm not sure that comforts me much, Mother." I smiled thinly. I thought about Rensi and feared for his safety. The high vizier remained in that inhospitable place where they found the barrier. Father told us the river overflowed its banks in a torrent to the east and west, unable to find its natural course. It made the task of reaching the obstruction perilous. I knew men had lost their lives, but I had not realized there had been so many.

"You will see a lot of dark days as a sovereign, my daughter." She smiled gently. "We have to do what needs to be done and learn to live with the results. Yet it is our burden to feel each drop of spilled blood in our hearts."

I looked down at my hands and fidgeted with the silver amulet I still wore. "I am not a ruler, Mother, nor will I ever be."

Mother did not hesitate. "I bore two kings on the day you and Merikare were born." She trained her eyes on me. "It is true that you are the eldest and the most capable and will have to be content to serve your younger brother. But you will marry Merikare and rule beside him. Your father and I are counting on that."

I poked idly at my food. "Father has made it clear I will not be co-regent. Therefore, I may sit beside Merikare one day, but he will never allow me to rule beside him."

"The kingship has remained unchanged for millennia. Your father is not likely to abandon the traditional view of one male pharaoh as the divine ruler over all of Egypt." She examined my face with clear golden amber eyes. "But we have such faith in you, Hagar. You have never had the airy dreams of a young girl. Your heart has always been set firmly on the future. We know you were born to rule. The entire realm knows this. Merikare would be wise to always seek your counsel." I frowned as she laid her hand on mine. "Sometimes I look at you and see a barely-grown child. The king sees you differently. He sees the blossoming young woman you have become. He believes it is time for you to become the mistress of your own house and has decided that as soon as the river flows completely free, you will wed Merikare."

My stomach suddenly turned over. "I praise the gods for my mother and my father who set me on the path of life. But, royal mother, do not rush to make me marry him. There is no profit for me to hurry. Imi will have the firstborn no matter what. If she has a girl, I agree, it will be time. If she has a boy, then you know he will grow to challenge any son I have."

"I admit, when the sisters first came to the palace, I did not see them as a threat. But they are shrewd and calculating. Imi has Merikare so twisted to her will that my recognition of him grows dim." Mother shifted in her seat. "He becomes as cruel and thoughtless as she is when they are together. Their treatment of anyone she believes is beneath her is inexcusable. Nobles, tradesmen, servants, they all fare alike under her conceit. And Merikare stands back and allows it." She shook her head. "Your father thinks it's amusing that I imagine a woman could hold sway over his son. He does not believe it. And it leaves me sadly perplexed."

"I don't want to marry Merikare, Mother," I replied firmly. "Let any of my half-sisters do it. He is quite fond of all his siblings, except me." My body felt heavy. "Let me give my life to the temple and become a priestess."

"We can't change what Pharaoh wants for you." Her tone was soothing, and she stroked my back. "A priestess may be what you want, but the eldest royal princess is what you are. It is your duty." She spoke as though every word pained her. "I am sorry I cannot do more for your happiness."

My heart ached for her and me. I looked up at the clear sky as yet another noontide slipped away. Merikare and Imi's grasp coiled around me, and I feared it would suffocate me and make me disappear into dark water as the belly crawler did to the kingfisher. I left the womb first—marked as ruler. But the gods deprived me of my portion and gave it to my brother instead.

There was nothing more I could do about that.

"Let's not let this rob us of our happiness today, Hagar," Mother said gently. "We've had so little of it lately. At this moment, there is life ... and food." She took another helping of lamb. "Pharaoh's attentions are diverted. So, perhaps we'll let his forgetfulness profit you and delay the marriage, for now."

I laughed lightly. "I will rejoice in that, Mother, and pray Father's thoughts stay diverted. I cannot control my fate, but I can keep it from taking my joy." *Sarai taught me that.*

A gray gull with a stout, long bill and webbed feet landed next to our table. I tore a small piece of bread from a loaf and threw it to him. He cocked his head, looked at me suspiciously, and then quickly gobbled it down.

"Hagar, don't encourage him. You know what pests they can be. And we should not be wasting bread."

"It's just a small bite—" The words were barely out of my mouth when the greedy bird swooped in and took the entire loaf of bread in its bill and flew away. Mother and I looked at each other and burst into uncontrollable laughter.

Not far from us, down the shore of the river, a woman turned her head. She held a basket in one hand and a small child by the other.

Sarai.

She smiled at us and nodded as she walked among our people sharing the sycamore figs I saw her fill a basket with that morning. It was a small gift of a sweet delicacy.

"Sarai seems at peace living and working among us," Mother said with quiet dignity. "We are the ones who enslaved her, yet she treats everyone she meets with love and compassion. She is genuinely the humblest person I have ever met."

"I agree. But she does not treat those who mistreat me with love and compassion. She was quite curt with Tameri in the beginning until the high vizier's wife and I mended our differences. And she was ready to plan a rebellion in the harem against Imi to protect me."

Mother considered me briefly and smiled. "I'm pleasantly surprised that the seemingly perfect Sarai has a contrary side."

I took a few pieces of lamb but pushed the onions aside. "Our people love her. She listens intently to each one that comes to her, no matter their station. She rises long before the sun to attend to those who have lost the most."

"Your father has gifted her with more jewelry than any other wife or concubine. I admit I was resentful." Mother looked at me and raised her eyebrows. She then turned her attention back to Sarai, who wore a modest linen tunic and walked barefoot like the commoners surrounding her. "I've never seen her wear one piece of it except at Wepet Renpet. Another would have flaunted it before the entire harem."

"Imi wears all the jewelry Merikare's given her at one time. If she fell into the river, she'd sink to the bottom." I expected a rebuke from my mother for my unpleasant words, but she smiled instead. I took a bite of lamb, then a sip of wine.

"I think Sarai would take the pieces apart and give away the stones and gold if she could," Mother said. "I have heard of her serving people while they awaited death, comforting others with unbearable diseases, and caring for those orphaned in the storm."

I nodded. "People who have forgotten how to smile do so at her touch. I have witnessed it all myself."

"There is something so beautiful about her, beyond her physical appearance. She shines with the light of the supernatural." Mother leaned forward and paused as if she contemplated Sarai's every movement. "A *presence* moves with her. Something my eyes cannot see, but my heart can feel."

I sat up straight, my stomach in knots. "I know," I whispered.

Sarai sat next to a group of women who mended nets for the fishermen. She picked up their tools and began to help. The faces of the women brightened. They all touched her as if a blessing would be theirs doing so. She humbly accepted their touch, laughed lightly, and went to work on the nets.

Watching her made me relax. "Mother, her gift is not the fruit in her basket. She bears the fruit of compassion toward those in the greatest need."

"How wise are your words, daughter," she said, and I smiled. "We have turned our backs on them for a very long time now. I have abdicated that responsibility to others and neglected my duty to the poor and powerless among us. I am thankful to Sarai for her example to me."

Servants approached and placed a bowl of cabbage boiled with vinegar and dill and a plate of berries and figs in front of us. They began to back away when one short, stout man bowed to my mother and said, "Your Majesty, may you drink from the middle of the river." It was an old blessing our people revived. The middle of the river held the coolest and freshest water.

Mother gave him a generous, amber-eyed smile. "Thank you, Amoy. It makes my heart rejoice to hear it."

Amoy beamed, bowed again, and backed away

Mother selected a few berries while I put a piece of green cabbage in my mouth. It was delicious. "The nobles are not happy that Father declared the homes of the common people be rebuilt first." I hoped to move the subject away from Sarai and the *presence* that tormented my soul. Sometimes, it seemed it spoke to me in my heart, saying words like, *"How long will you keep putting me off? How long shall I look for you to come to me?"* It overwhelmed me and often gave me gooseflesh.

"I know." Mother's eyes squinted with mischief. "Nobleman Nenwef complained the most and even accused the king of not caring about the nobles. Your royal father told him it was not true. He was deeply concerned about the nobles. To prove it, he sent Nenwef straight away to the dam to check on the wellbeing of the nobility who already served the court there." She chuckled. "There have been no more protests."

I giggled. "Rensi would have enjoyed that." I could imagine the high vizier dissolving into laughter if he'd seen it for himself. "It is hard to pity the nobles. They can afford to bring their building materials from afar. And the river is almost full enough to hold their barges."

"That is true, but they still deserve our sympathy. Imagine seeing your home crushed and reduced to tiny bits. As though it had never been."

I thought of the many fine houses lost—beautiful homes with reception areas, large living quarters, gardens, and private wells. But overall, the nobles had fared well. They had large retinues of servants to secure their belongings in the palace or temple. And most had other homes they could escape to in other parts of Egypt. I would save my sympathy for those who had suffered more.

"Father is doing the right thing. If I were king, I would do the same."

"Agreed."

I contemplated all the work accomplished in the short time since the storm. If one walked outside the walls of Henen-nesut, as far as the eye could see, beautiful new bricks laid basking in the sun. Not far from the quay, laborers worked tirelessly filling reed baskets with mud from the Nile while others filled leather buckets with water. They hoisted the buckets and baskets on their shoulders, emptied them in a pit to mix with straw, then poured the mixture into wooden brick-molds on the desert floor. The abundance of sunshine allowed them to be left where they were to bake.

It took one man five days to make enough bricks to build a typical one-story house. At the same time, many continued to clear the debris from the city. The mounds they built outside our walls grew enormously.

I walked around the city every morning, watching leveled sites being staked with measuring lines to mark off the building area before bricklayers descended on the lots like locusts. They raised a home in just a few days with three or four rooms and two cellars for storage.

A merchant's home took longer since they required two stories—their businesses occupied the first, and their families lived on the second. They were the men that traveled and bartered our grain, linen, gold, and papyrus to other countries and exchanged them for goods not native to Egypt.

A few merchants opened the outdoor marketplace again, but it was a remnant of what it had once been. There was little to barter for or with. No luxury items were available for sale, no fat goats or sweet honey cakes. People bartered for what they needed to survive and went back to work. No one stood and gossiped and socialized in the marketplace like they used to. But to see a few merchants crouched by their baskets, placing goods on one side of the scale and metal debens on the other until it balanced, arguing over price and finally agreeing, made life feel a little more normal.

Several people passed the royal quay and threw themselves on their bellies before the Great Royal Wife. I politely covered my mouth so they would not see me chew. They believed their devotion would please the gods, but none would consider approaching or touching her. She was semi-divine to them, having birthed Merikare, who they believed would take the form of Horus, son of Amun-Ra, when he became king.

Mother fell quiet watching them. I kept my mouth covered, munching on tender cabbage, and watched her.

"It's not true, you know. Amun-Ra did not impregnate me as they believe."

I swallowed the cabbage and followed it with a sip of wine.

"Some Great Royal Wives begin to believe it. Your father's mother did late in life. She became quite the demigoddess." Mother laughed. "But no one in the royal family holds power over the forces of nature. We have no supernatural abilities. Even so, the Egyptian kingship is based on the people believing it. Believing in the god-appointed right of the pharaoh to rule. And that he was created for that purpose only. It is how we uphold order and keep chaos at bay." She sounded like she was trying to convince herself.

I looked around with a clenched jaw, sensitive to every sound around me. I couldn't even consider what would happen if other ears heard what she said. I began to sweat and wished for royal fanbearers to relieve the rising heat in me and quiet the Great Royal Wife. She would never speak thus in front of them. She seemed to have surrendered to uncertainty about the gods of Egypt too, and it made me jittery. I bit my lip and twisted the silver amulet around my wrist.

I realized my mother's eyes remained fixed on Sarai, who still sat and mended nets with the fishermen's wives. I set mine on my mother. She sounded emotional, but there were no tears in her eyes. They were bright and alive.

"The spirit of a great god dwells with her," she said.

I swallowed hard. "Yes, Mother."

"I've not spoken to her about this. Nor can I. But I desire to know more about the god she serves." She sighed deeply. "I know how dangerous this is, Hagar. If anyone else caught my words, it would cost my position. And my life."

I nodded gravely.

"I saw the Nile completely dry up, yet a river of joy and hope flowed within me. I cannot explain it, but I will not deny it."

My heart thumped hard in my chest. *Would she be setting a trap to snare Sarai or me?* My face burned. How could I think such a thing? My mother would never seek to harm me or anyone else.

"The being moves through my rooms, Mother," I blurted. "It causes my arms to look like the skin of a goose after the cooks have plucked its feathers."

Mother laughed quietly. "I know what you mean. I too have had gooseflesh from it." She took a sip of wine and studied me over her cup. "We must search for a way to add her god to our temple."

"But she claims that he is hidden and that he chooses where and with whom to abide. How can such power be contained in any shrine?"

Tears welled in the eyes of the Great Royal Wife. "It is a vast mystery to me how a god can dwell beyond the sky and the stars and still touch the hearts of men. I do not understand it at all. But I know it is true."

Tears formed in my eyes too. *Should I tell her that Rensi feels it also? No. I should keep his confidence.*

"I want to understand her god," she said. "I've spoken to him, like I have seen her speak to him, on my knees. It's as though I have a thirst I can't quench. The *presence* disturbs me with happiness, elevates my thoughts, and makes my tears come easy. I can't sleep at night because I am restless to feel this *presence* again."

"Sarai calls that 'the dark night of the soul.' A time for searching, but not yet finding."

She nodded as though that made sense to her. So, I told her Abram's story how his soul grieved to know the truth about his god and the voice from the heavens that spoke as clear to him as the midsummer sun.

Mother barely moved, but she covered her mouth in shock at Abram's boldness when I told her he shattered his father's idols and blamed the largest one for committing the crime.

Her tears fell freely and sent the black kohl outlining her eyes running down her face. She looked at me, and by her wide grin, I realized my face was a mess as well. Once again, we burst into laughter until my sides hurt.

We took linen cloths, dampened them in the water bowl meant for our fingers, and rubbed our faces to remove the makeup.

"O, Hagar. You must be my agent in this. I cannot speak to anyone but you. Anything you learn from Sarai about her god, I want you to tell me. I crave any news of him. Any small bit of information makes my heart soar. Can you do this for me?"

"O, yes, Mother. Every word that slips from Sarai's lips, I will tell you."

She leaned over and wiped a spot of smeared makeup from my face.

"Mother, when Pharaoh reaches for Sarai, do you see—"

"His hand wither?"

Chapter Thirty-Two

SEVERAL NEW MOONS PASSED AND OUR beautiful city, fresh and new, had begun to bustle again. But judging from the grumbling of the women in the harem, one troublesome problem still made life uneasy. I continued to act unconcerned as my mind scrambled to find a solution.

Late one morning, Kiya startled me as she ran into my chambers in tears. A large red welt rose on her cheek.

Imi stormed in behind her. "I may have to come when the Great Royal Wife commands it, but I do not come at your command, Princess Hagar," she spat, spittle flying. Her lips pulled back and she bared her teeth. "Never send a servant to command my presence again."

My heart pounded. "I did not command, Imi. I invited you to share a meal." I turned to my servant. "Kiya, what did you say?"

"O, Princess, I said just that. That she was invited to join you for your midday meal." Her full body trembled.

"Liar," Imi screamed. "Your words said invited, but your tone said commanded. I knew exactly what you meant."

Kiya covered her face and sank to her knees, Dendera rushed to her side. A lump rose in my throat. I hated myself for drawing them into my struggle with Imi.

I took a couple of steps toward Imi and tried to appear at ease, looking her straight in the eyes. "There is no cause to accuse Kiya of lying. It was not a summons, I assure you. I invited you here so that we could try to find a good foot to stand on." I turned to Kiya and Dendera. "Both of you, go to the garden, cool yourselves in the pool."

Dendera helped Kiya to her feet, and they both hurried from the room, leaving me to face Imi alone.

Imi's hands clenched and unclenched. "Your slave insults a member of the royal household and you reward her with a dip in your pool?" Red flushed her chest. "She should be flogged."

"Princess Imi, please come in and sit. Let me pour you a glass of wine." I hoped using her rank and humbling myself would calm her. I poured a cup and breathed deeply. Bastet wandered in from outside, unaware of the row she strolled into.

Imi scowled and awkwardly tried to lower herself on my couch, her belly large and ripe, her feet planted wide apart.

"Here, let me help you." I reached out my free hand and she swatted it away. She dropped on her own, raised her arm, and snapped for her wine.

My vision clouded and I twitched. I wanted to smack her face and demand she walk right out my door. But instead, I took another deep breath and handed her the cup. "I thought we should talk and see if we can settle the strife that has stirred up between us. The entire harem feels the misery that comes from our discord. I don't know what I have done to cause you to dislike me so much. But I'm asking now. And I'd like to apologize, if I may. We will likely spend the rest of our lives together, Imi. Shouldn't we try to get on together?"

She sat silent and rigid, sipping her wine, her eyes cold and calculating.

I took a seat next to her. Bastet jumped on my lap and purred through her silver whiskers. I picked her up and set her beside me. "When you first arrived in Henen-nesut, you were so kind to me at the temple garden, offering to help when my maids were not with me. What has changed so much since then?"

Her mouth curled with dislike. "It is simple. I thought I might need you." She took a sip of wine. "But I don't."

My mouth fell open. "I'm sorry. I must have misheard you."

"I ... don't ... need ... you," she repeated slowly as though speaking to a fool, as her beautiful face hardened.

I sat for a moment—I believe my mouth remained open—listening to the beat of my heart. It had been an easy task avoiding Imi and her sister during what we called "the time of great activity" after the storm. They kept to themselves, sheltered most often in Merikare's opulent rooms, not once asking to help in any manner.

I toiled alongside my mother and father, doing whatever was necessary, until we saw Henen-nesut rising once again out of the dust. Pharaoh worked wonders for his people. He took a process that could have taken years and reduced it to less than one. And no one balked at the undertaking. Instead, they embraced it with enthusiasm.

Father vowed to abstain from all pleasure until the land was secure and rebuilt. For one thing, he delayed exercising his conjugal rights with any of his wives and concubines, including Sarai. He also postponed my impending marriage to Merikare. Both delays relieved my anxiety, but the time elapsed quickly. Now Henen-nesut looked like a city again, and the inundation came and withdrew, leaving behind rich soil and grateful hearts. The fellahin had sowed crops, and the harvest was upon us.

As well as Imi's time of delivery.

Pharaoh declared I would join Merikare's household at Wepet Renpet. I would ring in the new year as my brother's captive, and he came to my chambers to tell me the news himself. His two repulsive royal companions flanked him and howled at his vulgar descriptions of things he would do to me on our wedding night. I reminded him he and his wretched friends had no business disturbing me since that day had not yet come. The three had a good laugh at that and went on their way.

Regardless if Imi had a boy or girl, I had come to terms that it was a fate I could not avoid. For the sake of peace, the time had come to try to heal the rift between my brother's first wife and me.

If that was possible.

"Why do you hate me so much?" I finally said.

"I wondered when you would ask that." Her voice was coarse and lowborn. "That day at the temple was not the first time you and I have met."

Cold gripped my heart, sudden and unexpected.

"When we were small girls, Amisi and I came to Henennesut for Wepet Renpet. I was seven and Amisi was six. Our uncle asked my parents if he could bring us to see your famous temple gardens. He was my father's brother but was nothing like my father. My uncle was an evil pig of a man."

She stopped for a moment and stared straight ahead, her eyes dull and lifeless as if recalling something best left buried in the past.

"The Nomarch of Zoan put together an enormous caravan of merchants to bring their goods to trade at the large festival marketplace here." She blinked. "It was exhilarating, at first." Imi leaned back, her hands clasped and resting on her large belly. "Scores and scores of people traveled with us, including a lot of families with children our age. There were more donkeys than we could count. The line of them snaked farther than we could see in front or behind us. They transported all our food and water, along with exotic products to be traded. It was like a traveling fair, and I felt a sense of adventure for the first time in my life."

Her face grew dark and turned my skin into gooseflesh.

"Most of all, it was an escape from my mother and the horrible conditions at home. A break from spinning flax into thread from the moment the sun rose until it set at night. I couldn't believe my luck.

"It was the second night of our journey when Uncle told us we were going to be his wives." I gasped, and Imi looked at me through narrowed eyes. "Our mother had agreed to a brideprice for both of us. Half of what he made at the market would be hers. So, he believed the awful things he did to us in the middle of the night were his right as our future husband."

I swallowed in understanding.

"I was petting one of the feline skins he brought to sell when the words came from his mouth. I remember the dark spots of the pelt were perfectly even. It had a very long striped tail, and its claws stuck out of its paws. The skin was supposed to give special protection to the person who wore it, so Amisi and I slept under that fur every night even though the heat nearly suffocated us."

Her eyes found mine, not eyes of sadness, but cold and hostile. I couldn't hide my unease. I could sense something else coming. Almost taste it.

"It didn't work. Every night he drank, and every night he came to us for his pleasure. Don't look at me that way, Princess," she flared, her voice a guttural roar. "He did not take our virginity. He knew better than to enter a small girl that way. But his hands explored every other nook and cranny of our young bodies. Most of the time, I pretended to be asleep while he fondled me, but I wasn't." She shuddered. "I can still smell his stale beer breath and feel his rough, calloused hands on my skin."

For a flicker of a moment, I thought she appeared vulnerable and wounded. It was no wonder her behavior was so biting toward others after that kind of abuse. "Imi, I am so sorry," I said sincerely.

"Do not pity me, Princess," she snarled. "My time with that serpent has nothing to do with my feelings toward you." A sickening smile crossed her face. "Besides, he never made it home from that trip. He made so much money that he purchased us a ride back on a barge to sail up the river instead of crossing the desert by foot again. He was drunk one night and … tripped overboard. Amisi and I had the pleasure of seeing his limbs fought over by crocodiles."

From the look she gave, I doubted his stumble into the Nile had been an accident, but there would never be any proof. I wasn't sure I could blame the sisters even if I knew they pushed him. But Tameri's warning, *After you and Merikare wed, I would not let a thing pass my lips that has not been tasted by the one who serves it,"* slipped into my mind. I shuddered involuntarily. Thankfully, Imi had turned her face from me and did not notice it.

Bastet, sleeping beside me, now tried to crawl into my lap again. This time I pushed her to the floor and asked, "But I still don't understand why—"

Imi held up her hand to silence me. "While we were in Henen-nesut," she continued, "Amisi and I were playing in the temple gardens, running around with several other children. My uncle was at the market. Royal guards appeared to clear the way for royalty. They pushed all of us to the side and handled us very harshly. Like we were no more than animals. At first, I thought the king was coming, such a fuss was made. A row of guards stood elbow to elbow in front of us and looked so fierce that my child's heart felt real terror for the first time. Then, instead of the king, it was a little boy and little girl, no older than me, holding hands with the high priest. You and Merikare," she hissed scornfully. "You had on a finely braided wig and a small gold crown. Your wrists and forearms had wide bracelets on them, and a beautiful gold collar hung around your neck. It contained so many precious stones, nothing I had ever seen shined brighter in the sunlight.

"You walked with such an arrogant air, holding your head and neck high, and took small, even steps in the finest leather sandals I had ever seen. I was so little I slid between two of the guards to get a better look at you. Your eyes met mine, and you stopped in your tracks. You gave the guards a sharp look. They shoved me back so hard I fell on my bottom, stunned. I heard you say, 'Meti, I think that is the dirtiest peasant I have ever seen. Must we let them into the temple garden? Don't we have to be pure to come before the gods?' I did not hear what he said to you."

Knowing Meti, I got quite the scolding.

"Everyone around looked at me. We had just spent over a month traveling through the desert. I had bathed only a few times that entire time and was too young to understand purifying myself at the washbasins before entering the gardens. I sat on the ground and looked at my feet. They were calloused and dirty because I had never owned a pair of sandals. My coarse linen shift had not been freshly washed since we left the delta, and for the first time, I realized how soiled it was. The linen you wore was so fine, so sheer and white you could almost see through it. I ran my hand through my long-neglected hair, full of tangles."

She absently touched the neatly plaited wig she now wore.

"I had never seen a wig on a child before you." She paused a moment and again raised her eyes to me. "I realized my station in life for the first time that day. I looked around and saw merchants, fellahin, and others around me. I knew I was at the bottom of them all. Then someone lifted me roughly from the ground. It was one of the guards. He held Amisi by her arm, dragged us to the temple gate, and shoved us out."

I held my breath, stricken by her story. I had never heard such a dreadful thing.

"My uncle made me feel shame on that trip. But you." She jabbed a finger in my face. "You made me feel dirty. And I've hated you from that moment. You had everything. I had nothing. Something deep inside screamed that it was wrong. I was the one who should have everything," she said with reproach. "Then one day, I was spinning thread for my mother and looked up into your brother's eyes. I instantly knew who he was. I recognized him even after so many years. My mother did not know him, but she's a fool. I did not tell her she could have a fortune instead of a loom." She laughed spitefully. "I knew the gods had finally smiled on me. I knew my time had come."

There was a silence before Imi spoke so violently that Bastet hissed and ran from the room.

"Now that it has, I want it all. Everything you have will be mine, and I will be everything you were supposed to be." She leaned closer. "I will not stop until the day comes when I see you shoved to the side."

The anger she displayed was irrational, and worse, unstable. I believed her perplexing behavior was not all my fault. There was something seriously wrong with Imi.

Something my brother ignored because of her beauty. But he had to see the mood swings, the hostility, her lack of empathy toward others. I had read papyri about people in affected states like that, believed to be a symptom of a sick heart or uterus, all of a very mysterious nature.

I decided to tread as carefully as possible.

"Imi, I admit that my behavior was detestable," I said gently. "But I was a child. Surely you can't hold such things in your heart and let them ferment for so many years." I leaned toward her. "How can you hate me today for my thoughtless actions so many years ago?"

"I have a splendid memory, Hagar. To me, it is as though it happened only yesterday. I do hate you for it. And I always will." She eyed me contemptuously. "Until everything you have is mine. And then I'll never think about you again." She fell back against my cushy sofa. "Fortunately for me, your brother does not care for you either. We have bonded in our distaste for you."

My posture stiffened. "Do not scheme against me, Imi. My brother may be your fool for now, but he will get turned around." I could barely breathe. "Your situation may not be as firm as you believe. Merikare and I have been linked since the moment we emerged from our mother's womb. One does not escape what is fated. We have found our way to accept that. We have squabbled as siblings do our entire lives, but there has never been lasting hostility between us. Merikare will be king, and I will be the Great Royal Wife. I will be the one sitting next to him on the throne."

For a fleeting moment, Imi looked like a scared little girl, but the look changed so quickly it caused my heart to seize. I bit my lip and tried not to look away from her.

Sarai saved me. "Is everything all right?" she said.

She arrived rosy from the sun, carrying an empty basket that had been full of figs when she left that morning. Her linen dress clung tightly to her body from moisture on her skin, and a lock of tousled hair fell across her face as she glared at Imi.

She gave me courage. "Imi, please don't ever put me in the position of having to cause you pain and trouble again. I fear you don't fully understand the influence I have in the royal family."

Imi threw the faience cup in her hand on the limestone floor. Shards of delicate blue and green earthenware and red wine flew everywhere. The white kalasiris I wore appeared covered in blood. She spread her legs, jutted her significant stomach out, and lurched to her feet. "O, your days of influence are numbered. I promise you that. If this child in my womb is a boy, I will own everything you now call yours. I will take it all."

I looked at her in disbelief.

"Come in, Sarai. I'm leaving. I only came because Hagar commanded it. I had not intended on staying as long as I have."

She waddled past Sarai and out of the room.

Chapter Thirty-Three

"YOU COMMANDED HER?" SARAI ASKED. "THAT doesn't sound like you. The air in this room was thicker than the crowd of little ones who surrounded my basket of figs this morning. Only not as sweet."

"I invited her to join me for the midday meal. That is how she chose to take it."

My servants stepped lightly into the room and began to clean up the broken cup. Not a drop of water graced the skin of either of them. They had not taken my offer to cool off in the pool. My heart warmed, realizing they remained near the whole time.

"I wanted to find out why she dislikes me so. She gave me the answer I was looking for." I let out a deep sigh. "It's a story for another day, and not a good one." I shook my head slowly. "It is irrational how the hurts of our childhood follow us through our entire life if we let them."

"I don't think you should deal with Imi alone." Sarai crossed her arms and raised her eyebrows. "She means to see you suffer. She is a foolish woman and will tear this house down with her own hands if she can."

"I only want to do what is best for Egypt and the women in the harem. She is part of our lives now. For better or worse."

Tameri entered the room and flapped her handheld fan wildly, her face red. "Excuse me for interrupting, Princess Hagar. I thought you should know Princess Imi has taken your cat. She picked up Bastet down the hall while cursing your very name. I heard her say, 'you belong to me now' as she walked away, among other utterances I won't repeat. O, the gutter mouth on that one. She should not be allowed to show such open contempt of you."

"I deserve some of it," I admitted. "But I would not worry

about Bastet. She is capable of finding her way home when she is ready."

"Would she hurt your cat?" Sarai asked. "To hurt you?"

"Imi is impulsive. Even reckless at times," Tameri answered for me. "But cats are sacred to us and held in high esteem. The penalty for harming one is severe. Imi would not risk that."

"I agree," I said.

The three of us stayed silent for a moment.

Then I smiled.

Sarai and Tameri smiled.

My insides tickled and I started to laugh.

The two of them laughed with me. My servant girls looked at each other and laughed too. It was an odd way of behaving regarding the situation, but we had no other response. Stealing my cat just seemed silly.

"Laughter is good, Princess," Sarai said as she took a seat on the couch. "It is how I sometimes begin my prayers. It opens us to new possibilities."

Kiya stripped the wine-stained kalasiris off me.

"My prayers always begin 'help me!' to one god or the other," Tameri said.

We laughed again.

"I don't wish to spoil the light mood," Tameri added, "but be careful with that one. Imi's moods swing faster than a scarab can roll a ball of dung. Your brother is the boat, and that woman's lying tongue is the rudder."

Surprisingly, Kiya added a comment. "O, it is true. I have heard her falsify a person's words and accuse them of all sorts of wrongs. She makes untrue accusations against anyone who crosses her path."

Tameri nodded. "She's right. Imi thinks everyone slights her in some way and makes things up to prove her suspicions. Especially toward servants. I take a strong hand with my servants, but not like her. She can be outright brutal. Rensi said he stopped a young servant boy being whipped on Merikare's orders because of Imi. She alleged he looked at her suggestively. The boy claimed he just smiled at her."

Kiya finished fussing over me, and Dendera handed me a fresh cup of wine. I fingered its rim while I paced the room. "It's like she wishes to ruin everyone she can." *If only I had behaved better as a child.* "Merikare and I have been taught that it is our moral duty as royals to treat those who serve us well and justly. I can't believe the crown prince would treat them harshly." *Am I just as guilty for the pain inflicted upon them?* I turned toward Tameri, my voice thick with emotion. "Thank you, Tameri. You are a good friend to me. Please let me know if you hear of anyone mistreated at her hands. Perhaps I can intervene for them."

Tameri walked to the door, her fan-flapping more controlled now. "I wish I could stay. I heard you have a roasted leg of lamb coming. But I am the keeper of the vexed, and Imi left here upset. She behaves so rashly at times, and I'd better make sure she doesn't hurt herself. Or someone else." She stopped a moment and turned to Sarai. "I caught her making small cuts on her forearms with a piece of flint. She hides them under her thick bracelets. I've never witnessed such behavior. Have you ever seen anything like it?"

"Yes, unfortunately. In Ur, there was a young woman I caught cutting herself. I pulled her arms to me and noticed many leftover scars from other cuts. She told me the pain she felt from her body took away the pain she felt inside. It was only when she saw herself bleeding that she could feel and knew she was still alive. I believe she had no other way to express the anguish in her heart."

"Imi had a horrific childhood," I said with concern. "Unspeakable things happened to her."

"Keep a close eye on her, Tameri," Sarai said. "For the sake of the baby."

"Very well," Tameri agreed. "But do not blink or turn your back to her, Princess. And do not seek to take her hand in friendship. She will injure you when she can. Your brother has always been fond of stalking dangerous game, and Imi is as dangerous as they come."

I watched Tameri leave and was amazed at how our relationship had changed. She was a good friend, and I honestly did like her.

I turned to Sarai, ready to change the subject. "Do you really laugh before you pray? I've never heard of such a thing. I think the high priest would say the gods abhor such behavior."

Sarai pushed herself to her feet. "Walk with me?"

I followed her outside into the serene quiet of my private gardens. I marveled at how the sunshine made her skin glow and how it warmed mine. I should not have invited Imi to my chambers. I should have spent the day here, with Sarai, or had my midday meal with Mother on the royal quay. Imi rattled me. No doubt about that. But Sarai's natural peacefulness quickly steadied my spirit.

I loved being alone with Sarai. She often called me Hagar in her language, and it fell from her lips so beautifully. She freely taught me about El, as my desire to understand the depths of his nature had become insatiable. I probed her with questions that belonged to my mother as much as to me. What Sarai told me, I secretly shared with the Great Royal Wife.

"So, sometimes you laugh before you pray? Do you tell him a jest? Or does he share one with you?"

She threw back her lovely heart-shaped face and laughed. It crossed my mind that it wasn't fair that the gods had bestowed so much beauty on one woman *and* made laughing as much a part of her as breathing.

"Sarai, why doesn't your deity take offense when you come to him filled with mirth and not reverence?"

"O, Hagar. Life brings us times to be joyful and times to weep. God laughs with me and cries with me." She stopped and touched my arm. "He loves you too. I know you are worried about your life after you wed Merikare, but there is nothing secure in this world except a relationship with the one true God." Then she looked slightly abashed. "I used to worry about everything. I'd often get anxious looking for reasons why I was so anxious."

"You hide it well. But I am aware of your anxiety, even though you set up defenses to conceal it."

"I can worry and fret with the best of them. I am always aware of it. But it is not as bad as before. It took years before I became comfortable with just *being* me. I always needed someone to support and guide me and believed I was incapable of surviving on my own. God helped give my own feet the strength to stand with no one but Himself. I know that He is with me, wherever I am or whatever my circumstances."

"I've told your god that if he loves me and wanted to be with me, that I wanted that too," I whispered.

"Well and good," she announced. She turned among the rows of sweet and spicy wild roses starting to bloom again for the first time since the storm. Their intoxicating scent filled the hot air. I followed right behind her. She bent down and picked a small flower bud, and handed it to me. "This bud reminds me of you, Hagar. It is where you are in your spiritual journey."

I sniffed its delicate perfume.

"I know you are torn, Princess. But you cannot follow the Egyptian gods and my God. You must be ready to keep your face forward and serve only Him."

My brow furrowed.

I still served the gods of Egypt. I helped Meti every day in the temple with the daily ceremonial activities and every step of ritual worship. I twisted idly at my silver amulet.

I sniffed the bud again and walked down the crushed stone pathway, lost in thought. I never felt worthwhile unless my father, Meti, or Rensi saw me that way. But when I conversed with Sarai's god, I believed he accepted me just as I am. "I don't fully understand why, but your god makes me feel valued."

"Because He created you, and El cares for all of His

creation." Sarai paused beside a raised bed filled with little green sprouts, bent down, and plucked several from the soil.

"Why do you pull them out before they have grown?" I said, confused.

"I'm only pulling the weeds. It takes a while, but soon you begin to recognize the difference between the plants you want to cultivate and those that should be discarded. Those that are true and those that are false."

"Like the gods," I mused.

Sarai looked surprised. "You are clever, Hagar. Think on this. Gardens like yours don't grow naturally, but the weeds do. Your garden is beautiful because it's cultivated, and that doesn't happen by itself. I find I have to tend the garden of my soul as diligently as your caretakers tend this plot of soil. If I ignore the weeds, for example, they will grow unchecked and wild. So, I pluck them out, as I did these, and give God's spirit the room it needs to grow and flourish. As you become more firmly rooted in your belief in the one true God, you'll find it easier to discern His truth and pluck out the false."

"Rooted? Like a plant? In a god?" I shook my head. Sometimes Sarai made no sense to me. But I enjoyed her descriptive images and reflections about her god. Walking in the garden always brought them out in her. She used nature as the primary way to illustrate her relationship with her god.

We wandered to my ornamental pond. My gardeners only recently refilled it, but blue and white lotus already spread floating leaves and flowers across the surface. I sat beside the pond and dipped my hands in the cool water. Sarai took a seat beside me and did the same.

"It is hard for me to move from the comfortable place of what I know about the gods of Egypt. But I feel I am close to letting them go. I've worked my whole life for them, and they have never returned to me the same devotion I gave them. I believe it is time to focus solely on your god. To see where he is leading me. And Egypt."

"You are ready to make my God your God? Your only

God?" The sun caught her sky-blue eyes and made them shine even brighter.

I glanced down at the silver amulet on my wrist and then—slowly because it took more courage than I expected—returned my gaze to her face. "Yes. If you will show me how."

"What are you about to do, sister?" a menacing voice raged.

I flinched and whipped my head toward the voice.

Merikare stood a few feet from us, hands on his hips, his bare chest thrust out.

Chapter Thirty-Four

I SUCKED IN MY BREATH. IF Merikare had heard the words spoken between Sarai and me, our lives could be in real danger. "Brother, how long have you been here?"

"Long enough to hear your mind filled with blasphemy. You are infected with dangerous notions about our gods, Princess Hagar. You are being sickened by lies." He slowly reached up into the bough of my one remaining willow tree. His narrowed, blazing eyes stayed on mine. "I'm going to help you recover from your illness." He broke off a portion of the branch, unhurried, and stripped the leaves from it. His eyes never left mine.

"Merikare, you cannot strike Sarai." I moved between them. "She is the king's favorite. Only Pharaoh can punish her if he chooses to do so."

"I have no intention of striking Sarai," he said as he skillfully fashioned a weapon from the branch.

I forced my voice to remain steady to mask my fear. "Just turn and leave us, Merikare. I don't know what you think you heard, but—"

He took a step forward and struck in an instant. A force lashed across my body, so great my feet could not stand where they had been. Pain raced across my side, but I felt a more significant pain on the back of my head. The world blurred as I hit the crushed stones of the garden path.

I saw Sarai rise.

"No, Sarai, stay where you are," I whispered, grateful to see her lower herself. I rolled on my belly and absorbed the sting of Merikare's self-made whip again and again. The shock of it silenced my mouth, and I could not cry out. No one had ever struck me before.

I counted each blow and held my tears. I bit my lips so

hard I tasted warm blood in my mouth. Then, for some odd reason, an old poem came to mind.

I am the most beautiful tree in the garden,
And for all times, I shall remain.
The beloved and her brother
Stroll under my branches,
Intoxicated from wines and spirits
Steeped in oil and fragrant essences.

"I will never be the beloved," I murmured. "I will never be the beloved," I repeated over and over as the blows continued.

"Son, still your arm and drop your lash." Our mother's strong command managed to find its way to my ears.

The sting from the whip stopped, but the wounds it had inflicted began to throb instantly. I lifted my head and blinked to see through hazy confusion. Sarai stood behind Mother. She had not stayed on the bench but had bravely fled and sought help. I felt grateful again.

"She is to be my wife, Mother. I am free to discipline her as I see the need to do so."

"She is not your wife yet, Merikare. She is my daughter and a princess of Egypt. You will not strike her again. *Ever.* You stand in the royal women's residence and have no place here. You need to leave. Now."

Merikare threw the stick at me. It landed solidly on my back and rolled off. "We can take this up again on our wedding night, dear sister."

Sarai rushed to my side as he stormed away.

Mother grabbed Merikare by the arm as he started past her. "Son, I had high hopes that you would be a good king. What has happened to you? When did you grow so malicious?"

"Is it malicious to save her from herself? Would you rather see her body mutilated and impaled upon a stake? That is what happens to blasphemers in Egypt." He looked dangerously at Sarai.

Then darkness overtook me.

I woke to the smell of myrrh and frankincense and the most horrendous pain in my head.

Meti spoke incantations over me, magic chants, from a spell to Sekhmet, the goddess of physical healing who also cured possession by evil spirits. His voice changed from a whisper to a shout, and then a whisper again.

I wanted to sit up, but I couldn't. My own body wouldn't listen to me. I wondered why Meti was here and what the purpose was of the words he chanted. "Meti, have I been sleeping?" I croaked out, my mouth dry, my tongue thick.

"You speak. My daughter, it has been two days." Mother took my hand and gently squeezed it. "It is good to have you back."

My head ached fiercely. I couldn't remember what happened, and I was curiously immobile. I laid on my stomach, and from the earthy herb scent, I knew a poultice made from the leaves of a sycamore and honey covered my back. The heaviness meant fresh meat also laid on top of me, which suggested open wounds. "Am I going to die?" I whispered.

"We weren't sure for a while, Princess. You have a deep gash on your head, penetrating to the bone," Meti said. "You hit the stone bench by the pond when you fell. But if you can speak, then your mouth is not bound, and your jaw is not locked."

My mind cleared enough to understand that Meti would only be here because I was caught on that precarious, suspended scale that balanced life and death. Life in one pan and the heaviness of death added to the other pan—until one outweighed the other. But I was thankful for the high priest's attendance. There were no better hands to be in if sick or injured in Egypt.

Mother wept beside me.

"Do you promise, Meti?" I said, my voice hoarse. "That I'm not dying? Let your words be truthful to me, no matter what." I slanted my eyes to look at him. But the world blurred, and the light hurt. I closed them again.

Meti's tone was warm. "Someday, you will go to the house of your fathers, as we all will. But not today, Princess. Not today. That is the truth. I need you to lift your head a little for me if you can. Tell me if your neck is stiff."

I tried and screamed out. "It's not my neck, Meti. It's my head. It feels like everything burst inside."

"That's all right, Hagar. The pain will go away in time. It is an ailment that can be treated." His hand found mine, and I curled my fingers around it. "Think of shaking a goose egg. Your brain is like the yoke. It's been jangled, but the white part keeps it intact." He squeezed my fingers tenderly. "If your jaw had locked and your neck was stiff, there would have been nothing we could do for you." He released my hand. "Your silence is better than chatter now. You need to rest."

Meti spoke incantations over me again. I recognized them as part of my instruction in the temple. He was trying to determine what evil entity possessed me. Then he would drive it out.

Sarai's god. He is trying to remove the joy of him from my soul. But he has invited me to join him, and I will never look back.

"All-knowing Amun-Ra. Who is this god who has arrived? May this god be seized. Draw him out of our loved one, Amun-Ra," Meti chanted. "He is not welcome with us. May this god be seized, Amun-Ra. He is not welcome with us."

I tried to follow his words, to understand what he was asking of Amun-Ra, so that I could fight back. But my mind muddled. It hurt to think.

"Smite the evil spirit, and part the being from the one who loves you. May this god be seized, Amun-Ra, he is not welcome with us." Meti spoke in a singsong way, and I almost drifted back to sleep.

Had I slept for two days?

No. I had not been sleeping.

I drifted away from my body and hovered above Mother and Meti. I could hear Meti reciting spells and Mother crying. But I felt amazing peace and started toward a bright light. I wanted to run to it, to fly to it, but suddenly I returned to my body, and awful pain. That was when I strained to open my eyes, and my words were consumed whole, only allowing a small cry.

Something nudged my memory—something from the darkness I had been in. I struggled in my mind to recall it, my thoughts abnormally disordered. I remembered knowing that life ebbed within me. I had thought about my mother and father, and about how bright and blue the sky was. I remembered fighting to glimpse the sun and to see my family again.

I fought to live.

I laid there on my stomach, my head rested on my right cheek. Warm tears drifted down and puddled. My tongue reached for them and was glad to be able to taste their salt. I knew it meant I made it out of the darkness.

Something else tried to make its way out of the chaos of my mind. Bright blue eyes filled with light. "Where is Sarai? Someone intruded on us when we were speaking in the garden. I remember that now. Is she all right? Has she also been injured?"

Meti kept chanting.

Mother leaned in. "Sarai is fine. No harm has come to her. She was here in the beginning and helped wash the blood from your back and your head. There were handfuls of blood." She stifled a sob. "She has not taken food or drink since this happened and remains prostrate on the ground in grief."

"O, Mother! Now I remember everything." I began to shiver, cold to the depth of my being. "My injuries have been inflicted on me by the hand of my brother. Why would Merikare do this to me?"

Meti went silent.

Mother cried openly.

And the world fell dark again.

Gentle singing.

A lullaby. I opened my eyes. It was the song Mother sang to all the babes she brought into this world. I laid still a moment and listened, the sound so sweet I wished I could hear it every day as long as I lived.

My eyes adjusted to the light, and I realized the pain in my head had subsided. I rose, slow, unsteady. I gritted my teeth against the tight ache in my back.

The singing stopped. "You should not move yet, Hagar. Let me send for Meti first," Mother said.

"How long have I slept this time?" My voice rasped around a dry throat.

"Two days again."

"I'm thirsty and my stomach is in distress." I forced a smile for her. "Mother, I'm starving."

The Great Royal Wife didn't have to lift her hand. Bunefer already raced away. Mother removed the poultices and meat that covered my back and head. I winced as she lifted me gently and helped me lean against a large pillow. She poured water into a cup and held it while I took a sip. I gulped greedily, and she pulled the cup away. "Easy, Daughter, easy."

Bunefer returned, dragged a table next to me, and placed a large bowl full of savory waterfowl and lentil stew on it. I could smell the onions and garlic that flavored the rich broth it simmered in. Mother took a piece of flatbread and scooped a small bite of stew into my mouth.

"Don't go easy, Mother."

"You cannot eat too fast, Hagar."

"I can only obey my belly." I grinned, this time without effort. "And rejoice that I am among the living and able to sate my thirst and hunger."

Mother laughed, and I devoured every bite she brought to my lips.

"When I first saw the head injury, Hagar, I did not think you would make it. It cut the heart out of me. No one survives such a blow."

I tried to sit up further and grimaced, the skin on my back pulling against me.

She sprang up to help. "Your back is healing remarkably well. The swelling and redness are gone, and scabs are forming. Some of the stripes on your back are deep but will heal in time. Most of them won't leave a scar. But there are one or two you will probably carry the rest of your life."

Mother turned her head from me, but I saw the tears fall to the floor anyway.

Chapter Thirty-Five

SARAI ENTERED WITH TAMERI. THEY BOWED before my mother and rushed to me. Sarai kneeled and took my outstretched hands in hers. Her eyes, those brilliant gems, glistened with tears. "All things considered, you look wonderful, Hagar," she gushed. She lightly kissed my fingers, her face equally mixed with grief, love, and guilt. "I am so sorry. I know I brought this upon you."

"I won't bathe in self-pity, Sarai. Neither should you. Even the thought of it sickens me."

Tameri pushed my shoulders away from the pillow and inspected my injuries so close I could feel her warm breath on my back. "Pharaoh called for Meti, and my honorable husband, Rensi, the high vizier, to be present when Merikare brought his complaint about you."

My stomach fluttered. "Merikare complained to our father about me?"

"O, yes, Hagar. He claims he heard you willingly agree to let Sarai's god possess you, that you intended to turn your back on the gods of Egypt. On Pharaoh himself." She ran a finger across one of the wounds. I flinched.

"Noblewoman Tameri, that is a conversation for another day," the Great Royal Wife said.

"No, Mother. Please. I must hear this."

Mother raised her hands in surrender, and Tameri continued. "Rensi, the high vizier, my noble husband, tried to convince them that it is only your bright and curious mind at work. He explained that Sarai would have come to Egypt with her own opinions of the gods, as all foreigners do. That you are always curious about things you don't understand. 'Hagar has gained great respect through knowledge, and naturally, she would want to learn all she can about Sarai's culture.' Those are the exact words of Rensi, the high vizier. My husband."

So like Rensi to protect me.

Tameri stopped her inspection and reached in front of me, taking a large chunk of goose breast from my stew. I flinched again as warm broth dripped on my skin. She didn't seem to notice. "Meti agreed with him but offered to exorcise the spirit from you. Just in case." She popped the entire chunk into her mouth.

The Great Royal Wife gestured to Tameri and Sarai to take a seat. "Tameri, our princess does not need to become distressed over these matters. She needs to heal."

"It's all right, Mother. Really, I'm fine." I looked at Tameri. "Is there more?"

"Your brother claims your curious mind has turned dangerous. He has charged that you are treading on treason. He asked your father to allow your marriage to go on as soon as you are recovered. He wants full control over you. Whom you speak to…" She looked at Sarai. "Where you go and what you do."

Heat rushed to my cheeks. "I thought perhaps the king would see the danger I am in and not force this fate on me. If he allows the marriage, Merikare will make a prisoner of me in my own home. Why are Father's eyes blind to that? And what is causing my brother to be so hot-bellied toward me? I can't believe this all comes from his desire to please Imi."

"What Merikare claims is not the spouting of the hot-bellied," Mother said. "He did hear all that he reported to Pharaoh." She looked from me to Sarai and then back to me. "And he was fierce speaking of it. His countenance turned black as a thundercloud, his tongue so savage toward you, it caused fear to strike my heart. I don't know who he is anymore. But his claims upon you have become quite loud now."

I gathered my courage. "I observed him during the storm. He was strong and decisive, Mother. He was skillful and courageous in the fray. He was a king. I felt hope in what I saw. You should not lose faith in him."

"You and Merikare have been at odds with one another since before you could walk. He would reach over and pull your hair and you would swat him with whatever toy you had in your hand. He was always the first to cry. As you grew, that never seemed to change. He would seek to hurt you, you would strike back, and he would run for comfort or to tattle as though you started it." The face of the Great Royal Wife looked pale and beaten. "It seemed childish, and we even found humor in how you stood up to your brother. But we never saw this level of hostility or hatred between the two of you."

"It is the influence of the two sisters upon him," Tameri said. "They have possessed him with evil spirits. When they heard what Merikare did to you, they giggled."

I bit my lip. "Are you sure, Tameri? If you want our friendship to endure, please be silent if your words are not true."

"They giggled, Princess. I was with them. They were gleeful." She turned her face firmly toward mine. "Merikare has promised Imi your chambers as soon as you and he are wed. She told the crown prince that is all that will make her happy for now."

I looked down at my fingers.

"Until she can get her hands on my chambers," the Great Royal Wife said.

"Now that Merikare has raised a hand to me, will the king listen if I plead to break our betrothal?"

Mother lowered her head. "No. He judged what happened to you as an accident. And that Merikare believed he was doing the right thing. Merikare is not the first man to punish a woman with a beating."

"So, I wait for them to kill me?"

"He swore to the king he would not touch you again like this. But I have observed my son. He has become deceitful to men and the gods." Mother's shoulders drooped. "Merikare has always been jealous of you, Hagar. Your authority reaches wide, and he sees how much our people love and respect you.

He knows they prefer you to him. Imi is fuel to that hateful flame."

I looked at Sarai. She had been quiet through our discourse.

Tameri took a deep breath and let it out in a gush. "What worried Rensi, the high vizier, my noble husband, is that Merikare does not feel he was in the wrong raging at you. He acknowledged that it was unfortunate you lost your footing and hit your head. But he does not believe that he was at fault. He says it was the judgment of the gods. The high vizier, my husband, thinks Merikare sees marriage as his opportunity to be able to conquer you."

I looked at my mother. "And my father is willing to grant him such power?"

Her blank stare absorbed all the air in the room.

"Speaking of Father, has he been to see me?"

Mother placed her hand on my arm. "Your father has been here several times each day. I sent word to him that you are awake and sitting up and eating. He will come again soon."

I looked into her large amber eyes, the same eyes I saw in my reflection. "Will you plead for me for this wedding to be delayed?"

She nodded and smiled, but her gaze did not reveal any hope.

"Imi is not the only one good at scheming," Tameri said and looked at the Great Royal Wife, who gave a crisp nod. "We have solved part of your problem. The high vizier, my husband, found a nobleman willing to marry Amisi. He has lost two young wives in childbirth and desires the body of another. He is wealthy and the sisters have no good reason to object."

I was genuinely becoming quite fond of Tameri. "I know all the nobles of Henen-nesut," I said. "Who is the unfortunate fellow?"

"Masaharta," Mother said.

I smiled. "There is a man who can hold his own."

Masaharta was as stern a man as I had ever met. He wasn't

ruthless—at least, I had never heard an account when he was. But he was strict and abrasive, not one to give in to foolishness from a female. He was tall and slim, with a long nose and lips that always remained in a tight, perfect line.

"May the gods protect him while he sleeps," Mother said, and we all chuckled.

"When will this take place?" I closed my eyes, and a small amount of relief surrounded me.

"As we sit here," Tameri said. "His men arrived a short while ago to escort her to his house in Memphis. They will remain there until the reconstruction of his house in Henennesut. I have wished my ears were deaf many times since I've been the guardian of those girls. I've never heard such terrible yelling and cursing. Today was the worst of it." She smiled. "Is it wrong to greatly enjoy the distress of others?"

"Surely it could not have been all that bad," I said. "They knew the day would come when Amisi would marry and move away. It may have surprised them, but such a match for her will lift her high in rank."

"Those girls love an hour of fighting with each other more than a day of rejoicing. I have never met anyone like them. Merikare has plowed in a most disagreeable field." Tameri reached for the cup of wine Bunefer offered her. "Imi sent word for Merikare to come to her and then called him every name she could lay her tongue to."

This startled my mother. "An enemy has surely come among us in Imi. How can my son have eyes so blind and ears so unable to hear? I have voiced my objection regarding Imi since the day she arrived. Yet, it only vexes him if I speak against her. He is the crown prince, and she treats him like her servant. I know she possesses him with dark magic. Sadly, my royal husband is blind to it."

"I have never heard them speak magical words or chant spells, but I am quite sure I know what she holds over him," Tameri said. "She sent him a message this morning after Masaharta's men arrived. Our faithful Pentu was the scribe she employed to write it."

Pentu. I smiled, recalling the squat boy with the crooked nose and crooked teeth—Bunefer's only child. Years before, he saved my life when an enemy of my father, the King of Waset, sent someone to kidnap me. Pentu had screamed and pelted him with stones from a slingshot that was nothing more than a child's toy. The man tried to club Pentu with a mace but could not get close enough to the agile, small boy. I wiggled out of the man's grasp and ran. Royal guards heard Pentu screaming and apprehended the scoundrel. If it were not for Pentu's bravery, I would probably be living in that king's harem today. My father awarded Pentu a post as scribe to the royal household for life.

Tameri continued, "Pentu said the words he recorded for her were, 'Do anything, postpone everything, and come. If I endure your absence any longer, you will find me hanged.'" She let the words settle on us for a moment. "Imi often threatens to take her life. I once heard her claim she would throw herself to the crocodiles if Merikare did not do something she demanded."

"No wonder my son does not act wisely regarding her. She carries his first child, and it would hinder its soul's progress after death if she took her life," Mother said. "It would disqualify both mother and child from a proper burial." She looked at Tameri. "Do you believe her threats to be truthful?"

"I believe they are nothing more than the attention-seeking antics of an unstable young woman. Some mornings she refuses to rise from her bed. Other mornings she rises with the energy of an untamed force. If she carries that vigor into the crown prince's bed, there is no wonder he is her captive."

"Will Merikare be able to stop Amisi from becoming Masaharta's bride?" Sarai's eyes were still fogged with emotion.

"No," Mother said. "I alone rule the single women in the harem, and only Pharaoh can countermand my decision. Rensi has had his ear regarding this matter for the last few days. He will let it stand, no matter how much the crown prince bellows on his bride's behalf."

"Sarai," I said, "what troubles you? I know your heart is burdened. I assure you, this was not your fault, and I am recovering."

"I have never been more worried about anything, Princess. That is true." Sarai said. "I am grateful that you are improved and believe you will mend. I have …" Her voice cracked.

"Sarai has been ordered to Pharaoh's chambers this evening," Tameri finished. "Once the king heard you were out of danger, he sent word for her to come to him. Tonight, he is taking his rights as her husband."

Sarai hung her head as if all the shame of the world fell upon her.

"There is no dishonor in coupling," I said softly.

"And you need not be embarrassed in front of me," the Great Royal Wife said. "We all have the same duty to the king if he calls upon us. When a new woman comes to this harem, it is more my concern of how compatible she will be with the other women. We live in a small community, after all. You see how the drama Imi creates can disrupt the peace of the whole house. That is not the case with you, Sarai. You are a welcome addition."

I knew this to be partially true. Since I was a small child, I discerned unhappiness in my mother when a new bride or concubine came to my father. Mother truly loved the king, as a wife should. So how could she not grieve another in his bed?

"O, that I could turn back again to Canaan and not lie with him," Sarai cried, her outburst so sudden a jolt ran through me. "I am afraid it will only bring great woe. Sad woe."

"You sound as though you are facing a living death," Tameri countered. "Scores of virgins have rowed the king up and down the stream seated on the royal boat. I've never seen one bothered by it like you before. A good soak in the tub and some fine wine will calm the nerves."

"That will not be necessary." We all turned to see Rensi

entering Mother's chambers.

My spirits lifted quickly.

He bowed low before the Great Royal Wife. "Forgive me for intruding, but I came to see with my own eyes that it goes well for our beloved princess." He came close. "How happy I was when I heard of your recovery. It is said you will reach old age after all." His smile was infectious. I wanted to rise and give him a big hug. He turned to Sarai. "Unfortunately, the king took ill the moment he called for you. His stomach began to trouble him." Rensi looked at me and raised his eyebrows. "Meti assures us it is not serious, only a mild malady that will take a quiet night to remedy."

Hazy and confused thoughts entered my mind. Something Rensi said about the king taking ill troubled me. I tried hard to grasp what it was from my scrambled brain. I remembered that someone else was sick.

No.

A lot of people.

Charcoal. Limbs that looked like charcoal and cold, dead fingers gripping my body. I began to tremble. I looked at Sarai and saw the alarm on her face. "I had another vision."

"What did you see?" Sarai whispered.

"O, not another cursed dream," Tameri complained. "Give this message to that god you see. Tell him to depart and leave us in peace. We want to hear nothing more from him."

"Guard your tongue, foolish woman," Rensi said. "Her dream was the gift that saved us from the storm. Your words may only anger the god who sent it. Like they anger me."

Tameri pouted. "But if she doesn't give voice to it, maybe it will not come to be."

"The storm would have come with her warning or without it," Sarai said. "I know that much to be true."

"I cannot put it into place. The vision flees even though I am trying to hang on to it." As the words passed from my lips, I had the sensation that I was falling. Strong arms grabbed me and held me upright. I smelled mint and knew Rensi caught me again. He chewed peppermint leaves to relieve stomach pains.

"No one will discuss dreams and visions with my daughter until she is completely healed," the Great Royal Wife commanded in her imperial voice.

"My head took me for a spin, Mother," I said carefully. "I feel fine now."

Rensi relaxed his grip but remained close to me.

My words did not move the Great Royal Wife. "No more of this talk, Hagar. You cannot risk it. Your mouth will remain silent and everyone must leave."

Rensi bowed immediately, followed by his noble wife, Tameri, and Sarai. Rensi and Sarai wore troubled expressions as they departed. Tameri glanced sadly at my stew and the chunks of waterfowl she left behind.

Mother helped me lie down and kissed both of my cheeks. She pulled a light sheet over me. "Don't make me scold you, Hagar," she said tenderly. "You were on the edge of death. You are safe now. I want to keep you that way."

I delighted in her blissful attention toward me. "How good to know the love of a mother," I whispered and closed my eyes.

Chapter Thirty-Six

I INHALED THE HEADY AROMA OF lilies near my bath and
thanked Kiya. Anyone could see the worry in her wrinkled
brow, and I sincerely appreciated it. I was different from the
girl who almost died a few weeks before. I'd become a woman
who found inexpressible joy in small kindnesses, in the
everyday beauty of a sunrise and sunset, in every bird, flower,
or cry of an infant.

In being alive.

I gasped as the bathwater touched the wounds on my
back. I took a moment, pulled my knees up to my chin, feeling
the tug of the scabs, and let the sting subside. When I was
ready, I slid gently beneath the water and let it spread
pleasantly up to my neck. I closed my eyes, still sensitive to the
light, and soaked my bones and broken skin.

All the doors stood open, yet not a hint of a breeze
provided relief from the hot, dry air. I could hear activity in the
halls, women chatting, feet shuffling, while Dendera and Kiya
stood over me, fanning. I rarely allowed them to spend their
time in such a way, but they insisted, so great was their
happiness that I'd finally returned. Bastet moved between their
legs and purred. They said the clever cat found her way home
the very day after Imi made off with her.

I stayed in Mother's chambers until she decided I had
recovered enough to go to my own. She made sure I got my
rest, fussed over me, and asked me how I felt every time I
twitched a muscle. Her eyebrows drew tight together, and the
circles under her eyes darkened. So I told her, "Fine, Mother,
all better," even though my head ached and the world still
looked a little hazy.

Bunefer had dismissed my girls while I was convalescing
because she said they were in her way. But when Imi came and
curtly told her they would serve her until I mended, Bunefer

boldly told her no. She was a huge and intimidating woman, and it delighted me to hear that even Imi was reluctant to press her.

Bunefer had the largest hands I'd ever seen on a woman, and they had terrified me as a child. For no good reason. During my time in her care, I realized they were the gentlest hands in Egypt.

Bunefer had my servants check in with her daily and gave them tasks to do in the name of the Great Royal Wife. We all knew it was her way of protecting them from the predatory, scheming Princess Imi. She had them rock babies in the royal nursery or help our cooks, Bak-Mut and Ramose, in the kitchen. Bunefer and Bak-Mut were best friends and two of a kind. I once heard Bunefer say of Bak-Mut, "She is darker than midnight and larger than a hippopotamus. But don't tell her I said that. She'll never let me near her kitchen again." She laughed so hard, tears streamed down her face. I had smiled and thought she could have been describing herself.

Now, Dendera washed my hair and gently massaged my scalp but carefully avoided the head wound. "It looks so much better," she told me. She hummed sweetly, gushed about her time in the kitchen, and then hummed again. She had loved every moment of it. I knew she still stole off and helped knead dough, mix hearty stews, or gather fresh herbs. Kiya told me the cooks boasted that Dendera knew how to prepare any cut of meat delivered to the kitchen.

"There is no better baker than Ramose," Dendera said as she poured clear water through my hair, rinsing away the smoky, sweet scent of myrrh from the soap.

Ah, Ramose. There is that name again.

"He slaps dough on the inner wall of the clay oven and peels it off when it is done faster than anyone," she said, admiration in her voice. "He makes the very best Tigernut Sweets in the palace. And his flatbread, flavored with nuts and dates, is beyond description. Ramose is young and quick and curious about everything. He works very hard and is always happy for my extra pair of hands."

I bet he is. I smiled at her pretty face. "What does he look like?"

"Who?" she said innocently. "Ramose?"

I nodded and watched her eyes become warm pools.

"'Who? Ramose?'" Kiya mimicked. "It is the only name out of your mouth anymore."

Dendera blushed. "O, Kiya. That is not true."

Kiya giggled.

"What does he look like?" I repeated.

She cleared her throat. "Well, he is tall and thin but has very broad shoulders and strong arms." Her face sparkled as she spoke. "I don't know," she added, squirming. "He looks like a cook, I suppose." She helped me rise from the tub and dried me with a soft linen cloth.

The air felt cool, almost cold, as I stood damp under the easy rhythmic motion of Kiya and her great ostrich feather. Dendera looked away, but I could see she smiled. I knew Ramose was on her mind. *Good for you.* I remembered that quickening of love. There was nothing like it. A faint thought drifted into my head. *Abram.* I had tried to let them go, those thoughts of him, but once in a while, they crept in uninvited.

"Pardon me, Princess Hagar, but I need a moment."

I turned to see Imi at my door with two miserable-looking girls. One had a red welt on her cheek as Kiya had worn after dealing with Imi. The other had scratch marks on her arms as though she'd wrestled with a wild cat and lost.

My head instantly began to ache. "Of course, Princess Imi. Please come in." Dendera quickly pulled a linen kalasiris over my head and gently ran a comb through my hair. "Would you like to sit down? Can my girls get you a cup of wine?" I motioned at Kiya to stop fanning.

Imi stayed firmly planted by the door. She wore a long kalasiris so finely woven it was nearly transparent. An ornate wig and crown with a rearing cobra sat upon her head. "I want nothing from you," she seethed. "I've waited until you returned to let you know I am not a fool."

"You will have to pardon me now, Imi. I have no idea what you speak of. I have never called you a fool."

"It was because of you that Amisi was sent away." Her hand reached out unexpectedly, and both of her girls flinched. "I desired that my sister live with me and be my royal companion when my dear husband is away. It was a shameful deed sending her from the palace. It agitates my heart along with all else you have done to me."

"I understand you miss your sister. But how could I have arranged a marriage contract for her while I was unconscious?"

Her gaze was stony, revealing her contempt.

"The match will be good for Amisi. She has been lifted to a status I'm sure she never dreamed of before."

"O, so you claim to know what was in her dreams?"

"No. Of course not," I said cautiously, trying not to incite her. "But I pray she will find health and happiness there." I searched her face, attempting to assess how far I could go. "I am disappointed, Imi. I hoped your visit meant you were coming around to a reconciliation between us."

"I will never come around to that. We will never be on friendly terms, Princess. Not until I see you dead and buried in your tomb."

I raised my hand, and Dendera stopped combing. "Do not besmirch me, Imi." My head pounded. "You should know better than to wish ill on a member of the royal family. If I go to Pharaoh, you may find yourself dead and buried before sunset."

"Not while I carry this." She rubbed her large belly. "And not after I become the divine mother of a future pharaoh."

My eyes met Imi's and held there. "I have done nothing to you. Consider the good fortune that brought you here, count your many blessings, and stop trying to destroy the family who has embraced you."

Her fists grabbed the elegant wig she wore and wrenched it off her head. She threw the plaited human hair at my feet as

Sarai walked in from the garden with Kiya trailing her. I hadn't noticed Kiya slip out but had no doubt she followed instructions from the Great Royal Wife.

"Princess Imi," Sarai said. "Your tongue is like a spear. It cuts the silence and stabs at the soul. Do you know that a good nature is like heaven to a man? Perhaps you should try to befriend this town and praise its people, so your memorial will be of love and not of loathing."

"Save your skilled speech for my foe, Sarai," Imi hissed. "Your blasphemous teachings don't interest me. And being the king's favorite now won't save you forever."

"That, I don't know. But I do know my life will never be in your hands."

Their words clattered inside my throbbing head. I couldn't grasp what they were saying. If they slowed down, perhaps I could follow the conversation. The sun took up too much space in the room. The light bothered my eyes.

Then the world spun thick and heavy and filled with pain.

Chapter Thirty-Seven

SARAI AND KIYA GRASPED MY ARMS and helped me to the couch.

"Your head is swollen, Hagar," Sarai said as she gently moved my wet hair to inspect the wound. "These injuries take a long time to heal, and you are already doing too much."

Kiya trembled as she turned to Imi. "My apologies, Princess Imi, but the Great Royal Wife has instructed me to limit Princess Hagar's visitors. You don't mind coming back another time?"

Imi's face lit up like a torch. She took a step forward as though she meant to strike Kiya.

Sarai stood. "We all have the same instructions. I'm sure you understand."

Imi didn't say another word, turned, and stalked out. The two pathetic creatures with her lowered their heads and shoulders and followed her.

I looked at Kiya. "Really? My mother told you to stand against that one?"

She nodded. "And Bunefer, and the high priest, Meti. They told me not to fear her. But I can't stop my bones from shaking when they have a mind to."

"We've all conspired to keep her from you as long as we can," Sarai said.

"My harem of mother hens." I bid Kiya come closer, pulled her head down, and kissed the exact center of her lovely forehead. Then I decided on a lighter subject. "Before Imi came in, Sarai, we were discussing Ramose from the kitchen. Dendera seems to have taken quite a liking to him."

Dendera grabbed her cheeks and turned away. "O, mistress. You can't think—"

"I've seen that look before," Sarai said. "On your face, Hagar. Every time I mention Abram."

I blushed hearing Sarai charging me with affection toward her brother. And for a moment, I remembered the look he had given her last year at the festival. But the sound of his name caused my heart to flutter, and I found so much pleasure hearing it, I decided not to think about anything upsetting. "Let's not turn the tide toward me." I laid back against the pillows Kiya fluffed behind me. "We were discussing Ramose."

Dendera covered her face with her hands, but I could still see her smile.

Sarai sat near me and placed both hands in her lap. "Have you ever been enchanted by a man besides Abram before?"

My chest tightened. "I have a head injury, you know. You shouldn't make me feel like I need to take flight. It takes a vast amount of effort to spread wings and fly."

Kiya laughed timidly. "That is not a secret to any of us, Princess Hagar."

Dendera nodded. "It is no secret," she muttered and giggled.

"You are not the first to find my ... brother ... fascinating." She laid a tender hand on my arm. "But you are so young. I'm sure you've not been in love before. And trust me when I say, you probably are not now. I know Abram is attractive and extraordinary—"

"Appealing and alluring," I added. "He has great energy and a powerful mind."

Sarai nodded. "Men like that pull women like us in. I understand how you can feel drawn to him."

I looked into her knowing eyes and laughed. "I admit I was in awe when I first met him." I looked at Dendera and smiled. "It was a new feeling for me too."

Dendera reddened.

Kiya giggled again.

"Abram has done amazing things," I continued, "and I believe I could learn much from him."

"Your feelings may be intense but are probably not

romantic," Sarai said. "Not like our dear Dendera's are for Ramose."

Dendera half turned toward us, her face down, but she still smiled. "Royal women, this servant is not worthy of your attention. I admit he has sparked an emotion unfamiliar to me, and I have imagined my life with him, but it will pass."

"Only if it's gassiness and not true love, Dendera," I jested.

Kiya giggled more.

Sarai leaned toward me. "I did not want this between us, Hagar. I want us to be able to speak on all things and know it is safe to do so."

"I would like that too, Sarai."

Imi's pitiful servant, the one covered in scratches, rushed through the door. "Please come. Please help me," she said and turned and ran out again.

I looked at Sarai. We rose and followed the girl down the hallway and found Imi hunched on the ground. "It's my belly," she cried.

Sarai knelt by her side. "Did this just happen now?"

"No," Imi yelled. "It has kept sleep from me all night. But the pains were not as they said they would be. They were only small cramps, like before my monthly blood. But now I cannot get up. There is an awful pain in my back. Annoying, uncomfortable pain. And I need to push."

"Imi," Sarai said, urgent. "Try and resist that urge for now."

Imi's breasts leaked fluid on her fine linen kalasiris and a pool of bloody water puddled around her on the floor.

"You have been in labor, Imi. I believe your time is here," I said. "Your child is coming today. Now." I looked at Sarai. "We need to get her to the birthing pavilion."

Dendera ran off in the direction of my mother's chambers. Kiya dashed off for the royal midwives.

We helped Imi up and walked slowly, frequently stopping, her pains rhythmic and close together. Sweat beaded and dripped down her face. She groaned loud and screamed profanities when a birth spasm ripped through her body. I tried to rub her back, but she screamed that she did not want to be touched.

She cursed my brother.

She cursed me.

She shook and shivered.

My head pounded in my skull. I knew we would never make it to the pavilion.

The birthing pavilion sat in a quiet corner away from all other activities. It had a matted roof for shade and birthing bricks for the delivering mother to squat on. Carved images circled all around it of Hathor and Taweret, the goddesses who assisted with childbirth. But Imi would have to deliver without the protection from their magic. It was on the other side of the harem and may as well have been on the other side of the Nile.

The Great Royal Wife caught up with us quickly with Bunefer and Dendera.

I gave a massive sigh of relief. "Royal Mother, I am not sure we will make it to the pavilion."

"I will not have my child here, with you," Imi objected and looked at me darkly. "I must be in the pavilion surrounded by midwives and the gods of Egypt. It is the proper way for a future pharaoh to come into the world."

"Let's not put the crook and flail into this child's hands just yet, Imi," the Great Royal Wife said.

"You care nothing for my child," Imi cried as she doubled over with pain.

Mother let the spasm pass without a word, her face stoic through all of Imi's screaming and cursing. "This is my first grandchild, Imi," the Great Royal Wife finally said. "He or she is very important to me, regardless of the circumstances of birth. But I assure you that you are delivering your child now, and until the midwives arrive, we will have to do."

Imi's red face streamed with tears. "I ... have ... to ...

push …"

Dendera helped me raise her linen kalasiris over her head, and we tossed it to the side. Bunefer and Sarai each gripped one of her hands and helped Imi to squat. Her two servants huddled together across from us. Dendera ran off again. I knew she looked for a servant whose monthly blood flowed. We would rub it over the infant to keep away demons who sought to harm newborns.

Kiya had still not returned with the midwives.

Mother saw Imi's two terrified servant girls. "Run to the kitchen and ask the cooks for Nile perch stewed in oil. They keep it on hand when women are expecting in the harem." The girls stood still and did not move. "Quickly," Mother shouted.

They scampered off.

Sarai looked at me curiously.

"It's used to massage a new mother's back so her milk will come in. But it has to be done as soon as the baby is delivered."

Sarai nodded. "Royal women nurse their infants?"

"Not all. But Imi has requested to do so."

"I will not give anyone a chance to murder my son," Imi screeched.

"No one would seek to harm the crown prince's child," the Great Royal Wife said softly. "And do not be disappointed if it's a girl. Daughters are a blessing to the soul." She looked at me and smiled.

"It is not a girl," Imi insisted as she gritted her teeth, clenched Sarai and Bunefer's hands, and pushed. She leaned over and vomited. The smell made me heave involuntarily. Imi wailed and begged the gods for help.

Sarai and Bunefer moved her back several paces to avoid the mess.

I went to my knees in front of Imi. I reached up and felt the crown of her child's head. "Push one more time, Imi. Make it a good one."

A series of vile words followed my plea. Some I had never

heard before. Again, she cursed my brother, as well as the entire royal family, shivered uncontrollably, but gave one more hard push.

Imi's infant son slid into my waiting arms. His wrinkled little body was greasy and covered in something cheese-like. My heart pounded. He was blue and didn't move. I quickly wiped out his mouth with my fingers, and his face turned red, his lips quivered, and he bellowed loudly.

The cries took my breath away.

Chapter Thirty-Eight

I STEPPED LIGHTLY INTO MERIKARE'S CHAMBERS and spied my nephew in the arms of his mother. I had not seen him since the day his slippery body plunged into my hands. Now, protective amulets circled his little arms and legs, and a small crown sat upon his head. My lips parted, and everything in me softened. Babies had shared the harem with me my entire life, but I never gave them much thought. Yet this one I found interesting. I had marveled at how perfectly formed he was when he took his first breath in my arms. But when he curled his tiny fingers around mine—I became undone.

Father and Mother were already there, Meti and Rensi too. Mother took her grandson from Imi and swayed and cooed. The black kohl around her eyes smudged from proud tears gushed over the child. Pharaoh stood with the high priest and high vizier a few steps away, his hands clasped behind him.

I bowed before my royal parents. "Life, health, and strength be to you," I said, stood and kissed both of them, then nodded at Meti and Rensi. I looked at my nephew's adorable face and leaned over for a long, deep sniff of his head. I wished I could capture his intoxicating, newborn scent in one of my alabaster flasks.

Imi smiled, but her teeth set against me. "I'm surprised to see such affection from you toward my son, Princess Hagar." Her short wig just brushed her bare shoulders and prettily framed her square and perfect face as the bangs softened her broad forehead. "The high priest just told us a magician from Saqqara uttered a prophecy to him before I gave birth. 'Imi, First Wife of Merikare, will bear a son. One day, he will rule in Egypt.' I hope your love for him will last now that you have heard the foretelling."

My mother raised her eyes to me.

I smiled pleasantly. "I believe I will always have a

particular fondness for him."

Imi muttered something under her breath that I could not hear. However, from her pinched expression and the way she crossed her arms over her chest, I believed she cursed me. But her face transformed into something enchanting when she turned toward the others. She treated them kindly, as guests, and offered them wine.

I backed against a long wall with a painted relief of Merikare being embraced by a goddess. I peered at the rendering of my brother's handsome face, midnight-black eyes, and well-crafted, dimpled chin. His son had that same striking face and dimple in his chin. I tried to melt into it, letting the dry air swallow me, remembering the feel of holding the infant.

This was Merikare's first son's name day, and my brother summoned me here to observe but not take part. I guessed that his wife insisted I be present so she could bask in her superior position over me. I imagined she thought I hated her child for being a boy.

I wasn't sorry I disappointed her.

Merikare took his son from our mother and lifted him high over his head. "Akhtoy," he said. "I have named him Akhtoy." The high priest murmured a blessing. Merikare lowered the child, and Meti anointed Akhtoy with sweet-smelling sacred oil believed to originate from the eyes of the gods. Merikare turned to Imi and handed Akhtoy to her. "She gave birth to this baby that you see. His name will be entered into the House of Life, and her name will be revered forever." Imi gave her son a warm smile and clucked and fussed over him as all good mothers do. Then she wallowed in the glow and fawning of my parent's approval.

I watched the scene, detached, with a lack of emotion for Merikare or Imi. Only for Akhtoy did my heart quicken. I secretly wished he was mine. "It pleases me more than bread or beer, like ointment to my soul, that you have a goodly inheritance in the land of Egypt, Princess Imi," I said, quoting an old proverb from my place against the wall. "And may

Akhtoy be the eldest of many sons." The skin twitched around my mouth, and I pretended to lift a cup of wine that I had not been offered.

Feigning happiness for Imi did not fool anyone. Mother gave me *that* look. Rensi's mouth turned up at the edges, while Meti gazed at me similar to the way my mother did. Imi snorted loudly. Merikare smirked.

My father didn't regard me one way or the other.

I smiled pleasantly again, as though I genuinely meant every word, and pressed a little harder into the wall.

Honestly, it did not bother me that Imi had a boy. It relieved me and sealed my desire not to marry the crown prince. Imi was welcome, as far as I was concerned, to become the Great Royal Wife. I would ask my brother today to release me. Merikare could choose another royal bride, any of our sisters—even Ana, who he was so fond of—to ensure his succession to the throne. I would promise never to marry, live my days in the temple or simply slip away to whatever exile he thought acceptable. A complication out of their lives forever. I knew that meant I would never hold children of my own in my arms. A deep pit plunged in my stomach thinking about Akhtoy, but in the end, the sacrifice would be worth it.

For the sake of peace.

A fat, squat woman with heavy breasts entered and stood with her head down in the corner—a wet nurse. Imi had obviously decided to do what most royal women did and entrust their child to another. The realities of caring for an infant probably quickly overtook her paranoia that someone would seek to do him harm.

The king and his wife departed after we all bowed again, followed by Meti and Rensi. I remained against the wall, hoping to find a moment with Merikare.

Imi barked at the woman with heavy breasts, who scampered over to take her charge. Imi roughly pushed Akhtoy into her arms. My mouth fell open. Akhtoy started to complain, but the wet nurse gave him a nipple, and he took it with passion. Merikare didn't blink, as though nothing was wrong with Imi's abrupt change in behavior.

The crown prince gave Imi an impassioned kiss on the lips, for my benefit, I supposed and turned to leave. Precisely what I had hoped for. I forced a smile and nodded at Imi—who flicked one hand toward me as if to dismiss me. I stole another glance toward my nephew and followed Merikare out.

"Merikare, may we speak a moment?"

"Make it fast, sister." He looked at me with narrowed eyes and a clenched jaw. "I have much to celebrate, and libations are flowing freely. My royal companions, and the women they have chosen, are waiting to entertain me."

I flushed from the sting of his harsh manner and forced myself to take a slow, deep breath to calm myself. "Dear brother." My tone dripped sweetness and light. "You are the champion of our people, the son praised by the king, standing high since birth. You have no need of me in your life. I am only a difficulty to you. I ask that you consider picking amongst our sisters—someone who does not distress your wife as much as I do. Let me live my life unmarried, in the temple, or wherever you wish me to go." Before I could stop it, a tear dropped on my linen kalasiris. And then another. "Please, Merikare. Let me go."

His abrupt halt startled me. "We all have a duty to Egypt, Hagar." He gritted his teeth. "Yours is to marry me and become the next Great Royal Wife. At least in appearance. It is the condition I gave, before the scribes, so Father would allow me to marry Imi. It may as well be set in stone." He stepped close to me, the pungent smell of onions and garlic on his warm breath. "We will marry on Wepet Renpet, and at the start of the new year, you will be mine to control." He laughed callously. "O, mighty sage. How is it you discerned the fate of Egypt, yet failed to see your own future in your dreams?"

My heart jumped in my chest. "But we could talk to Father—"

"Set. In. Stone." He leaned even closer. "Why do the gods

hate you so much? All they had to do was make you a boy. Instead, they stole the crook and flail from you and placed them in my hands." His laughter echoed in the hall as he strutted away.

I did not follow him further. I recalled words Meti had said to Merikare when we were children. *"Young fellow, how vain you are. You do not listen when I speak, and your heart is denser than a great obelisk."* I watched him swagger away, likely feeling the same way Meti had that day.

Then my vision blurred, and my face grew hot thinking about how I'd turned soppy and cried in front of him. *Imi would have loved to have seen that.*

I wandered home and into my garden, drenched in self-pity and defeat. I inhaled the bloomy scent of scores of flowers starting to blossom. I touched several of them gently, as though saying goodbye. They would all belong to Imi soon.

I found a quiet place near my pond where the blue and white lotuses drifted. The same spot I had fallen when Merikare struck me. I went to my knees, and the crushed stones of the pathway dug into my skin. I lifted my hands heavenward and bowed my head. I sat still and waited for Sarai's god, hoping to be overcome by his unseen *presence* that settled on one soft as a breeze. I wanted him to tell me what to do and show me how to get what Sarai had.

Peace and joy.

Even when life appeared miserable and bleak.

Sarai always began her prayers with, "I will do and I will hear." It struck me as odd, and I told her so.

"That makes no sense," I had said. "Don't you mean exactly the opposite? Don't you hear first, and then do?"

"You have to *do this*, come before His *presence* in faith, before you can hear and understand His will for your life."

"O, Sarai. You are teaching me to pray."

"O, Hagar. You do learn quickly."

We had laughed.

After that, I sought the purest gold in Egypt, along with

extraordinary and brilliant precious stones. I believed that as soon as I understood Sarai's god, I could put an image to him, even give him a name, if I enticed him properly.

"You cannot limit El to a temple," Sarai said when I told her my plan. "And He doesn't need your gold or jewels. He is worth far more than all of them, and they all belong to Him anyway. He only wants you to seek Him and love Him." She had smiled so sweetly. "Think on this. You live in a palace made of stone, and the God of Abram reached you here. If you had wings and soared as high as the eagle and built your nest in the stars, El would have reached you there."

Now, I bowed before him. I could deny him no longer, no matter what. He was the only God worthy of following. I said so and promised to leave the old gods of Egypt forever.

I remained like that for a long time, clearly and completely surrendering to something bigger than myself. Admittedly, out of deep need and a feeling of hopelessness. The gravel under my knees cut further into my skin, but I didn't care. I waited patiently for my deliverance.

A childlike sense of awe filled my spirit.

He was with me now, his *presence* surrounding the whole mass of air around me. So palpable, I swear I could feel his hand upon me. And then I heard a more resonant voice than my own, like a whisper in my heart. "I see you, Hagar."

It was all El said as I experienced a peace that passed all understanding.

Chapter Thirty-Nine

I LAY ABED THAT NIGHT, SMILING. Bastet snuggled with me and emitted a deep, guttural purr as I scratched behind her ears. I thought about how hard I tried to understand God with my mind, but now that I knew El saw *me* from His home in heaven, it all seemed so simple. But at the same moment, complex. A sweetness filled my soul knowing El was no longer just Sarai's God or Abram's—El was my God.

And I would serve Him forever.

I closed my eyes and drifted off.

"No," I screamed and sat up confused. The dream was so clear, the terror so real, my heart hammered my chest. I was there again, with *Him.* But this time, hideous crocodiles filled their wide mouths with human limbs and dragged them to the bottom of the river.

Kiya rushed in, tousled and ruffled after rising quickly from a deep sleep. "Princess, are you having a nightmare?"

"Where am I? What time is it?"

"You are in your bed. And it is long before dawn."

The light from the clay oil lamp she held illuminated my senses and the worry in her brown eyes. "Sarai. Go. Bring her to me."

Kiya ran off. Bastet stretched, jumped down, and wandered out of the room as I waited for Sarai.

When she finally entered my bedchamber, she held an oil lamp and appeared very young in the muted light. "Kiya, go back to bed. I will stay with Hagar," she said.

"Can I get you anything first?" Kiya asked through a yawn.

"No, please, go back to sleep," I said. "And Kiya …"

She turned to me. "Yes?"

"Thank you for coming so quickly."

She smiled sleepily and padded out of the room.

"Your God was in my dream tonight. No, *my* God was in my dreams. He spoke to me and showed me what was to come."

Sarai sat on the edge of my bed. "Tell me everything you remember."

"It was the vision lost in the disorder of my mind after Merikare beat me. The showing was quick but so real. I saw Him again, the man who stood beside me under the ankh. It was so pleasant being with Him because I believed He approved of me."

Sarai bent closer.

"We stood on a boat in the middle of the river. I spoke to the man and said I desired to look upon His face. 'Gaze at the sun,' the man told me. But I replied that I couldn't. 'You admit you cannot look at the sun. How much more beyond your power must it be to look upon God Himself?' The wind became unfriendly, and I thought I had angered Him. The boat tossed about like a toy in the large waves. But being so close to Him, filled me with comfort and my heart was entirely blissful." I shivered. "Then crocodiles appeared everywhere, hideous and dreadful. They filled their wide mouths with human limbs and dragged them to the bottom of the river. I thought of Zadah and believed my dream was a haunting of her."

"Yes," Sarai said. "It is normal to have nightmares for a long while after something tragic happens to us."

"But that was not all, Sarai. When I looked at the river again, it flowed with vomit, thick and rancid. The limbs that floated on its surface were blackened and looked like charcoal. Blisters bubbled up all over them and burst before my eyes." I reached out and she took my hands. "It fouled the air, and I covered my nose and heaved. Then the man spoke these words, 'Let me declare it and set it in order for you. A great wrong has occurred in the land of Egypt. But do not be afraid because you are my witness.' Then He disappeared, and that's when I woke."

Sarai bit her lip and turned her face from me. "All the troubles in the land of Egypt lay at my feet." Her voice cracked.

"You put too much on yourself, Sarai. Surely this is between Egypt and the one true God. He desires to make His presence known here, and it is not your fault if they will not listen."

"I hope, when the truth is revealed, you will be able to lend me a small portion of the understanding you now show."

"Truth? What truth?"

"O, Hagar. It is not mine to tell. But send for Meti. Now. Tell him what you have told me. He will know what it means and what is to come. He has seen it before, and I have too." She stood and moved toward the door.

"Where are you going?"

"To pray for Egypt, Hagar. Your people are in danger again."

"But Sarai …"

She stopped and turned toward me. "Yes, Hagar?"

"Why me?"

"Because you seek him busily."

I followed her out and went to rouse Kiya again, but Dendera was awake and volunteered to run to the temple for the high priest. Nonetheless, our activity woke Kiya, and she helped me dress for Meti's visit.

The high priest appeared faster than I expected and refused to sit or take refreshment, anxious to hear every word of my dream. He stood tall on long ebony legs and wore his spotted leopard robe across his broad shoulders, making him appear larger than he was. I smelled the familiar warm, musky scent of him from temple incense.

I told him the terrible, awful things I had seen but left out the words God had spoken. They were meant for me. The high priest did not have the ears to hear them.

"It is called the Black Sickness, Princess." His eyes turned dark and heavy.

"Why have I not heard of it before, Meti?"

"It is a disease that has slept for years. One your age would not remember. It vanished as quickly as it emerged but took many people with it. The gods are stirring again. I feared as much. I have felt it too."

"But blackened limbs and boils?"

He slid his fur off, and Kiya sprang up and took it from him. A large amulet hung from his neck, the image of Amun-Ra himself, carved from lapis lazuli. "First there were fever and chills, and usually a swelling in the armpit or groin. It filled with rotten pus until it burst. Fingers, noses, even lips turned black and looked, as you said, like charcoal." He paced the room restlessly in front of me. "It spreads easily, we think by touch or breathing the air around an infected person. Once you do, you are likely dead." He shook his head. "What you have seen is unthinkable. May this god be seized who attacks our people." He placed his tense hands on my shoulders. "What have we done to anger him so?"

"I don't know what vexes Him, dear teacher. But if the boils do appear, you must send for Sarai's brother, Abram. Seek the answer from him on how to save us." I thought of the guilt on Sarai's divine face. "I don't know why, but in my soul, I believe he will know." I absently twisted the amulet on my wrist. It seemed a natural part of my body, like an arm or a leg. Yet, I wanted to cast it away.

I gazed at the heavy blue amulet that hung from Meti's neck, so close to my face, so close to his heart. I wanted to ask the high priest, *Do you hear Amun-Ra's voice? Does he speak to you as the one true God speaks to me? Does he call you by name or simply dangle there in silence?* Instead, I flushed under Meti's in-depth scrutiny and did not utter a word.

The high priest took his robe back from Kiya, slung it over his shoulders, and left my chambers in haste for my father.

Pharaoh took the vision as seriously as he had the first one, but this time he told me so. He abstained from all pleasure and mandated that everyone in his household do the same. He spent his days in the temple, before the gods of Egypt, and required me to go to the temple daily too. I complied with every request from the king and high priest, but in my heart, even as I bowed before the silent stone figures of Osiris, Isis, Horus, and Set, I spoke to the one living God. I prayed for my people, but mostly for my king. That God would give him eyes to see and ears to hear. And I begged Him to take the vision and judgment of the Black Sickness from me.

From Egypt.

Kiya or Dendera slept on the floor near my bed every night in case I woke in terror. Sleep did not come easily, held at bay by my fear of seeing the vision again. But the dream did not return, and I began to believe that God had listened and answered my prayers. After a few weeks, I began to sleep with no trouble, and my dreams remained undisturbed.

Having Pharaoh and Meti take my dream seriously made Merikare's mood curdle darker toward me than ever before. I tried to keep away from him and Imi, but returning from the temple one day, I nearly ran into them while walking through the palace forecourt. My head had been down, deep in my thoughts, when I heard Imi say, "Here she is, my husband, your troublemaking sister. The inciter of your citizens."

I froze as a cold sweat swept over me, and growing nausea filled the pit in my stomach.

The crown prince stepped in front of me and crossed his arms. "Peace be upon you, Hagar."

"Peace be upon you, Merikare."

"Have you been avoiding me while stirring up trouble for our city?"

"Of course not. I have been following our king's instructions. I would see plenty of you if you spent any time in the temple as a future king should."

He flinched, and I knew I hit my mark. "Your talk of black limbs and boils caused alarm among our people. And because our father allowed no pleasure for anyone in his household, it has caused extreme frustration for my royal companions and me."

The severity of his voice made me dizzy. My eyes and head still fatigued on occasion, and my thoughts turned hazy and fought for details. I stood before him in a sweat-soaked kalasiris and struggled to clear my mind. "Let me pass, Merikare," was all I could summon.

"It is a crime," Imi said, "that you can cause so much trouble and get away with it. May you be justified before the gods. My royal husband and I see no acceptable reason for you to cause such fear and force us to refrain from our desires." She pressed herself against my brother and skimmed her fingers lightly down his arm.

"I hope I am not justified before the gods, Imi. If I am, no peasant or royal would be safe. I pray daily the vision was nothing more than a nightmare and there is no truth to it."

"There is no truth in anything that comes from your mouth. Only inventions you create for attention." She tucked her hand inside Merikare's bent elbow. "You should be punished."

I opened my mouth but thought better of saying anything more. "Brother, again, let me pass."

Merikare stood firm. "Sister, unlike our father, I will not tolerate or listen to the foolishness you claim to see in your sleep. The new year is quickly upon us, and for the sake of my people, they will never hear words from you again."

"I suggested we cut your tongue out," Imi said.

I thought about how ugly she looked at that moment. How vile her opened mouth, how cold her eyes. But I ignored her and stared steadily at Merikare. "You will be my husband, dear brother, and I will be your Great Royal Wife. I will live my life obedient to your wishes and for your pleasure only. If it secures your happiness, I promise you will not have to force me. I will live my days in silence."

Merikare frowned as beads of sweat gathered on his forehead. He hadn't expected me to submit so quickly, and it seemed he couldn't conjure another word.

We both stood immovable.

Unwilling to give in.

Unable to let the other one go—our fate bound together by the accidental outcome of sharing a womb.

Chapter Forty

TWO FULL MOONS PASSED WITHOUT SWELLINGS filled with rotten pus or blackened limbs. As the new year approached, each disease-free day brought a lightness to my spirit when I should have been anxious about my future with Merikare. I often wandered in my garden among the fading blossoms of the henna bushes. The fragrant small, white flower clusters still generously released a scent of pure sweetness. There I would reflect on the God of Abram until the last bit of sunshine gave way to the vivid colors of dusk. I found surprising joy in my union with Him and knew that God would never leave me no matter what trials and conflicts I faced.

Life moved on peacefully.

Until Imi came to visit the day before Wepet Renpet.

"These will be my chambers after tomorrow," she said, her manner disturbingly relaxed. "I want to look around and decide what changes to make and what will remain the same." Her two hopeless-looking servant girls stood behind her, faces to the ground. They were both very young, tiny little things, and bronzed as though they'd spent time in the sun.

I had just sat down to my midday meal, famished, but my appetite fled in haste. To appear unruffled, I picked at lemon chicken and figs and smiled. "Please, be my guest."

She pointed to my wine, and one of her girls leapt to pour her a cup. "Be my guest," I said again, even though my permission was not sought.

Then she rooted through everything.

She instructed her servants to lift the lids of my storage chests, her voice cold and steady as she commanded them to remove the contents. They spread my possessions all over the limestone floor as Imi stood erect, shoulders back, her neck exposed. She had them present every item for her inspection.

Her remarks were loud and curt. "Not worthy of me," and "Merikare has given me superior jewels already." And even, "It won't do for me, but I will send it to Amisi."

From outside my door came the sound of childish laughter, light and carefree—a stark contrast to the mood in my chambers. I tore a small piece of flesh from the chicken, nibbled, and kept quiet while Imi examined my royal linens, counted the gold cups on my table, and noted the number of lamps in the room. She even had one of her girls measure the oil used to fuel them.

"There is much to be improved," she muttered. "Sarai will be moving on too. The king has arranged for chambers closer to his. If you ask me, the two of you should have been separated a long time ago."

"I don't recall asking you, Imi," I said, thinking I should be careful, but I couldn't hold back.

She sneered at me. "Your conversations with her are coming to an end, Princess. I assure you of that."

I shrugged.

Then she shouted at my girls. "Both of you. Line up before me."

My skin prickled.

They looked at me. I nodded. They stood and faced her but looked straight ahead, as though they could see right through her. She poked their skin. Examined their mouths as though they were animals. Made them turn while she viewed every inch. "I may keep this one," she said, standing in front of Kiya. "But I will sell the fat one to the slave traders."

She got the response she desired.

The girls began to shake and tears filled in their eyes.

I had to look away.

Then she forced them to their bellies. "Bow before me."

Dendera hesitated a second too long and got slapped for it. Her face turned ashen, except for the red welt from Imi's hand that had become a common sight in the harem. She fell face down.

Imi's large brown eyes burned into mine, but now they looked black.

This was more than I could take. "Does it make you feel powerful when you abuse the powerless? The girls have been together since they were children. Surely there is no reason to separate them now."

Dendera and Kiya sobbed gently on the floor, and my chest tightened. "Please do not take your dislike of me out on them, Imi. They will serve you faithfully. That I assure you."

Imi studied me carefully with a predatory stare—then her smile sent chills through my soul. *I have given myself away. She found what she was looking for, what would strike my heart the deepest.*

"On second thought, I won't keep either of them. They will both be sold."

The girls wept openly.

I stood and walked toward them. "That would be an impulsive and extreme measure, Imi. Something I notice you often struggle with. Girls, both of you stand this instant."

They peeked up, realized I was quite serious, and scrambled to their feet.

"I promise you, neither of you will ever bow before the likes of this interloper again." I turned toward Imi. "Remove yourself from my chambers. Do not dare to cross this threshold until it is yours to do so."

"I will sell them, Hagar, because I won't need them. I will have a princess of Egypt to do my bidding soon. Do you know what I intend for you?" The words tumbled without effort from her foul mouth. "You will make up my marriage bed with the finest linen in the land and stand outside the door every time I go in to please the crown prince. And since I spend more time there than anywhere, you will remain for long hours at that door."

"I will gladly be your doorkeeper, Imi, and with good spirits. I will bid you goodnight when you go in and bid you a good day when you come out. You will never be a cause of distress to me, no matter what you do. My soul is at peace." I pointed to my door. "Now, get out."

"Don't talk to me like that. You have gone too far, Hagar. I *will* make you suffer."

"But not today. Get. Out."

O, the fury that flew from the room.

"Kiya," I said. "Find Pentu, the scribe, and bring him back quickly. There is something I must do, and I must do it now."

I had taken my concerns regarding my marriage to my mother and father several times—the threats made against me by Imi and the dark promises from Merikare of what my life would be like once we married. Mother grieved and sympathized and believed every word I said. I knew she spoke to Father on my behalf. But the king had deaf ears when it came to Merikare. He refused to believe Imi could influence the crown prince or that my brother would make me a prisoner in my own home. And Pharaoh instructed my mother that, regardless of what happened, they would not interfere in our lives once we were married. "Who are we to meddle with another man and his wife?" he had said. "The throne goes to the man who marries the heiress princess, the eldest daughter of my Great Royal Wife. He must marry Hagar to take my throne without dispute."

The matter was settled.

The high vizier commiserated with me and researched any legal way out. But the king's desires ruled above all else. Rensi had taken my hands in his. "It is strange, really," he said. "Every common woman has the legal right to divorce her husband if she is mistreated. But being royal, you have fewer rights than the wives of the fellahin."

"Yes," I said. "Duty above all else. I have lived my life in luxury, for want of nothing. Perhaps I'm selfish and thoughtless to complain. Better is my calling than the calling of so many others." I squeezed his hands to reassure him, but his eyes remained somber, and his face pained.

Kiya and Dendera—both with free-falling tears—dressed me in a long, flowing white kalasiris, cinched at the waist with a simple gold belt. Dendera's hands trembled as she placed an unadorned, plaited wig on my head. She sniffled and adjusted the thin gold crown with a rearing cobra on the wig.

I let my hand rest on the silver cuff Meti had attached to me the year before. I ran my fingers across the smooth red jasper stones that represented the blood of Isis. It made my heart heavy. *How odd.* I had wanted to be rid of it for some time. This talisman was the only thing left that bound me to the gods of Egypt. Yet, after tonight, it would my sole possession. No one could take it from me except the high priest, not even my new husband or his greedy first wife. I shook my head softly and let my hand fall away.

I sat and let Bastet curl up in my lap one last time. I wrestled tears as I scratched behind her ears. Then I kissed her head, her nose, and even her mouth. I hugged her tight, which she had never allowed before. But she passively accepted my parting affection, as though she knew this was the end for us.

I cast a final glance at my girls, my cat, my lovely furnishings, and whispered goodbye to the walls that had been home for most of my life. I roamed, alone and unseeing, through the columned halls of the palace. I wished I could take flight and disappear forever as I struggled to breathe in the stuffy, warm air. The night had trapped the heat inside and imprisoned it, just like me.

My father had arranged a small celebration in his royal living quarters—no grand banquet like the previous year. It would be unseemly after the storm had claimed so many lives and resources. But any gathering with the royal household, and the highest-ranking nobles, was a significant event. A sumptuous meal and the king's most refined wine would be served.

There was much to celebrate—the new year, the king's

first grandson, my marriage to Merikare, and the king's intent to consummate his marriage to Sarai.

I walked into the magnificent residence of our king and stood a moment. Rensi and Tameri were already there and seated at a long table lavishly set with gold tableware. Bowls of white lilies, placed at even distances down the center, perfumed the room.

The high vizier stood when he saw me, his significant belly hanging on a frame that was otherwise slim, and motioned for me to join them.

I took a seat next to Rensi, breathed in the fragrant scent of the lilies, and tried to relax. He leaned toward me and peered into my eyes.

"High Vizier, why do you stare at me like that?" I reached up to make sure my wig and crown were straight.

"Be still, Princess," he jested. "Let me look in thine eyes and behold what is to come." He squinted to see me better. "I see stalks of grain aplenty. And cows, fine looking and fat."

"I see someone sated with too much beer and bread," I said and smacked his large, round stomach.

Tameri looked us both over and rolled her dark weasel eyes as servants placed tiny roasted birds on the table—quail perhaps. She ignored us and sampled the delicacy.

Rensi laughed warmly. "If that is all you see, Princess, I am happy for it." He reached for a large piece of griddlecake, dipped it in honey that dripped down his hand, and stuffed the whole thing in his mouth. He licked the sticky sweetness from his fingers. "In all seriousness, Hagar, how are you doing on this night that you will wed? You have not come to me for counsel for some time. Have you found peace in your fate?"

"Yes, I have found peace. It is not in my hands. And I will accept what comes without complaint."

I looked up to see Sarai standing next to my father on a terrace that overlooked the Nile. A breeze moved the plaits in her black wig that covered her long sable hair. She wore a pleated linen kalasiris, modestly covered with a wide purple scarf. Gold threads, woven through the scarf, picked up the light from the torches that lit the balcony and shimmered like stars. My father leaned in toward Sarai, and I sucked in my breath. Their heads almost touched. They were so engrossed in conversation, his desire fixed on his handsome face.

Tameri followed my gaze. "Observe the way he looks at her. Pharaoh is not letting his affection for Sarai be delayed any longer. Although she is unripe in experience, her perfume will spread its fragrance throughout his chambers." She laughed.

"O, wife. Guard your tongue." Rensi shook his head. "That is our king and his favorite you speak of in such a common manner."

"I only speak the truth, my beloved. Look at the desire on his lips when he talks to her. I am the one who has prepared Sarai for his bedchamber. He will find her love more pleasant than all other fruit on his vine."

I could not help but laugh with Tameri. "Your wife's descriptions are always quite colorful, Rensi," I said. "She told Sarai to 'be like a gazelle, and he will be your stag.' And, you will never forget 'when the time of singing has come.'"

Rensi rubbed his bald head and sighed heavily. Then he relaxed the exasperated line between his eyebrows and chuckled. "Tameri, where do you come up with such things?"

Strangely, it had been one of the things that bonded Sarai and me. We often giggled late into the night after Tameri left my chambers, repeating the pictures she drew so well with her words.

For a moment, I forgot the fate that waited for me this evening.

But I remembered quickly when Merikare entered the room with Imi on his arm.

Soon, by simple decree from the king—and one night spent in the crown prince's chambers—it would be official. I would belong to him, and my life would change forever.

Imi scanned the room until her eyes fixed on me with raw hatred. She raised her hand, and the woman with the heavy breasts hurried in carrying little Akhtoy. He was greeted by oohs and ahhs from other members of the royal family. Imi kept her neck tilted up and her eyes on me.

She did it. She took it all from me, just as she promised she would. But my life is not in your hands, Imi. I will not let my heart sink. Wailing saves no man from the pit.

Chapter Forty-One

I LOOKED AROUND FOR MY MOTHER. "Where is the Great Royal Wife?"

"She is ill," Tameri said. "A fever and chills overtook her earlier this evening."

I rose to my feet. "Why didn't anyone tell me?" Absolute terror seized my heart. "No, no, no," I muttered under my breath.

Rensi gripped my arm. "What is it, Princess?"

"My dream, Rensi."

He paled instantly. "The Black Sickness? Surely not, Hagar."

"Let's not make more of this than it is," Tameri scolded.

My cheeks heated up. "I need to know and need to see her." I lifted my long kalasiris to my knees and fled the room. "O, God of Abram and Sarai, not my mother," I cried, running all the way to the chambers of the Great Royal Wife.

I arrived breathless and panting. Meti was already there, by her door. The royal physician stood next to him, worry wrinkles spread deep around his eyes. The very tall man stayed silent, and looked at Meti.

"He called for me the moment he found swelling in her secret parts," Meti said gravely. "I was just on my way to alert your father."

I nodded at him. "Go. I will stay with her."

"You can't go near her, Hagar. We cannot allow this to spread. Bunefer is with her. She wouldn't allow us to part her from your mother. She must remain isolated now too. Until we see what happens."

"Meti, teacher. Thank you for your concern. But I will see my mother, and I will see her *now*."

The physician was firm. "You won't leave the room again, Princess."

The high priest stood still a moment and then laid a gentle hand on my arm. "May the gods protect you, my child." He turned to leave, then stopped and added, "May the gods protect us all."

I lifted my head to meet the physician's eyes. "Tell me everything."

"She is burning up, and small tumors, the size of dates, cover her body. It will not be long before they begin to burst and discharge the pus that forms on top of them."

I straightened. "We had our morning meal together. Mother was fine, except agitated by a slight headache."

"She caught a chill this afternoon. Bunefer piled blankets on her, but she could not get warm. Then she would throw them off, feeling hot, as though her entire body was inflamed. And Bunefer would pile them back on because she was so cold again." He sighed.

I knew the answer but asked anyway. "The Black Sickness?"

He nodded.

I entered her bedroom and smelled kyphi, the compound incense used in sick rooms. It filled the air with the scent of cinnamon and calamus. Mother lay on her bed motionless, eyes closed. Bunefer sat at her side, humming softly.

I approached slowly.

Bunefer looked up and shook her head. "Child, you shouldn't be here," she said, but not harshly. Her heart wasn't in it.

Small lumps covered Mother's hands that lay on top of a thin linen sheet. I gasped. Her fingers, lips, and the tip of her nose were blackened. I lifted the sheet by her feet. Her toes were discolored as well.

"Princess, don't touch her. It is for your safety," the physician said with firm courtesy.

"Your pleas will come to no avail," said Bunefer. "This one does as she pleases. She won't listen if her heart tells her not to."

"But this is the Black Sickness. If it leaves this room, leaves this palace, it will sweep across Egypt. I must insist."

"I will not leave this room. No matter what comes," I said, breathless. "A slight headache at sunrise to this by sunset? Does anyone survive once they become infected?" I looked at the physician hopefully.

"There are records of many who survived," he said gently. "Your mother is a strong woman and is fighting it. We won't know if this is the end for a while yet."

Mother coughed, and the physician laid a soft linen rag over her mouth. Deep red blooms quickly covered the white, sun-bleached cloth.

I began to sob.

Bunefer pulled a chair next to hers and led me to it, holding me in her large, gentle hands. I sank down, and she draped her arms around me. I pressed my face into her and moaned.

"My daughter," the Great Royal Wife said weakly. "You should not be here. The risk is too great."

I leaned toward her. "Hush now, Mother." I wiped my eyes on a cloth Bunefer handed me. "Save your strength. We can talk about it in the morning. When you are well."

"Apologize to the royal physician, my strong-willed child. I'm sure he tried to keep you out." Her voice trailed off.

"Shh," I said softly. "We'll talk later."

"I love you, Hagar. We had such fun together," she said and fell silent.

I sang the familiar lullaby Mother had sung to her children after they were born. I even heard her hum it while holding Akhtoy on his name day. It was believed it had magic and protected the one it was sung to. I didn't know what else to do.

"Comest thou to kiss this child?
I will not let thee kiss her.
Comest thou to soothe her?
I will not let thee soothe her.
Comest thou to harm her?

I will not let thee harm her.
Comest thou to take her away?
I will not let thee take her from me."

My voice choked with tears. I could not continue the song of magic. It bridled my soul to do so. I fell to my knees beside my mother's bed and whispered her name. There was no response. I lifted my hands toward heaven. "God of Abram and Sarai, show favor to me and let my words please your heart. My mother festers with fever, and boils are devouring her. Reach out your hand to this great woman, the noblest person in the land. She has felt your *presence*. Let us feel it now. Lay your healing hand upon her and show her mercy." For an instant, a wave of belonging, of pure love, washed over me. I knew God's *presence* was with us. "May you do what you have set out to do," I added and ended the same way Sarai always did. "Amen, amen." Sarai said it meant "truly, truly" in her language.

I looked up, and Bunefer had her head bowed too. The physician had slipped from the room. I thought perhaps appealing to a god not known in Egypt alarmed him. But he returned a few moments later and said Kiya had brought food, and Meti sent disturbing news.

"The king and crown prince have been isolated in their chambers. Meti said the king is in a state of profound grief for his wife. He is also upset but not surprised that his eldest daughter is with her. He believes he will lose you both this very night." He brought a shaky hand to his forehead. "The malady has already spread. The gods have struck down many in the palace with fever."

May you do what you set out to do. I wondered if I could live with the consequences of that without complaint. I wondered if I would even live.

Returning to my vigil beside Mother's still and dignified body, I discerned pain on her face and knew she suffered. The boils that covered her began to erupt. The pus bubbled up and boiled over, spewing what looked like raw egg yolk across her skin. The wretched smell reached my nose, and I heaved involuntarily. Bunefer handed me another linen cloth, this one drenched in perfume. I buried my face in it.

Time passed slowly.

Days and nights blurred together, but I remained on the chair by Mother's bed. Dazed, spent, edgy. I wept and apologized. "This was all my fault. I had the dream."

"Now, now, dear girl," Bunefer said. "You did not cause this. We are in the hands of the one mightier than all of us. The sole thing necessary to us is the will of the one true God." I studied her face a moment and understood. She knew El too.

But soon, Bunefer lay on a cot beside my mother. Her face turned ghostly pale, sweat dripped off her large body, and she vomited blood. She was hot, then cold, then hot again.

My new faith faltered. It took all of my will not to cry out to the gods of Egypt. I began to plead with the God of Abram relentlessly and struck many bargains with Him. *Is it disrespectful to bargain with God?* We bartered for everything in life. Shopkeepers expected customers to argue for a lower price. Or did one just agree that God knew best and simply accept the price set? I knew so little about Him. I had no answers.

But He answered.

Again, a fleeting moment of pure love poured into my soul. With that more resonant voice than my own, He reminded me that my mother and Bunefer also knew the one true God. He had seen them, and they had been aware of His *presence*. He was their hope too.

Swellings quickly grew like mushrooms in the dark, damp places of Bunefer's body. Miserable sores covered her arms, legs, and face. She moaned quietly, as though she didn't want to disturb anyone.

Natural light filled the room as another new morning dawned. Mother hadn't uttered a sound through the long, dark night, but now she struggled to breathe. The sound oddly reminded me of the sistrum rattle.

The physician, who hovered near, whispered the words, "Her end is here."

I rested my head beside her, lifted her lifeless, cold fingers, and laid them on my cheek. I wanted to embrace her more than anything in the world. I wanted her eyes to open and her smile to fall upon me once more.

The physician gently lifted her fingers and pulled me from the bed. "You should not touch her, Princess Hagar. But it is time to cry out to this god you have spoken to all night. For the Great Royal Wife of Egypt is dead." His voice quaked. "Your mother is gone."

I couldn't breathe.

People died all the time. It was a fact of life. But I never imagined my mother would end like this. It simply wasn't possible for my mind to perceive. An unearthly scream came from my mouth as despair captured a princess. "The one who loved me most in this world has perished," I sobbed. "How can I endure such a loss?"

"Your mother was a great woman," said the physician. "She is worth great sorrow."

I stared at her still body and realized I had never considered the possibility of her actually leaving me. Not even as she lay dying before my eyes. All the dire words from the physician had fallen on deaf ears. I had not believed him even when he said the end was near. Perhaps if he had slapped me in the face, I would have heard. Maybe if he shook me, I would have understood. Or possibly there was nothing he could have done to make me believe that I would never see my mother again in the land of the living. That her easy laughter and bright smile were gone forever, and her genuinely kind heart had stopped beating. I would never share another lunch with her on the royal quay. And I would never again hear her call my name.

She told me she loved me. I told her to hush. We would talk later.

There was no later.

And there was no boundary to my grief. I had seen this in a dream. I knew it was coming. Was there anything I could have done to save her life? Had I not fought hard enough for her? I knew this guilt and ache in my heart would be bound to me for the rest of my life.

I put my face in my hands and wailed.

Chapter Forty-Two

BUNEFER QUICKLY FOLLOWED THE GREAT ROYAL Wife. My forehead rested in my palms when the royal physician gave me the news. I shrugged clumsily—there were no tears left. I thought of her big hands and bigger heart. I thought of her son Pentu and decided to visit him if he survived this.

If I survived this.

"People are fleeing the city, but they will not escape," the royal physician said solemnly. "They will only take this determined demon with them." He handed me a cup of something that smelled like rancid oil. "Meti delivered this for you. A preventative potion he says tastes like donkey urine, but he assures me it is not."

I wondered how Meti would know what donkey urine tasted like. I took a sip and wrinkled my nose, then gagged on the greasy feel in my mouth. I knew it contained fat from a hippopotamus. I had concocted many such potions during my schooling with Meti. "Actually, it tastes like nuts that have gone bad, and then went bad again, and then were mixed with donkey urine." I forced a smile. "Why aren't you drinking this?"

He shifted from side to side. "I have a lump. Under my arm, Princess. As small as a quail's egg, but I know what it is."

I took a good look at him. O, what a change! His body appeared diminished and bent, bereft of rest, pale and clammy. Clearly sick. I steadied my breath and reached out my hand. "I am sorry." My voice cracked.

Why had I been given this vision? And why am I so useless to do anything to save my people?

He stepped out of my reach. "It grieves me to add to your sorrow." He scratched the dark stubble under his chin that added to his look of fatigue. "I know you are close to the high vizier, Rensi, and his noble wife, Tameri. They are both ill."

I stood, shaking. "It is like death came to us starved and sated himself on my loved ones."

"Many have passed to the afterlife already. Countless names are being whispered down the halls. Old, young, rich, and poor. It is not discriminating." He looked down and rubbed his brow. "Nothing I could have done would have prepared me for this."

"I must go to the high vizier."

He nodded. "There is no one left in the halls. You may go."

"Your name, noble physician. What name may I pray for?"

"Bomani." He smiled kindly.

"It means warrior." I returned his smile. "Keep fighting, Bomani. Do not surrender."

The foul, sickening smell of death hung over the room. I covered my nose with the perfumed linen cloth I carried from the Great Royal Wife's chambers. My steps were uncertain, as though I'd had too much wine. Tameri lay on a woven mat on the ground in the corner. Sarai was on her knees beside her. Tameri rolled back and forth, writhed and whimpered and moaned. I pressed the cloth hard against my mouth to keep from crying out. She was severely disfigured, almost unrecognizable. Her nose was black like her fingers, as though they'd been burned, her neck covered in growths as large as figs.

She looked at me and shrieked, "Curse the gods and let us die. Is there no refuge from their anger? Death has visited my home and snared us." Then she closed her dark eyes and groaned.

I stood stiff and unmoving. Through blurry eyes, I saw Sarai walk toward me. She took my hand and led me to Rensi. I gasped and stopped mid-stride at the sight of the miserable sores that covered him. Large as apples, they oozed stomach-turning yellow yolk. His fingers, toes, nose, and lips, all charcoal black. My mind could not grasp how fast this happened.

"It feels as though it was just last night we sat together laughing, teasing Tameri."

Sarai's remarkable eyes had lost their light. She sighed sadly, shook her head, and shuffled back to Tameri.

Rensi heard me. "Princess Hagar," he said weakly. "You expose yourself too readily." He coughed into a cloth already covered in blood.

"I am not in danger coming to you. The royal physician gave me a potion that will prevent me from becoming ill."

"The one Meti said tasted like donkey urine? We suffered it too. It was nearly as bad as this malady. But it did not work for us." He coughed again. "Will you find out for me how the high priest knew what donkey urine tasted like?"

"I wondered the same thing." I smiled. Our minds were so alike. My smile quickly faded when I realized his voice had the same rattle my mother's had at the end. "Don't speak, Rensi. Just listen to me for a moment." My voice choked. "You have been my dearest friend and confidant. I don't know what life will be like if you leave me. But I want you to know I love you, and your noble wife."

He smiled faintly. "I was a young man when I married Tameri, Hagar. She has always been my companion. Perhaps even now. In death." He coughed more blood. "Many men discard their lowborn wives after they rise in the world. I rose to the highest rank in the land and did not desert her. She can be difficult and demanding. She can be hard to love at times, but she is always worth the effort." He sighed. "I could never keep all of her adversaries straight. She had more than your royal father." Another cough. More blood. "Do you know she demanded that people prostrate themselves before her and bring her gifts after I became high vizier?"

"Yes, Rensi. I remember that." I looked toward Tameri, relieved to see the small rise and fall of her chest. She had not yet passed.

"I acted like I was mad. But your father and I had a good belly laugh about it." He opened his eyes, and they held concern but no fear. "My life has never been boring with her." A tear slipped down his cheek and shattered my heart. "I weep not for myself, but I weep to leave her. If she survives, who will have the patience for her that I have had? Who will love her?"

"Tameri is part of the royal family. And we will take care of her. I promise."

He smiled. "Let me advise you one more time, dear girl," he said. Then a spasm hit and caused his teeth to clench. He looked to be in great pain.

"Rest, Rensi. I can hear your words of wisdom later."

"No, now."

I leaned toward him, placing the perfumed rag over my nose, so great was the stench.

"There is only one God," he whispered through the death rattle. "I called to Him and said, 'Are you there?' He answered me in my heart, 'I am here.'" Rensi expelled one last ragged breath on earth and was gone. His eyes remained open, but he could not see.

I howled in grief and Sarai hurried to me. She closed the eyes of my beloved friend and covered him with a white sheet. Rensi's belly tented the rest of his body. The belly that shook when he laughed would never shake again. "I cannot bear this, Sarai. Surely joy has left Egypt forever. Death surrounds me and I am so afraid."

Tameri groaned, and we both turned toward her.

"The mattress was too soft and caused her back to hurt," Sarai said as if I had asked why she lay on the ground. "She is more comfortable on the hard floor. And there is good news. Her fever seems to have broken, and none of her swellings have erupted. She may survive this."

My heart throbbed in pity for her. "She does not realize yet that the man who loved her is gone. I remember when Tameri delivered her first son and fell sick. Rensi could not eat or drink, so great was his misery. So great was his love."

"She will need a lot of care if death does not take her," Sarai said. "She may wish it did. Not only has she lost Rensi, but she will be maimed for life. There is no way to save the limbs once they have turned black."

"Her fingers?"

"And her nose."

I shook my head. "Where are their servants? And their children?" For the first time, I realized we were the only ones in the high vizier's substantial chambers.

"At the first sign of swelling under his arm, Rensi had the servants take his children away on one of the royal barges. They are instructed not to return until they hear that it's safe to do so." She looked at Tameri. "She would not leave with them."

"And where are the priests? Or the royal physicians? Why did no one tend this noble family?"

"I sent them away. There are so many others to watch over. There was nothing more to do for Rensi or Tameri. Except to pray and wait."

"Is this the price we pay to love one another? Does all love end in such pain?"

"Loving and being loved is a gift. It is the very essence of our Creator. Don't let fear ever keep you from it." She turned her head as if to consider her words. "Unfortunately, the longer we live, the more grief we must suffer. Loss is a path our feet will take no matter how much we try to avoid it."

We moved near Tameri and sat on the ground, looking at her in silence for a long while. I lowered my head into Sarai's lap, and she stroked my hair. Her tears dropped softly on my cheek. "I wish I could unravel for you what goes on here. But I cannot. I ache for you, for Rensi, for your mother. They shone so brightly on this earth and it will be forever dimmed without them."

I sat up. "Why *is* God doing this to us, Sarai? I know it is God. Why has He hurt me beyond all I could have imagined?

You have said He is a loving God, but how can a loving God do this to His people? My throat is dry from endless appeals to Him that remain unanswered. And now, the losses are too much to bear."

"My experience with God is this. He doesn't react to our suffering by making it vanish. Sometimes we have to go through pain, even when we want to go around it. But He gives us His very *presence* so we may approach God in our grief."

I thought of the undeniable waves of pure love that washed over me beside my mother's deathbed. They had given me strength in the moment.

"Times like these tend to awaken things in us we weren't even aware we had. Like courage and compassion. After you lost Zadah, there was a new kindness and consideration in you. You grew from it and in it." She took my hand and squeezed. "But most of all, it always awakens our need for God. And with faith in Him you will persevere. And there you will find hope, and in that hope is peace. I promise you that."

I looked at Tameri thoughtfully. "They had a funny way about them, didn't they? Rensi appeared hard on the outside toward her, but he was so soft inside. I wonder what it would be like to be loved like that." I lowered my eyes. "Rensi and my mother discovered your God too. Are they with Him now?"

"We don't discover God, Hagar. We remember He is already there. We retrieve what our soul knows is truth. And yes, they are with Him now. Most assuredly. They are in divine union with the one true God. And nothing can ever come between them."

Tameri stirred, turned, and peeked at us through swollen eyes. "Is there any comfort to be found in this world?" She started to cry. "My Rensi is gone, isn't he?"

"Yes, my dear Tameri," I whispered. "He is gone. But we believe your children are safe. They fled on a royal barge."

"Yes, yes, I know." She sighed deeply. "Rensi insisted I go with them since I didn't have a fever or swellings yet. But I could not leave him." She sobbed openly now. "So how could he leave me? Come back, Rensi. Come back." Then, mercifully, she rolled over and drifted to sleep.

"Hagar, you're exhausted. Go home," Sarai said. "I will stay with Tameri."

I had no strength to protest. I forced myself up and out into the large columned hallway. My footsteps echoed off the high ceilings, the lone sound that broke an eerie silence. No other person was about, not even a palace guard. The only beings were musicians and dancers painted on the walls, frozen in place while practicing their art. And they didn't care that I hurt beyond my worst imaginings.

The stillness caused gooseflesh to cover me from head to toe, so I quickened my pace and ran to my chambers, breathing heavily as I entered. Both of my girls were there and rose abruptly as I entered.

Kiya ran to me first. "Princess, how good to see your face. Are you sick?"

My hands went to my neck and searched for signs of the illness. It was smooth. At the same moment, relief and guilt engulfed me. "No. I am well. Both of you are too?"

They nodded and smiled. "We are well. We are well," they said in unison, bobbing their heads.

I smiled in relief. "The doctor said if we were not afflicted during the first night, we should be all right. But my mother, Rensi, Bunefer, probably soon even Tameri …"

Fingers touched the parted lips of my servants.

"None of them breathe any longer. They are gone." I shivered and moaned, then bent over and wept.

Dendera moved to my side. Kiya filled my bath. I stood impassively as Dendera removed my clothes, my wig, and my amulet. I offered no resistance while the girls washed me quickly, dried me, and slipped a fresh kalasiris over my head. Dendera slipped out and returned with lamb and wild spinach soup. They tried to spoon feed me as they would a young child. But I had no stomach for it. They led me to bed, where the midday sun filled the warm room with light. I lay there for a long time, my knees drawn tightly into my stomach. I forced my eyes to shut, and eventually fell asleep.

I woke to a searing, red-hot jolt of pain in my heart. Night had fallen and contributed cool air to the darkness. I thrashed about, my hands clenched into fists, and I pounded my bed. *It was real. They are all gone.* My head beat with a thunderous throb. I leaned over the side and retched across the floor. And then came long, hard tears of agony.

Sarai returned the next day at dusk and entered my room where I remained abed. "Tameri will survive," she whispered, and nearly collapsed in Kiya and Dendera's arms.

They washed her too. Tried to feed her—she refused—and then helped her to bed.

In the early morning hours, a disheveled Kiya shook me, but I was already awake. "A messenger came. Her brother is coming."

"Whose brother?"

"Sarai's. You are both to go now. Straight away. To the Great Audience Hall." She dropped her voice low. "Dendera and I are summoned with you."

I began to tremble. "What do you know, Kiya? Tell me all quickly."

"I know nothing more. A courier came and left no other words, except that we were all to rise and go to the king immediately. He said the brother of Sarai was expected at any moment, and we were to be there when he arrives."

Couldn't she have started with that? I scrambled out of bed and ran to Sarai's room. She was nearly dressed. "Why would Abram be coming?"

"Your father summoned him." She gazed at me with clear

blue eyes. "Hagar, I am not sure Abram and I will survive this day."

I lifted an eyebrow and cocked my head. "Why would you say such a thing?" And then I remembered. "No. It was me. I told Meti to go to Abram if the Black Sickness came. He went for help, Sarai. That is all." I smiled. "And this means your brother survived."

Dendera entered, combing her mussed coal-black hair with one hand and carrying a linen kalasiris for me in the other. "Another messenger," she said. "A boat hailed at the royal quay. Sarai's brother is here."

Dendera slid the linen kalasiris over my head, then Kiya stuffed my hair under a plaited wig and tried to apply makeup with shaking hands. "So sorry, Princess, so sorry. Why does the king call for us too?" she mumbled.

She wiped off the makeup and tried again, but her hands continued to quiver.

"Never mind, Kiya, I will do it." I took her hands in mine. "I don't know why the king wants you girls too. But you need to find Pentu." And then a terrible thought struck my heart. "Did he survive?"

She nodded. "As far as I know."

"Dendera, go with her. Bring Pentu with you and meet us there. In case the time has arrived. He'll know what that means, what to do, and what to bring."

Sarai and I rushed to the Great Audience Hall. The only sound in the empty predawn came from our sandals scuffing the floor. The only light emanated from oil lamps on pedestals, making our shadows dance unnervingly on the walls. But the air smelled fresh and clean and carried no lingering stench of the Black Sickness.

We reached the limestone-corbelled arch at the entrance of the hall. I stopped and twisted the silver amulet on my wrist. For the first time, it struck me that Pharaoh called us *here*— where he assembled his advisors, his highest officers, and even the priests to determine serious matters of state and religion.

Why?

My heart thumped in my chest as we entered slowly.

I couldn't believe how Sarai maintained her composure, her beautiful head held high. I couldn't read if she was excited or scared.

Then, at once, Sarai and I halted.

What is going on? God in heaven, what is going on?

Chapter Forty-Three

I SAW MY FATHER AND RECOILED.

Even though formally dressed and embellished with all symbols of kingship, he appeared small and broken. Pharaoh— half man and half god—now looked barely half man. I remembered the last time I saw him, at Wepet Renpet, leaning toward Sarai on the balcony, so much passion and desire written on his handsome face.

I looked to his right in a daze and saw Meti in his long leopard robe and white papyrus sandals. He looked bent on his long legs, his shoulders slumped. The young, ambitious Hyrcanos stood beside him, his tall, thin frame upright and proud, his prominent eyes alert and attentive. Rensi's unexpected death elevated him to high vizier. I was thankful Tameri was not here to see it.

My breathing slowed when I looked at my mother's throne—the chair that should have been vacant. Imi sat in it erect, chin jutted out, arms crossed, looking so comfortable it turned my blood cold. A delighted smirk sullied her pretty face.

I wanted to rush forward and pull her off. I wanted to scream at my father, "How can you banish my mother's memory so effortlessly?" But I remained silent, as sick-hearted as it made me.

Merikare stood to Imi's left, one hand casually on her shoulder, but his body appeared rigid. I recognized the false smile on his face from childhood, the one that appeared when he'd been naughty. He fixed his gaze on a man kneeling before the king, flanked by Merikare's royal companions.

I leaned into Sarai and grabbed her arm. "Abram," I whispered in her ear.

I swallowed hard and pinched my lips together, realizing Merikare's two mountainous soldiers were Abram's escorts. One attractive. One ugly. Both brutish. The day the hideous one grabbed me roughly with his enormous hand and left deep red marks on my skin, had left deep marks on my memory as well. It was the same day Sarai and Imi had come into my life. I recalled Merikare hesitated before ordering the man to release me, as though he enjoyed seeing me hurt and humiliated.

I inhaled the familiar woody aroma of frankincense that burned in ceremonial braziers around the hall. It calmed me a little as I dragged my feet toward the king. All eyes were upon us. My hand clutched the silver amulet on my wrist and turned it round and round.

The royal companions raised Abram roughly to make way, but the king's brusque gesture with his hand made them stop.

We stopped too.

Abram's mesmerizing gaze found Sarai. She turned away.

My brows knitted as I looked from Sarai to Abram's waiting eyes.

He wore a knee-length yellow linen tunic, a brown-striped vesture, and a scarf that encircled his head like a turban. He was leaner than I remembered. His bones pushed through his skin, and his eyes sunk deep into his head. Although, he had not diminished so much that I couldn't see the comely, larger-than-life man that still made my heart leap.

"What is this you have done to me?" Pharaoh's voice echoed through the hall. "Why did you not tell us she was your wife? Why did you tell my son that she was your sister?"

I inhaled sharply and gaped at Sarai.

Her lovely face fell, and tears instantly dropped to the floor.

Abram answered. "It is true. She is my sister. My half-sister." He spoke humbly. "But it is also true she is my wife. Yet a half-truth is a whole lie." He nodded toward Merikare. "I believed your son would have murdered me had I told him the truth. He was so taken with her extraordinary beauty that he insisted she belonged in your harem. He didn't bother to inquire if she were free." Abram pressed his hands hard against his chest, his voice thick and anguished. "Fear overtook me. I had no doubt he intended to take her … one way or the other."

Pharaoh turned abruptly to give Merikare a hard, sharp look. "A man's fear can always bring a snare, my son. Many are driven to uncharacteristic acts by the threat of death. It is not an appropriate tool for a wise ruler."

Merikare scowled as though the king had clouted him across his head.

No one breathed.

"But you, Abram," Pharaoh said. "What an improper thing you have done regardless of my son's behavior. How unbecoming of a man I greatly admired and respected."

"You are justified in reproving and upbraiding me, Your Majesty. My feet are made of clay. I have shown great weakness by implying a husband's life is worth more than a wife's honor. I exposed Sarai and you to great sin. But worse than that, I disregarded my faith in the promises of God."

"But if you felt threatened by the behavior of my son, then am I not also at fault? I am the one in authority, and if someone harms another in my name, I am guilty too." Pharaoh glanced at Sarai, and his eyes softened. "O, Sarai. How deeply sorry I am that I may have violated your virtue. This king begs your forgiveness."

"May I approach, Pharaoh?" Sarai said.

He nodded.

Abram and the royal companions moved aside, and Sarai stepped gracefully toward the king.

He rose and met her halfway.

She knelt before him. "I ask for your forgiveness and understanding. I was directed to claim Abram as my brother and nothing more. I was not free to sort the truth out for you. God delivered us from our folly, but at great cost to you and your people. My soul is wholly distressed."

The king reached out, and his hands did not wither. Sarai placed her hands in his. It was the first time he had ever touched her. He helped her to her feet. "In these," he said, lifting her fingers to his lips and lightly kissing them, "you hold the heart of a king."

"And you and your people will reside in my heart forever," Sarai said.

Merikare and Imi pouted in perfect harmony.

Pharaoh released her and walked back to his throne. "Abram, I almost took her as my wife." He squeezed his eyes shut for a moment. "But I restore Sarai to you with her honor intact. Take your wife and go."

"Impossible," Merikare shouted. Blue veins bulged from his thick neck. "We let them go? Enriched with the spoils of Egypt? They deceived the throne, and that is a crime. They should not leave with their heads. Their entire tribe should be impaled on stakes or drowned in the river."

Our father's fury climbed and fell at once. "I see perhaps Abram was more justified in his fear of you than I thought," the king said. "But can't you see, Merikare? They are a particular favorite of the gods. I believe it is at our peril to touch one hair on their heads. And therefore, we must take special care they receive no further injury. Have we not lost too much already?"

"Let me deal with them, Father," Merikare begged. "I brought her to you. I will see they are punished, as a warning to others, beyond anything Egypt has ever seen."

"Yes, brother," I said, finding my voice and stepping toward the throne. "You brought her here and broke our laws of hospitality to do so. Just as I alleged a year ago."

"He would have fled with her—" Merikare began.

Pharaoh blanched. "You knew something was amiss, Merikare? A storm flattened our city and dried up the river. A grievous plague has entered my house, taken your mother, and threatens to spread into all the land." His mouth twisted. "Mice now abound and have eaten half our grain. Locusts have descended on what remains in the field. And you continued to cling to your silence?"

Mice? Locust? I had heard nothing about them.

Merikare's face fired like a torch, and he opened his

mouth. But the king waved a hand, dismissing anything that might come from it.

Imi moved slightly in my mother's chair. She turned her face to the crown prince and gave him a stern look as his shoulders slumped.

Pharaoh's eyes met mine. "Did you know they were married?"

"No, I did not." My face burned. "Do you think I would have kept such a secret from you?"

"You and Sarai are quite close. Hyrcanos suggested I summon you and your servants to see if you were guilty of keeping her secret."

"That would have been a very serious crime, my king."

"You have no idea the relief in my heart, my daughter."

"But Merikare," Meti spoke for the first time. "You have angered the gods and brought their wrath upon us. You must make things right before them."

"He only angered one God, High Priest," I said and stopped. My heart tightened.

Merikare straightened. He and Imi smiled like cats that caught their mouse.

Meti stiffened. "And which one of our gods is that, Princess?"

There was no place to go but forward. "It was none of the false gods of Egypt, dear teacher. It is the one true God. The God of Abram and Sarai. Father, you have seen His power. How can you deny Him? He is a God who is neither blind nor deaf, nor chiseled and carved, nor created by the hands of man."

Pharaoh's eyes bored into me.

Sarai linked her arm with mine. "O, Hagar," she whispered. "Do you wish to perish this day?"

A rashness took hold of me akin to madness. "They must see the truth. His power has kept my father's hand from touching you. Your God brought a mighty storm, dried up the Nile, and sent the Black Sickness. All to keep you from my father's bed. Your God is real. Surely they understand that." It seemed so obvious to me.

I exhaled and looked at Meti, expecting him to acknowledge at least a small part of my words. Instead, he lowered his head and turned his back to me. But not before I saw the tears in his eyes.

The hair lifted on my neck and arms. *Should I have kept quiet? It had seemed the perfect time to declare it.*

"Blasphemy," shouted Imi.

My brother nodded. "Treason. And that *is* a crime, Father. One that requires she be burned alive."

My breath burst in and out of my chest, and I trembled violently.

"Do you want to take back your words, Princess Hagar?" Pharaoh asked miserably.

I could not lie to him. "How can I continue to worship the created when I have met the Creator, Father? How can I disbelieve what I believe?" My knees weakened, and I was not sure how much longer I could stand.

Pharaoh's fists slammed the carved lion heads on his armrests. "How can I endure more loss? And command with my voice the destruction of my beloved daughter?" He pressed a palm over his heart as though it would help it stop breaking.

"You have no choice, Pharaoh," Merikare said.

"Are you made of stone, my son? The words are impossible for me to utter."

"Your Majesty," Sarai said. "Do butterflies continue to walk among the caterpillars once they have sprouted wings? Hagar's beliefs have altered, but should she die for that? Allow her to leave Egypt, with us." She wrapped her arm around my shoulder.

I looked up, hopeful.

The king exhaled quietly and studied her. He motioned to Hyrcanos. "High Vizier, a pharaoh has never given a princess of Egypt to a foreigner. Is there any prior instance that would allow that to happen?"

"No, Your Majesty."

I will burn today. Tossed in flames until my flesh hisses and splits and turns to ash.

"However ..." Hyrcanos leaned over and whispered in Pharaoh's ear.

The king sat quietly for a moment. He raised his hand to silence Merikare when he moved to protest. Meti remained with his back to us.

"It would be better," Pharaoh said finally, "if Hagar lived and served a woman like you, Sarai. As a *handmaiden*. Far better for her even than if she remained here, as a princess of Egypt." He sat up straight and made a decree in a tone that no one dared argue with. "Hagar, and all that she owns, now belongs to you, Sarai of Ur. Furthermore, I remove from her any title or claim of royalty for the remainder of her life, and from any offspring she may have."

"O, Father," I cried, both relieved and heartbroken. I stepped toward the throne, and brawny royal guards, standing stock-still in front of the platform, now thrust their bare chests in front of me. They raised the flat leather clubs they carried, ready to strike.

"No slave may approach the priestly person of Pharaoh," said Hyrcanos.

Chapter Forty-Four

THE FULL WEIGHT OF THE NEW high vizier's words settled hard on me. I had made my choice. I would not die for it, but I would live with the consequences for the rest of my life.

Imi beamed and looked up at Merikare and whispered to him.

"Father," Merikare said. "I have a request. If one leaves Egypt, their soul is in peril of losing the afterlife if they die in a foreign country and are not buried properly. Hagar's servants have done nothing wrong. So why should they be subjected to such punishment? My wife, Princess Imi, has become quite fond of the girls. She graciously requests they serve her instead. Thus, they will not be forced to forfeit the next world."

I looked behind me to where Kiya and Dendera huddled together. Beside them was Pentu, with his crooked nose and crooked teeth. I sighed in relief.

He boldly walked forward and prostrated himself before the king. "Life, health, and strength be to you, Pharaoh."

"You may rise," Pharaoh said.

"There is a legal matter which pertains to the request of the crown prince and his royal wife. May I address it, my king?"

"You may."

Pentu unrolled a scroll in his hands and read clearly. "Whereas, on the day of Wepet Renpet, my two servants, Kiya and Dendera, held as slaves by me, shall from that day forward be free persons in the country of Egypt."

Imi gasped.

I turned my head to see the girls. They gazed at me in wonder.

Pentu continued. "No one, in any capacity as royal or noble, may act to repress either of them for the remainder of their lives. Everything I own, except one silver bucket, I have divided equally between them and is regarded as payment for their years of faithful service. I also entrust my beloved cat, Bastet, to Kiya. My noble friend, Pentu, holds all in trust. Signed, The King's Daughter, Hagar, Princess of Egypt. Witnessed and recorded by Pentu, Scribe of the Royal Household."

A shocked silence followed.

"But she is no longer a princess," Imi cried. "Surely that is not valid."

My father motioned to Pentu. He stepped forward and handed Hyrcanos the scroll.

The high vizier looked it over quickly. "She was titled when she had Pentu write this," he said. "It is a legal and binding document." He handed it to Pharaoh.

Imi's head jerked back. Merikare stood with his elbows wide from his body, shook his bright red face, and pierced me with cold, hard eyes.

The king took his time to read it through, his eyebrows gathered in. He stared hard at Imi sitting on my mother's throne—as though he saw her for the first time—and realized the seat she occupied. "What evil deed have I done? My faithful Great Royal Wife warned me of you." Imi's eyes were wide as full moons. "My royal daughter begged me to release her from your grasp. I didn't listen. I failed to believe my royal son was such a fool to be led by the nose by a woman like you." He shook his head slowly. "I didn't save Hagar from you, but she shrewdly saved those she cared about." His eyes blazed. "Now remove yourself from the throne that belonged to the noblest woman in the land."

Imi obeyed quickly and vacated the chair, her face ashen. She stood, twisting as if caught in Pharaoh's grip with no place to go.

"High Vizier."

"Yes, Your Majesty?"

"Have a decree written that if Princess Imi ever sits on the throne of the Great Royal Wife, she is to be taken out immediately and slaughtered like an ox. This decree is to stand in perpetuity." The king's voice was rich, measured, and controlled.

"Yes, Your Majesty."

Imi shook visibly. As soon as Pharaoh turned toward us, she slithered behind Merikare. She stretched her hand out and laid it on his arm. He shook it off as if he'd been stung by an insect.

"The servants of Hagar are free women now," Pharaoh declared. "And wealthy ones. Although I see a formal promise here, you did not yet read, Pentu."

"Yes, Your Majesty. Hagar wanted me to discuss that with Dendera first. It is permission for her to marry a cook named Ramose."

Dendera squealed and hugged Kiya.

The king cleared his throat, and the hall fell silent.

Meti still stood with his back to me.

"Abram," Pharaoh commanded. "Take your wife and her handmaid." His voice broke, and he swallowed hard, as though trying to regain composure. "And depart from my palace and my country. I assure you safe passage. And I will fill the royal barge with riches to appease your god. However, you are never to return to the land of Egypt again."

My girls rushed toward me, tears in their eyes. I saw Merikare nod. His royal companions grabbed me forcefully by the arms and ushered me, hanging like a limp rag between them, out of the great pillared hall.

I bent my neck far enough back for one more glance at my father, but all my eyes found was an empty throne.

Out we went from the palace into the cool blackness of early morning air, the light of torches leading the way. Sarai's pleas for the royal companions to release me went unheeded, so now the only sound was the stony courtyard crunching under footsteps. I took a deep breath and caught the rich, sweet fragrance of night-blooming jasmine that grew like a weed around the palace. By dawn, its scented star-shaped flowers would close and be gone.

Like me.

My sandals slipped from my feet. "May I retrieve my foot coverings?" I said in a voice that had no power.

Neither of the royal companions slowed or spoke but kept a steady pace toward the royal quay while my legs ached and my arms went numb. We neared the spot Mother and I had gathered for our midday meals to watch the Nile and its wildlife returning. It seemed so much time had passed since then. A tear slipped down my cheek. My time with Mother was one of many precious memories I would not leave behind.

The royal companions dumped me, unceremoniously, once we reached the high-water pier used during the inundation. They guffawed and walked away, leaving me without breath, limbs weak from the final humiliation by my twin brother. I covered my face with my hands. My dull, heavy chest and knotted belly made standing nearly impossible.

A hand lightly touched my shoulder, and I opened my eyes to see my sandals in Kiya's hands. Sarai stood next to her, reached out her hand, and lifted me to my feet. Dendera immediately straightened my wig and linen kalasiris.

Kiya knelt and gently placed a sandal on each foot, then stood, tall and willowy. "There are no words for the goodly thing you have done for us."

Dendera bobbed her head and clucked her gratefulness with tear-filled eyes.

"There is one last thing you can both do for me," I said.

"Anything, anything." They nodded in unison.

"Make sure Tameri is well cared for. You are women of substance now, and with that comes a voice and the right to be heard. I leave her in your care." My body sagged thinking about Rensi's wife, how much I had grown to love her, and knowing I would not be there for her. "Tell Tameri my last thoughts and concern were of her."

"We promise it will be done, Princess Hagar," Kiya said.

"Our roles have changed, Kiya. I am no longer a princess. I am now the servant and you are a noblewoman."

"You will always be royalty to me, Princess," she said.

We all embraced in a way previously unthinkable in our different stations in life.

I heard a shout and looked up to see Pentu running down the royal quay, my silver bucket in hand. He handed it to Sarai. "It is all she owns, but it is yours," he said.

Sarai placed a hand on my elbow and drew me close. I could smell earthy, sweet lily and myrrh from the perfume on her skin. She steered me onto the royal barge. I took one glance back as Abram walked down the quay, his broad, powerful shoulders slumped over his chest.

And then I saw Kiya leaning against Pentu, her head tilted on his shoulder, his crooked nose resting on her hair. It was a good last look.

I would not turn around again.

Abram embarked and filled the deck, filled the entire boat with his bearing. As strikingly handsome as always, even though he was bent to the point of collapsing. I took in his long silver beard, his fair olive skin, and his uncompromising air of manliness. Beneath his turban, his face appeared gaunt, and dark circles weighed down haunted brown eyes. I had a strong desire to go to him, touch him, and comfort him.

But he was not mine to console. He was Sarai's. *Her husband.* I shook my head slowly, taking in the depth of their deception and the cost to Egypt. But there was no doubt that Merikare bore the blame for most of it. He had threatened Abram's tribe, and they had done what they needed to do to survive.

Male servants, dressed in simple linen kilts, boarded the barge behind Abram laden with an astonishing amount of goods. A massive offering sent to appease their foreign God. Bronze jars and baskets filled with amethysts and emeralds, jasper and lapis lazuli, gold, silver, flasks of perfume, incense, shrouds of fine linen, jugs of oil, and the king's most exceptional wine and beer.

But Abram didn't look once to savor the abundance of it all. He kept his focused eyes on Sarai, the silence between them thick and onerous.

As soon as the servants went ashore, the barge pilot, a dark, muscular man in a knee-length tunic, his eyes outlined in black kohl, positioned himself at the bow with a long pole to measure the depth of the river. He shouted orders to the helmsman. Sailors swiftly pulled anchor and untied the ship from the pier. There was still no hint of sunlight, and generally, one did not travel the Nile at night, but darkness was not an obstacle for my father's skilled royal crew. The force of the current pressed against the stern, and in a rapid, controlled movement, the three score oarsmen pulled us quickly from shore. We floated away from Henen-nesut and into the unknown.

My heart stopped beating as Abram made his way to us and reached out his hand to Sarai.

She looked away.

I couldn't breathe.

Abram fell to his knees and grabbed the hem of her long kalasiris. Enormous sobs came from the great man. "Forgive me, Sarai. You are the only thing that matters in my life. You have consumed my thoughts since I sailed from this place a year ago. I have not slept without seeing you in my dreams. Your beautiful eyes, your creamy white skin, even the scent of you. I missed your counsel, your smile, and the way you make me laugh. I've lived in fearful expectation of judgment, and a fury of guilt still devours me. Please free me, Sarai. Please forgive me."

Sarai, stiff and silent, crossed her arms and tilted her head toward the heavens. Her chest heaved in and out as Abram wept profoundly and wrapped his arms around her legs.

My stomach quivered. I didn't want to stare but couldn't take my wide eyes off them. It seemed as if time slowed, then ceased altogether.

Sarai rocked back and forth and moaned. Then she collapsed upon Abram and took him in her arms. "I'm releasing you, Abram, to restore my soul. If I hold this in my heart, I will destroy myself and give in to sadness and resentment. I will not place that yoke of bondage around my neck."

My face flushed at the sight of their intimate embrace. And then something bitter rose in the back of my throat. Thankfully, only a few torches flickered around us, so the light was murky enough to hide me. My fingers played with my silver amulet, turning it this way and that, and for an instant, I wished Sarai had remained in Henen-nesut.

From where did that arise?

I quickly moved away from them, toward the port side of the royal barge. *How could I think such thoughts after Sarai saved my life?* My face grew hot and my throat thick. I leaned against the weathered wooden rail and shuddered.

One red gash of sunlight wrested its way out of darkness along the horizon. The sun would soon rise beyond the eastern desert and shine its golden light on a new and different world, a world I'd never imagined seeing. This splendid boat would move through the regions of Egypt and deliver me far away from my home, now filled with the ghosts of my newly departed loved ones. Two tears slipped down my cheek. *One for Mother. One for Rensi,* I thought as I wiped them with my fingers and kissed the wet tips.

I grabbed the side of the planked vessel and envisioned holding a plough like the fellahin. *O, God of Abram, I have stepped my feet on your path. I will not look back. Amen and amen.*

The river was high but not nearly at its peak. Gentle waves rolled into the barge but were pushed down and sideways and thrown behind us in a large wake. I thought of how like the waves of the river I was. I too had been pushed down and sideways and thrown out in a large wake. But past the wake, the river gathered back together as smooth and calm as my own spirit.

My fingers found my silver amulet. "From this day forward," I whispered, "I am no longer Hagar, Princess of Egypt." I took a deep breath. "I am Hagar, the handmaid of Sarai of Ur, and maidservant of the God of Abram. I will take flight across the desert sands of Egypt and see what lies in the country so close to where the sun sets." I slipped the cuff from my wrist and hurled it into the Nile. The shackle that bound me to the false gods of Egypt slipped powerless beneath the dark water. The sight exhilarated me.

I turned my face north as the river's strong current swept the royal barge quickly away from Henen-nesut … and surprised myself with a smile.

Author Note

The Egyptian Princess is a work of fiction based on Rabbinical Literature and the Hebrew and Arabic tradition of Hagar being the daughter of a pharaoh before becoming a handmaid in Abram's—Abraham's tribe. The idea of Hagar being a princess of Egypt is well known in Hebrew and Arabic beliefs, although it is a new idea for modern-day Christians.

When I first read the Midrashim tradition of Hagar, I realized I knew nothing about her and became overcome with finding out as much as possible. My thought was, *how did a princess of Egypt become a handmaid in the first Hebrew tribe?*

My sources came from The Midrash (Gen. R. xlv.), which states: Hagar was the daughter of Pharaoh, who, seeing what great miracles God had done for Sarah's sake (Gen. xii. 17), said: "It is better for Hagar to be a handmaid in Sarah's house than a mistress in her own." In this case, Hagar's name is interpreted as a *reward* (Ha-Agar = this is a reward).

The Jewish Women's Archive cites both the Midrash and the Aggadah as saying: After the Lord afflicted Pharaoh and his household with mighty plagues, the king sees the miracles performed to protect Sarah. He gives her his daughter, Hagar, saying, "It would be better for my daughter to be a handmaiden in Sarah's house than a noblewoman in another." The Midrash is an ancient Rabbinic interpretation of scripture, and the Aggadah is a Rabbinic narrative.

My book's premise is also found in the Ancient Book of Jasher, known as The Book of Wisdom. Although Jasher was in the original King James Version of 1611 AD and the Dead Sea Scrolls, it is no longer in the Bible. However, we find references regarding Jasher in Joshua 10:13; 2 Samuel 1:18; and 2 Timothy 3:8.

Jasher 15:32 says: And the king said to his daughter, "It is better for thee my daughter to be a handmaid in this man's house than to be mistress in my house after we have beheld the evil that befell us on account of this woman (Sarai)."

The Bible gives us another clue regarding Hagar being a princess. Genesis 25:6 (KJV) refers to Ishmael's twelve sons as *princes*. But neither of Isaac's sons nor the six sons Keturah—the wife Abraham took after Sarah passed away—have royal titles.

Mohammedans tell legends about Hagar, which agree with the Hebrew tradition. Hagar and Ishmael are considered the ancestors of their prophet Mohammed, and they attribute many miracles to Hagar, of which neither the Torah nor the Midrashim speak on.

Dating Abraham was one of the biggest obstacles I faced in researching this book. Many people will have different views, but I concluded that no one knows for certain from varied opinions. Figuring out when Abraham was in Egypt became as uncertain an endeavor as guessing which king's harem Sarai landed in. I found a five-hundred-year span when different scholars placed Abraham in Egypt, as his timeline has been re-dated many times.

The Atlas of Bible History by Harper Collins states: Scholars disagree about the date of Abraham's journey to Canaan, but the milieu of the biblical accounts suggest that the Middle Bronze Age provides the most suitable background. John MacArthur's Study Bible and Commentary state that Abraham was born in 2165 BC. There was enough evidence for me to comfortably place Abraham in Egypt in the Mid-Bronze Age, which included the First Intermediate Period of ancient Egypt that lasted between 2181 BC to 2055 BC.

Egypt had divided into two kingdoms, with a king in Upper Egypt (the south) and a king in Lower Egypt (the north). The country also separated into nomes (like states), with a nomarch (governor) ruling in each. The First Intermediate Period took place during the ninth and tenth dynasties. The kings in Lower Egypt are believed to be Kheti, Merikare, and Ity sometimes referred to as Akhtoy. They ruled from Henen-nesut, which was renamed Herakleopolis Magna during the Greco-Roman period.

Mentuhotep II c. 2061-2010 BC of Waset, later renamed Thebes by the Greeks (now known as Luxor), eventually united ancient Egypt and initiated the Middle Kingdom period. But it is almost impossible to date events in Egyptian history. The kings-list is in poor shape, and large parts of Egyptian chronology are missing. What we do have appears deficient and unclear.

With a rough idea of when the events between Sarai and the King of Egypt may have occurred, I switched my research to what life as a princess in ancient Egypt may have looked like and how a *princess* could become a *handmaid* in Abraham's tribe.

That became the seed for my fictional account of Hagar's story.

According to the Dead Sea Scrolls and the Midrash, Hagar's association with the first Hebrews began when Abraham moved his tribe from Canaan to Egypt to escape a great famine. Abraham thought the Egyptians would kill him to claim Sarah, so he deceived them by saying she was his sister and not his wife. When Sarai ended up a part of Pharaoh's household, she may have met Hagar in the harem, or adequately termed, the Royal House of Women, at that time.

Egyptian "harems" were not as we picture them from the medieval Ottoman Empire as a place where eunuchs guarded women who waited for their master to call upon them. In ancient Egypt, a harem—or Royal House of Women—was where the wives, concubines, single women, and the king's male and female children lived. They also employed men and sometimes became critical economic institutions. These royal women's quarters often had farms of their own, livestock, large estates, and produced products like textiles.

I chose a specific dynasty to place my story in; still, a few perennial threads woven through history support the idea that life didn't change much for royal families over the years. As well as royal daughters receiving formal and equal educations as their male counterparts, Egyptian princesses never married below their station. Which meant they married their father, a brother, or remained single. Some became priestesses and served the gods in the temple.

Kings of Egypt often married foreign daughters for political reasons. However, their daughters were *never* married to foreigners. There is one famous correspondence from King Amenhotep III, of the eighteenth dynasty, to the king of Babylon. Amenhotep refused to allow one of his daughters to marry the foreign monarch. Amenhotep states, "From time immemorial, no daughter of the king of Egypt is given to anyone." This is believed to have been the tradition of Egyptian kings "from time immemorial" and ensured no foreigner could prove a claim to Egypt's throne.

But somehow, a royal princess did end up as a handmaid in the tribe where the story of the first Hebrews begins. Also, she left Egypt, which brought to my attention another exciting fact about ancient Egyptians. It concerned the strong beliefs they held about death and the afterlife, and they spent a great deal of their time living preparing for immortality. It was crucial to be appropriately buried—and *in* Egypt. If you weren't, you forfeited the afterlife altogether. For this reason, few ancient Egyptians traveled out of the country. The risk of ending up in a grave on foreign soil was simply too significant. Yet, somehow—against tradition—Hagar left Egypt forever, became a handmaid, and then a foreigner's wife.

I began to imagine Hagar as an educated, sophisticated, royal Egyptian princess—as opposed to a victimized, oppressed slave exploited by a power couple. And I uncovered information that leads me to believe Hagar and Sarah were not always dueling rivals. That, in fact, they probably began their relationship tightly bonded in trust and mutual respect.

To me, Hagar is one of the most fascinating women in history. I hope to provide added dimension to an often over-looked figure whose life had layers and layers of meaning. Her story is filled with spiritual value, transcends centuries, and is as relevant today as it was four thousand years ago.

Questions for Conversation

1. Are you familiar with the story of Hagar, Abram, and Sarai in Genesis 16? Abram decides, two chapters before, and against God's will, to journey into Egypt to escape a famine in Canaan. Who, besides Sarai, paid the most significant price for Abram's sin? Do you believe others are affected by our sins?

2. If you are not Hebrew or Arabic, did their tradition of Hagar being a princess surprise you? For most Christians, this will likely be a new thought. Does knowing that all Egyptian royal children, regardless of gender, were educated help give you a different perspective of the woman Hagar may have been?

3. If you were familiar with Hagar's story before reading this book, have you ever thought of her as a woman of faith? We see her stand boldly, proclaim God as her own, and disavow Egypt's gods, even though her father is considered half-god. Do you think you would ever have that kind of courage? To stand up for your faith, knowing it may cost you your life? Hagar didn't die, but have you heard stories of others who died for what they believed?

4. Imi's character is based on a mental illness called Borderline Personality Disorder. Have you ever known anyone that behaved as she did? If you know someone who has a mental illness, can you separate your feelings toward them and realize it is the illness that makes them the way they are? Understanding mental illness has been at the forefront of discussion in the United States. Since the beginning of time, human beings have likely suffered from PTSD, depression, and other mental diseases too. Have you ever heard of examples from ancient societies about the way they were treated or mistreated?

5. Hagar had—what we would call—a crush on Abram. Do you believe that had anything to do with her "father issues" and her need to feel valued? Did you feel appreciated by your parents? If not, how did you seek their attention?

6. Did you make the connection between the amulet on Hagar's wrist and her struggle between the gods of Egypt and the one true God? Can you identify anything in your life that keeps you apart from a relationship with God?

7. What did you think when Hagar secretly wished Sarai had stayed in Henen-nesut? What did that reveal about her feelings toward Sarai and toward Abram? Did it tell you anything new about Hagar?

8. Does the author succeed in giving Hagar a new voice? Did she bring to life a vibrant, strong, intelligent woman, known to most as merely a handmaid? Will thinking of Hagar as a sophisticated, educated woman change the way you feel about her?

9. There is renewed interest in Hagar. During a time when America is championing strong women, do you enjoy reading about them in fiction? Would you recommend this book to a friend? Are you curious enough to continue with Hagar on her journey into Canaan in book two of the Women of Valor series in 2022?

Made in the USA
Middletown, DE
17 March 2021